“We do not know what
where it came from i
created it. But we know

Constance waited.

“It was created to wreak a
world.”

“Vengeance? What kind of vengeance?”

“To cleanse the earth.”

For a reason she could not quite explain, Constance wasn’t sure she wanted the monk to continue. She forced herself to speak. “Cleanse it—how?”

The man’s anxious expression now turned almost sorrowful. “I am very sorry to burden you with this difficult knowledge. When the earth is drowning in selfishness, greed, violence, and evil, the Agozyen will cleanse the earth of its human burden.”

Constance swallowed. “I’m not sure I understand.”

“It will cleanse the earth *entirely* of its human burden,” the monk said in a very low voice. “So that all might start afresh.”

Douglas Preston and Lincoln Child are the co-authors of a string of bestselling suspense novels, including the Agent Pendergast adventures. Douglas Preston and his family live on the coast of Maine, while Lincoln Child lives with his wife and daughter in New Jersey. Find out more at www.prestonchild.com.

By Douglas Preston and Lincoln Child

The Wheel of Darkness
The Book of the Dead
Dance of Death
Brimstone
Still Life with Crows
The Cabinet of Curiosities
The Ice Limit
Thunderhead
Riptide
Reliquary
Mount Dragon
Relic

By Douglas Preston

Tyrannosaur Canyon
The Codex
Ribbons of Time
The Royal Road
Talking to the Ground
Jennie
Cities of Gold
Dinosaurs in the Attic

By Lincoln Child

Deep Storm
Death Match
Utopia
Tales of the Dark 1–3
Dark Banquet
Dark Company

The Wheel of Darkness

DOUGLAS PRESTON
& LINCOLN CHILD

An Orion paperback
First published in Great Britain in 2007
by Orion
This paperback edition published in 2008
by Orion Books Ltd,
Orion House, 5 Upper St Martin's Lane,
London WC2H 9EA

An Hachette Livre UK company

A CIP catalogue record for this book is available from the British Library.

Printed and bound in the UK by CPI Mackays, Chatham ME5 8TD

The Orion Publishing Group's policy is to use papers that are natural, renewable and recyclable products and made from wood grown in sustainable forests. The logging and manufacturing processes are expected to conform to the environmental regulations of the country of origin.

www.orionbooks.co.uk

Lincoln Child dedicates this book to his daughter, Veronica

Douglas Preston dedicates this book to
Nat and Ravida,
Emily, Andrew, and Sarah

Acknowledgments

Douglas Preston and Lincoln Child would like to express their great appreciation to the following people for their invaluable help: Jaime Levine, Jamie Raab, Eric Simonoff, Eadie Klemm, Evan Boorstyn, Jennifer Romanello, Kurt Rauscher, Claudia Rülke, and Laura Goeller. We also express our thanks to Captain Richard Halluska of ISM Solutions and to Videotel Marine International, UK.

This is a work of fiction. All characters, corporations, locales, events, vessels, and religious practices, rituals, and iconography described in these pages are fictitious or used fictitiously, and any resemblance to actual events, ships, persons, religious establishments, government entities, or corporations is unintentional and coincidental. In particular, North Star Lines, the *Britannia*, and all who serve or sail aboard her are caprices of our imaginations.

1

The only things moving in the vastness of the Llölung Valley were two black specks, barely larger than the frost-split boulders that covered the valley floor, inching along a faint track. The valley was a desolate place, devoid of trees; the wind chuckled and whispered among the rocks, the cries of black eagles echoed from the cliffs. The figures, on horseback, were approaching an immense wall of granite, two thousand feet high, from which poured a slow plume of water—the source of the sacred Tsangpo River. The trail disappeared into the mouth of a gorge that split the rock face, reappeared at higher altitude as a cut angled into the sheer wall of rock, and finally topped out on a long ridge before disappearing once again into the jagged peaks and fissures beyond. Framing the scene, and forming a backdrop of stupendous power and majesty, stood the frozen immensity of three Himalayan mountains—Dhaulagiri, Annapurna, and Manaslu—trailing plumes of snow. Beyond them, a sea of stormclouds rose up, the color of iron.

The two figures rode up the valley, cowled against the chill wind. This was the last stage of a long journey, and despite the rising storm they rode at a slow pace, their horses on the verge of exhaustion. As they approached the mouth of the gorge, they crossed a rushing stream once, and then a second time. Slowly, the two entered the gorge and vanished.

Inside the gorge, they continued following the faint trail as it climbed above the roaring stream. Hollows of blue ice lay in the shadows where the rock wall met the boulder-strewn floor. Dark clouds scudded across the sky, pushed before a rising wind that moaned in the upper reaches of the gorge.

The trail changed abruptly at the base of the great rock wall, mounting upward through a steep and terrifying cut. An ancient guard station, built on a projecting tongue of rock, lay in ruins: four broken stone walls supporting nothing more than a row of blackbirds. At the very foot of the cut stood a huge *mani* stone, carved with a Tibetan prayer, rubbed and polished by thousands of hands of those wishing a blessing before attempting the dangerous journey to the top.

At the guard station, the two travelers dismounted. From here they were forced to proceed on foot, leading their horses up the narrow trail as the overhang was too low to admit a rider. In places, landslides had peeled away the sheer rock wall, taking the trail with it; these gaps had been bridged by rough planks and poles drilled into the rock, forming a series of narrow, creaking bridges without railings. Elsewhere, the trail was so steep that the travelers and their mounts were forced to climb steps carved into the rock, made slick and uneven by the passage of countless pilgrims and animals.

The wind shifted now, driving through the gorge with a booming sound, carrying flakes of snow with it. The stormshadow fell into the gorge, plunging it into a gloom as deep as night. Still the two figures pushed up the vertiginous trail, up the icy staircases and rock pitches. As they rose, the roar of the waterfall echoed strangely between the walls of stone, mingling with the rising wind like mysterious voices speaking in an unknown tongue.

When the travelers at last topped the ridge, the wind almost halted them in their tracks, whipping their robes and biting at their exposed skin. They hunched against it and, pulling their reluctant horses forward, continued along the spine of the ridge until they reached the remains of a ruined village. It was a bleak place, the houses thrown down by some ancient cataclysm, their timbers scattered and broken, the mud bricks dissolving back into the earth from which they had been formed.

In the center of the village, a pile of prayer stones rose, topped by a pole from which snapped dozens of tattered prayer flags. To one side lay an ancient cemetery whose retaining wall had collapsed, and now erosion had opened the graves, scattering bones and skulls down a long scree slope. As the two approached, a group of ravens flapped up in noisy protest from the wreckage, their scratchy cries rising toward the leaden clouds.

At the pile of stones, one of the travelers stopped and dismounted, gesturing for the other to wait. He bent down, picked up an old stone, and added it to the pile. Then he paused briefly in silent meditation, the wind lashing at his robes, before retaking the reins of his horse. They continued on.

1

Beyond the deserted village the trail narrowed sharply along a knife-edge ridge. Struggling against the violence of the wind, the two figures crept along it, arcing around the shoulder of a mountain—and then at last they could just begin to spy the battlements and pinnacles of a vast fortress, standing dully against the dark sky.

This was the monastery known as Gsalrig Chongg, a name that might be translated as "the Jewel of the Awareness of Emptiness." As the trail continued around the side of the mountain, the monastery came fully into view: massive red-washed walls and buttresses mounting the sides of a barren granite rock, ending in a complex of pinnacled roofs and towers that shone here and there with patches of gold leaf.

The Gsalrig Chongg monastery was one of very few in Tibet to have escaped the ravages of the Chinese invasion, in which soldiers drove out the Dalai Lama, killed thousands of monks, and destroyed countless monasteries and religious structures. Gsalrig Chongg was spared partly because of its extreme remoteness and its proximity to the disputed border with Nepal, but also due to a simple bureaucratic oversight: its very existence had somehow escaped official attention. Even today, maps of the so-called Tibet Autonomous Region do not locate this monastery, and the monks have taken great pains to keep it that way.

The trail passed by a steep scree slope, where a group of vultures picked away at some scattered bones.

"There appears to have been a recent death," the man murmured, nodding toward the heavy birds, which hopped about, utterly fearless.

"How so?" asked the second traveler.

"When a monk dies, his body is butchered and thrown to the wild animals. It is considered the highest honor, to have your mortal remains nourish and sustain other living things."

"A peculiar custom."

"On the contrary, the logic is impeccable. *Our* customs are peculiar."

The trail ended at a small gate in the massive encircling wall. The gate was open and a Buddhist monk stood there, wrapped in robes of scarlet and saffron, holding a burning torch, as if expecting them.

The two huddled travelers passed through the gate, still leading their horses. A second monk appeared and silently took the reins, leading the animals off to stables within the encircling wall.

The travelers stopped before the first monk, in the gathering darkness. He said nothing, but merely waited.

The first traveler pulled back his cowl—revealing the long, pale face, white-blond hair, marble features, and silvery eyes of Special Agent Aloysius Pendergast of the Federal Bureau of Investigation.

The monk turned toward the other. The second figure removed its cowl with a tentative movement, brown hair spilling out into the wind, catching the swirling snowflakes. She stood, head slightly bowed, a young woman who appeared to be in her early twenties, with a delicate face, finely formed lips, and high cheekbones—Constance Greene, Pendergast's ward. Her penetrating violet eyes darted around, taking in everything quickly, before dropping again to the ground.

The monk stared at her for only a moment. Making no comment, he turned and gestured for them to follow him down a stone causeway toward the main complex.

Pendergast and his ward followed the monk in silence as he passed through a second gate and entered the dark confines of the monastery itself, the air laden with the scent of sandalwood and wax. The great ironbound doors boomed shut behind them, muffling the howling wind to a faint whisper. They continued down a long hallway, one side of which was lined with brass prayer cylinders, creaking and turning round and round, driven by some hidden mechanism. The hall forked, and turned again, driving deeper into the monastic depths. Another monk appeared in front of them carrying large candles in brass holders, their flickering light revealing a series of ancient frescoes lining both walls.

The mazelike turnings brought them at last into a large room. One end was dominated by a gold statue of Padmasambhava, the Tantric Buddha, illuminated by hundreds of candles. Unlike the contemplative, half-closed eyes of most depictions of the Buddha, the Tantric Buddha's eyes were wide open, alert and dancing with life, symbolizing the heightened awareness achieved by his study of the secret teachings of Dzogchen and the even more esoteric Chongg Ran.

The Gsalrig Chongg monastery was one of two repositories in the world preserving the discipline of Chongg Ran, the enigmatic teachings known to those few who were familiar with them as the Jewel of the Mind's Impermanence.

At the threshold to this inner sanctum, the two

travelers paused. At the far end, a number of monks reposed in silence, sitting on tiered stone benches as if awaiting someone.

The uppermost tier was occupied by the abbot of the monastery. He was a peculiar-looking man, his ancient face wrinkled into a permanent expression of amusement, even mirth. His robes hung from his skeletal frame like laundry draped on a rack. Next to him sat a slightly younger monk, also known to Pendergast: Tsering, one of only very few of the monks who spoke English, who acted as the "manager" of the monastery. He was an exceptionally well-preserved man of perhaps sixty. Below them sat a row of twenty monks of all ages, some teenagers, others ancient and wizened.

Tsering rose and spoke in an English shot through with the strange, musical lilt of Tibetan. "Friend Pendergast, we welcome you back to monastery of Gsalrig Chongg, and we welcome your guest. Please sit down and take tea with us."

He gestured to a stone bench set with two silk-embroidered cushions—the only cushions in the room. The two sat, and moments later several monks appeared carrying brass trays loaded with cups of steaming buttered tea and *tsampa*. They drank the sweet tea in silence, and only when they had finished did Tsering speak again.

"What brings friend Pendergast back to Gsalrig Chongg?" he asked.

Pendergast rose.

"Thank you, Tsering, for your welcome," he said quietly. "I'm glad to be back. I return to you in order to continue my journey of meditation and enlightenment.

Let me introduce to you Miss Constance Greene, who also has come in hopes of study." He took her hand and she rose.

A long silence ensued. At last, Tsering rose. He walked over to Constance and stood before her, looking calmly into her face, and then reached up and touched her hair, fingering it delicately. Then, ever so gently, he reached out and touched the swell of her breasts, first one, then the other. She remained standing, unflinching.

"Are you a woman?" he asked.

"Surely you've seen a woman before," said Constance dryly.

"No," said Tsering. "I have not seen woman since I come here—at age of two."

Constance colored. "I'm very sorry. Yes, I am a woman."

Tsering turned to Pendergast. "This is first woman ever to come to Gsalrig Chongg. We never accept woman before as student. I am sorry to say it cannot be permitted. Especially now, in middle of funeral ceremonies for Venerable Ralang Rinpoche."

"The Rinpoche is dead?" Pendergast asked.

Tsering bowed.

"I am sorry to hear of the death of the Most High Lama."

At this, Tsering smiled. "Is no loss. We will find his reincarnation—the nineteenth Rinpoche—and he will be with us again. It is I who am sorry to deny your request."

"She needs your help. *I* need your help. We are

both . . . *tired* of the world. We have come a long way to find peace. Peace, and healing."

"I know how difficult journey you make. I know how much you hope. But Gsalrig Chongg exist for thousand year without female presence, and it cannot change. She must leave."

A long silence ensued. And then Pendergast raised his eyes to the ancient, unmoving figure occupying the highest seat. "Is this also the decision of the abbot?"

At first, there was no sign of movement. A visitor might have even mistaken the wizened figure for some kind of happy, senile idiot, grinning vacantly from his perch above the others. But then there was the merest flick of a desiccated finger, and one of the younger monks climbed up and bent over the abbot, placing his ear close to the man's toothless mouth. After a moment he straightened up and said something to Tsering in Tibetan.

Tsering translated. "The abbot asks woman to repeat name, please."

"I am Constance Greene," came the small but determined voice.

Tsering translated into Tibetan, having some difficulty over the name.

Another silence ensued, stretching into minutes.

Again the flick of the finger; again the ancient monk mumbled into the ear of the young monk, who repeated it in a louder voice.

Tsering said, "The abbot asks if this real name."

She nodded. "Yes, it is my real name."

Slowly the ancient lama raised a sticklike arm and pointed to a dim wall of the room with a fingernail that extended at least an inch from his finger. All eyes turned toward a temple painting hidden under a draped cloth, one of many hanging on the wall.

Tsering walked over and lifted the cloth, holding up a candle to it. The glow revealed a stunningly rich and complex image: a bright green female deity with eight arms, sitting on a white moon disk, with gods, demons, clouds, mountains, and gold filigree swirling about her, as if caught in a storm.

The old lama mumbled at length into the ear of the young monk, his toothless mouth working. Then he sat back and smiled while Tsering again translated.

"His Holiness ask to direct attention to *thangka* painting of Green Tara."

There was a murmuring and shuffling of the monks as they rose from their seats and respectfully stood in a circle around the painting, like students waiting for a lecture.

The old lama flapped a bony arm at Constance Greene to join the circle, which she hastily did, the monks shuffling aside to afford her space.

"This is picture of Green Tara," Tsering continued, still translating at one remove the mumbled words of the old monk. "She is mother of all Buddhas. She have constancy. Also wisdom, activity of mind, quick thinking, generosity, and fearlessness. His Holiness invite female to step closer and view mandala of Green Tara."

Constance stepped forward tentatively.

"His Holiness ask why student given name of Green Tara."

Constance looked around. "I don't know what you mean."

"Your name Constance Greene. This name contain two important attribute of Green Tara. His Holiness ask how you get name."

"Greene is my last name. It's a common English surname, but I've no idea of the origin. And my first name, Constance, was given to me by my mother. It was popular in . . . around the time I was born. Any resemblance of my name to the Green Tara is obviously a coincidence."

Now the abbot began to laugh, shakily, and struggled to stand with the help of two monks. In a few moments he was standing, but just barely, as if the slightest nudge would jostle him into a loose heap. He continued to laugh as he spoke again, a low, wheezy sound, displaying his pink gums, his bones almost rattling with mirth.

"Coincidence? No such thing. Student make funny joke," Tsering translated. "The abbot like good joke."

Constance glanced at Tsering to the abbot and back again. "Does that mean I'll be allowed to study here?"

"It mean your study is already begun," said Tsering, with a smile of his own.

2

In one of the remote pavilions of the Gsalrig Chongg monastery, Aloysius Pendergast rested on a bench beside Constance Greene. A row of stone windows looked out over the gorge of the Llölung to the great Himalayan peaks beyond, washed in a delicate pink alpenglow. From below came the faint roar of a waterfall at the head of the Llölung Valley. As the sun sank below the horizon, a *dzung* trumpet sounded a deep, drawn-out note that echoed among the ravines and mountains.

Almost two months had passed. July had come, and along with it spring in the high foothills of the Himalayas. The valley floors were greening, speckled with wildflowers, while a furze of pink wild roses flowered on the hillsides.

The two sat in silence. They had two weeks until the end of their stay.

The *dzung* sounded again as the fiery light died on the great triumvirate of mountains—Dhaulagiri, Annapurna, and Manaslu—three of the ten highest peaks in the world. Twilight came swiftly, invading the valleys like a flood of dark water.

Pendergast roused himself. "Your studies are going well. Extremely well. The abbot is pleased."

"Yes." Her voice was soft, almost detached.

He laid a hand on hers, his touch as light and airy as a leaf's. "We haven't spoken of this before, but I wanted to ask if . . . everything went well at the Feversham Clinic. If there were no complications to the, ah, procedure." Pendergast seemed uncharacteristically awkward and at a loss for words.

Constance's gaze remained aimed deep into the cold, snowy mountains.

Pendergast hesitated. "I wish you would have let me be with you."

She inclined her head, still remaining silent.

"Constance, I care for you very much. Perhaps I haven't expressed myself strongly enough on that point before. If I didn't, I apologize."

Constance bowed her head further, her face flushing. "Thank you." The detachment vanished from her voice, replaced by a faint tremor of emotion. She stood abruptly, looking away.

Pendergast rose as well.

"Excuse me, Aloysius, but I feel the need to be alone for a while."

"Of course." He watched her slim form move away from him until it vanished like a ghost into the stone corridors of the monastery. Then he turned his gaze to the mountainous landscape beyond the window, falling deep into thought.

As darkness filled the pavilion, the sounds of the *dzung* stopped, the last note sustained as a dying echo among the mountains for many long seconds. All was still, as if the coming of night had brought with it a kind of stasis. And then a figure materialized in the inky shadows at the foot of the pavilion: an old monk in a saffron robe. He gestured at Pendergast with a withered hand, using the peculiar Tibetan shake of the wrist that signified *come.*

Pendergast walked slowly toward the monk. The man turned and began to shuffle off into the darkness.

Pendergast followed, intrigued. The monk took him in an unexpected direction, down dim corridors toward the cell that held the famed immured anchorite: a monk who had voluntarily allowed himself to be bricked up in a room just large enough for a man to sit and meditate, walled up for his entire life, fed once a day with bread and water by means of moving a single loose brick.

The old monk paused before the cell, which was nothing more than a featureless dark wall. Its old stones had been polished by many thousands of hands: people who had come to ask this particular anchorite for wisdom. He was said to have been walled up at the age of twelve. Now he was nearly one hundred, an oracle famed for his unique gift of prophecy.

The monk tapped on the stone, twice, with his fingernail. They waited. After a minute, the one loose stone in the façade began to move, ever so slightly, scraping slowly over the joint. A withered hand appeared, white as snow, with translucent blue veins. It rotated the stone into a sideways position, leaving a small space.

The monk bent over to the hole and murmured something in a low voice. Then he turned to listen. Minutes passed, and Pendergast heard the faintest whisper from within. The monk straightened up, apparently satisfied, and gestured for Pendergast to step close. Pendergast did as requested, watching the stone slip back into position, guided by an unseen hand.

All of a sudden, a deep scraping sound seemed to come from within the rock next to the stone cell, and a seam opened up. It enlarged to become a stone door, which grated open on some unseen mechanism. A peculiar scent of some unknown incense wafted from within. The monk held out his hand in a gesture for Pendergast to enter, and when the agent had passed over the threshold, the door slid shut. The monk had not followed—Pendergast was alone.

Another monk appeared out of the gloom, holding a guttering candle. During the past seven weeks at Gsalrig Chongg, as well as in his previous visits, Pendergast had come to know the faces of all the monks—and yet this one was new. He realized he had just entered the inner monastery, whispered about but never confirmed—the hidden sanctum sanctorum. Such access—which, he'd understood, was absolutely forbidden—was apparently guarded by the immured anchorite. This was a monastery within the monastery, in which a half dozen cloistered monks passed their entire lives in the profoundest meditation and unceasing mental study, never seeing the outside world or even coming in direct contact with the monks of the outer monastery, guarded by the unseen anchorite. They had so withdrawn from the world, Pendergast once heard it said, that the light of the sun, should it fall upon their skin, would kill them.

He followed the strange monk down a narrow

corridor, leading into the deepest parts of the monastic complex. The passages became rougher and he realized that they were tunnels cut out of the living rock itself: tunnels that had been plastered and frescoed a thousand years before, their paintings now almost obliterated by smoke, humidity, and time. The passage turned, and turned again, passing small stone cells containing Buddhas or thangka paintings, illuminated by candles and drifting with incense. They passed no one, saw no one—the warren of windowless rooms and tunnels felt hollow, damp, and deserted.

Finally, after what felt like an endless journey, they came to another door, this one bound in bands of oiled iron, riveted into thick plates. Another key was brandished, and with some effort the door was unlocked and opened.

The room beyond was small and dim, illuminated by a single butter lamp. The walls were lined in ancient, hand-rubbed wood, meticulously inlaid. Fragrant smoke drifted in the air, pungent and resinous. It took Pendergast's eyes a moment to adjust to the extraordinary fact that the chamber was packed full of treasure. Against the far wall sat dozens of caskets in heavy repoussé gold, their lids tightly locked; next to them stood stacks of leather bags, some of which had rotted and split, spilling their contents of heavy gold coins—everything from old English sovereigns and Greek staters to heavy gold mughals. Small wooden kegs were stacked around them, the staves swollen and rotted, spilling out raw and cut rubies, emeralds, sapphires, diamonds, turquoises, tourmalines, and peridots. Others seemed filled with small gold bars and oval Japanese kobans.

The wall to his right contained a different kind of treasure: shawms and kangling horns made of ebony, ivory, and gold, and encrusted with gems; dorje bells of silver and electrum; human skullcaps trimmed in precious metals and glowing with turquoise and coral inlay. In another area stood a crowd of statues in gold and silver, one adorned with hundreds of star sapphires; nearby, nestled in wooden crates and straw, he could see translucent bowls, figures, and plaques of the finest jade.

And to his immediate left, the greatest treasure of all: hundreds of cubbyholes stuffed with dusty scrolls, rolled thangkas, and bundles of parchment and vellum tied in silk cords.

So astonishing was the display of treasure that it took Pendergast a moment to realize a human being was sitting, cross-legged, on a cushion in the near corner.

The monk who had brought him now bowed, hands together, and withdrew, the iron door clanging behind him, the lock turning. The cross-legged monk gestured toward a cushion beside him. "Please sit down," he said in English.

Pendergast bowed and seated himself. "A most remarkable room," he replied. He paused a moment. "And a most unusual incense."

"We are the guardians of the monastery's treasures—the gold and silver and all other transitory things the world considers wealth." The man spoke in a measured and elegant English, with an Oxbridge accent. "We are also stewards of the library and the religious paintings.

The 'incense' you note is the resin of the *dorzhan-qing* plant—burned ceaselessly to keep the worms at bay—ravenous woodworms indigenous to the high Himalayas that seek to destroy everything in this room made of wood, paper, or silk."

Pendergast nodded, taking the opportunity to examine the monk more closely. He was old, but wiry and astonishingly fit. His red-and-saffron robes were tightly wound, and his head was shaven. His feet were bare and almost black with dirt. His eyes gleamed in a smooth, ageless face that radiated intelligence, anxiousness, and grave concern.

"No doubt you're wondering who I am, and why I have asked you to come," the monk said. "I am Thubten. Welcome, Mr. Pendergast."

"Lama Thubten?"

"We have no distinguishing titles here in the inner temple." The monk leaned toward him, peering closely at his face. "I understand that your business in life is to—I am not sure how to put it—to pry into the affairs of others, to put right what has been wronged? To solve riddles, shine light onto mystery and darkness?"

"I have never heard it put quite that way. But yes, you're correct."

The monk sat back, relief evident on his face. "That is good. I feared perhaps I was mistaken." Then his voice fell almost to a whisper. "There is a riddle here."

There was a long silence. Then Pendergast said, "Go on."

"The abbot cannot speak of this matter directly. That

is why they have asked me to do so. Yet even though the situation is dire, I find it . . . difficult to talk about."

"You have all been kind to me and my ward," said Pendergast. "I welcome the opportunity to do something in return—if I can."

"Thank you. The story I am about to tell you involves revealing some details of a secret nature."

"You can count on my discretion."

"First I will tell you a little of myself. I was born in the remote hill country of Lake Manosawar in western Tibet. I was an only child, and my parents were killed in an avalanche before my first birthday. A pair of English naturalists—a husband-and-wife team doing an extensive survey of Manchuria, Nepal, and Tibet—took pity on such a young orphan and informally adopted me. For ten years I stayed with them as they traveled the wilds, observing, sketching, and taking notes. Then one night a roving band of soldiers came upon our tent. They shot both the man and the woman, and burned them with all their possessions. I alone escaped.

"Losing two sets of parents—you can imagine my feelings. My lonely wanderings took me here, to Gsalrig Chongg. In time I took a vow and entered the inner monastery. We devote our lives to extreme mental and physical training. We occupy ourselves with the deepest, the most profound, and the most enigmatic aspects of existence. In your study of Chongg Ran, you have touched upon some of the truths that we plumb to an infinitely greater depth."

Pendergast inclined his head.

"Here in the inner monastery, we are cut off from all

existence. We are not permitted to look upon the outside world, to see the sky, to breathe fresh air. All is focused on turning within. It is a very great sacrifice to make, even for a Tibetan monk, and that is why there are only six of us. We are guarded by the anchorite, not allowed to speak to an outside human being, and I have violated that sacred vow to speak with you now. That alone should help impress upon you the seriousness of the situation."

"I understand," Pendergast said.

"We have certain duties here as monks of the inner temple. In addition to being keepers of the monastery's library, relics, and treasure, we are also the keepers of . . . the Agozyen."

"The Agozyen?"

"The most important object in the monastery, perhaps in all of Tibet. It is kept in a locked vault, over in that corner." He pointed to a niche carved in the stone, with a heavy iron door, which was hanging ajar. "All six monks gather here once a year to perform certain rituals of warding over the vault of the Agozyen. When we performed this duty in May, a few days before you arrived, we found the Agozyen was no longer in its place."

"Stolen?"

The monk nodded.

"Who has the key?"

"I do. The only one."

"And the vault was locked?"

"Yes. Let me assure you, Mr. Pendergast, that it is quite impossible for one of our monks to have committed this crime."

"Forgive me if I am skeptical of that assertion."

"Skepticism is good." He spoke with peculiar force and Pendergast did not reply. "The Agozyen is no longer at the monastery. If it was, we should know."

"How?"

"That is not to be spoken of. Please believe me, Mr. Pendergast—we *would* know. None of the monks here have taken the item into their possession."

"May I take a look?"

The monk nodded.

Pendergast rose and, taking a small flashlight from his pocket, went over to the vault and peered at the round keyhole of the lock. After a moment he examined it with a magnifying glass.

"The lock's been picked," he said, straightening up.

"I am sorry. Picked?"

"Coaxed open without the use of a key." He glanced at the monk. "Forced, actually, by the looks of it. You say none of the monks could have stolen it. Have there been other visitors to the monastery?"

"Yes," said the monk with a ghost of a smile. "In fact, we know who stole it."

"Ah," said Pendergast. "That makes things much simpler. Tell me about it."

"A young man came to us in early May—a mountaineer. His was a strange arrival. He came from the east—from the mountains on the Nepalese border. He was half dead, a man in mental and physical collapse. He was a professional mountaineer, the lone survivor of an expedition up the unclimbed west face of Dhaulagiri. An avalanche swept all to their deaths save him. He'd been forced to cross and descend the north face, and from there make his way over the Tibetan frontier illegally, through no fault of his own. It took him three weeks of walking and finally crawling down glaciers and valleys to reach us. He survived by eating berry rats, which are quite nourishing if you catch one with a stomach full of berries. He was on the verge of death. We nursed him back to health. He is an American—his name is Jordan Ambrose."

"Did he study with you?"

"He took little interest in Chongg Ran. It was strange—he certainly had the power of will and activity of mind to succeed, perhaps as much as any westerner we have seen . . . besides the woman, that is. Constance."

Pendergast nodded. "How do you know it was him?"

The monk did not answer directly. "We would like you to trace him, find the Agozyen, and bring it back to the monastery."

Pendergast nodded. "This Jordan Ambrose—what did he look like?"

The monk reached into his robes and pulled out a tiny, scrolled parchment. He untied the strings binding it and unrolled it. "Our thangka painter made a likeness of him at my request."

Pendergast took the scroll and examined it. It showed a young, fit, and handsome man, in his late twenties, with long blond hair and blue eyes, and a look on his face of physical determination, moral casualness, and high intelligence. It was a remarkable likeness that seemed to capture both the outer and inner person.

"This will be very useful," said Pendergast, tying it up and slipping it into his pocket.

"Do you need any more information to find the Agozyen?" the monk asked.

"Yes. Tell me exactly what the Agozyen is."

The change that came over the monk was startling. His face grew guarded, almost frightened. "I cannot," he said in a quavering voice pitched so low it was barely audible.

"It's unavoidable. If I'm to recover it, I must know what it is."

"You misunderstand me. I cannot tell you what it is because *we don't know what it is.*"

Pendergast frowned. "How can that be?"

"The Agozyen has been sealed within a wooden box ever since it was received for safekeeping by our monastery a thousand years ago. We never opened it—it was strictly forbidden. It has been passed down, from Rinpoche to Rinpoche, always sealed."

"What kind of box?"

The monk indicated with his hands the dimensions, about five inches by five inches by four feet.

"That's an unusual shape. What do you think might have been stored in a box that shape?"

"It could be anything long and thin. A wand or sword. A scroll or rolled-up painting. A set of seals, perhaps, or ropes with sacred knots."

"What does the name *Agozyen* mean?"

The monk hesitated. "Darkness."

"Why was opening it forbidden?"

"The founder of the monastery, the first Ralang Rinpoche, received it from a holy man in the east, from India. The holy man had carved a text on the side of the box which contained the warning. I have a copy of the text here, which I will translate." He took out a tiny scroll, written with Tibetan characters, held it at arm's length in his slightly trembling hands, and recited:

Lest into the dharma you unchain
An uncleanness of evil and pain,
And darkness about darkness wheel,
The Agozyen you must not unseal.

"The 'dharma' refers," said Pendergast, "to the teachings of the Buddha?"

"In this context it implies something even larger—the entire world."

"Obscure and alarming."

"It is just as enigmatic in Tibetan. But the words used are very powerful. The warning is a strong one, Mr. Pendergast—very strong."

Pendergast considered this for a moment. "How could an outsider know enough about this box to steal it? I spent a year here some time ago and never heard of it."

"That is a great enigma. Surely none of our monks ever spoke of it. We are in the greatest dread of the object and never talk of it, even amongst ourselves."

"This fellow, Ambrose, could have scooped up a million dollars' worth of gemstones in one hand. Any ordinary thief would have taken the gold and jewels first."

"Perhaps," said the monk after a moment, "he is not an ordinary thief. Gold, gemstones . . . you speak of earthly treasures. *Passing* treasures. The Agozyen . . ."

"Yes?" Pendergast prompted.

But the old monk simply spread his hands, and returned Pendergast's gaze with haunted eyes.

3

The black shroud of night had just begun to lift when Pendergast made his way through the ironbound doors of the monastery's inner gate. Ahead, beyond the outer wall, the bulk of Annapurna reared up, adamant, a purple outline emerging from the receding darkness. He paused in the cobblestone courtyard while a monk silently brought his horse. The chill predawn air was heavy with dew and the scent of wild roses. Throwing his saddlebags over the animal's withers, he checked the saddle, adjusted the stirrups.

Constance Greene watched wordlessly as the FBI agent went through his final preparations. She was dressed in a monastic robe of faded saffron, and, were it not for her fine features and her spill of brown hair, could almost have been mistaken for a monk herself.

"I'm sorry to leave you early, Constance. I have to get on our man's trail before it gets cold."

"They really have no idea what it is?"

Pendergast shook his head. "Beyond its shape and its name, none."

"Darkness . . . ," she murmured. She glanced at him, her eyes troubled. "How long will you be gone?"

"The difficult part is already done. I know the thief's name and what he looks like. It's simply a matter of catching up to him. Retrieving the artifact should be the work of a week, perhaps two at the most. A simple assignment. In two weeks, your studies will be completed and you can rejoin me to finish up our European tour."

"Be careful, Aloysius."

Pendergast smiled thinly. "The man may be of questionable moral character, but he does not strike me as a killer. The risk should be minimal. It's a simple crime, but with one puzzling aspect: why did he take the Agozyen and leave all that treasure? He seems to have no previous interest in things Tibetan. It suggests the Agozyen is something remarkably precious and valuable—or that it is in some way truly extraordinary."

Constance nodded. "Do you have any instructions for me?"

"Rest. Meditate. Complete your initial course of study." He paused. "I'm skeptical that no one here knows what the Agozyen is—somebody must have peeked. It's human nature—even here, among these monks. It would help me greatly to know what it was."

"I'll look into it."

"Excellent. I know I can count on your discretion." He hesitated, then turned toward her. "Constance, there's something I need to ask you."

Seeing his expression, her eyes widened, but when she spoke her voice remained calm. "Yes?"

"You've never spoken of your journey to Feversham.

At some point you may need to talk about it. When you rejoin me . . . if you're ready . . ." Again, his voice fell into atypical confusion and indecision.

Constance looked away.

"For weeks now," he went on, "we haven't spoken of what happened. But sooner or later—"

She turned on him abruptly. *"No!"* she said fiercely. "No." She paused a moment, mastering herself. "I want you to promise me something: never mention him or . . . Feversham . . . in my presence again."

Pendergast remained motionless, looking at her carefully. It appeared that his brother Diogenes's seduction had affected her even more deeply than he realized. At last, he nodded again, faintly. "I promise."

Then, withdrawing his hands from hers, he kissed her on both cheeks. Taking hold of the reins, he swung up in the saddle, kicked his horse, passed through the outer gate, and set off down the winding trail.

1

In a barren cell deep in the Gsalrig Chongg monastery, Constance Greene sat in the lotus position, her eyes closed, visualizing the exceedingly complex knotted silk cord that lay on a cushion in front of her. Tsering sat behind her in the dim light, her only awareness of him the low sound of his voice, murmuring in Tibetan. She had been studying the language intensively for nearly eight weeks and had developed a halting fluency, acquiring a modest vocabulary along with some phrases and idioms.

"See the knot in your mind," came the low, mesmerizing voice of her teacher.

At will, the knot began to materialize, about four feet before her closed eyes, radiating light. That she was sitting on the bare, cold floor of a nitre-encrusted cell receded from her consciousness.

"Make it clear. Make it steady."

The knot came into focus, sharply, wavering a little or going fuzzy when her attention wavered, but always returning to focus.

"Your mind is a lake in twilight," the teacher said. "Still, calm, and clear."

A strange sense of being there and yet not being there enveloped Constance. The knot she had chosen to visualize remained in front of her. It was one of medium complexity, tied over three hundred years ago by a great teacher. It was known by the name of the Double Rose.

"Increase the image of the knot in your mind."

It was a difficult balance of effort and letting go. If she concentrated too hard on clarity and stability, the image began to break up and other thoughts intruded; if she let go too much, the image faded into the mists of her mind. There was a perfect balancing point; and gradually—very gradually—she found it.

"Now gaze upon the image of the knot you have created in your mind. Observe it from all angles: from above, from the sides."

The softly glistening coils of silk remained steady in her mind's eye, bringing her a quiet joy, a mindfulness, that she had never before experienced. And then the voice of her teacher disappeared entirely, and all that was left was the knot itself. Time vanished. Space vanished. Only the knot remained.

"Untie the knot."

This was the most difficult part, requiring immense concentration—being able to trace the coils of the knot, and then mentally untie it.

Time passed; it could have been ten seconds, or ten hours.

A gentle hand touched her shoulder and her eyes

opened. Tsering was standing before her, robe tucked around an arm.

"How long?" she asked in English.

"Five hours."

She rose, and found her legs so wobbly she could barely walk. He grasped her arm and helped her steady herself.

"You learn well," he said. "Be sure no take pride in it."

She nodded. "Thank you."

They walked slowly down an ancient passageway, turned a corner. She could hear, up ahead, the faint sound of the prayer wheels echoing down the stone passageway.

Another corner. She felt refreshed, clear, alert. "What drives those prayer wheels?" she asked. "They never cease turning."

"There is a spring of water under monastery—source of Tsangpo River. It pass over wheel, turn gears."

"Ingenious."

They passed by the wall of creaking, rattling brass wheels, like some Rube Goldberg confection. Constance could see, behind the wheels, a forest of moving brass rods and wooden gears.

They left the wheels behind and came into one of the outer corridors. Ahead loomed one of the far pavilions of the monastery, the square pillars framing the three great mountains. They entered the pavilion and Constance drank in the pure high-altitude air. Tsering indicated a seat and she took it. He sat down next to her. For a few minutes they gazed over the darkening mountains in silence.

"The meditation you are learning is very powerful.

Someday, you may come out of meditation and find the knot . . . untied."

Constance said nothing.

"Some can influence the physical world with pure thought, create things out of thought. There is story of monk who meditate so long on rose that when he open his eyes, there is rose on the floor. This is very dangerous. With enough skill and meditation, there are those who can create things . . . other than roses. It is not something to desire, and it is a grave deviancy from Buddhist teaching."

She nodded her understanding, not believing a word of it.

Tsering's lips stretched into a smile. "You skeptical person. That very good. Whether you believe or not, choose with care image you meditate on."

"I will," said Constance.

"Remember: Though we have many 'demons,' most not evil. They are attachments you must conquer to reach enlightenment."

Another long silence.

"Have question?"

She was quiet for a moment, recalling Pendergast's parting request. "Tell me. Why is there an inner monastery?"

Tsering was silent for a moment. "Inner monastery is oldest in Tibet, built here in remote mountains by group of wandering monks from India."

"Was it built to protect the Agozyen?"

Tsering looked at her sharply. "That is not to be spoken of."

"My guardian has left here to find it. At this monastery's request. Perhaps I can be of some help, too."

The old man looked away, and the distance in his eyes had nothing to do with the landscape beyond the pavilion. "Agozyen carried here from India. Taken far away, into mountains, where it not threaten. They build inner monastery to protect and keep Agozyen. Then, later, outer monastery built around inner one."

"There's something I don't understand. If the Agozyen was so very dangerous, why not just destroy it?"

The monk was silent for a very long time. Then he said, quietly, "Because it has important future purpose."

"What purpose?"

But her teacher remained silent.

5

The jeep came careening around the corner of the hill, bumped and splashed though a series of enormous, mud-filled potholes, and descended onto a broad dirt road toward the town of Qiang, in a damp valley not far from the Tibet-Chinese border. A gray drizzle fell from the sky into a pall of brown smoke, which hung over the town from a cluster of smokestacks across a greasy river. Trash lined both shoulders.

The driver of the jeep passed an overloaded truck, honking furiously. He swerved past another truck on a blind curve, slewing within a few feet of a cliff edge, and began descending into town.

"To the railroad station," Pendergast told the driver in Mandarin.

"Wei wei, xian sheng!"

The jeep dodged pedestrians, bicycles, a man driving a pair of oxen. The driver screeched to a halt in a crush of traffic at a rotary, then inched forward, leaning continuously on the horn. Exhaust fumes and a veritable symphony of claxons filled the air. The windshield wipers slapped back and forth, streaking the mud that covered the jeep, the anemic rainfall sufficient only to spread it around.

Beyond the rotary, the broad avenue ended at a low gray cement structure. The driver stopped abruptly before it. "We are here," he said.

Pendergast stepped out and opened his umbrella. The air smelled of sulfur and petroleum fumes. He entered the station and made his way through hordes of people, pushing, yelling, lugging huge sacks and wheeling baskets. Some carried live, trussed-up chickens or ducks, and one even wheeled along a piteously squalling pig tied up in an old wire shopping cart.

Toward the back of the station, the throngs thinned and Pendergast found what he was looking for: a dim passageway leading to the officials' offices. He passed by a half-sleeping guard, walked swiftly down the long corridor, glancing at the names on the doors as he passed. At last he stopped before a particularly shabby door. He tried the handle, found it unlocked, and walked in without knocking.

A Chinese official, small and rotund, sat behind a desk heaped with papers. A battered tea set stood to one side, the cups chipped and dirty. The office smelled of fried food and hoisin sauce.

The official leapt up, furious at the unannounced entry. "Who you?" he roared out in bad English.

Pendergast stood there, arms folded, a supercilious smile on his face.

"What you want? I call guard." He reached to pick up the phone, but Pendergast quickly leaned over and pressed the receiver back into its cradle.

"Ba," said Pendergast in a low voice, in Mandarin. "Stop."

The man's face reddened at this further outrage.

"I have some questions I would like answered," said Pendergast, still speaking in coldly formal Mandarin.

The effect on the official was pronounced, his face reflecting outrage, confusion, and apprehension. "You insult me," he finally shouted back in Mandarin. "Barging into my office, touching my telephone, making demands! Who are you, that you can come in here like this, behaving like a barbarian?"

"You will please sit down, kind sir, remain quiet, and listen. Or"—Pendergast switched to the insulting informal—"you will find yourself on the next train out of here, reassigned to a guardpost high in the Kunlun Mountains."

The man's face edged toward purple, but he did not speak. After a moment he sat stiffly down, folded his hands on the desk, and waited.

Pendergast also seated himself. He took out the scroll Thubten had given him and held it out to the official. After a moment, the man took it grudgingly.

"This man came through here two months ago. His name is Jordan Ambrose. He was carrying a wooden box, very old. He bribed you, and in return you gave him an export permit for the box. I would like to see a copy of the export permit."

There was a long silence. Then the official laid the painting on the table. "I do not know what you are speaking about," he said truculently. "I do not take bribes. And in any case a lot of people come through this station. I wouldn't remember."

Pendergast removed a flat bamboo box from his pocket, opened it, and tipped it upside down, depositing a neat stack of fresh hundred-yuan renminbi notes on the table. The man stared at them, swallowed.

"You would remember this man," Pendergast said. "The box was large—a meter and a half long. It was obviously old. It would have been impossible for Mr. Ambrose to have taken the box through here or gotten it out of the country without a permit. Now, kind sir, you have a choice: bend your principles and take the bribe, or stick to your principles and end up in the Kunlun Mountains. As you may have guessed from my accent and fluency in the language, although I am a foreigner, I have very important connections in China."

The official wiped his hands with a handkerchief. Then he extended a hand, covering the money. He pulled it back toward him and it quickly disappeared into a drawer. Then he rose. Pendergast rose likewise, and they shook hands and exchanged polite, formal greetings, as if meeting for the first time.

The man sat down. "Would the gentleman like some tea?" he asked.

Pendergast glanced at the filthy, stained tea set, then smiled. "I would be greatly honored, kind sir."

The man shouted roughly into a back room. An underling came trotting out and removed the tea set. Five minutes later he brought it back, steaming. The bureaucrat poured out the cups.

"I remember the man you speak of," he said. "He had

no visa to be in China. He had a long box. He wanted both an entry visa—which he would need to leave—as well as an export permit. I gave him both. It was . . . very expensive for him."

The tea was a long gin green and Pendergast was surprised at its quality.

"He spoke no Chinese, of course. He told me a quite incredible story of having crossed from Nepal into Tibet."

"And the box? Did he say anything about it?"

"He said it was an antiquity he had bought in Tibet—you know, these dirty Tibetans, they'd sell their own children for a few yuan. The Tibet Autonomous Region is awash in old things."

"Did you ask what was in it?"

"He said it was a phur-bu ritual dagger." He rummaged in a drawer, rifled through some papers, and brought out the permit. He pushed it to Pendergast, who glanced at it.

"But the box was locked and he refused to open it," the official continued. "That cost him quite a bit more, avoiding an inspection of the contents." The bureaucrat smiled, exposing a row of tea-stained teeth.

"What do you think was in there?"

"I have no idea. Heroin, currency, gemstones?" He spread his hands.

Pendergast pointed at the permit. "It states here he would be taking a train to Chengdu, then a China Air flight to Beijing, transferring on to a flight to Rome. Is this true?"

"Yes. He was required to show me his ticket. If he

followed any other route leaving China, he would be in danger of being stopped. The permit is only for Qiang–Chengdu–Beijing–Rome. So I am sure that is how he went. Of course, once in Rome . . ." Again he spread his hands.

Pendergast copied down the travel information. "What was his demeanor? Was he nervous?"

The bureaucrat thought for a moment. "No. It was very strange. He seemed . . . euphoric. Expansive. Almost radiant."

Pendergast stood. "I thank you most kindly for the tea, *xian sheng*."

"And I thank you, kindest sir," said the official.

An hour later, Pendergast had boarded a first-class car of the Glorious Trans-China Express, headed to Chengdu.

6

Constance Greene knew that the monks of the Gsalrig Chongg monastery lived according to a fixed schedule of meditation, study, and sleep, with two breaks for meals and tea. The sleeping period was set: from eight in the evening to one o'clock in the morning. This routine never varied, and it had probably remained the same for a thousand years. She thus felt certain that at midnight she would be unlikely to encounter anyone moving about the vast monastery.

And so at twelve o'clock sharp, just as she had done the last three nights in a row, she folded back the coarse yak skin that served as her blanket and sat up in bed. The only sound was the distant moaning of the wind through the outer pavilions of the monastery. She rose and slipped into her robes. The cell was bitter cold. She went to the tiny window and opened the wooden shutter. There was no glass, and a chill flow of air came in. The window looked out into the darkness of night, upon a single star shivering high in the velvety blackness.

She shut the window and went to the door, where she paused, listening. All was quiet. After a moment she opened the door, slipped into the hall, and walked down the long outer corridor. She passed the prayer wheels, endlessly creaking their blessings to heaven, then passed through a corridor that plunged deep into the riddle of rooms, searching for the immured anchorite who guarded the inner monastery. Although Pendergast had described its proximate location, the complex was so vast, and the corridors so labyrinthine, that it was proving nearly impossible to locate.

But this evening, after many turns, she came at last to the polished stone wall indicating the outside of his cell. The loose brick was in place, its edges abraded and chipped from being moved countless times. She tapped on it a few times and waited. Minutes went by, and then the brick moved just a little; there was a small scraping noise and it began to turn. A pair of bony fingers appeared like long white worms in the darkness, grasped the brick's edge, and moved it around so that a small opening appeared in the darkness.

Constance had carefully worked out beforehand what she wanted to say in Tibetan. Now she leaned toward the hole and whispered.

"Let me into the inner monastery."

She turned and placed her ear against the hole. A faint, whispery, insectlike voice answered. She strained to hear and understand.

"You know it is forbidden?"

"Yes, but—"

Before she could even finish, she heard a scraping noise and a piece of the wall beyond the cell began to move, opening along an old stone seam to reveal a dark corridor. She was taken aback—the anchorite hadn't even waited to hear her carefully crafted explanation.

She knelt, lit a dragon joss stick, and proceeded inside. The wall closed. A dim corridor stretched ahead, exhaling the smell of damp air, wet stone, and a cloying, resinous scent. The air was hazy with incense.

She took a step forward, holding up the joss stick. The flame flickered, as if in protest. She moved down the long passageway, its dark walls dimly frescoed with disturbing images of strange deities and dancing demons.

The inner monastery, she realized, must have once held far more monks than it did now. It was vast, cold, and empty. Not knowing where she was going, and without even a clear idea of what she was doing—beyond finding the monk Pendergast had spoken to and questioning him further—she turned several corners, passing through large, vacant rooms, the walls painted with half-glimpsed thangkas and mandalas, almost obliterated by time. In one room, a lone, forgotten candle guttered in front of an ancient bronze statue of the Buddha eaten away by verdigris. The joss stick she was using for light began to fizzle and she pulled another from her pocket and lit it, the scent of sandalwood smoke filling the passageway.

She turned another corner, then halted. A monk stood there, tall, gaunt, in a ragged robe, his eyes hollow and staring with a strange, almost fierce intensity. She faced him. He said nothing. Neither moved.

And then Constance reached up to her hood, drew it back, and let her brown hair fall across her shoulders.

The monk's eyes widened, but only slightly. Still he said nothing.

"Greetings," Constance said in Tibetan.

The monk faintly inclined his head. His large eyes continued staring at her.

"Agozyen," she said.

Again, no reaction.

"I have come to ask: what is Agozyen?" She spoke haltingly, continuing in her poor Tibetan.

"Why are you here, little monk?" he asked quietly.

Constance took a step toward him. "What is Agozyen?" she repeated more fiercely.

He closed his eyes. "Your mind is in a turmoil of excitement, young one."

"I must know."

"Must," he repeated.

"What does Agozyen do?"

His eyes opened. He turned and began walking away. After a moment, she followed.

The monk wound his way through many narrow passages and convoluted turnings, down and up staircases, through rough-cut tunnels and long, frescoed halls. Finally he paused before a stone doorway curtained in frayed orange silk. He drew it aside and Constance was surprised to see three monks seated on stone benches, as if in council, with candles arrayed in front of a gilded statue of the seated Buddha.

One of the monks rose. "Please come in," he said in surprisingly fluent English.

Constance bowed. Had they been expecting her? It seemed impossible. And yet there was no other logical explanation.

"I'm studying with Lama Tsering," she said, grateful to switch to English.

The man nodded.

"I want to know about the Agozyen," she said.

He turned to the others and began speaking in Tibetan. Constance strained to catch the thread of what he was saying, but the voices were too low. At last the monk turned back to her.

"Lama Thubten told the detective all we knew," he said.

"Forgive me, but I don't believe you."

The monk seemed taken aback by her directness, but he recovered quickly. "Why do you speak this way, child?"

The room was freezing and Constance began to shiver. She pulled her robe tightly about her. "You may not know exactly what the Agozyen is, but you know its purpose. Its *future* purpose."

"It is not time to reveal it yet. The Agozyen was taken from us."

"Taken prematurely, you mean?"

The monk shook his head. "We were its guardians. It is imperative that it be returned to us, before . . ." He stopped.

"Before what?"

The monk merely shook his head, the anxious lines of his face gaunt and stark in the dim light.

"You *must* tell me. It will help Pendergast, help *us*, in locating the object. I won't reveal it to anyone but him."

"Let us close our eyes and meditate," said the monk.

"Let us meditate, and offer prayers for its speedy and safe return."

She swallowed, tried to calm her mind. It was true, she was acting impulsively. Her behavior was no doubt shocking to the monks. But she had made a promise to Aloysius and she was going to keep it.

The monk began chanting, and the others took it up. The strange, humming, repetitive sounds filled her mind, and her anger, her desperate desire to know more, seemed to flow from her like water from a pierced vessel. The strong need to fulfill Pendergast's request faded somewhat. Her mind became wakeful, almost calm.

The chanting stopped. She slowly opened her eyes.

"Are you still passionately seeking the answer to your question?"

A long silence passed. Constance remembered one of her lessons—a teaching on desire. She bowed her head. "No," she lied. She wanted the information more than ever.

The monk smiled. "You have much to learn, little monk. We know quite well that you need this information, that you desire this information, and that it will be useful to you. It is not good for you personally that you seek it. The information is extremely dangerous. It has the potential of destroying not just your life, but your very soul. It may bar you from enlightenment for all of time."

She looked up. "I need it."

"We do not know what the Agozyen is. We do not know where it came from in India. We do not know who created it. But we know *why* it was created."

Constance waited.

"It was created to wreak a terrible vengeance on the world."

"Vengeance? What kind of vengeance?"

"To cleanse the earth."

For a reason she could not quite explain, Constance wasn't sure she wanted the monk to continue. She forced herself to speak. "Cleanse it—how?"

The man's anxious expression now turned almost sorrowful. "I am very sorry to burden you with this difficult knowledge. When the earth is drowning in selfishness, greed, violence, and evil, the Agozyen will cleanse the earth of its human burden."

Constance swallowed. "I'm not sure I understand."

"It will cleanse the earth *entirely* of its human burden," the monk said in a very low voice. "So that all might start afresh."

7

Aloysius Pendergast stepped off the vaporetto at Ca' d'Oro and paused, leather briefcase in hand. It was a warm summer day in Venice, and sunlight sparkled off the waters of the Grand Canal and glowed on the intricate marble façades of the palazzi.

He consulted a small piece of paper, then walked down the quay toward a little warren of streets leading northeast to the Chiesa dei Gesuiti. Soon he had left the bustle and noise behind and was deep in the shadowy coolness of the side streets running behind the palaces along the Grand Canal. Music spilled from a restaurant, and a small motorboat plied the back canal, leaving behind the sound of water lapping against the marble and travertine bridges. A man leaned out a window and called across the canal to a woman, who laughed.

A few more turns brought Pendergast to a door with a worn bronze button, labeled simply *Dott. Adriano Morin.* He pressed once and waited. After a moment he heard the creak of a window opening above and looked up. A woman gazed out.

"What do you want?" she asked in Italian.

"I have an appointment to see *il Dottore*. My name is Pendergast."

The head ducked back in, and after a moment the door was opened. "Come in," she said.

Pendergast entered a small foyer with walls of red silk brocade and a floor of black and white marble squares. Various exquisite works of Asian art decorated the room—an ancient Khmer head from Cambodia; a Tibetan dorje in solid gold, inlaid with turquoises; several old thangkas; an illuminated Mughal manuscript in a glass case; an ivory head of the Buddha.

"Please sit down," the woman said, taking her place behind a small desk.

Pendergast seated himself, placed his briefcase on his knees, and waited. He knew that Dr. Morin was one of the most notorious dealers in "unprovenanced" antiquities in Europe. He was, essentially, a high-level black-market dealer, one of many who received looted antiquities from various corrupt Asian countries, supplied them with phony paperwork, and then sold them on the legitimate art market to museums and collectors who knew better than to ask questions.

A moment later Morin appeared in the doorway, a neat, elegant man with exquisitely trimmed and polished fingernails, tiny feet encased in fine Italian shoes, and a carefully barbered beard.

"Mr. Pendergast? How delightful."

They shook hands. "Please come with me," the man said.

Pendergast followed him into a long *salone,* with a wall of Gothic windows looking out over the Grand Canal.

Like the foyer, it was filled with extraordinary examples of Asian art. Morin indicated a seat and they settled down. The man slipped a gold cigarette case from his pocket, snapped it open, offered it to Pendergast.

"No, thank you."

"Do you mind if I do?"

"Of course not."

Morin plucked a cigarette from the case and threw one elegant leg over the other. "Now, Mr. Pendergast. How may I be of service to you?"

"You have a lovely collection, Dr. Morin."

Morin smiled, gestured around the room. "I sell only through private placement. We are not, obviously, open to the public. How long have you been collecting? I haven't run across your name before, and I pride myself in knowing most everyone in the field."

"I'm not a collector."

Morin's hand paused as it was lighting the cigarette. "Not a collector? I must have misunderstood you when we spoke over the phone."

"You did not misunderstand me. I lied."

Now the hand had gone very still, the smoke curling into the air. "I beg your pardon?"

"I'm actually a detective. Working privately, tracing a stolen object."

The very air in the room seemed to freeze.

Morin spoke calmly. "Since you admit you are here in no official role, and as you have gained entrance under false pretenses, I am afraid this conversation is at an end." He stood up. "Good day, Mr. Pendergast. Lavinia will show you out."

As he turned to leave the room, Pendergast spoke to his back. "That Khmer statue in the corner comes from Banteay Chhmar in Cambodia, by the way. It was looted only two months ago."

Morin paused halfway to the door. "You are mistaken. It comes from an old Swiss collection. I have the papers to prove it. As I have for all the objects in my collection."

"I have a photograph of that very object, in situ, in the temple wall."

Morin called out. "Lavinia? Please call the police and tell them I have an undesirable in my house who refuses to leave."

"And that sixteenth-century Sri Chakrasamvara and Vajravarahi from Nepal was exported with a forged permit. Nothing like that could have left Nepal legally."

"Shall we await the police, or are you on the way out?"

Pendergast checked his watch. "I'm happy to wait." He patted his briefcase. "I've got enough documents in here to keep Interpol busy for years."

"You have nothing. All my pieces are legal and carefully provenanced."

"Like that kapala skull cup, trimmed in silver and gold? It's legal—because it's a modern copy. Or are you trying to pass it off as original?"

Silence descended. The magical light of Venice filtered in through the windows, filling the magnificent room with a golden sheen.

"When the police come, I will have you arrested," Morin said finally.

"Yes, and no doubt they will confiscate the contents of my briefcase—which they will find most interesting."

"You're a blackmailer."

"Blackmailer? I seek nothing. I am merely stating facts. For example, that twelfth-century Vishnu with Consorts allegedly from the Pala dynasty is also a forgery. It would bring you a small fortune if it were real. Pity you can't sell it."

"What the devil do you want?"

"Absolutely nothing."

"You come here, you lie, you threaten me in my own home—and you want nothing? Come now, Pendergast. Do you suspect that one of these objects is stolen? If so, why don't we discuss it like gentlemen?"

"I doubt the stolen object I seek is in your collection."

The man dabbed his brow with a silk handkerchief. "Surely you came to visit me with some goal in mind, some request!"

"Such as?"

"I have no idea!" the man erupted furiously. "You want money? A gift? Everybody wants something! Out with it!"

"Ah well," said Pendergast diffidently. "As long as you're insisting, I've a little Tibetan portrait I'd like you to look at."

Morin turned swiftly, the ash falling from his cigarette. "For God sakes, is that all? I'll look at your damned portrait. There's no need for all these threats."

"I'm so glad to hear it. I was concerned you might not be cooperative."

"I *said*, I'd cooperate!"

"Excellent." Pendergast took out the portrait given him by the monk and handed it to Morin. The man unrolled it, flicked open a pair of glasses and put them on, then examined it. After a moment, he pulled the glasses off and handed the scroll back to Pendergast. "Modern. Worthless."

"I'm not here for an evaluation. Look at the face in the portrait. Did this man visit you?"

Morin hesitated, took back the painting, and examined it more closely. A look of surprise crossed his face. "Why, yes—I do recognize this man. Who in the world made this portrait? It's done in perfect thangka style."

"The man had something to sell?"

Morin paused. "You're not working with this . . . individual, are you?"

"No. I'm looking for him. And the object he stole."

"I sent him and his object away."

"When did he come?"

Morin rose, consulted a large daybook. "Two days ago, at two o'clock. He had a box with him. He said he'd heard I was a dealer in Tibetan antiquities."

"Was he selling it?"

"No. It was the strangest thing. He wouldn't even open the box. He called it an Agozyen, which is a term I'd never heard of—and I know as much about Tibetan art as anyone alive. I would have thrown him out immediately, except that the box was real, and very, *very* old—quite a prize in and of itself, covered with an archaic Tibetan script that dated it to the tenth century or before. I would have liked to have that box, and I was very curious about what was inside it. But he wasn't a seller. He wanted to go into some kind of partnership with me. He needed financing, he said. To create some kind of bizarre traveling exhibit of the item in the box, which he claimed would astound the world. I think *transfigure* was the word he used. But he absolutely refused to show the item until I met his terms. Naturally, I found the whole proposition absurd."

"How did you respond?"

"I tried to talk him into opening the box. You should have seen him. He began to frighten me, Mr. Pendergast. He was a madman."

Pendergast nodded. "How so?"

"He laughed maniacally and said I was missing the opportunity of a lifetime. He said he would take it to London, where he knew a collector."

"The opportunity of a lifetime? Do you know what he meant by that?"

"He babbled some nonsense about changing the world. *Pazzesco*."

"Do you know which collector he planned to go to in London?"

"He didn't mention a name. But I know most of them." He scribbled on a piece of paper, handed it to Pendergast. "Here are a few names to start with."

"Why did he come to you?" Pendergast asked.

Morin spread his hands. "Why did you come to me, Mr. Pendergast? I am the premier dealer in Asian antiquities in Italy."

"Yes, it's true; no one has better pieces than you do—because no one is less scrupulous."

"There's your answer," Morin said, not without a touch of pride.

The door chimes rang insistently, repeatedly, and there was a banging sound. *"Polizia!"* came a muffled voice.

"Lavinia?" Morin called. "Please send the police away with my thanks. The undesirable has been taken care of." He turned back to Pendergast. "Have I satisfied your curiosity?"

"Yes, thank you."

"I trust those documents in your briefcase won't fall into the wrong hands."

Pendergast flipped the briefcase up and opened it. Out spilled a number of old newspapers.

Morin looked at him, his face reddening, and then a sudden smile broke out. "You are as unscrupulous as I am."

"One fights fire with fire."

"You made all that up, didn't you?"

Pendergast snapped the briefcase shut. "Yes—except for my comment on that Vishnu with Consorts. But I'm sure you will find some rich businessman who will buy it and enjoy it, and be none the wiser."

"Thank you. I intend to." Then he stood and ushered Pendergast toward the door.

8

A recent rain had slicked the streets of Croydon, a grim commercial suburb on the southern fringes of London. It was two o'clock in the morning, and Aloysius Pendergast stood on the corner of Cairo New Road and Tamworth. Cars rushed along the A23 and a train flashed past on the London-to-Southampton railway. An ugly, seventies-era hotel rose up at the corner of the block, its poured-cement façade streaked with soot and damp. Pendergast adjusted his hat and tightened his Burberry around his neck, tucked his Chapman game bag under his arm, and then approached the glass entry doors of the hotel. The doors were locked and he pressed a buzzer. A moment later an answering buzz unlocked the door.

He entered a brightly lit lobby smelling of onions and cigarette smoke. Stained polyester carpeting in blue and gold covered the floor, and the walls were encased in a waterproof-finished textured gold wallpaper. A Muzak version of "Strawberry Fields Forever" drifted through the lobby. At one end, a clerk with long hair, mashed a bit on one side of his skull, waited sullenly for him at the reception desk.

"A room, please." Pendergast kept his collars turned up and stood in a way that blocked most of his face. He spoke in a gruff voice with a Midlands accent.

"Name?"

"Crowther."

The clerk shoved a card over to Pendergast, who filled it in with a false name and address.

"Mode of payment?"

Pendergast took a sheaf of pound notes from his pocket and paid in cash.

The man gave him a swift glance. "Luggage?"

"Bloody airline misplaced it."

The clerk handed him a card key and disappeared into the back, no doubt to go back to sleep. Pendergast took his card key and went to the bank of elevators.

He took the elevator to his floor—the fourth—but did not get off. After the doors closed again, he remained on the elevator while it waited at the floor. He opened his bag, took out a small magnetic card-reading device, swiped his card through it, and studied the readout that appeared on the small LCD screen. After a moment he punched in some other numbers, slowly repassed the card through the reader, and tucked the device back into his bag. Then he pressed the button for the seventh floor and waited while the car rose.

The doors rolled back on a hall that was brightly lit with fluorescent tubes. It was empty, the same blue-and-gold rug stretching the length of the building, doors lining both walls. Pendergast exited the elevator, walked quickly to room 714, then paused to listen. It was quiet within, the lights out.

He inserted his key card, and the door snapped ajar with a little trill and a green light. He slowly eased it open and stepped inside, quickly shutting it behind him.

With any luck, he would simply locate the box and steal away without waking the inhabitant. But he was uneasy. He had done a bit of research into Jordan Ambrose. The man came from an upper-middle-class family in Boulder, Colorado; he was an expert snowboarder, climber, and mountain bike rider who had dropped out of college to climb the Seven Summits. It was an accomplishment claimed by only two hundred people in the world, summiting the highest peak on each of the seven continents, and it took him four years. After that, he had become a highly paid professional mountaineer, guiding trips to Everest, K2, and the Three Sisters. During the winter he made money doing extreme snowboarding stunts for videos and also collected money from endorsements. The expedition to Dhaulagiri had been a well-organized and -financed attempt to scale the unclimbed west face of the mountain, one of the last epic climbs left in the world, a staggering twelve-thousand-foot sheer face of rotten rock and ice swept by avalanches, high winds, and temperature swings from day to night of fifty to sixty degrees. Thirty-two climbers had already died in the attempt, and Ambrose's group would add five more fatalities to the list. They hadn't even made it halfway up.

That Ambrose had survived was extraordinary. That he had made it to the monastery was nothing short of miraculous.

And then, everything he had done since the monastery had been out of character—beginning with the theft.

Jordan Ambrose didn't need money, and up to this point had shown little interest in it. He wasn't a collector. He had no interest in Buddhism or any kind of spiritual seeking. He had been an honest and highly intelligent man. He had always been focused—one might say obsessed—with climbing.

Why had he stolen the Agozyen? Why had he carted it all over Europe, not looking to sell it, but trying to arrange for some kind of partnership? What was the purpose of this "partnership" he sought? Why had he refused to show it to anyone? And why had he made no effort to contact the families of the five dead climbers—who were all close friends of his—something utterly at variance with the climbing ethic?

Everything Jordan Ambrose had done since the monastery had been completely out of character. And this concerned Pendergast deeply.

He stepped past the foyer, took a dogleg, and entered the darkened room. The rusty-iron smell of blood hit him immediately and he could see, in the harsh light of the motorway that filtered through the curtains, a body splayed on the floor.

Pendergast felt a swell of dismay and annoyance. The simple resolution he had hoped for was not to be.

Keeping his raincoat tight about him and his hat on his head, he reached out and turned on a light with a gloved hand.

It was Jordan Ambrose.

Pendergast's dismay increased when he saw the condition of the body. It lay on its back, arms thrown wide, mouth open, blue eyes staring at the ceiling. A small bullet hole in the center of the forehead, with powder burns and tattooing, indicated the man had been executed at point-blank range with a .22. There was no exit wound: the .22 had rattled around inside the skull, no doubt killing Ambrose instantly. But it appeared the murderer had not been content merely to kill—he had indulged himself in an utterly gratuitous orgy of knife play with the victim's corpse, cutting, stabbing, and slicing. It did not bespeak a normal mind, or even an average killer.

Pendergast quickly searched the room and determined the Agozyen was gone.

He went back to the body. The clothes had been badly cut up in the brutal postmortem knife work, but several partially turned-out pockets indicated the killer had searched the body before going into a bloody frenzy. Careful to touch the corpse as little as possible, Pendergast slipped the man's wallet out of his back pocket and looked through it. It was full of cash—Ambrose had not been robbed of his money. Rather, Pendergast guessed, the man had been searched to make sure he had not written anything down about the fateful appointment.

He slipped the wallet into his game bag. Then he stood back and examined the room again, taking in everything. He noted the bloodstains, the marks in the carpet and on the bed, splashed across the suitcase.

Ambrose was well dressed, in a suit and tie, as if expecting a visitor of some importance. The room was neat, the bed carefully made, the toiletries arranged in the bathroom. A new bottle of scotch and two nearly full glasses stood on a table. Pendergast examined the sweating on the sides of the glasses, dipped in a finger and tasted the liquor, estimating the amount of ice that had been present and had subsequently melted. Based on the dilution of the whisky and the temperature of the glasses, he estimated that the drinks had been poured four or five hours before. The glasses had been wiped clean—no fingerprints.

Once again he was struck by the bizarre dichotomy of the killer's actions.

He placed his bag on the bed, extracted some test tubes and tweezers, knelt, and took samples of blood, fibers, and hair. He did the same in the bathroom, on the off-chance the visitor had used it. But the visitor appeared to have been careful, and a cheap, perfunctorily cleaned hotel room was one of the worst places to conduct forensic evidence gathering. Nevertheless, he did a thorough job, dusting the doorknobs and other surfaces for prints—even underneath the Formica table—only to find that every surface had been meticulously wiped clean. A damp spot in the corner near the door indicated an individual had placed an umbrella there, which had dripped water, and then retrieved it.

The rain had started at nine and stopped by eleven.

Pendergast knelt again at the body, slipped his hand inside the suit, and felt the temperature of the skin. Based on body temperature, the evidence of the drinks, and the timing of the rain shower, death had taken place around ten o'clock.

Carefully, Pendergast rolled the body over. The carpet underneath was marked by cuts where the knife had gone clear through the body into the floor. Taking his own knife, he cut out a square of carpet, peeled it up, and examined the marks in the plywood subfloor, probing into them with the tip of his knife. They were remarkably deep.

Pendergast retreated to the door, then gave the room a final look over. There was nothing more to see. The general outlines of what had happened were now plain: the killer had arrived for an appointment around ten; he'd placed his wet umbrella in the corner and his wet raincoat over a chair; Ambrose had poured out two scotches from a bottle he had purchased for the occasion; the man had taken out a .22 Magnum, pressed it to Ambrose's head, and fired a bullet into his brain. Next, he had searched the body and the room; then savagely and senselessly stabbed and cut up the corpse—and then, still apparently calm, had wiped down the room, taken the Agozyen, and left.

Behavior well outside the bell curve of most murderers.

The hotel wouldn't discover the corpse until checkout time or later. Pendergast had plenty of time to get far away.

He turned off the light, exited the room, and took the elevator to the lobby. He went to the desk and gave the bell a pair of sharp rings. After a long wait, the clerk came slouching out of the back, his hair mashed even further.

"Problem?" he asked.

"I'm a friend of Jordan Ambrose, registered in room 714."

The clerk scratched his skinny ribs through his shirt. "So?"

"He had a visitor about ten this evening. Do you recall him?"

"I'm not likely to forget *that*," said the clerk. "Man came in around ten, said he had an appointment with the gentleman in 714."

"What did he look like?"

"Had a bloody patch over one eye, along with some bandages. Wore a cap and raincoat, it was tiddling down outside. Didn't get a closer look and didn't want to."

"Height?"

"Oh, about average."

"Voice?"

The man shrugged. "American, I think. Kind of high. Soft-spoken. Didn't say much."

"When did he leave?"

"Didn't see him go. Was in the back doing paperwork."

"He didn't ask you to call him a cab?"

"No."

"Describe what he was wearing."

"Raincoat, like yours. Didn't see what he had on his feet."

"Did he come by car or cab?"

The clerk shrugged and scratched again.

"Thank you," Pendergast said. "I'll be going out for a few hours. Call me a cab from your standard pool, please."

The clerk made a call. "Just buzz when you return," he said over his shoulder, as he went back to his "paperwork."

Pendergast stood outside. In about five minutes, a cab came. He got in.

"Where to?" the driver asked.

Pendergast took out two fifty-pound notes. "Nowhere yet. Can I ask you a few questions?"

"You a copper?"

"No. Private detective."

"A regular Sherlock, eh?" The cabbie turned, his red, bloodshot face lighting up with excitement and pleasure. He took the note. "Thanks."

"A man left here about a quarter past ten or half past ten this evening, most likely in one of your cabs. I need to locate the driver."

"Right." He plucked his radio off the dash, spoke into it. The exchange went on for a few minutes, and then he pressed a button and handed the mike back to Pendergast. "Got your bloke on the line."

Pendergast took the mike. "You're the man who picked up a fare in front of the Buckinghamshire Gardens Hotel this evening about ten-twenty?"

"I'm your man," came the raspy voice, in a heavy Cockney accent.

"Where are you? Can I meet you?"

"I'm driving back from Southampton on the M3."

"I see. Can you describe your fare for me?"

"To tell the truth, guv, your man 'ad an eye that warn't too lovely. A patch over it, oozing blood like, didn't want to take too close a butcher's, if you get my meaning."

"Was he carrying anything?"

"A big, long cardboard box."

"His accent?"

"American, southern or something."

"Could he have been a woman in disguise?"

A raspy laugh followed. "With all the nancy boys around today, I suppose it's possible."

"Did he tell you his name or pay by credit card?"

"Paid in cash and never said a bleedin' word the whole way—after telling me where he was going, that is."

"Where did you take him?"

"Southampton. To the quay."

"The quay?"

"Right, guv. To the *Britannia*."

"North Star's new ocean liner?"

"You got it."

"Was he a passenger?"

"Think so. He had me drop him off at the customs building, and he had what looked like a ticket in his hand."

"Could he have been crew?"

Another raspy laugh. "Not bloody likely. It were a two-'undred-pound cab ride."

"He had no luggage other than the box?"

"No, sir."

"Was there anything else unusual about him?"

The driver thought for a moment. "He had a strange smell about him."

"Smell?"

"Like he worked in a tobacconist, like."

Pendergast paused for a moment, thinking. "Do you know when the *Britannia* is sailing, by any chance?"

"They said it were sailing at noon, with the tide."

Pendergast handed the mike back to the cabbie and

thought for a moment. And in that moment his cell phone rang.

He flipped it open. "Yes?"

"It's Constance."

Pendergast sat up, surprised. "Where are you?"

"I'm at the Brussels airport, I've just deplaned from a nonstop flight from Hong Kong. Aloysius, I've got to see you. I've some critical information."

"Constance, your timing is excellent. Listen to me carefully. If you can get to Heathrow in four hours or less, I'll pick you up at the airport. Can you do that—four hours, not one minute more? Otherwise I'll be forced to leave without you."

"I'll do my best. But what's this about leaving? What's happening?"

"We're about to set sail."

9

The black London cab tore along the M3 motorway at one hundred and forty kilometers per hour, passing cars and lorries in a blur. In the distance, the squat, cream-colored tower of Winchester Cathedral was visible amidst a tangle of gray urban landscapes.

In the rear seat, Pendergast, sitting next to Constance, glanced at his watch. "We need to be at the Southampton docks in fifteen minutes," he told the driver.

"Impossible."

"There's another fifty pounds in it for you."

"Money won't make 'er fly, sir," the driver said.

Still, the vehicle accelerated even further, tires squealing as the cabbie negotiated the ramp onto the southbound A335. The Winchester suburbs quickly gave way to greenery. Compton, Shawford, and Otterbourne passed by in heartbeats.

"Even if we do make the ship," Constance said at last, "how are we going to board? I read in *Le Monde* this morning that every stateroom's been booked for months. They're calling this the most sought-after maiden voyage since the *Titanic*."

Pendergast shuddered. "A rather unfortunate comparison. As it happens, I've already secured us acceptable accommodations. The Tudor Suite, a duplex at the ship's stern. It has a third bedroom we'll be able to use as an office."

"How did you manage that?"

"The suite had been booked by a Mr. and Mrs. Prothero of Perth, Australia. They were happy to exchange the tickets for an even larger suite on the *Britannia*'s world cruise this coming fall, along with a modest monetary consideration." Pendergast allowed himself the briefest of smiles.

The cab shot over the M27 interchange, then began to slow as the traffic inbound to Southampton grew heavier. They passed through a dreary industrial zone, then row after row of semidetached brick houses, as they approached the maze of streets in the old town center. They made a left onto Marsh Lane, then an immediate right onto Terminus Terrace, the big vehicle dipping and swerving deftly through the traffic. The sidewalks were thick with people, most of them holding cameras. From ahead came the sound of cheering and shouting.

"Tell me, Constance, what it is you discovered that caused you to leave the monastery with such precipitation?"

"It's quickly said." She lowered her voice. "I took your parting request to heart. I made inquiries."

Pendergast lowered his own voice in turn. "And how does one 'make inquiries' in a Tibetan monastery?"

Constance suppressed a grim smile. "Boldly."

"Which means?"

"I went into the inner monastery and confronted the monks."

"I see."

"It was the only way. But . . . oddly enough, they seemed to be expecting me."

"Go on."

"They were surprisingly forthcoming."

"Indeed?"

"Yes, but I'm not sure why. The monks in the inner monastery truly don't know what the artifact is or who created it—Lama Thubten was honest in that regard. It was carried up from India by a holy man to be secreted away, protected, in the high Himalayas."

"And?"

Constance hesitated. "What the monks didn't tell you is that they know the *purpose* of the Agozyen."

"Which is?"

"Apparently, it is a instrument to wreak vengeance upon the world. *Cleanse* it, they said."

"Did they hint as to what form this 'vengeance,' this 'cleansing,' might take?"

"They had no idea."

"When is this to happen?"

"When the earth is drowning in selfishness, greed, and evil."

"How fortunate, then, that the world has nothing to fear," said Pendergast, his voice heavy with irony.

"The monk who did most of the talking said it was not their intent to release it. They were its *guardians*, there to ensure it didn't escape prematurely."

Pendergast thought for a moment. "It appears that one of his brothers might not agree with him."

"What do you mean?"

Pendergast turned to her, his gray eyes luminous. "I would guess that one particular monk felt the earth *was* ripe for cleansing. And he contrived for Jordan Ambrose to steal the Agozyen—and ultimately unleash it upon the world."

"What makes you think that?"

"It's very clear. The Agozyen was extraordinarily well protected. I spent more than a year at the monastery and never even knew it existed. How is it that a casual visitor, a mountain climber not even there for study, managed to find and steal it? That could only happen if one or more of the monks *wanted* it stolen. Lama Thubten told me he was certain none of the monks had the object in their possession. But that doesn't mean a monk couldn't have helped an outsider obtain it."

"But if the artifact is as terrible as they say—what kind of a person would want to see it *deliberately* unleashed?"

"Interesting question. When we return the Agozyen to the monastery, we'll have to seek out the guilty monk out and ask him directly." Pendergast thought for a moment. "Curious that the monks didn't simply destroy the object. Burn it."

"That was the last question I asked. The monks grew very frightened and said it was impossible for them to do so."

"Interesting. In any case, to business. Our first task will be to get a list of passengers—and when they boarded."

"You think the killer is a passenger?"

"I'm quite sure. All crew and hospitality staff were required to be on board ship well before the hour of Ambrose's death. I find it significant that he disguised himself with this bloody bandage *before* going to see Ambrose."

"Why? He was disguising himself so he wouldn't be traced to the crime."

"I doubt he intended to commit a crime when he went to the hotel. No, Constance—the killer disguised himself even before he knew what Ambrose was offering, which suggests he's a well-known, recognizable person who wished to remain incognito."

Their conversation was cut short as the taxi pulled up at the foot of Queen Dock. Pendergast leapt from the car, Constance following. To the left lay the Customs and Departures building; to the right, a perfect Babel of onlookers and well-wishers, camera crews and media types. Everyone was waving British flags, throwing confetti, and cheering. To one side a band was playing, adding to the general din.

And over everything towered the *Britannia*. It seemed to dwarf not only the dock, but the entire city, its black hull rising toward a glittering snow-white superstructure more than a dozen decks high, all glass and balconies and mahogany brightwork. It was a vessel larger and grander than anything Constance had ever imagined, and its bulk threw an entire neighborhood—Platform Road, the Banana Wharf building, Ocean Village marina—into shadow.

But the shadow was moving. The horns were blasting. The dockworkers had slipped the hawsers and retracted the boarding gantry. High overhead, hundreds of people stood at its railing or on the countless balconies, taking pictures, throwing streamers, and waving good-bye to the crowd. With a final ground-shaking blast of its horn, the *Britannia* slowly, ponderously, inexorably began to move away from the dock.

"Ever so sorry, guv," the driver said. "I did my best, but—"

"Bring the bags," Pendergast interrupted. Then he dashed off through the crush of onlookers toward a security checkpoint. As Constance watched, he stopped only long enough to flash his badge at the police, then he was off again, heading past the band and the camera crews toward a scaffold covered with bunting, on which stood a thick press of dignitaries and—Constance assumed—North Star corporate officers. Already the group was beginning to break up; men in dark suits were shaking each other's hands and stepping down off the scaffold.

Pendergast darted through a sea of lesser functionaries that surrounded the scaffold and singled out one man standing at its center: a portly gentleman with an ebony walking stick and a white carnation on his dove-gray vest. He was being congratulated by those around him, and he was clearly surprised and taken aback when Pendergast inserted himself into the little group, uninvited. The man listened to Pendergast for a moment, a mixture of impatience and irritation on his face. Then, abruptly, he frowned and began to shake his head furiously. When Pendergast continued to talk urgently, the man drew himself up and began to gesticulate, poking his finger first at the ship, then at Pendergast, his face flushing a deep red. Security personnel began to crowd around them and they were lost from sight.

Constance waited by the taxi, the driver at her side. He had not bothered to retrieve the luggage, and she was not surprised; the huge bulk of the *Britannia* was still gliding along the dock, moving slowly but picking up speed. There would be no more stops until it reached New York after a crossing of seven days and six nights.

As she watched, the ship's horn let out another blast. Abruptly, large jets of water began to boil around the bows. Constance frowned: it almost seemed as if the vessel was slowing down. She glanced back in Pendergast's direction. He was visible again now, standing beside the man with the carnation, who was talking into a cell phone. The man's face had gone from red to purple.

Constance returned her attention to the ship. It was no illusion: the ship's bow thrusters had reversed, and the *Britannia* was creeping backward toward the dock. The earsplitting cheering around her seemed to falter as the crowds looked on with increasing perplexity.

"Blimey," the driver muttered. Then, walking around to the rear of the taxi, he opened the boot and began to pull out their baggage.

Pendergast gestured to Constance, indicating that she should meet him at the security checkpoint. She made her way through the buzzing crowds, the driver at her heels. On the dock itself, workers were hastily extending the lower boarding gantry again. The band faltered, then gamely started up again.

The horn gave yet another blast as the gangway was maneuvered into position against the ship's black flanks.

Pendergast ushered her through the checkpoint and together they walked quickly down the dock.

"No need to make haste, Constance," he said, taking her arm lightly and slowing her down to a leisurely stroll. "We might as well enjoy the moment—of keeping the world's largest ocean liner waiting, that is—not to mention its more than four thousand passengers and crew."

"How did you manage it?" she asked as they stepped onto the gantry.

"Mr. Elliott, principal director of the North Star Line, is a warm acquaintance of mine."

"He is?" she asked dubiously.

"Well, even if he wasn't ten minutes ago, he certainly is now. The gentleman and I are recently acquainted, and he is warm now—*very* warm."

"But delaying departure? Getting the ship to return to the dock?"

"When I explained just how much it would be to his advantage to accommodate us—and how much to his *personal disadvantage* not to—Mr. Elliott was most eager to be of assistance." Pendergast glanced up at the ship, then smiled once again. "You know, Constance, under the circumstances I think I'm going to find this voyage tolerable—perhaps even agreeable."

10

For Roger Mayles, cruise director of the *Britannia*, one of the earliest and most important decisions of the voyage had been at which table to dine on First Night. It was always a prickly question, very prickly, made all the more so by the fact that this was First Night on the maiden voyage of the world's largest ocean liner.

A difficult question indeed.

As cruise director, his job was not only to know the names and needs of all the passengers, but to mingle with them as well. At all times. If he disappeared during dinner, it would send a message to them that he didn't love them, that his was just a job.

It wasn't just a job.

But then, what do you do with a passenger list that is almost three thousand names long, spread over eight dining rooms and three seatings?

Mayles had fussed and fussed. First he had decided on the restaurant: it would be Oscar's, the movie-themed dining room. It was a spectacular art deco room, one wall a single curtain of Venetian cut crystal, with a waterfall behind, the whole thing backlit. The whisper of water was designed to raise the ambient white noise, which had the curious effect of lowering the apparent volume of sound. Two other walls were of real gold leaf, and the final one was of glass, looking out into the darkness of the ocean. It wasn't the biggest restaurant on the ship—that was the King's Arms, with its three opulent levels—but it had the smartest decor.

Yes, Oscar's it would be. Second seating, naturally. The first seaters were to be avoided at all costs; they were generally cretins who, no matter how rich they were, had never managed to shed the barbaric habit of eating before seven.

Then came the question of the table itself. It would, of course, be one of the "formal" tables—the large ones where guests could, on request, still observe the old-fashioned tradition of assigned seating, in which they would be mingled with strangers, as in the glory days of ocean liners. Formal dress, of course. To most, this meant black tie. But Mayles was very fussy about such things and he always dressed in a white dinner jacket.

Next, he'd had to choose the guests at his table. Roger Mayles was particular and he had many private, admittedly vicious prejudices to satisfy. His list of guests to avoid was a long one: topping it were CEOs, anyone involved in the stock markets, Texans, fat people, dentists, and surgeons. His preferred list included actresses, titled nobility, heiresses, television talk show hosts, airline stewards, mobsters, and what he called "mysteries"—people who defied placing—as long as they were intriguing, very rich, and X-class.

After hours of poring over the guest lists he had come

up with what he considered to be a brilliant party for First Night. He would put together tables for himself every night of the voyage, of course, but this one was special. This would be a dinner to remember. It was certain to prove an excellent diversion. And Mayles was always in need of diversion at sea, because—and this was his biggest secret among many—he had never learned to swim and was deathly afraid of the open ocean.

And so it was with great anticipation and not a little trepidation that he arrived at the gold-leafed entrance to Oscar's, dressed in a thousand-dollar Hickey Freeman dinner jacket purchased especially for the voyage. He paused at the door, letting all eyes fall on his impeccably tailored form. He beamed a gracious smile at the room and made his way to the head formal table.

As the guests arrived he seated them with handshakes, warm words, and various gestures and flourishes. Last to arrive were the two "mysteries"—a gentleman named Aloysius Pendergast and his "ward," a designation that in Mayles's mind conjured up all sorts of deliciously salacious ideas. Pendergast's file had intrigued him because it was so utterly devoid of information, and the fellow had managed to book himself into one of the aft duplex suites—the Tudor, at a cost of fifty-thousand pounds—at the last minute, even though the entire ship had been fully booked for months. On top of that, he had delayed the "sailaway" by nearly half an hour. How had he done it?

Most intriguing.

As the man approached, Mayles took a second, longer look. He liked what he saw. The man was refined, aristocratic, and strikingly handsome; he was dressed in a splendid cutaway with an orchid boutonniere on his lapel. His face was shockingly pale, as if he were recovering from a deathly illness, and yet there was a hardness, a vitality, in his lithe frame and gray eyes that showed anything but physical weakness. His face was as finely chiseled as a Praxiteles marble. He moved through the crowd like a cat threading its way across a set dining table.

But even more striking than Pendergast was his so-called ward. She was a beauty, but not in any way common or modern—no, hers was a Pre-Raphaelite beauty, the spitting image of Proserpine in the famous painting by Rossetti, but with her straight hair cut in a flapperish bob. She wore a formal gown by Zac Posen that Mayles had admired in one of the galleries along St. James's on Deck 6—the costliest one there. Interesting that she would purchase her First Night dress on board rather than select one from her own wardrobe.

He quickly recalculated the seating and placed Pendergast at his side, and Constance opposite. Mrs. Dahlberg went on the other side of Pendergast; Mayles had put her on the list because she had divorced two English lords in a row and ended up with an American meatpacking mogul, who then died a few months after the nuptials, leaving her a hundred million richer. Mayles's febrile imagination had gone riot with that one. But as he contemplated her in person he was disappointed to see she did not look like the vulgar fortune-hunter he had imagined.

He sprinkled the others about—a dashing young English baronet and his French wife; a dealer of impressionist art; the lead singer for the Suburban Lawnmowers and her boyfriend; the author and bon vivant Victor Delacroix; and a few others who, Mayles hoped, would make for a brilliant and amusing table. He'd wanted to include Braddock Wiley, a movie star aboard for the mid-Atlantic premiere of his new film, but his stature as an actor was waning and Mayles had ultimately decided he could invite him on the second night.

As he seated people, Mayles deftly introduced them to each other, to obviate the need for a round of vulgar introductions once they were seated. Soon everyone was in place and the first course arrived: crêpes Romanoff. They chatted about nothing for a moment as the waiters laid down the plates and poured the first wine of the evening.

Mayles broke the ice. "Do I detect a New Orleans accent, Mr. Pendergast?" He prided himself in his ability to tease out even the most reluctant conversationalist.

"How clever of you," responded Pendergast. "And for my part, do I detect, behind your English accent, a touch of Far Rockaway, Queens?"

Mayles felt the smile freeze on his face. How in the world did the man know *that*?

"Don't be concerned, Mr. Mayles—I've made a study of accents, among other things. In my line of work I find it useful."

"I see." Mayles took a sip of the Vernaccia to cover up his surprise and quickly turned the conversation away. "Are you a linguist?"

A certain amusement seemed to lurk in the man's gray eyes. "Not at all. I investigate things."

Mayles had his second surprise of the dinner. "How interesting. You mean, like Sherlock Holmes?"

"Something like that."

A rather unpleasant thought ran through Mayles's head. "And are you . . . investigating now?"

"Bravo, Mr. Mayles."

Some of the others were now listening, and Mayles didn't quite know what to say. He felt a twinge of nerves. "Well," he went on with a light laugh, "I know who did it: Mr. Mustard in the pantry. With the candlestick."

As the others laughed politely, he again turned the conversation away from this potentially difficult line. "Miss Greene, have you ever seen the painting *Proserpine,* by Rossetti?"

The woman turned her eyes on him, and he felt a shiver of disquiet. There was something distinctly strange in those eyes. "I have."

"I do believe you resemble the woman in the painting."

She continued to look at him. "Should I be flattered to be compared to the mistress of the lord of the underworld?"

This bizarre answer, its intensity—and her resonant, old-fashioned voice—put Mayles out. But he was an expert at riding any vagary of conversation, and he had a ready reply. "Pluto fell in love with her because she was so beautiful, so vital—as you are."

"And as a result Pluto kidnapped her and dragged her into hell to be his mistress."

"Ah well, some people have all the luck!" Mayles glanced around and received an appreciative laugh for his little bon mot—even Miss Greene smiled, he was relieved to notice.

The dealer, Lionel Brock, spoke: "Yes, yes, I know the painting well. It's in the Tate, I believe."

Mayles turned a grateful face toward Brock. "Yes."

"A rather vulgar work, like all the Pre-Raphaelites. The model was Jane Morris, the wife of Rossetti's best friend. Painting her was a prelude to seducing her."

"Seduction," said Miss Greene. She turned her strange eyes on Mayles. "Have you ever seduced, Mr. Mayles? Being cruise director on a luxury ocean liner must be a marvelous platform from which to do it."

"I have my little secrets," he said, with another light laugh. The question had cut rather closer to the bone than he was accustomed to. He didn't think he would put Miss Greene at his table again.

"Afar from mine own self I seem, and wing strange ways in thought, and listen for a sign," Greene recited.

This was followed by silence.

"How lovely," said the meatpacking heiress, Mrs. Emily Dahlberg, speaking for the first time. She was a strikingly aristocratic woman in a gown, draped in antique jewels, slender and well-kept for her age, and—Mayles thought—she looked and spoke exactly like the Baroness von Schräder in *The Sound of Music*. "Who wrote that, my dear?"

"Rossetti," said Greene. "The poem he wrote about Proserpine."

Brock turned his gray eyes on Constance. "Are you an art historian?"

"No," she replied. "I'm a pedant and an obscurantist."

Brock laughed. "I find pedants and obscurantists charming," he said with a smile, leaning toward her.

"Are you a pedant as well, Dr. Brock?"

"Well, I . . ." He laughed off the question. "I suppose some might call me that. I've brought along some copies of my latest monograph, on Caravaggio. I'll send a copy over to your stateroom—you can decide for yourself."

A hush fell over the table as a distinguished man with silver hair, in uniform, came up to the table. He was slender and fit, and his blue eyes sparkled under his cap. "Welcome," he said.

Everyone greeted him.

"How is everything going, Roger?"

"Just shipshape, Gordon. So to speak."

"Allow me to introduce myself," the new arrival said to the table, gracing them with a charming smile. "My name is Gordon LeSeur and I'm the first officer of the *Britannia*." He had a charming Liverpudlian accent.

A murmuring of introductions went all around.

"If you have any questions about the ship, I'm your man." He smiled again. "How's dinner?"

Everyone assured him it was excellent.

"Fine! We're going to take good care of you, I promise."

"I've been wondering," asked Mrs. Dahlberg. "They say the *Britannia* is the largest cruise ship in the world. How much bigger is it than the *Queen Mary 2*?"

"We're fifteen thousand tons heavier, thirty feet longer, ten percent faster, and twice as pretty. But Mrs. Dahlberg,

I have to correct one thing you said: we're not a cruise ship. We're an ocean liner."

"I didn't know there was a difference."

"A world of difference! The point of a cruise ship is the cruise itself. But an ocean liner's job is to transport people on a schedule. The *'B'* has a much deeper draft and a more pointed hull form than a cruise ship, and it is capable of serious speed: over thirty knots, which is more than thirty-five miles an hour. The hull has to be a lot stronger than a cruise ship and good at seakeeping, able to cross the open ocean in all weathers. You see, a cruise ship will run away from a storm. We don't divert—we just plough right through."

"Really?" asked Mrs. Dahlberg. "We might encounter a storm?"

"If the weather reports are correct, we *will* encounter a storm—somewhere off the Grand Banks of Newfoundland." He smiled reassuringly. "Nothing to worry about. It'll be great fun."

The first officer said his good-byes to the table and moved to another nearby, one populated with loud dot-com billionaires. Mayles was grateful for the momentary silence from those braying asses while the first officer repeated his spiel.

"Finest first officer in the fleet," Mayles said. "We're lucky to have him." It was his standard line; and, in fact, LeSeur was a decent fellow. Not your typical first officer, who were usually arrogant, conceited, with a chip on their shoulders because they weren't captain.

"He looks rather like a graying Paul McCartney," said Lionel Brock. "No relation, is there?"

"It's the accent," said Mayles, "and you're not the first to make that observation." He winked. "Don't let him hear you say that; our first officer, I'm sorry to say, is not a Beatles fan."

The main course had arrived along with another wine, and the volume of simultaneous talk at the table intensified. Mayles had his radar out. Even as he himself spoke, he could listen to several other conversations simultaneously. It was a useful skill.

Mrs. Dahlberg had turned to Pendergast. "Your ward is a remarkable young woman."

"Indeed."

"What is her background?"

"She is self-educated."

A loud guffaw of laughter from the next table caught Mayles's ear. It was Scott Blackburn, the dot-com wunderkind, with his two sycophantic buddies and their hangers-on, all in Hawaiian shirts, slacks, and sandals, in utter disregard of the ship rules and the sartorial traditions of First Night. Mayles shuddered. On every crossing there seemed to be at least one group of rich, loud businessmen. Very high-maintenance. According to their files, Blackburn and his group had been on a wine tour of the Bordeaux country, where they had spent millions of dollars creating instant wine cellars. And, as billionaires frequently were, they were demanding and eccentric: Blackburn had insisted on redecorating his extensive suite with his own art, antiques, and furniture for the seven-day crossing.

Mrs. Dahlberg was still talking to Pendergast. "And how did she happen to end up as your ward?"

Miss Greene interrupted. "My first guardian, Dr. Leng, found me abandoned and wandering the streets of New York City, an orphan."

"Heavens, I didn't know such things happened in modern times."

"When Dr. Leng was murdered, Aloysius, his relative, took me in."

The word *murdered* hung heavily in the air for a moment.

"How tragic," said Mayles. "I'm so sorry."

"Yes, it's a tragic story—isn't it, Aloysius?"

Mayles detected an edge in her voice. There was something going on there. People were like icebergs—most of what really went on, especially the ugliness, was submerged.

Mrs. Dahlberg smiled warmly at Pendergast. "Did I hear earlier that you're a private investigator?"

Oh no, thought Mayles. *Not that again.*

"At the present moment, yes."

"What was it you said you were investigating?"

"I'm afraid I didn't say."

"Investigating?" Brock, the dealer, said with an alarmed look. He apparently had missed the earlier conversation.

"How deliciously mysterious." Dahlberg smiled and laid a hand on Pendergast's. "I love a good mystery. Do you read murder mysteries, Mr. Pendergast?"

"I never read novels. I find them ridiculous."

Dahlberg laughed. "I *adore* them. And it strikes me, Mr. Pendergast, that the *Britannia* would make a splendid setting for a murder." She turned to Mayles. "What do you think, Mr. Mayles?"

"A murder would be splendid, as long as nobody got hurt." This witticism elicited a round of laughter, and Mayles once again prided himself on his ability to keep a conversation at a charming, superficial level, where social etiquette demanded it remain.

Pendergast leaned forward. "I can't promise a murder on the voyage," he said, his voice like honey, "but I can tell you this: there *is* a murderer on board."

11

Pendergast relaxed in the salon of their suite, leafing through the *Britannia*'s oversize wine list. Nearby, a flat-screen television was tuned to the ship's information channel and a muted voice was extolling the virtues of the ocean liner to a succession of images.

"The *Britannia* is a grand vessel in the old tradition," the cultured British voice intoned. "With sweeping staircases, vast public areas, two ballrooms, eight restaurants, three casinos, and five swimming pools. She has a passenger manifest of 2,700, a crew of 1,600, and a gross tonnage of 165,000. In terms of accommodations she is the roomiest vessel on the high seas, and the crew-to-passenger ratio is unmatched by any other luxury ship. Several features are unique to the *Britannia*, such as the eight-story Grand Atrium, the 'Sedona SunSpa®,' the upscale shopping arcades of Regent Street and St. James's, the thousand-seat Belgravia Theatre, and the heated pool modeled after a Roman bath excavated at Pompeii. It boasts the crystal and gilt King George II ballroom, the largest ballroom afloat. The ship is longer than the Empire State Building is tall, and its whistle is audible for fifteen miles. In the tradition of the *Titanic* and the great ships of the past, the *Britannia* is distinguished by the extraordinary amount of 'brightwork' used in its trimming, inside and out, involving more than a million board-feet of teak, mahogany, Port Orford cedar, gum, iroko, and Queen Island beech . . ."

On the second floor of the suite, a door opened. Constance emerged from her room and came down the stairs.

Pendergast shut off the television and put the wine list aside. "I had no idea the ship's wine cellar was so extensive," he said. "One hundred and fifty thousand bottles laid down. Their selection of pre-1960 Pauillacs is particularly impressive."

He glanced up as she came over. She had changed out of her formal dinner clothes and into a pale yellow dress. "Your new wardrobe suits you, Constance," he said.

"You helped pick it out," she replied, settling into a chair opposite him.

"You were rather sharp this evening," he said.

"So were you."

"I'm trying to smoke out a killer. What were you doing?"

Constance sighed. "I'm sorry if I was difficult. After the monastery, I find all this opulence—dispiriting."

"Be in the world but not of it." Pendergast quoted the ancient Buddhism maxim.

"I'd rather be in my home, reading a book by the fire. This"—she gestured around— "is grotesque."

"Keep in mind we're working."

She shifted restlessly in her chair and gave no reply.

Privately, Pendergast noted that a change had come over his ward in the past few weeks. Her time in the monastery had worked wonders on her. He was glad to see she had continued her Chongg Ran discipline in her stateroom, rising at four every morning and meditating for an hour, meditating in the afternoon, and not overindulging in food and drink. Most importantly, she was no longer listless, drifting. She was more purposeful, relaxed, more interested in the world around her than she had been since the death of his brother. This little mission of theirs, this unsolved mystery, had given her a new sense of direction. Pendergast had high hopes she was well on the way to recovery from the terrible events of March and the procedure at the Feversham Clinic. She was no longer in need of protection from others. Indeed, after her sharp display at dinner, he wondered if it wasn't now the other way around.

"What did you think of our dinner companions?" he asked.

"Very little, alas. Except for Mrs. Dahlberg—there's something attractively genuine about her. She seems interested in you."

Pendergast inclined his head. "I'm not the only one who made an impression." He nodded at a slim manuscript that lay on a side table, entitled *Caravaggio: The Riddle of Chiaroscuro*. "I see that Dr. Brock wasted no time sending his monograph over to you."

Constance glanced at the manuscript, frowned.

"Despite their shortcomings, I suspect a few of our dinner guests may prove useful," he went on.

"Mr. Mayles, for instance. Now there is a man who notices everything."

Constance nodded and they fell into silence.

"So," she finally said, changing the subject, "the thief and murderer killed Jordan Ambrose with a small-caliber pistol. Then committed gratuitous violence to the body."

"Yes."

"But the rest of the modus operandi you described—the careful checking of the pockets, the meticulous wiping and cleaning of all surfaces—doesn't fit."

"Precisely."

"I'm not aware of any precedent in any of the casebooks I've read."

"Nor am I. Except, perhaps, for a singular case I handled in Kansas not so long ago."

There was a knock on the door and Pendergast went to answer it. Their cabin stewardess stood in the hall outside.

"Come in," Pendergast said, waving his hand.

The woman made a small curtsey and stepped inside. She was thin and middle-aged, with black hair and deep-set black eyes. "Pardon me, sir," she said in an Eastern European accent. "I was wondering if I could be of assistance in any way at present?"

"Thank you, no. We are fine for the time being."

"Thank you, sir. I'll be back to turn down the beds." And with another small curtsey, she ducked out of the room.

Pendergast closed the door and returned to the sofa.

"So how *are* we going to spend the evening?" Constance asked.

"There are any number of postprandial entertainments available. Are you in the mood for anything in particular?"

"I thought perhaps the muster drill."

"How droll. Actually, before we do anything, there's one chore to complete." Pendergast gestured toward a large computer printout that lay beside the wine list. "There are twenty-seven hundred passengers on board this ship and only seven days in which to find the murderer and retrieve the Agozyen."

"Is that the passenger list?"

Pendergast nodded. "Direct from the ship's database. Including occupation, age, sex, and time of boarding. As I told you earlier, I've already ruled out members of the crew."

"How did you obtain that?"

"With great ease. I located a low-level computer maintenance tech and told him I was a North Star auditor, evaluating crew performance. He couldn't furnish the list quickly enough. I've already made considerable progress thinning the pool of suspects." And he pulled a sheet of paper from his jacket pocket.

"Go on."

A long white finger touched the paper. "The murder was committed at ten, the cab arrived at the dock at half past midnight, and so the killer must have boarded after that point. That alone removes one thousand four hundred seventy-six names."

The finger touched the paper again. "The murderer is a man."

"How in the world do you know that?" asked Constance, as if the assumption were an offense to womanhood.

"The bottle of scotch. A man like Ambrose would hardly have chosen that if his visitor were a woman. And then there is the knife that was driven clean through the body, through half an inch of carpet, and almost an inch into plywood flooring. That must have taken great strength. Finally, Ambrose himself was a mountain climber in superb physical condition, not an easy man to kill. It implies our killer is strong, fit, and fast—and male."

"I'll concede the point."

The finger moved down the sheet. "For these same reasons, we can bracket the age: over twenty, under sixty-five. On a ship like this, that latter fact is most useful. In addition, he's not traveling with a wife: the messy murder, cab ride, disguise, boarding ship with the Agozyen—all these are the actions of a man unencumbered by a wife. The psychopathology of the murder, the keen pleasure taken in the violence, also points strongly toward a single man. A single male, of a certain age: one thousand and twelve more names removed. Which gives us two hundred and twelve left."

The finger moved again. "All the evidence shows that Ambrose contacted a known collector, perhaps not of Asian antiquities per se, but a collector nonetheless. And a man whose face might be recognizable to members of the general public. Which leaves us with twenty-six."

He glanced up at Constance. "The murderer is clever. Put yourself in his shoes. He has to get this awkward box on board ship without being conspicuous. He would not have boarded immediately, carrying the box—that would be remembered. And besides, he was covered with blood from the murder; he'd have to change his clothes and wash up in a secure place. So what would he do?"

"Go to a hotel room, wash, repack the Agozyen in a larger steamer trunk, and then board at the height of the final crush."

"Precisely. And that would be around nine this morning."

Constance smiled wryly.

The finger lifted from the paper. "Which leaves us with just eight suspects—right here. You'll note a curious coincidence: two were at our table." He pushed the paper over. She read the names:

Lionel Brock. Owner of Brock Galleries, West 57th Street, New York City. Age 52. Prominent dealer of impressionist and post-impressionist paintings.

Scott Blackburn, former President and CEO, Gramnet, Inc. Age 41. Silicon Valley billionaire. Collects Asian art and 20th-century painting.

Jason Lambe, CEO, Agamemnon.com. Age 42. Technology mogul, Blackburn a major investor in his company. Collects Chinese porcelain and Japanese woodcuts and paintings.

Terrence Calderón, CEO, TeleMobileX Solutions. Age

34. Technology mogul, friend of Blackburn. Collects French antiques.

Edward Smecker, Lord Cliveburgh, reputed cat burglar. Age 24. Collects antique jewelry, silver and gold plate, reliquaries, and objets d'art.

Claude Dallas, movie star. Age 31. Collects Pop art.

Felix Strage, chairman of the Department of Greek and Roman Art, Metropolitan Museum of Art, New York City. Collects Greek and Roman antiquities.

Victor Delacroix, author and bon vivant. Age 36. Eclectic art collector.

Pendergast reached over with a pen and drew a line through the last name. "This one we can eliminate right away."

"How?"

"I noticed at dinner he was left-handed. The killer is right-handed."

She looked at him. "You've eliminated two thousand six hundred and ninety-three suspects—and you haven't even resorted to cleverness yet."

"Eliminating the last seven might prove more challenging. This is where we must divide if we are to conquer." He glanced at her. "I will undertake the investigation abovedecks, among the passengers and ship's officers. I'd like you to handle the belowdecks portion of our search."

"Belowdecks? If it's not a member of the crew, then why bother?"

"The best place to hear gossip and rumor on the passengers is belowdecks."

"But why me?"

"You have a better chance of convincing crew members to talk than I do."

"And what am I looking for, exactly?"

"Generally, anything your instincts tell you would be helpful. Specifically, a box. A long, awkward box."

She paused. "How am I to get belowdecks?"

"You'll find a way." He placed a cautionary hand on her elbow. "But I must warn you, Constance—I don't understand this killer. And that worries me. As it should you."

She nodded.

"Make no moves on your own. Observe, then come to me. Agreed?"

"Yes, Aloysius."

"In that case, the *game*, as they say, is afoot. Shall we toast the hunt with a fine old port?" Pendergast once again picked up the wine list. "The '55 Taylor is drinking exceptionally well right now, I understand."

She waved her hand. "I'm not in the mood for port, thank you, but please yourself."

12

Juanita Santamaria wheeled her maid's trolley down the elegant gold carpeting of Deck 12, her lips pursed in a slight frown, her eyes locked straight ahead. The trolley, piled high with fresh linens and scented soap, squeaked as it moved over the plush nap.

As she rounded a bend in the corridor, a passenger approached: a well-preserved woman of about sixty with a violet rinse. "Excuse me, my dear," the woman said to Juanita. "Is this the way to the SunSpa?"

"Yes," the maid replied.

"Oh, and another thing. I'd like to send the captain a note of thanks. What's his name again?"

"Yes," said Juanita, without stopping.

Ahead, the hall ended in a plain brown door. Juanita pushed the trolley through and into a service area that lay beyond. Large canvas bags of soiled laundry lay to one side, along with stacks of gray plastic tubs full of dirty room-service dishes, all waiting to be transported to the bowels of the ship. To the right lay a bank of service elevators. Wheeling the trolley up to the nearest elevator, Juanita extended her arm and pressed the down button.

As she did so, her finger trembled ever so slightly.

The elevator doors whispered open. Juanita pushed the trolley inside, then turned to face the control panel. Once again, she reached out to press a button. This time, however, she hesitated, staring at the panel, her face slack. She waited so long that the doors slid shut again and the elevator hung in its shaft, motionless, waiting. At last—very slowly, as if zombified—she pressed the button for Deck C. With a hum, the car began to descend.

The main starboard corridor of Deck C was cramped, low-ceilinged, and stuffy. It was as crowded as Deck 12 had been empty: busboys, maids, croupiers, hostesses, technicians, stewards, manicurists, electricians, and a host of others scurried past, intent on the innumerable errands and assignments required to keep a grand ocean liner running. Juanita pushed her trolley out into the ant-farm bustle, then stopped, staring back and forth as if lost. More than one person glared at her as they passed: the corridor was not wide, and the trolley, parked in the middle, quickly created a jam.

"Hey!" A frowsy woman wearing a supervisor's uniform came bustling up. "No carts allowed down here, get that up to housekeeping right away."

Juanita had her back to the woman and did not respond. The supervisor grabbed her by the shoulder and wheeled her around. "I said, get that—" Recognizing Juanita, she stopped.

"Santamaria?" she said. "What the *hell* are you doing down here? Your shift doesn't end for another five hours. Get your ass back up to Deck 12."

Juanita said nothing, made no eye contact.

"You hear me? Get back abovedecks before I have you written up and docked a day's pay. You—"

The supervisor stopped. Something in Juanita's vacant expression, the dark hollows of her eyes, made her fall silent.

Abandoning the maid's trolley in the middle of the corridor, Juanita walked past the woman and made her way unsteadily through the crowds. The supervisor, spooked, simply watched her go.

Juanita's quarters were in a cramped, oppressive warren of cabins near the ship's stern. Although the turbine/diesel power plant was three decks beneath, the thrumming vibration and smell of fuel haunted the air like a drifting infection. As she approached the cabin, her step grew slower still. As crew members passed by, they frequently turned back to look at her, shocked by her unfocused eyes and the drawn, spectral look on her face.

She stopped outside her door, hesitant. A minute passed, then two. Suddenly, the door opened from within and a dark, black-haired woman began to step out. She wore the uniform of the waitstaff for Hyde Park, the informal restaurant on Deck 7. Seeing Juanita, she stopped abruptly.

"Juanita, girl!" she said in a Haitian accent. "You surprised me."

Again, Juanita said nothing. She stared past the woman as if she weren't there.

"Juanita, what's wrong? You're all staring, like you saw a ghost."

There was a splatter as Juanita's bladder gave way.

Yellow coils of urine trickled down her legs and puddled on the linoleum of the corridor.

The woman in the waitress uniform jumped back. "Hey!"

The loud voice seemed to rouse Juanita. Her glassy eyes focused. They swiveled toward the woman in the doorway. Then, very slowly, they moved down her face, to her throat, where a gold medallion hung from a simple chain. It depicted a many-headed snake, crouched below the rays of a stylized sun.

Suddenly, Juanita's eyes widened. Thrusting out her hands as if to ward something off, she half staggered, half fell back into the hallway. Her mouth yawned open, showing an alarming cavern of pink.

That was when the screams began.

13

Roger Mayles walked across the plushly carpeted floor of the Mayfair Casino, nodding and smiling as he went. The *Britannia* had been in international waters for less than five hours, but already the casino was buzzing: the din of slot machines, blackjack and roulette dealers, and craps players drowned out the floor show currently playing in the Royal Court, just forward in the bow of Deck 4. Almost everybody was wearing a tux or a black evening gown: most had rushed straight down here after the First Night dinner without bothering to change.

A cocktail waitress carrying a salver laden with champagne stopped him. "Hello, Mr. Mayles," she said over the noise. "Care for a glass?"

"No thank you, darling."

A Dixieland band was wailing almost at their elbows, adding to the sensation of frantic merriment. The Mayfair was the most boisterous of the *Britannia*'s three casinos, and, Mayles thought, was a giddy spectacle to greed and Mammon. The first night at sea was always the most gleefully chaotic: nobody had yet been sobered by large casino losses. Mayles winked at the waitress and continued on, glancing from table to table. A small dome of smoked glass had been discreetly set into the ceiling over each one, almost invisible among the dazzling crystal chandeliers. The decor was fin de siècle London, all crushed velvet and rich wood and antique brass. In the center of the vast room rose a bizarre sculpture carved out of pale pink ice: Lord Nelson, clad rather perversely in a toga.

Reaching the casino's bar, Mayles took a right and stopped before an unmarked door. Pulling a passcard from his pocket, he swiped it through an adjoining reader and the lock popped open. He glanced from left to right, then slipped quickly inside, away from the noise and bustle.

The room beyond had no overhead lights. Instead, it was illuminated by a hundred small CCTV monitors set into all four walls, each displaying a different perspective of the casino: bird's-eye views of tables, banks of slot machines, cashiers. This was the "pit" of the Mayfair Casino, where the casino staff vigilantly monitored gamblers, croupiers, dealers, and money handlers alike.

Two technicians in chairs with rollers studied the displays, their faces spectral in the wash of blue light. Victor Hentoff, the casino manager, stood behind them, also frowning at the monitors. He would spend most of the next six days shuttling between the ship's casinos, and he had spent so many years staring at screens that his face had acquired a kind of perpetual squint. At the sound of Mayles's entrance, he turned.

"Roger," he said in a gruff voice, holding out his hand.

Mayles reached into his pocket and pulled out a sealed envelope.

"Thanks," Hentoff said. He slit open the envelope with a fat finger and pulled out several sheets. "My God," he said, flipping through them.

"Lots of low-hanging fruit," Mayles said. "Ripe for the picking."

"Care to give me an executive summary?"

"Sure." Along with everything else Mayles had to do, the casino staff expected him to provide them, discreetly, with a list of potential high rollers—or easy marks—for special cultivation and buttering up. "The Countess of Westleigh is back for another fleecing. Remember what happened on the maiden voyage of the *Oceania*?"

Hentoff rolled his eyes. "I can't believe she'd return after that."

"She has a weakness for maiden voyages. And baccarat dealers. Then there's—"

Suddenly, Hentoff wasn't looking at Mayles anymore. He was looking over the cruise director's shoulder. At the same moment, Mayles noticed that the noise level in the room had gone up tremendously. He turned to follow Hentoff's gaze and with a thrill of dismay saw that his dinner guest, Pendergast, had somehow let himself into the pit and was now closing the door behind him.

"Ah, Mr. Mayles," Pendergast said. "Here you are."

The feeling of dismay deepened. The cruise director rarely made poor choices for his dining companions, but selecting Pendergast and his "ward" had been a mistake he didn't intend to repeat.

Pendergast swept his gaze around the walls of monitors. "Charming view you have in here."

"How did you get in?" Hentoff demanded.

"Just a little parlor trick." Pendergast gave a dismissive wave.

"Well, you can't stay here, sir. This area is off-limits to passengers."

"I just have a request or two to make of Mr. Mayles, then I'll be on my way."

The casino manager turned to Mayles. "Roger, you know this passenger?"

"We dined together. How can I help you, Mr. Pendergast?" Mayles asked, with an ingratiating smile.

"What I'm about to tell you all is confidential," Pendergast said.

Oh no, Mayles thought, feeling his sensitive nerves tense up. He hoped this wasn't going to be a continuation of Pendergast's morbid dinner conversation.

"I'm not just aboard the *Britannia* to relax and take the air."

"Indeed?"

"I'm here as a favor to a friend. You see, gentlemen, my friend has had something stolen from him—something of great value. That object is currently in the possession of a passenger on this ship. It is my intention to retrieve the object and return it to the rightful owner."

"Are you a private investigator?" Hentoff asked.

Pendergast considered this a moment, his pale eyes reflecting the light of the monitors. "You could certainly say that my investigations are private."

"So you're a freelancer," Hentoff said. The casino

manager was unable to keep a note of disdain from his voice. "Sir, once again I must ask you to leave."

Pendergast glanced around at the screens, then returned his attention to Mayles. "It's your job, isn't it, Mr. Mayles, to know about the individual passengers?"

"That's one of my pleasures," Mayles replied.

"Excellent. Then you are just the person to provide me with information that can help me track down the thief."

"I'm afraid we can't share passenger information," Mayles said, his voice edging into winter.

"But this man could be dangerous. He committed murder to obtain the object."

"Then our security staff would handle the matter," said Hentoff. "I'd be happy to direct you to a security officer who could take down the information and keep it on file."

Pendergast shook his head. "Alas, I can't involve low-level staff in my investigation. Discretion is paramount."

"What *is* this object?" Hentoff asked.

"I'm afraid I can't be specific. It is an Asian antique of great value."

"And how do you know it's on board ship?"

In response, Pendergast's lips merely twitched in what might have been a faint smile.

"Mr. Pendergast," Mayles said in the voice he reserved for humoring the most truculent of passengers. "You won't tell us what you're looking for. You won't tell us how you're sure it's aboard the *Britannia*. You aren't here in any official capacity—and in any case we are now in international waters. Our own security staff is the law—

U.S. and British law no longer applies. I'm sorry, but we simply can't sanction your investigation or help you in any way. On the contrary, we will take it seriously amiss if your investigation disturbs any of our guests." To ease the sting of this refusal, he gave Pendergast his most winning smile. "I'm sure you understand."

Pendergast nodded slowly. "I understand." He gave a little bow, then turned to go. And then, hand on the doorframe, he stopped.

"I suppose," he said casually, "you're aware that a group of card counters is active on your floor?" And he nodded his head vaguely toward a cluster of screens.

Mayles glanced over, but he wasn't trained in pit observation and all he saw were swarms of men and women at the blackjack tables.

"What are you talking about?" Hentoff asked sharply.

"Card counters. Highly professional and well organized, too, based on how successful they've been at not drawing, ah, *heat*."

"What rot," Hentoff said. "We've seen nothing of the sort. What is this, some kind of game?"

"It's not a game to them," Pendergast said. "At least, not in the sense you'd like it to be."

For a moment, Pendergast and the casino manager looked at each other. Then, with a hiss of irritation, Hentoff turned to one of his technicians. "What's the running take?"

The technician picked up the phone, made a quick call. Then he glanced up at Hentoff. "Mayfair's down two hundred thousand pounds, sir."

"Where—across the board?"

"At the blackjack tables, sir."

Quickly, Hentoff looked back at the screens and stared for a moment. Then he turned back to Pendergast. "Which ones are they?"

Pendergast smiled. "Ah! I'm afraid they've just left."

"How convenient. And just how, exactly, were they counting cards?"

"They appeared to be running a variant of the 'Red-7' or the 'K-O.' It's hard to be certain, given that I wasn't really studying the screens. And their cover is good enough that they obviously haven't been caught before: if they had been, you'd have had mug shots in your database and your facial recognition scanners would have picked them up."

As he listened, Hentoff's face grew increasingly red. "How in the world would you know something like this?"

"As you said yourself, Mr.—Hentoff, is it? I'm a *freelancer*."

For a long moment, nobody spoke. The two technicians sat as if frozen, not daring to look away from their screens.

"It's clear you could use some assistance in this matter, Mr. Hentoff. I'd be happy to provide it."

"In exchange for our help with your little problem," Hentoff said sarcastically.

"Precisely."

There was another strained silence. At last, Hentoff sighed. "Jesus. What exactly is it you want?"

"I have great faith in Mr. Mayles's abilities. He has access to all the passenger files. His job is socializing with everyone on board, asking questions, soliciting information. He's in an excellent position to help. Please don't worry, Mr. Mayles, about disturbing the passengers—I'm interested in a handful of passengers only. I'd like to know, for example, if any of this handful consigned items to the central safe, if their cabins are on the 'no entry' list for housekeeping . . . that sort of thing." Then he turned to Hentoff. "And I might need your help as well."

"With what?"

"With—let's see, what is the expression?—greasing the wheels."

Hentoff glanced from Pendergast to Mayles.

"I'll consider it," Mayles muttered.

"For your sakes," said Pendergast, "I hope you don't take too long. Down two hundred thousand pounds in five hours—that's a rather nasty trend." He rose with a smile and slipped out of the pit without another word.

14

Constance Greene drifted down the broad thoroughfare of boutiques and upscale shops on Deck 6 known as St. James's. Although it was past midnight, the *Britannia* showed no signs of settling down for the night: beautifully dressed couples strolled along, gazing at the window displays or chatting in low tones. Large vases of fresh flowers lined the passages, and a string quartet could be heard sawing learnedly over the chatter and laughter. The air smelled of lilac, and lavender, and champagne.

Constance moved slowly on, passing a wine bar, jeweler, and art gallery, the latter featuring original signed prints by Miró, Klee, and Dalí at astronomical prices. Inside the doorway, an ancient woman in a wheelchair was scolding the young blonde woman pushing her. Something about the young woman gave Constance pause: the girl's downcast eyes and faraway expression, hinting of some private sorrow, could have been her own.

Past the arcade of St. James's, a set of ornate double doors opened onto the Grand Atrium: a vast eight-story space in the heart of the ship. Constance stepped up to the railing, glanced first upward, then down. It was a remarkable vista of terraced balconies and sparkling chandeliers and countless vertical rows of lights and exposed elevators of stained glass and crystal. Below, at the King's Arms restaurant on Deck 2, knots of people were sitting around red leather banquettes, dining on Dover sole, oysters Rockefeller, and tournedos of beef. Waiters and sommeliers wound their way among them, one setting down a plate brimming with delicacies, another bending solicitously over a diner to better hear his request. Tiers of balconies on Decks 3 and 4 overlooking the Atrium held additional tables. The clatter of silverware, the murmur of conversation, the ebb and flow of music, all drifted up to Constance's ears.

It was a hothouse atmosphere of luxury and privilege, a huge floating city-palace, the grandest the world had ever seen. And yet Constance remained utterly unmoved. Indeed, there was something repellent to her in all this desperate pursuit of pleasure. How different was this frantic activity, this coarse consumption and anxious attachment to the things of the world, from her life in the monastery. She longed to return.

Be in the world but not of it.

Turning away from the railing, she walked over to a nearby elevator bank and ascended to Deck 12. This deck was almost entirely given over to passenger accommodations; while still a picture of elegance, with its thick oriental carpets and gilt-framed landscapes in oils, its atmosphere was much more sedate. She moved forward. Ahead, the corridor ended, making a ninety-degree turn to the left. Straight ahead was the door to her suite, the

Tudor, situated at the aft port corner of the ship. Constance began to reach for her passcard, then froze.

The door to the suite was ajar.

Instantly, her heart began to beat furiously, as if it had been waiting for just such an event. Her guardian would never have been so careless—it had to be somebody else. *It can't be him*, she thought. *It can't. I saw him fall. I saw him die.* A part of her knew that her fears were irrational. Yet she could not ease the sudden racing of her heart.

Reaching into her bag, she pulled out a slender box, snapped it open, and removed a gleaming scalpel from its plush nest. The scalpel *he* had given her.

Holding the blade before her, she advanced silently into the stateroom. The main salon of the suite was oval in shape, ending in a large two-story plate-glass window overlooking the black Atlantic roiling far below. One door to the left led to a convenience pantry, another to the right opened onto the room she and Aloysius used as a study. The room was lit by a dim courtesy light. Beyond she could see moonlight painting a glittering trail across the heaving ocean, throwing jewels into the ship's wake. It illuminated a sofa, two wing chairs, the dining area, a baby grand piano. Twin staircases curved up the walls to the left and right. The left led to Pendergast's bedroom; the right to Constance's. Taking another silent step forward, she craned her neck, looking upward.

The door to her room was ajar. Pale yellow light streamed out from beneath it.

She took a fresh grip on the knife. Then—slowly, and in complete silence—she crossed the room and began ascending the stairs.

During the course of the evening, the seas had steadily grown stronger. The slow roll of the ship, once barely perceptible, was becoming distinct. From above and far forward came the long, mournful cry of the ship's whistle. Sliding one hand up the banister, Constance took slow, careful steps.

She gained the landing, stepped toward the door. There was no sound from beyond. She paused. Then she violently pushed the door open and darted inside.

There was a startled cry. Constance whirled toward the sound, knife extended.

It was the cabin stewardess, the dark-haired woman who had introduced herself earlier. She had been standing by the bookcase, apparently engrossed in the book she had just dropped in surprise. Now she looked at Constance, her expression a mixture of shock, dismay, and fear. Her eyes fastened on the gleaming scalpel.

"What are you doing here?" Constance demanded.

The shock was slow to leave the woman's face. "I'm sorry, miss. Please, I just came in to turn down the beds . . ." she began in her thick Eastern European accent. She continued to stare at the scalpel, terror distorting her face.

Constance slipped the scalpel back in the case and returned it to her bag. Then she reached for the bedside phone to call security.

"No!" the woman cried. "Please. They'll abandon me at next port, leave me in New York with no way of getting home."

Constance hesitated, hand on the phone. She eyed the woman warily.

"I'm so sorry," the woman went on. "I come in to turn down bed, put chocolate on pillow. And then I saw . . . I saw . . ." She pointed at the book she had dropped.

Constance glanced at it. To her vast surprise, she saw it was the thin volume titled *Poems of Akhmatova*.

Constance was not quite sure why she had brought this book along. Its history—and its legacy—was painful to her. Just to look upon it now was difficult. Perhaps she'd carried it as a penitent carries a cilice, hoping to atone for her misjudgment through pain.

"You like Akhmatova?" she said.

The woman nodded. "When I came here, I could bring no books. I have missed them. And then, turning down your bed, I saw—I saw yours." She swallowed.

Constance continued to gaze at her speculatively. *"I have lit my treasured candles,"* she quoted Akhmatova. *"One by one, to hallow this night."*

Without taking her eyes from Constance, the woman replied, *"With you, who do not come, I wait the birth of the year."*

Constance stepped back from the phone.

"Back home, in Belarus, I taught the poetry of Akhmatova," the woman said.

"High school?"

The woman shook her head. "University. In Russian, of course."

"You're a professor?" Constance asked, surprised.

"I was. I lost my job—as did many others."

"And now you work on board . . . as a *maid*?"

The woman smiled sadly. "It is the same for a lot of us

here. We lose many jobs. Or our countries have few jobs. Everything is corrupt."

"Your family?"

"My parents had a farm, but it was taken away by the government because of the fallout. From Chernobyl. The plume drifted west, you see. For ten years I taught Russian literature at university. But then I lost my position. Later I heard of work on the big boats. So I come here to work, send money home." She shook her head bitterly.

Constance took a seat in a nearby chair. "What's your name?"

"Marya Kazulin."

"Marya, I am willing to forget this breach of privacy. But in return, I would like your help."

The woman's expression grew guarded. "How can I possibly help you?"

"I would like to be able to go belowdecks from time to time, chat with the workers, the stewards, the various members of the crew. Ask a few questions. You could introduce me, vouch for me."

"Questions?" the woman became alarmed. "You work for the shipping line?"

Constance shook her head. "No. I have my reasons, personal reasons. Nothing involving the company or the ship. Forgive me if I'm not more specific at this point."

Marya Kazulin seemed to relax slightly, but she said nothing. "This could get me into trouble."

"I'll be very discreet. I just want to mingle, ask a few questions."

"What kind of questions?"

"About life on board the ship, any unusual goings-on, gossip about the passengers. And whether or not anyone has seen a specific item in one of the cabins."

"Passengers? I do not think this is good idea."

Constance hesitated. "Ms. Kazulin, I'll tell you what it's about, if you promise not to speak of this to anyone."

After a hesitation, the maid nodded.

"I'm looking for something hidden on board the ship. An object, sacred and very rare. I was hoping to mingle with the housekeeping staff, to see if anyone has seen something like it in a stateroom."

"And this item you mention? What is it?"

Constance paused. "It's a long, narrow box, made of wood, very old, with odd writing on it."

Marya considered this a moment. Then she straightened up. "Then I will help you." She smiled, her face betraying a certain excitement. "It is *horrible* to work on cruise ship. This make it more interesting. And it for good cause."

Constance held out her hand and they shook.

Marya eyed her. "I will get you uniform like mine." She waved a hand over her front. "You cannot be seen below the waterline dressed as passenger."

"Thank you. How will I contact you?"

"I will contact you," Marya said. She knelt, retrieved the book, and handed it to Constance. "Good night, miss."

Constance held her hand for a moment, and pressed

the book into it. "Take it. And please don't call me 'miss.' My name is Constance."

With a fleeting smile, Marya retreated toward the door and let herself out.

15

First Officer Gordon LeSeur had served on dozens of ship's bridges in his career at sea, from admiralty cutters to destroyers to cruise ships. The bridge of the *Britannia* resembled none of them. It was quieter, ultramodern, spacious—and curiously unnautical in feeling, with its many computer screens, electronic consoles, dials, and printers. Everything on the bridge was a model of beyond-state-of-the-art technology. What it most resembled, he mused, was the sleek control room of a French nuclear power plant he'd toured the prior year. The helm was now called an "Integrated Bridge System Workstation" and the chart table the "Central Navigation Console." The wheel itself was a glorious affair in mahogany and polished brass, but it was there only because visiting passengers wanted to see it. The helmsman never touched it—LeSeur sometimes wondered if it was even connected. Instead, the helmsman maneuvered the ship using a set of four joysticks, one for each of the propulsion pods, plus a pair controlling the bow thrusters and midthrusters. The main engine power was controlled with a set of jetliner-style throttles. It was more like a super-sophisticated computer game than a traditional bridge.

Below the huge row of windows that stretched from port to starboard, a bank of dozens of computer workstations controlled and relayed information about all aspects of the ship and its environment: engines, fire suppression systems, watertight integrity monitors, communications, weather maps, satellite displays, countless others. There were two chart tables, neatly laid out with nautical charts, which nobody seemed to use.

Nobody except him, that is.

LeSeur glanced at his watch: twenty minutes past midnight. He glanced out through the forward windows. The huge ship's blaze of light illuminated the black ocean for hundreds of yards on all sides, but the sea itself was so far below—fourteen decks—that if it were not for the deep, slow roll of the vessel they might just as well have been atop a skyscraper. Beyond the circle of light lay dark night, the sea horizon barely discernible. Long ago they had passed the slow pulsing of Falmouth Light, and shortly thereafter Penzance Light. Now, open ocean until New York.

The bridge had been fully manned since the Southampton pilot, who had guided the ship out of the channel, had departed. Overmanned, even. All the deck officers wanted to be part of the first leg of the maiden voyage of the *Britannia*, the greatest ship ever to grace the seven seas.

Carol Mason, the staff captain, spoke to the officer of the watch in a voice as quiet as the bridge itself. "Current state, Mr. Vigo?" It was a pro forma question—the new marine electronics gave the information in continuous readouts for all to see. But Mason was traditional and, above all, punctilious.

"Under way at twenty-seven knots on a course of two five two true, light traffic, sea state three, wind is light and from the port quarter. There is a tidal stream of just over one knot from the northeast."

One of the bridge wing lookouts spoke to the officer of the watch. "There's a ship about four points on the starboard bow, sir."

LeSeur glanced at the ECDIS and saw the echo.

"Have you got it, Mr. Vigo?" asked Mason.

"I've been tracking it, sir. It looks like a ULCC, under way at twenty knots, twelve miles off. On a crossing course."

There was no sense of alarm. LeSeur knew they were the stand-on ship, the ship with the right of way, and there was plenty of time for the give-way ship to alter course.

"Let me know when it alters, Mr. Vigo."

"Yes, sir."

It always sounded odd in LeSeur's ear to hear a female captain addressed as "sir," although he knew it was standard protocol both in the navy and in civilian shipboard life. There were, after all, so few female captains.

"Barometer still dropping?" Mason asked.

"Half a point in the last thirty minutes."

"Very good. Maintain present heading."

LeSeur shot a private glance at the staff captain. Mason never spoke about her age, but he guessed she was forty, maybe forty-one: it was hard to tell sometimes with people who spent their lives at sea. She was tall and statuesque, and attractive in a competent, no-nonsense kind of way. Her face was slightly flushed—perhaps due to the stress of this being her first voyage as staff captain. Her brown hair was short, and she kept it tucked up beneath her captain's cap. He watched her move across the bridge, glance at a screen or two here, murmur a word to a member of the bridge crew there. In many ways she was the perfect officer: calm and soft-spoken, not dictatorial or petty, demanding without being bossy. She expected a lot of those under her command, but she herself worked harder than anybody. And she exuded a kind of magnetism of reliability and professionalism you found only in the best officers. The crew was devoted to her, and rightly so.

She wasn't required on the bridge, and nor was he. But all of them had wanted to be here to share in the first night of the maiden voyage and to watch Mason command. By rights, she should have been the master of the *Britannia*. What had happened to her had been a shame, a real shame.

As if on cue, the door to the bridge opened and Commodore Cutter entered. Immediately, the atmosphere in the room changed. Frames tensed; faces became rigid. The officer of the watch assumed a studious expression. Only Mason seemed unaffected. She returned to the navigation console, glanced out through the bridge windows, spoke quietly to the helmsman.

Cutter's role was—at least in theory—largely ceremonial. He was the public face of the ship, the man the passengers looked up to. To be sure, he was still in charge, but on most ocean liners you rarely saw the captain on the bridge. The actual running of the ship was left to the staff captain.

It was beginning to seem that this voyage would be different.

Commodore Cutter stepped forward. He pivoted on one foot, then—hands clasped behind his back—strode along the bridge, first one way, then back, scrutinizing the monitors. He was a short, impressively built man with iron gray hair and a fleshy face, deeply pink even in the subdued light of the bridge. His uniform was never less than immaculate.

"He's not altering," said the officer of the watch to Mason. "CPA nine minutes. He's on a constant bearing, closing range."

A light tension began to build.

Mason came over and examined the ECDIS. "Radio, hail him on channel 16."

"Ship on my starboard bow," the radio engineer said, "ship on my starboard bow, this is the *Britannia,* do you read?"

Unresponsive static.

"Ship on my starboard bow, are you receiving me?"

A silent minute passed. Cutter remained rooted to the bridge, hands behind his back, saying nothing—just watching.

"He's still not altering," said the officer of the watch to Mason. "CPA eight minutes and he's on a collision course."

LeSeur was uncomfortably aware that the two ships were approaching at a combined speed of forty-four knots—about fifty miles an hour. If the ULCC supertanker didn't begin to alter course soon, things would get hairy.

Mason hunched over the ECDIS, scrutinizing it. A sudden feeling of alarm swept the bridge. It reminded LeSeur of what one of his officers in the Royal Navy had told him: *Sailing is ninety percent boredom and ten percent terror*. There was no in-between state. He glanced over at Cutter, whose face was unreadable, and then at Mason, who remained cool.

"What the hell are they doing?" the officer of the watch said.

"Nothing," said Mason dryly. "That's the problem." She stepped forward. "Mr. Vigo, I'll take the conn for the avoidance maneuver."

Vigo retired to one side, evident relief on his face.

She turned to the helmsman. "Wheel aport twenty degrees."

"Aye, wheel aport twenty—"

Suddenly Cutter spoke, interrupting the helmsman's confirmation of the order. "Captain Mason, we're the stand-on ship."

Mason straightened up from the ECDIS. "Yes, sir. But that ULCC has almost zero maneuverability, and it may have passed the point where—"

"Captain Mason, I repeat: *we are the stand-on ship.*"

There was a tense silence on the bridge. Cutter turned to the helmsman. "Steady on two five two."

"Aye, sir, steady on two five two."

LeSeur could see the lights of the tanker on the starboard bow, growing brighter. He felt the sweat break out on his forehead. It was true that they had the clear right of way and that the other ship should give way, but sometimes you had to adjust to reality. They were probably on autopilot and busy with other things. God knows, they might be in the wardroom watching porn flicks or passed out drunk on the floor.

"Sound the whistle," said Cutter.

The great whistle of the *Britannia,* audible over fifteen miles, cut like a deep bellow across the night sea. Five blasts—the danger signal. Both bridge lookouts were at their stations, peering ahead with binoculars. The tension grew excruciating.

Cutter leaned into the bridge VHF repeater. "Ship crossing on my starboard bow, this is the *Britannia*. We are the stand-on ship and you must alter. Do you understand?"

The hiss of an empty frequency.

The whistle sounded again. The lights on the ULCC had resolved themselves to individual points. LeSeur could even see the faint bar of light of the tanker's bridge.

"Captain," said Mason, "I'm not sure that even if they altered now—"

"CPA four minutes," said the officer of the watch.

LeSeur thought, with utter disbelief, *Bloody hell, we're going to collide.*

The silence of dread descended on the bridge. The *Britannia* sounded the danger signal again.

"He's altering to starboard," said the lookout. "He's altering, sir!"

The whistle of the ULCC sounded across the water, three short blasts indicating it was backing down in an emergency maneuver. *About frigging time*, thought LeSeur.

"Steady on," said Cutter.

LeSeur stared at the ECDIS. With excruciating slowness the ARPA vector radar overlay recalculated the ULCC's heading. With a flood of relief, he realized they were moving out of danger; the ULCC would pass to starboard. There was a palpable relaxation on the bridge, a murmur of voices, a few muttered curses.

Cutter turned to the staff captain, utterly unperturbed. "Captain Mason, may I ask why you reduced speed to twenty-four knots?"

"There's heavy weather ahead, sir," Mason replied. "Company standing orders state that on the first night out, passengers are to be acclimated to the open sea by—"

"I know what the standing orders say," Cutter interrupted. He had a slow, quiet voice that was somehow immeasurably more intimidating than bluster. He turned to the helmsman. "Increase speed to thirty knots."

"Aye-aye, sir," the helmsman said, his voice dead neutral. "Increasing speed to thirty knots."

"Mr. Vigo, you may resume the watch."

"Aye, sir."

Cutter continued staring at Mason. "Speaking of the standing orders, it has come to my attention that one of the officers of this ship was seen leaving the stateroom of a passenger earlier this evening."

He paused, letting the moment build.

"Whether or not there was a sexual liaison is irrelevant.

We all know the rules regarding fraternization with passengers."

With his hands behind his back, he made a slow turn, looking into each officer's face in turn, before ending with Mason.

"May I remind you that this is not the Love Boat. This kind of behavior will not be tolerated. Let the passengers be responsible for their own indiscretions; my crew must not indulge themselves in this way."

LeSeur was startled to see that the flush on Mason's face had deepened considerably.

Couldn't be her, he thought. *She's the last one who would break the rules.*

The door to the bridge opened and Patrick Kemper, the chief security officer, stepped in. Seeing Cutter, he moved toward him. "Sir, I—"

"Not now," Cutter said. Kemper stopped, fell silent.

On every large cruise ship LeSeur had served on, the captain's prime responsibilities were to schmooze with the passengers, preside over long, jolly dinners at the captain's table, and be the public face of the ship. The staff captain, while nominally second in command, was the chief operating officer. But Cutter had a reputation for disdaining the glad-handing duties, and it appeared he was going to carry this habit into his first captaincy. He was an officer of the old school, a former commodore in the Royal Navy from a titled family, who LeSeur suspected had been advanced somewhat beyond his competencies. A few years before, the captaincy of the *Olympia* had gone to Cutter's most bitter rival, and it had stuck in his craw ever since. He'd pulled strings in high places to get command of the *Britannia*—which should by rights have gone to Mason—and now his intentions were obvious. He was going to do everything in his power to make sure this maiden voyage was the crossing of his career—including breaking the *Olympia*'s own fastest crossing, set just the year before. Rough weather would have no effect on him, LeSeur thought grimly, other than to steel his resolve. Cruise ships fled weather; but an ocean liner, a *real* ocean liner, toughed it out.

LeSeur glanced at Mason. She was looking ahead through the forward windows, calm and poised; the only hint of something amiss was the rapidly disappearing flush. So far, through the shakedown cruise and today's departure, she'd taken the commodore's heavy-handedness and second-guessing with equanimity and grace. Even being passed over as master of the *Britannia* seemed not to have ruffled her feathers. Perhaps she'd gotten used to the high-seas chauvinism and developed a thick skin. The captaincies of the great ships seemed to be one of the last male bastions in the civilized world. She was no doubt aware of the unspoken rule: in the passenger ship business, the so-called teak ceiling remained: no matter how competent, a woman would never make master of one of the great liners.

"Speed under the hull thirty knots, sir," the helmsman said.

Cutter nodded and turned to the chief security officer. "All right, Mr. Kemper, what is it?"

The small, bulletlike man spoke. Despite his heavy Boston accent and inescapable American-ness, LeSeur thought of Kemper as a kindred soul. Maybe it was because they both came from working-class neighborhoods in port cities on the Atlantic. Kemper had once been a cop, shot a drug dealer who was about to pull the hammer on his partner, become a hero—but left the force anyway. Couldn't deal with it, apparently. Still, he was a bloody good security officer, even if he did lack self-confidence. LeSeur guessed that lack was one of the by-products of killing a man.

"Captain, we've got an issue in casino operations."

Cutter turned away from Kemper and spoke to the man as if he weren't there. "Mr. Kemper, the casinos are incidental to the operation of ship. The first officer will handle it." Without even glancing at LeSeur, he turned to the officer of the watch. "Call me if you need me, Mr. Vigo." He strode crisply across the bridge and disappeared through the door.

" 'This is not the Love Boat,' " LeSeur muttered. "What a prig."

Mason said crisply, but not unkindly, "Commodore Cutter was correct to say what he did."

"Yes, sir." LeSeur turned to Kemper with a friendly smile. "All right, Mr. Kemper, let's hear about the problem in the casino."

"It seems we got a bunch of card counters working the blackjack tables."

"Oh, Lord."

"First Mayfair was down two hundred thousand pounds, and then Covent Garden dropped by a hundred thousand."

LeSeur felt a slight twinge: this was just the kind of

thing that would really steam Corporate. "Did you identify them?"

"Obviously, we know who the winners are, but we don't know who's just lucky and who's counting. They work as a team: players and counters. The counters don't play—they watch and signal their players. As you know, they're the brains."

"I don't know, actually. Not a coincidence?"

"Not likely. Hentoff's worried they might be like that team of MIT students a few years back who took Vegas for three million."

The sick feeling in the pit of LeSeur's stomach deepened. The *Britannia,* he knew, wasn't Las Vegas, where you could give a chap the bum's rush if you caught him counting cards. These were paying passengers. And passenger ship companies relied heavily on gambling profits: a row in the casino might discourage other passengers from gambling. But something had to be done. A successful maiden voyage into New York with a fanfare of adoring publicity wouldn't matter a damn to Corporate if there were huge losses in the casino. It was about money—first, last, and always.

"What do you propose we do about it?" he asked.

"Well, sir. There was this . . ." Kemper hesitated. "This *unusual* passenger. A rich guy who styles himself a private investigator. He's the one first spotted the card-counting operation. He's offered to help identify the individuals involved."

"In return for what?"

"Well, you see . . ." Kemper stammered a moment. "It appears he's on board to track down an artifact he claims was stolen from a client of his. If we give him some information on his suspects, he'll help us with the card counters . . ." His voice trailed off.

"For all we know," said LeSeur briskly, "this might be a coincidence and we'll be up a hundred thousand pounds in Mayfair by the end of the night. Let's wait a few more hours, see if the losses continue. Whatever you do, please deal with it *quietly*. No melodrama."

"Right, sir."

LeSeur watched Kemper go. He felt sorry for the guy—and sorry for himself. Good Christ, if only he were back in the Royal Navy, where they didn't have casinos, card counters, and neurotic passengers.

16

"You made the bathwater too hot again," the elderly woman said, her shrill voice far too loud for the cabin. "And you put in too little bath oil."

Inge Larssen struggled to help the old woman—who weighed twice what she did—into her nightwear. "Sorry, mum," she murmured.

"And how many times do I have to tell you?" The hectoring voice went on as the ancient skin, wrinkled and flaccid as a rooster's wattle, mercifully disappeared beneath layers of silk and cotton. "Leaving dinner tonight, you put my handbag on the right side of my wheelchair. It goes on the left! The *left*!"

"Very well, mum." Wincing at the tight grip the ancient claw had on her shoulder, Inge handed the old woman her cane. Immediately, she received a painful rap on the knuckles with it. "Stand up straight, girl. Do you want me to take a tumble?"

"No, mum." Inge looked away as she spoke. Looking at her employer only seemed to incite additional criticism.

"Really, you are the *worst* companion I've ever had—

and I've had more than my share, I can tell you. If you don't shape up I'll simply have to let you go."

"I'm very sorry if I'm not giving satisfaction, mum," Inge replied.

It was the work of half an hour to get the woman into bed, lift her feet into position and tuck them in, apply lotion to her hands and vanishing cream to her face, comb and pin her hair, and fluff up the pillows just so.

"I don't want to hear a sound out of you, now," came the croaking voice. "You know how hard I find it to fall asleep."

"Very well, mum."

"And leave the door open. I'm a light sleeper and there's no telling when I might need you."

"Very well." As softly and slowly as she could, Inge crept out of the bedroom and took up her position in a chair just outside, in the living room. It was here that she slept, on the couch. The old woman insisted that her beddings be put away first thing in the morning and not brought out until late at night; it seemed to annoy her that Inge had to sleep as well.

She waited, barely daring to breathe, while the old lady muttered and murmured fretfully. Gradually, the sounds died away and the breathing became more regular. Inge sat listening until the loud snoring began, as it always did: despite what the crone said, she was the heaviest of sleepers and never woke up during the night.

Now, very carefully, Inge rose from her chair and moved stealthily past the open bedroom door. The snoring continued unabated. Moving to the entryway, she passed a mirror, and stopped just a moment to make sure she was presentable. A serious young woman with straight blonde hair and sad, almost frightened eyes looked back. She ran a quick hand over her hair. Then, moving to the front door of the suite, she opened it cautiously and exited out into the hall.

She walked down the elegant carpeted corridor, feeling better almost immediately. It was like a dark mist disappearing in the heat of the sun. Reaching the central stairway, she made her way down to the public levels of the ship. It was so much cheerier here: people chatted, laughed. More than one man smiled at her as she walked past the shops, cafés, and wine bars: although shy and a little awkward, Inge was attractive, and her Swedish heritage was unmistakable.

She had been working for the old woman for two months now, and it was unlike anything she had anticipated. Orphaned at an early age, she had led a sheltered childhood, growing up in convent schools. When it was time to find a job, she had secured a position as a ladies' companion through an agency that was affiliated with the convent. It seemed perfect. Her spoken English was impeccable, and the school provided her with excellent references. She had no place to live, and being a companion would provide both room and board. And better yet, traveling with a wealthy lady would allow her to see the outside world she had daydreamed about so often.

But the reality could not have been more different. Her employer was critical of her every move; Inge couldn't think of a single word of praise she had been given. While she was awake, the old woman required constant attendance and demanded that her every whim be carried out instantly. Inge was not allowed to leave her side. It was like being in prison—with a two-year sentence, based on the contract she'd signed. Her only freedom came late at night, when the woman slept. And she always woke at dawn, querulous and demanding.

Inge wandered through the elegant spaces, drinking in the music, the conversation, the sights and smells. She had a rich imagination—her daydreams were her only escape—but the *Britannia*, at least, lived up to all her hopes. It was the most beautiful thing she had ever seen. She stopped outside a grand casino, peering in at the wealthy and powerful as they gambled and carried on in their finery. Seeing such sights made her forget the living hell she endured by day.

She lingered in the doorway a few moments more. Then she roused herself and moved on. It was late now, very late, and she needed to get some sleep herself—the old lady did not allow her to nap or take any breaks. But she would come here again tomorrow night, soaking up the sights—sights to fuel the dreams and fancies that, in turn, would help her make it through the days to come. Dreams of the day when she too could travel in such luxury and elegance, unfettered by poverty or cruelty, when she would have a husband and a closet full of beautiful clothes. And no matter how wealthy she became, she would always speak softly to her servants and treat them with kindness, remembering that they, too, were human beings.

17

Special Agent Pendergast glided silently through the opulent public spaces of the *Britannia*, his silver eyes taking in every possible detail, fixing the layout of the ship in his mind. He had been walking for almost three hours now, through salons and spas and restaurants and pubs and casinos and arcades and vast echoing theaters. Dressed in an impeccably tailored black suit, he blended in with the tuxedo-clad crowds and was conspicuous mainly for his blond-white hair and pallid complexion.

He knew his target was awake and about. At 4 A.M. he finally found him, strolling aimlessly along Deck 7, the highest of the public decks, threading his way through a maze of lounges and galleries, heading amidships. Directly over their heads were close to eleven hundred passenger compartments. In order to earn back the enormous cost of building such a huge and heavily framed vessel, North Star had cut back on single cabins and made all of the seaward passenger accommodations into spacious—and expensive—stateroom suites with private balconies. The balconies required that the staterooms be placed as high in the ship's superstructure as possible, far above the spume-heavy waterline, thus forcing the public spaces into the lower decks.

The crowds had thinned. The ship was rolling ponderously, deep slow rolls that took several minutes to complete. They were coming from a storm center far to the east. It was quite possible that many of the passengers were regretting the expansive dinners they had enjoyed earlier in the evening. His target appeared to be one of them.

Pendergast paused as he consulted a fold-out map of the ship, now covered with neat annotations of his own. He looked around and saw what he was looking for: a hatchway leading to the promenade deck. Although other levels of the *Britannia* had external patios, public balconies, and pool decks, only Deck 7 had a promenade that encircled the entire vessel. And sure enough, there went his target: the man was opening the hatch and stepping out into the open air.

At the door, Pendergast took a swig of bourbon from a silver hip flask, let it linger briefly in his mouth, then swallowed it, opened the door, and slipped through. He found himself in what seemed like the teeth of a gale. The wind blasted him full in the face, pulling his tie from beneath his jacket and whipping it out behind him. Even though he was eight levels above the surface of the ocean, the air was full of atomized spray. It took him a moment to realize this wasn't entirely due to the approaching storm; the ship was moving at over thirty miles an hour, which even on a windless sea created its own gale on any exposed deck. It was as the first officer, LeSeur, had said:

A cruise ship will run away from a storm. We don't divert—we just plough right through.

He saw his target standing at the rail about fifty yards off, in the lee. Pendergast strode forward, his hand raised in jovial greeting.

"Jason? Jason *Lambe*?"

The man turned. "What?" His face looked green.

Pendergast surged toward him, seized his hand. "By God, it *is* you! I thought I recognized you at dinner! How the hell are you?" He pumped his hand, clasping the man's left in an enthusiastic greeting, drawing him close.

"Uh, fine." Jason Lambe did not look at all fine. "Excuse me, but do I know you?"

"Pendergast! Aloysius Pendergast! P.S. 84, Riverdale!" Pendergast clapped an arm around the man's shoulders, gave an affectionate squeeze while breathing heavily in his face, giving him a good dose of bourbon-breath. Lambe seemed to freeze, flinching and making an effort to disentangle himself from the obnoxious, clinging embrace.

"I don't remember any Pendergast," he said dubiously.

"Come on! Jason, think back to the old days! Glee club, varsity basketball!" Another squeeze, harder this time.

Lambe had had enough. With a strenuous effort, he tried to twist from the agent's limpet-like grasp.

"Getting senile in your old age, Jason?" Pendergast gave Lambe's upper arm an affectionate grope.

Lambe finally wrenched himself free, shook off his hand, and took a step back. "Look, Pendergast, why don't you head back to your cabin and sober up? I don't have the slightest idea who you are."

"Is that any way to treat an old buddy?" Pendergast whined.

"Let me make it even plainer. Fuck off, pal." Lambe brushed past him and headed back inside, still looking seasick.

Pendergast leaned on the rail, shaking briefly with silent mirth. After a moment he straightened up, cleared his throat, adjusted his suit and tie, wiped his hands with a silk hankie, and, with a disdainful frown, dusted himself off with a few flicks of his manicured fingers. He then took a stroll around the deck. The rolling motion of the ship was still more pronounced, and he bent into the wind as he headed forward, one hand on the rail.

He glanced overhead at the rows of balconies above him, all empty. It seemed a supreme irony: the bulk of the *Britannia*'s passengers paid a hefty premium to obtain a balconied suite, but because of the extraordinary speed of the ship they were next to impossible to use.

It was the work of almost ten minutes to stroll the length of the ship. At last he paused in the relative calm of the stern. He walked to the rail and looked out over the roiling wakes: four lines of white froth subsumed into an angry ocean. The spray and spume raised by the wind and sea had started to congeal into a light mist, wrapping the ship in an eerie, damp shroud.

The ship's horn gave a mournful blast and Pendergast turned, leaning thoughtfully against the rail. On the decks above him, twenty-seven hundred passengers were housed in luxurious surroundings. And far below his feet, in the deep spaces below the waterline, were the quarters of the sixteen hundred men and women whose job it was to cater to those passengers' every whim.

Over four thousand people—and among them was a bizarre murderer and the mysterious object he had killed to possess.

In the shelter of the lee, Pendergast removed the list from his pocket, slipped out a fountain pen, and slowly drew a line through the name of Jason Lambe. His assessment of the man's physical condition—which he had examined rather thoroughly under the pretext of the drunken reunion—assured him that Lambe's stick-like arms and puny frame could not have overwhelmed Ambrose, let alone committed an act of such savage violence.

Six more to go.

The horn sounded again. As it did, Pendergast paused. Then he straightened up, listening intently. For an instant, he thought he had heard another cry, superimposed over the shriek of the horn. He waited, listening, for several minutes. But there was nothing save the rushing of the wind. Wrapping his dinner jacket tightly around himself, he made his way toward the entrance hatchway and the welcoming warmth of the ship. It was time to retire for the night.

18

A dirty sun struggled up through the mists lying on the eastern horizon, the watery rays of dawn flooding the ship with yellow light. First Officer Gordon LeSeur stepped out of the Admiral's Club and walked down the plushly carpeted starboard corridor of Deck 10. A few passengers were standing at the elevator bank and he greeted them good morning with a cheerful hello. They nodded back, looking a little green around the gills. LeSeur, who had not been seasick in over twenty years, tried to feel sympathetic but found it difficult. When passengers got seasick, they got cranky. And this morning they were bloody cranky.

For a brief moment, he indulged himself in nostalgia for the Royal Navy. Normally a cheerful, easygoing bloke, he was getting weary of the flashy cruise ship lifestyle—especially the antics of spoiled passengers desperate to "get their money's worth," indulging themselves in an orgy of eating and drinking, gambling and bonking. And these American passengers always made the same asinine comment about him looking like Paul McCartney. Wanting to know if he was related to Paul McCartney.

He was no more related to McCartney than Queen Elizabeth was related to her corgis. Perhaps he should have followed his father's footsteps into the merchant marine. Then he could be working on a nice, quiet, and blessedly passenger-free VLCC.

He smiled ruefully to himself. What was wrong with him? It was way too early in the crossing to start having thoughts like these.

As he continued sternward, he pulled a radio from its holster, set to the ship's frequency, and pressed the transmit button. "Suite 1046, right?"

"Yes, sir," Kemper's Boston accent rasped over the radio. "A Mr. Evered. Gerald Evered."

"Very well." LeSeur returned the radio. He paused outside the door, cleared his throat, adjusted his uniform, then raised his hand and rapped once.

The door was quickly opened by a man in his late forties. Automatically, LeSeur took in the details: paunch, thinning hair, expensive suit, cowboy boots. He didn't look seasick and he didn't look cranky. He looked scared.

"Mr. Evered?" he asked the man. "I'm the first officer. I understand you wished to speak with someone in command?"

"Come in." Evered ushered him inside, then closed the door. LeSeur glanced around the cabin. The closet door was open and he saw both suits and dresses hanging within. Towels were strewn across the bathroom floor, which meant housecleaning hadn't yet cleaned the room. Strange, though—the bed was perfectly made.

That meant nobody had gone to sleep the night before. A cowboy hat rested on the pillow.

"My wife is missing," Evered said, the heavy Texas accent not surprising LeSeur.

"For how long?"

"She didn't come back to the cabin last night. I want the ship searched."

LeSeur quickly arranged his face into its most sympathetic expression. "I'm very sorry to hear that, Mr. Evered. We'll do all we can. May I ask a few questions?"

Evered shook his head. "No time for questions. I've waited too long as it is. You need to organize a search!"

"Mr. Evered, it'll help immeasurably if I could just gather a little information first. Please sit down."

Evered hesitated a moment. Then he took a seat on the edge of the bed, drumming his fingers on his knees.

LeSeur sat down in a nearby armchair and removed a notebook. He had always found it helped if he took notes—it seemed to calm people. "Your wife's name?"

"Charlene."

"When did you last see her?"

"About ten-thirty last night. Maybe eleven."

"Where?"

"Here, in our cabin."

"Did she go out?"

"Yes." A hesitation.

"Where was she heading?"

"I can't rightly say."

"She didn't mention that she wanted to go shopping, or to the casino, something like that?"

Another hesitation. "Well, see, we had a bit of an argument."

LeSeur nodded. So that's how it was. "Has this ever happened before, Mr. Evered?"

"Has what ever happened before?"

"Your wife leaving after an argument."

The man laughed bitterly. "Hell yes. Doesn't it happen to everybody?"

It had never happened to LeSeur, but the first officer chose not to mention this. "Has she stayed away overnight before?"

"No, never. She always comes back eventually, tail between her legs. That's why I called." He swiped his brow with a handkerchief. "And now I think you better get going with that search."

LeSeur knew he had to delicately get the passenger's thoughts away from a search. Fact was, the *Britannia* was too large to be searched completely. And even if they wanted to, they didn't have the manpower to undertake one: passengers had no idea just how small the security staff really was on an ocean liner.

"Pardon my asking, Mr. Evered," he said as gently as he could, "but are you and your wife . . . generally on good terms?"

"What the hell's that got to do with my wife missing?" the man flared up, almost rising off the bed.

"We have to consider all the possibilities, Mr. Evered. She might be sitting in a lounge somewhere, still angry."

"That's what I'm talking about—go find her!"

"We'll do that. We'll start by paging her on the public address system." LeSeur already had a pretty good idea of how things stood. The couple had hit middle age, were having trouble in their marriage, and took the crossing to try to put some magic back into life. Maybe the husband been caught boning someone at the office, or she herself had been tempted by a little afternoon delight with a neighbor. So they went on a romantic ocean voyage to patch things up, and instead of finding the magic ended up fighting their way across the Atlantic.

Evered frowned again. "It was just an argument, nothing serious. She's never stayed out all night. Damn it, you need to get your people together and start a—"

"Mr. Evered," LeSeur interrupted smoothly, "I wonder if you'd mind my saying something? To reassure you."

"What?"

"I've been working aboard passenger ships for many years now. I see this kind of thing all the time. A couple quarrels, one steps out. It isn't like your wife just walked out of your house, Mr. Evered. This is the *Britannia*, the largest passenger ship afloat. There are hundreds, thousands of things on board that could have distracted your wife. Perhaps she's in one of the casinos—they're open all night, you know. Maybe she's in the spa. Or shopping. Perhaps she stopped someplace to rest her feet, then fell asleep—there are two dozen lounges on board. Or perhaps she ran into somebody she knew; a woman, perhaps, or . . ."

LeSeur let his voice trail off decorously, but he knew the meaning was clear.

"Or what? Are you implying that my wife might've met another man?" Evered rose from the bed in a sad, middle-aged fury.

LeSeur stood as well and smiled disarmingly. "Mr. Evered, you misunderstood me. I certainly didn't mean to imply anything of the sort. It's just that I've seen this happen a hundred times before, and it always works out in the end. Always. Your wife is just out enjoying herself. We'll make a few announcements over the PA system and ask her to contact us or you. I guarantee you she'll be back. Tell you what: why don't you order breakfast for two, served en suite? I'll bet you anything she'll be here before it arrives. I'll send up a bottle of Veuve Clicquot, on the house."

Evered was breathing heavily, making an effort to control himself.

"In the meantime, have you got a picture of your wife I could borrow? We have your ID photos from embarkation, of course, but it always helps to have more than one image. I'll circulate them among our security staff, so they can keep an eye out."

Evered turned away, walked into the bathroom. LeSeur heard a zipper opening, the sound of shuffling and rummaging. A minute later Evered emerged again, a photo in his hand.

"There's nothing to worry about, Mr. Evered. The *Britannia* is probably one of the safest environments in the world."

The man glared back at him. "You better damn well be right."

LeSeur forced a smile. "Now, order that breakfast for two. And have a good day." He let himself out of the stateroom.

In the hall, he paused to examine the photo. To his

surprise, he found that Ms. Evered was something of a babe. Not outrageously stunning, of course, but he wouldn't throw her out of bed: a dozen years younger than her husband, thin and blonde and stacked and wearing a two-piece swimsuit. Now he was more certain what had happened: the missus, pissed off, had met someone and was shacked up with him. He shook his head. These luxury liners were like one big floating orgy. Something happened to people when they got away from land—they started acting like a bunch of sybarites. If Mr. Evered knew what was good for him, he'd go out and do the same: there were plenty of rich widows aboard . . .

LeSeur chuckled quietly at the thought. Then he pocketed the picture. He'd be sure to send it down to security: after all, Kemper and his boys were connoisseurs of hot-looking women, and no doubt they'd appreciate an eyeful of the curvaceous Ms. Evered.

19

The chief of security's office was in the central security complex, a tangle of low-ceilinged rooms on Deck A, at the *Britannia*'s waterline. Asking directions, Pendergast passed first a manned checkpoint, then a series of holding cells, a locker room and showers, and then a large circular room filled with dozens of closed-circuit televisions cycling through hundreds, maybe thousands, of surveillance cameras sprinkled about the ship. Three bored security officers kept a listless eye on the walls of flat-panel screens. Beyond that stood a closed, faux-wood door marked *Kemper*. The ship's legendary brightwork, Pendergast noticed, did not extend belowdecks.

He knocked.

"Enter," came a voice.

Pendergast stepped inside, closing the door behind him. Patrick Kemper was behind his desk, ear to a telephone. He was a short, burly man with a large, heavy head, thick knotty ears, a brown hairpiece, and a perpetual put-upon expression stamped on his features. His office was remarkably bare: other than a framed picture of the *Britannia* and some internal North Star promotional posters, there were hardly any furnishings or decoration. The clock on the wall behind Kemper read twelve noon exactly.

Kemper put down the phone. "Have a seat."

"Thank you." Pendergast sat in one of the two unpadded seats facing the desk. "You asked to see me?"

Kemper's put-upon expression deepened. "Not exactly. Hentoff requested it."

Pendergast winced at the accent. "So the casino manager has agreed to my little proposal? Excellent. I'll be most happy to return the favor tonight, when the card counters turn out for their evening's work."

"You work out those details with Hentoff."

"How kind."

Kemper sighed. "I have a lot on my plate at the moment. So I hope we can keep this brief. What, exactly, do you need?"

"Access to the ship's central safe."

Abruptly, the security chief's weary attitude evaporated. "No frigging way."

"Ah—and here I was under the misapprehension we had an agreement."

Kemper's look changed to disbelief. "Passengers are not authorized to enter the vault, much less snoop around in it."

Pendergast's reply, when it came, was mild. "It's not hard to imagine what might happen to a security director who presided over a million-pound loss in the casinos on a mere seven-day crossing. Hentoff may be in charge of the casinos, but when it comes to security, the, ah, *chip* stops with you."

Several moments passed in which the two men looked at each other. Then Kemper licked his lips. "Only the first officer, the staff captain, and the commodore have access to the vault," he said in a low voice.

"Then I suggest you phone the officer of your choice."

Kemper continued to stare at Pendergast for another minute. At last—without taking his eyes off him—he picked up the phone and dialed. A brief, murmured conversation ensued. When Kemper put down the phone, the expression on his face had not quite cleared. "The first officer will meet us there now."

It was the work of five minutes to make their way to the vault, located one level below on Deck B, in a heavily reinforced section of the ship that also housed the master guidance control system and the server farms controlling the *Britannia*'s internal network. Here, below the waterline, the vibration of the diesels was more pronounced. The first officer was already waiting at the security station, looking every inch a ship's commander with his silver hair and smart uniform.

"This is Mr. Pendergast," Kemper said, a distinct lack of grace in his voice.

LeSeur nodded. "We met last night. At Roger Mayles's table."

Pendergast smiled thinly. "My reputation precedes me, thanks to the good Mr. Mayles. This is the situation, gentlemen: a client has engaged me to find an object that was stolen from him. I know three things about this object: it is a unique Tibetan artifact; it is somewhere on this ship; and its current owner—who, by the way, is also on the ship—murdered a man to obtain it."

He patted the breast pocket of his suit jacket. "My list of suspects contains three names of passengers who, according to Mr. Mayles, consigned items to the ship's vault. I would like to give those items a cursory inspection, if you please."

"Why?" Kemper asked. "Each suite is equipped with its own safe. If what you say is really true, the thief wouldn't stash the thing there."

"The object is over four feet long. That makes it too large for in-room safes, other than the ones in the very largest suites."

LeSeur frowned. "Let's make this brief. Mr. Pendergast: you can look, but you are not to touch. Mr. Kemper, get one of your men in here, please. I'd like three pairs of eyes to witness this."

They passed the security station and went down a short corridor, which dead-ended in an unmarked door. The first officer reached into his pocket, pulled out a key on a steel chain, and unlocked the door. Kemper swung it open and they entered.

Although the room beyond was small, the rear wall was completely taken up by a massive circular vault door of polished steel. LeSeur waited while one of the guards from the security station entered the room. Then, extracting another key from his pocket, he inserted it into a lock in the vault door. This was followed by an identity card slipped into a card reader to one side of the safe. Next, LeSeur pressed his palm into a hand geometry scanner beside the card slot. There was a metallic *thunk* and a red light above the door went on.

LeSeur walked to a large combination dial set into the far side of the vault door. Shielding the dial from the other occupants of the room, he spun it left and right several times. The light above the door turned green; the first officer turned a wheel set in its center, then pulled it toward him, and the massive door swung open.

The interior was illuminated in a watery green light. Beyond the door lay a chamber about twelve feet square. The rear part of the vault was secured by a steel curtain, behind which lay numerous metal boxes, racked in sliding frames, shoulder high. The two facing walls were covered in safe doors, some quite large, their flush front panels gleaming dully in the pale light. Each had a key slot in its center, with a number etched into the steel directly above.

"A safe of safes," said Pendergast. "Most impressive."

"Right," said LeSeur. "Who are we looking for?"

Pendergast pulled the sheet out of his pocket. "The first is Edward Robert Smecker, Lord Cliveburgh." He paused for a second, reading. "It seems that once his ancestral fortune was exhausted, he resorted to creative ways to make ends meet. Hangs out with the jet set, makes the rounds of Monaco, St. Tropez, Capri, and the Costa Smeralda. Jewelry tends to disappear when he's around. None of the jewelry he supposedly stole was ever recovered, and he's beaten every rap. It is assumed he recuts the gems and melts down the metal for bullion."

The first officer turned to a terminal in the near wall, typed briefly on its keyboard. "That would be number

236." He walked over to a small safe. "This isn't big enough for the object you mention."

"Perhaps the object's profile can be reduced in size by cutting or folding. If you'd be so good as to open it?"

With an almost imperceptible tightening of the lips, LeSeur inserted a key and turned it. The door swung open to reveal a large aluminum suitcase with a dial lock.

"Interesting," Pendergast said. He prowled around the open door for a moment, rather catlike himself. Then he reached out and, with utmost delicacy, began turning the dials, one after the other, with a long, spidery finger.

"Just a minute!" Kemper cried. "I told you, touch *nothing*—"

"Ah!" Pendergast raised the lid on the suitcase. Inside were many bricks of aluminum foil and cellophane wrap, each coated with a thick layer of wax.

"Oh, Jesus," said Kemper. "I hope this isn't what it looks like." He slipped a penknife out of his pocket, stabbed it through the layers of wax and foil, and drew it down, revealing a crusty white powder. He reached in, dabbed a fingertip into the powder, took a taste.

"Cocaine," he said.

"It would appear," Pendergast murmured, "our good Lord Cliveburgh has started a new and even more lucrative business venture."

"What do we do?" said LeSeur, staring at the white powder.

"Nothing, for now," said Kemper, shutting the suitcase and spinning the dial. "Believe me, this isn't going anywhere. We'll radio ahead to U.S. Customs. When we come into port, Cliveburgh will collect his trunk and they'll nail him quayside with the stuff—*off* the ship."

"Very well," said LeSeur. "But how will we explain that we opened—?"

"We don't need to," said Kemper grimly. "Leave the details to me."

"What a stroke of luck," said Pendergast cheerfully, as the gloom deepened in the room. "It seems rather fortunate I came along!"

No one else seemed to share his view in this matter.

"Next on my list is the movie star, Claude Dallas."

LeSeur noticed that Kemper had begun to sweat. If this ever got out . . . He turned to the terminal without bringing the thought to completion. "Number 822."

They approached a larger vault. "Promising," murmured Pendergast.

LeSeur opened it with his key. Inside were several old steamer trunks, covered with stickers for such destinations as Rio de Janeiro, Phuket, and Goa. The hasps were protected by fist-sized padlocks.

"Hmm," Pendergast said. He bent before the trunk, massaging his chin curiously.

"Mr. Pendergast," the security chief said in a warning tone.

Pendergast reached out two lean hands, one of which held a tiny, gleaming tool; he massaged the lock, turning it between his fingers. It sprang open with a click.

"Mr. Dallas should have this lock replaced," he said. And before Kemper or LeSeur could object, he swung it away, opened the hasp, and raised the lid.

A rubber suit lay on top, along with some braided

horsehair whips, chains, manacles, ropes, and various leather and iron devices of an obscure nature.

"How curious," said Pendergast, reaching in. This time LeSeur said nothing as Pendergast pulled out a Lycra Superman cape and suit, with the crotch cut out. He examined it carefully, plucked something from the shoulder, placed it in a test tube that seemed to appear from nowhere and disappear into nowhere, and then gently laid the garment back down. "I'm not sure it's necessary to check Mr. Dallas's other boxes."

"It is certainly *not* necessary," said LeSeur dryly.

"And last," Pendergast said, "is Felix Strage, chairman of the Greek and Roman department at the Met. He is returning from a rather unpleasant trip to Italy, where he was questioned by the Italian authorities over some purchases his museum made back in the 1980s of illegally acquired antiquities."

LeSeur gave Pendergast a long, hard look. Then he turned back to the keyboard. "Number 597," he said. "Before I open the safe, let's get one thing straight. Keep your hands off. Mr. Wadle here will do the handling." He nodded to the guard. "If you open any of the contents, this fact-finding mission of yours will end abruptly and prematurely. Understood?"

"Perfectly," the agent replied good-naturedly.

LeSeur moved to a safe on the lowest tier of the right wall, one of the largest in the entire vault. He paused, fishing for a different key. Then he knelt, unlocked the steel door, and pulled it open. Inside were three massive, squat wooden crates. The safe was quite deep, and the light was too dim to make the objects out with any success.

Pendergast stared at the crates a moment, motionless. He turned and slipped a screwdriver out of his pocket. "Mr. Wadle?"

The security guard looked with uncertainty at Kemper, who nodded curtly.

Wadle took the screwdriver and unscrewed the side of the crate—eight screws in all—and then removed it. Inside was bubble wrap and foam-in-place. He eased aside the bubble wrap and removed two blocks of foam to reveal the side of a Greek vase.

Pendergast slipped a penlight from his pocket and shined it into the open crate. "Hmm. We seem to have a calyx-crater. Undoubtedly genuine. It seems our Dr. Strage is up to his old tricks, smuggling more antiquities for his museum." He straightened up, replacing the penlight in his pocket. He stepped back from the wall of safes. "Thank you for your time and patience, gentlemen."

LeSeur nodded. Kemper said nothing.

"And now, forgive me if I leave in haste." And with that he bowed, turned, and stepped out of the vault.

In the elevator, ascending to Deck 12, Pendergast paused to remove the list from his pocket. He drew a line through Lord Cliveburgh and another through Dallas. He did not draw a line through Strage.

20

Constance Greene walked down the elegant corridor, Marya Kazulin at her side. She felt an unaccustomed thrill—the thrill of mystery, deceit, and investigation.

"The uniform fits you perfectly," Kazulin whispered in her thick accent.

"Thank you for bringing it to my suite."

"Is nothing. Uniforms are the only thing we have in plenty. Except for dirty laundry maybe."

"I'm unfamiliar with this type of shoe."

"Work shoes. The kind that nurses wear. They have a soft sole, like sneakers."

"Sneakers?"

"Is that not the word?" Marya frowned. "Now remember, as cabin steward you are not to speak to passengers except when in their cabins on business. Do not make eye contact with anyone we pass. Step to one side and look down."

"Understood."

Marya led the way around a corner, then through an unmarked hatchway. Beyond lay a linen room and a bank of two service elevators. Marya walked up to the elevators, pressed the down button. "Who is it you wish to speak to?"

"The people who clean the large suites, the duplexes and triplexes."

"They are the ones who speak better English. Like me."

The elevator doors slid open and they entered. "Some of the workers don't speak English?" Constance asked.

Marya pressed the button for Deck C and the elevator began to descend. "Most of the crew speak no English. The company likes it better that way."

"Cheaper labor?"

"Yes. Also, if we cannot speak to each other, we cannot form union. Cannot protest work conditions."

"What's wrong with the work conditions?"

"You shall see for yourself, Ms. Greene. Now, you must be very careful. If you are caught, I will be fired and put off ship in New York. You must pretend to be foreign, speak broken English. We must find you a language nobody else speaks so you will not be questioned. Do you have any language other than English?"

"Yes. Italian, French, Latin, Greek, German—"

Marya laughed, genuinely this time. "Stop. I think no Germans in crew. You will be German."

The doors slipped open onto Deck C and they stepped out. The difference between the passenger decks and the service decks was apparent immediately. There was no carpeting on the floor, artwork on the walls, or brightwork trim. It looked more like a hospital corridor, a claustrophobic landscape of metal and linoleum. Fluorescent tubes, hidden behind recessed ceiling panels, threw a harsh light over the scene. The air was stuffy and uncomfortably warm, freighted with numerous scents: cooked fish, fabric softener, machine oil. The deep thrum of the diesel engines was far more pronounced here. Crew members, some in uniform, some in T-shirts or dirty sweats, bustled past, intent on their duties.

Marya led the way down the narrow corridor. Numbered, windowless doors of imitation wood grain lined both sides. "This is dormitory deck," Marya explained in a low voice. "Women in my bunk do some large cabins, you speak with them. We say you are friend I met in laundry. Remember, you are German and your English is not good."

"I'll remember."

"We need reason why you ask questions."

Constance thought a moment. "What if I say I do the smaller rooms and want to better my position?"

"Okay. But do not be too eager—people here will stab you in back for a job with better tips."

"Understood."

Marya turned down another corridor, then stopped before a door. "This my room," she said. "Ready?"

Constance nodded. Marya took a deep breath, then opened the door.

The room beyond was as small as a prison cell, perhaps fourteen feet by ten. Six narrow lockers were set into the far wall. There were no chairs or tables, no adjoining bath. The walls to the left and right were occupied entirely by spartan bunks, set three high. At the head of each bunk was a small shelf, topped by a light. As Constance looked around, she noticed that each of these shelves was filled with books, photos of loved ones, dried flowers, magazines—a small, sad imprint of the individual who occupied the bunk.

"There are *six* of you in here?" she asked incredulously.

Marya nodded.

"I had no idea conditions were so cramped."

"This nothing. You should see Deck E, where the NPC staff sleep."

"NPC?"

"No Passenger Contact. Crew who do laundry, wash engine rooms, prepare food." Marya shook her head. "Like prison. They no see daylight, no breathe fresh air, for three, four months maybe. Work six days week, ten hours a day. Pay is twenty to forty dollars a day."

"But that's less than minimum wage!"

"Minimum wage where? We are nowhere—in middle of sea. No wage law here. Ship registered in Liberia." She looked around. "My bunkmates in mess already. We find them there."

She traced a circuitous path through the narrow, sweat-fragrant corridors, Constance close behind. The crew dining area was located amidships, a large, low-ceilinged room. Crew members, all in uniform, sat at long cafeteria-style tables, heads bent over their plates. As they took their places in the buffet line, Constance looked around, shocked at the plainness of the room—so very different from the opulent dining rooms and grand salons the passengers enjoyed.

"It's so quiet," she said. "Why aren't people talking?"

"Everyone tired. Also, everyone upset about Juanita. Maid who went crazy."

"Crazy? What happened?"

She shook her head. "Is not uncommon, except it usually happen at end of long tour. Juanita go crazy . . . rip out own eyes."

"Good God. Did you know her?"

"A little."

"Did she seem to have any problems?"

"We all of us have problems," Marya said, quite seriously. "Otherwise not take this job."

They made their lunch choices from an unappetizing variety—fatty slices of boiled corned beef, waterlogged cabbage, mushy rice, gluey shepherd's pie, anemic-looking squares of yellow sheet cake—and Marya led the way to a nearby table, where two of her bunkmates picked listlessly at their plates. Marya made the introductions: a young, dark-haired Greek woman named Nika, and Lourdes, a middle-aged Filipina.

"I have not seen you before," Nika said in a thick accent.

"I'm assigned to cabins on Deck 8," Constance replied, careful to add a German accent of her own.

The woman nodded. "You must be careful. This isn't your mess. Don't let *her* see you." She nodded toward a short, hirsute, thickset woman with frizzy bottle-blonde hair, standing in a far corner and surveying the room with a scowl.

The women made small talk in a strange mixture of languages with a lot of English words thrown in, apparently the lingua franca of the *Britannia*'s service decks.

Most of it focused on the maid who had gone crazy and mutilated herself.

"Where is she now?" Constance asked. "Did they medevac her off the ship?"

"Too far from land for a helicopter," said Nika. "They lock her in infirmary. And now I have to do half her rooms." She scowled. "Juanita, I knew she was heading for trouble. She is always talking about what she see in the passengers' rooms, poking her nose where it not belong. A good maid sees nothing, remembers nothing, just does her job and keeps her mouth shut."

Constance wondered if Nika ever took her own advice on the latter point.

Nika went on. "Yesterday, how she talk at lunch! All about that stateroom with the leather straps on bed and vibrator in drawer. What is she doing looking in drawer? Curiosity killed the cat. And now I have to clean half her rooms. This Jonah ship."

Her mouth set firmly into an expression of disapproval and she sat back and crossed her arms, point made.

There were murmurs and nods of agreement.

Nika, encouraged, uncrossed her arms and opened her mouth again. "Passenger disappear too on ship. You hear that? Maybe she is a jumper. This Jonah ship, I tell you!"

Constance spoke quickly to stem the flow of words. "Marya tells me you work in the larger cabins," she said. "You're lucky—I just have the standard suites."

"Lucky?" Nika looked at her incredulously. "For me is twice as much work."

"But the tips are better, right?"

Nika scoffed. "The rich ones give you smallest tips of all. They always complain, want everything just so. That ρυπαρός in the triplex, he make me come back three times today to remake his bed."

This was a piece of luck. One of the people on Pendergast's list—Scott Blackburn, the dot-com billionaire—had taken one of only two triplex suites. "Do you mean Mr. Blackburn?" she asked.

Nika shook her head. "No. Blackburn even worse! Has own maid, she get linens herself. Maid treat me like dirt, like I *her* maid. I have to take that triplex also, thanks to Juanita."

"He brought his own maid along?" Constance asked. "Why?"

"He bring *everything* along! Own bed, own rugs, own statues, own paintings, own piano even." Nika shook her head. "Bah! Ugly things, too: ugly and ρυπαρός."

"I'm sorry?" Constance feigned ignorance of the word.

"Rich people crazy." Nika cursed again in Greek.

"How about his friend, Terrence Calderón, next door?"

"Him! He okay. Give me okay tip."

"You clean his stateroom, as well? Did he bring his own things?"

She nodded. "Some. Lot of antiques. French. Very nice."

"The richer they are, the worse they are," said Lourdes. She spoke excellent English with only a faint accent. "Last night, I was in the suite of—"

"Hey!" a voice boomed right behind them. Constance

turned to see the supervisor standing behind her, hands on copious hips, glaring.

"On your feet!" the woman said.

"Are you speaking to me?" Constance replied.

"I said, on your *feet*!"

Calmly, Constance rose.

"I haven't seen you before," the woman said in a surly tone. "What's your name?"

"Rülke," Constance said. "Leni Rülke."

"What's your station?"

"The Deck 8 cabins."

A look of bitter triumph came over the woman's fat features. "I thought as much. You know better than to eat here. Get back down to the Deck D cafeteria where you belong."

"What's the difference?" Constance asked in a mild tone. "The food's no better here."

Disbelief took the place of triumph on the supervisor's face. "Why, you impudent bitch—" And she slapped Constance hard across her right cheek.

Constance had never in her life been slapped before. She stiffened for a moment. Then she took an instinctive step forward, hand closing tightly over her fork. Something in her movement made the supervisor's eyes widen. The woman stepped back.

Slowly, Constance laid the fork back on the table. She thought of Marya and the pledge of secrecy she owed her. She glanced down. Marya was staring at them, her face white. The other two women were looking studiously at their plates.

Around them, the low murmur of apathetic conversation, which had stopped for the altercation, resumed. She looked back at the supervisor, committing her face to memory. Then—cheek burning—she stepped away from the table and left the cafeteria.

21

First Officer Gordon LeSeur felt a rising sense of concern as he stepped into Kemper's monastic office. The missing passenger had not shown up, and the husband had demanded to meet with all the senior officers. Commodore Cutter had been cloistered in his cabin for the last eight hours, in one of his black moods, and LeSeur wasn't about to disturb him for Evered or anybody else. Instead, he'd assigned the watch to the second officer and rounded up the staff captain, Carol Mason, for the meeting.

Evered was pacing back and forth in the cramped confines, his face red, his voice shaking. He looked like he was teetering on the brink of hysteria. "It's past four in the afternoon," he was saying to Kemper. "It's been eight goddamn hours since I alerted you to my wife's disappearance."

"Mr. Evered," Kemper, the chief of security, began. "It's a big ship, there's a lot of places she could be—"

"That's what you all said before," Evered said, his voice rising. *"She's not back yet.* I heard the PA announcements like everyone else, I saw the little picture you posted on the

TVs. This isn't like her, she would never stay away this long without contacting me. I want this ship searched!"

"Let me assure you—"

"To hell with your assurances! She could have fallen somewhere, be hurt, unable to call out or get to a phone. She could have . . ." He stopped, breathing heavily, savagely brushed away a tear with the back of his hand. "You need to contact the Coast Guard, contact the police, get them here."

"Mr. Evered," Staff Captain Mason said, quietly taking charge, much to LeSeur's relief. "We're in the middle of the Atlantic Ocean. Even if the police or the Coast Guard had jurisdiction—which they don't—they could never reach us. Now, you must believe me when I say we have time-tested procedures for dealing with this kind of situation. The chances are almost one hundred percent that, for some reason, she's unwilling to be found. We have to consider the possibility that she may be in somebody else's company."

Evered jabbed a trembling finger at LeSeur. "I told him this morning, my wife's not like that. And I won't take that kind of insinuation, not from you or anybody else."

"I'm not insinuating anything, Mr. Evered," said Mason, her voice firm and quiet. "I'm simply saying there's no reason to get upset. Believe me, statistically you're safer on board this ship than even in your own home. Having said that, we take security seriously, and given the nature of the problem, we *will* institute a search of the ship. Immediately. I'll supervise it myself."

The staff captain's low, competent voice and her soothing words had the intended effect. Evered was still flushed and breathing heavily, but after a moment he swallowed and nodded. "That's what I've been asking from the beginning."

After Evered had left, the three stood in silence. Finally, the security chief fetched a deep sigh and turned to Mason. "Well, Captain?"

The staff captain was staring thoughtfully at the empty doorway. "Is there any way we could get a psychiatric background report on Mrs. Evered?"

A silence. "You don't think—?" Kemper asked.

"It's always a possibility."

"Legally we'd have to go through her husband," Kemper said. "That's a step I'd be most reluctant to take until we're really sure she's . . . no longer on the ship. Son of a *bitch*. We've already got a problem with crew morale over that crazy housekeeper—I hope to God we find her."

Mason nodded. "Me too. Mr. Kemper, please organize a level-two search." She glanced at LeSeur. "Gordon, I'd like you to work with Mr. Kemper personally."

"Certainly, sir," LeSeur said. Inwardly, he cringed. A level-two search meant every public space, all the crews' quarters, and the entire belowdecks section of the ship—everything, in fact, but the staterooms. Even with the entire security staff mobilized, it would take a full day, at least. And there were some spaces deep in the bowels of the ship that simply couldn't be searched successfully.

"I'm sorry, Gordon," she said, reading the look on his face. "But it's a step we have to take. Standing orders."

Standing orders, he thought a little morosely. And that's all it was, really: an exercise in formality. Passenger cabins could only be examined in a level-three search, and Commodore Cutter would have to authorize that personally. No such search had ever been conducted on a ship LeSeur had worked on, not even when there had been a jumper. And that's what LeSeur privately figured Mrs. Evered was: a jumper. Suicide at sea was more common than the passengers ever realized. Especially on high-profile maiden voyages, where some people wanted to go out in style. That was a huge irony, because it was the way of the cruise industry to sweep them under the rug and do everything to keep the news from the rest of the passengers. Instead of going out in style, Mrs. Evered might simply be five hundred miles behind them and a thousand fathoms deep—

LeSeur's thoughts were interrupted by a knock. He turned to see a security officer standing in the doorway. "Mr. Kemper, sir?"

"Yes?" Kemper asked.

"Sir," the man said nervously, "two things." He shifted, waiting.

"Well?" Kemper snapped. "Can't you see I'm in a meeting?"

"The maid who went crazy—she, ah, just killed herself."

"How?"

"Managed to get free of her restraints and . . ." He faltered.

"And what?"

"Pried a sharp piece of wood free from her bedframe and jammed it into her eye socket. Went up into her brain."

There was a short silence as this bit of information was digested. Kemper shook his head.

"Mr. Kemper," LeSeur said, "I think you might want to have a word with the passenger in the last suite she cleaned before she went off the deep end. There might have been some kind of unpleasant encounter, an accident, perhaps . . . I was on a cruise ship once where a passenger brutally raped the maid that came in to clean."

"I'll do that, sir."

"Be circumspect."

"Of course."

There was a silence. Then Kemper turned back to the nervous security officer. "You mentioned a second thing?"

"Yes, sir."

"Well? What is it?" Kemper asked brusquely.

"There's something you should see."

"What?"

The man hesitated. "I'd rather you saw it directly, sir. It might pertain to the missing passenger."

"Where is it?" Mason interrupted, her voice sharp.

"The weather deck aft of the St. James's shopping arcade."

"Lead the way," said Mason crisply. "We'll all go together."

Kemper headed toward the door, then glanced back at LeSeur. "You coming, sir?"

"Yes," LeSeur said reluctantly with a sinking feeling.

The deck was raw and damp. There were no passengers—the few hardy souls who ventured out into the open air usually sought out the unbroken circuit of the promenade on Deck 7, directly above. There was a buffeting wind that tore froth from the ship's bow far into the air, and within moments LeSeur's jacket was soaked.

The security officer led the way to the railing. "It's down there," he said, pointing over the side.

LeSeur joined Kemper and Carol Mason at the rail. He glanced over, staring down at the water seven decks below. It boiled angrily along the smooth flank of the ship.

"What are we looking at?" Kemper asked.

"There, sir. I just noticed it as I did a visual inspection of the hull. Do you see the damage to the brightwork below the toe-rail there, just to the left of that scupper?"

Keeping a tight grip on the railing, LeSeur leaned farther over, peering carefully. Then he saw it: a six-inch scrape along the teak brightwork that hid the deck joint.

"Sir, if that damage was there before we sailed yesterday, I would have noticed it. I'm sure of it."

"He's right," the staff captain said. "This vessel is much too new to be dinged up like that." She peered more closely. "And if I'm not mistaken, there's something clinging to that splintered section, almost the same color as the wood."

LeSeur squinted. The starboard hull was deep in afternoon shadow, but he thought he saw it, too.

Mason turned to the security officer. "See if you can retrieve it."

The man nodded, then lay flat on the deck. While LeSeur and Kemper held his feet, the man ducked his head under the railing, then reached over the edge with his hand. He moved his arm around, grunting. Just when LeSeur thought he couldn't get any wetter, the man cried out. "Got it!" he said.

They pulled him back from the edge of the deck and he

got to his feet, something balled protectively in his hand. As the three crowded around, he slowly uncurled his fist.

Lying in his palm was a small cluster of fine threads, matted and soaked with spray. LeSeur heard Mason catch her breath. As she did so, he realized that the threads were all connected at one end to what looked like a small patch of skin. With a thrill of dismay he realized these were not threads at all, but hair—human hair, by the look of it, and platinum blonde.

"Mr. Kemper," Mason said in a low, even voice. "Do you have that photograph of the missing woman?"

He removed a small portfolio from his pocket, opened it, drew out the photo, and handed it to the staff captain. She held it up, looked at it carefully, then looked back at the hair in the officer's cupped palm.

"Oh, shit," she murmured.

22

Special Agent Pendergast stepped out of his stateroom, closed the door, and started down the corridor. He was smartly dressed in a black tuxedo, and that, along with his purposeful stride and the eight o'clock hour, gave the distinct impression he was on his way to dinner.

But Pendergast would not be having dinner this evening. Rather, he would use the dinner hour to accomplish some business of his own.

Reaching a bank of elevators, he pressed the up button. When the doors slid open, he stepped in and pressed the button for Deck 13. In less than thirty seconds he was walking briskly down another corridor, headed forward.

Most of the passengers were at dinner or in the casinos, or taking in a show. Pendergast passed only two people, a maid and a cabin steward. At last the passage doglegged first right, then left, ending in the forward transverse corridor. This corridor was much shorter, and there were only two doors to his left: each led to one of the ship's royal suites.

Pendergast stepped up to the first door, labeled *Richard II Suite*, and knocked. When there was no answer, he slipped an electromagnetic card out of his bag. The card was attached by a coiled wire to a palmtop computer concealed within the bag. He inserted the card into the door's passkey slot, examined a readout on the unit's tiny screen, then punched a series of numbers into the keypad. There was an electronic chirp and the LED on the doorlock went from red to green. With one more glance down the corridor he slipped inside and, closing the door behind him, paused to listen intently. He had already confirmed that Lionel Brock was at dinner; the suite appeared empty, silent and dark.

Pulling a small flashlight from his jacket, he made his way into the cabin. The four royal suites were not as large as the duplex or triplex apartments, but each was quite broad, occupying half of the forward superstructure of Deck 12 or 13 and overlooking the forecastle. According to the deck plan Pendergast had examined, the suites consisted of a large living room, dining room, kitchenette, lavatory, and two bedrooms with a connecting bath.

He stepped through the living room, shining his light over the surfaces. The room looked barely used; the maid had been in recently. The wastebasket was empty. The only thing even remotely curious about the room was that a freshly changed pillow lay at one side of the leather couch. On the passenger manifest, Brock was occupying the room by himself. Perhaps the man suffered from piles.

The only sign of occupancy was an unopened bottle of Taittinger sitting in a pedestal champagne bucket, the ice half melted.

Slipping on a pair of latex gloves, he went through

the drawers of the side tables and the desk, finding only ship's literature and remote controls for the television and DVD player. He lifted the wall paintings, peered behind each in turn, finding nothing. Stepping to the forward picture window, he quietly drew back the curtain. Far, far below, the *Britannia*'s bow sliced through the spume-tossed waves. The weather had steadily grown worse and the ship's slow roll was now more pronounced.

Stepping back from the window, Pendergast moved to the kitchenette. It too looked unused: Brock was clearly taking his meals in the many ship's restaurants. The refrigerator held only two more bottles of champagne. Quickly, Pendergast searched the drawers, finding nothing but cutlery and glassware. Then he moved to the dining room, then lavatory, giving them a quick examination. Next, the coat closet. None held anything of interest.

He stepped back out into the living room and paused to listen. All was silent. He glanced at his watch: quarter after eight. Brock had been scheduled for the eight o'clock seating at the King's Arms and would not be back for at least ninety minutes.

The bedrooms lay to starboard. One door was closed, the other open. Pendergast stepped over to the open door, listened once again, then stepped inside. The bedroom was rather similar to his own: a king-sized bed with an extravagant canopy, two side tables, an armoire, writing desk and chair, a closet, and a door that no doubt led to the connecting bathroom. The room was clearly Brock's.

It was the work of fifteen minutes to give the room

a thorough search. More quickly now, he moved into the shared bathroom and gave the toiletries a brief inspection. Once again, he discovered little other than a confirmation of what he had already suspected: Brock's cologne of choice was Floris Elite.

At the far end of the bathroom was a small dressing room with a door that connected to the second bedroom. Pendergast reached for the knob, intending to give the room only a cursory search—it seemed more and more likely that, if Brock was guilty of anything, the evidence would be found elsewhere than on the *Britannia*.

The door was locked.

Pendergast frowned. Returning to the living room, he tried the other door to the second bedroom. It, too, was locked.

Most intriguing.

He kneeled, examining the mechanism with his flashlight. It was a simple tumbler lock that would offer little resistance. He reached into his pocket and drew out a lockpick that resembled a small wire toothbrush. He inserted it into the lock, and in a moment the soft click of a tumbler signified success. Grasping the doorknob, he eased the door open into the dark room.

"Move and you're dead," came a harsh voice out of the blackness.

Pendergast went motionless.

A man stepped into view from behind the door, gun in hand. A woman's sleepy voice came from the darkness of the bedroom: "What is it, Curt?"

Instead of answering, the man gestured at Pendergast with the gun, stepped through the door, shut and locked it behind him. He was a dark-haired man with acne scars and olive skin, handsome in a gangsterish way, very muscular. He carried himself like a prizefighter, but for a big man he could clearly move with consummate stealth. He was not a steward: he wore a dark suit rather than a uniform, and the material barely managed to stretch across his broad shoulders.

"All right, pal, who are you and what are you doing here?" Curt asked.

Pendergast smiled, nodded to a sofa chair. "May I? I've been on my feet all day."

The man stood there, scowling, while Pendergast sat down and made himself comfortable, crossing one knee daintily over the other.

"I asked you a question, motherfucker."

Pendergast pulled the bottle of champagne out of the melting ice, let the excess water drain off the outside, and with a deft twist unseated the cork. Two empty flutes stood to one side. He filled them both to the brim.

"Care to join me?" he asked.

The man raised the gun. "I'm just about out of patience. You got a problem, and it's getting worse."

Pendergast took a sip. "That makes two of us with a problem. If you would sit down, we could discuss them in comfort."

"I don't got a problem. You do. You got a *big* fucking problem."

"I'm well aware of my problem. *You* are my problem. You're standing in front of me with a gun pointed at my head, and you seem to be losing your temper.

Yes, a definite problem." Pendergast took a sip, sighed. "Excellent."

"You got one more chance to tell me who you are before I plaster your brains on the wall."

"Before you do that, I might just point out that you have a far more serious problem than I."

"Yeah? And what the hell's that?"

Pendergast nodded toward the bedroom door. "Does Mr. Brock know you are entertaining a lady in his suite?"

An uneasy hesitation. "Mr. Brock's got no problem with me entertaining ladies."

Pendergast raised his eyebrows. "Perhaps. Perhaps not. But on top of that, if you attempt to 'plaster' anything on the wall, you'll find yourself the unfortunate center of attention on this ship. If you're lucky, you'll end up with a murder charge. If you're not, it will be *your* brains decorating the wallpaper. I'm also armed, you see."

Another hesitation. "I'm calling ship's security."

Pendergast took another sip. "You're not thinking this through, Mr. Curt."

The man jabbed the gun at him. "It's Johnson. Curtis Johnson. Not 'Mr. Curt.' "

"Excuse me. Mr. Johnson. Even if it's true Mr. Brock doesn't mind you entertaining ladies while on duty, if you call security there may be questions raised about the cargo Mr. Brock has stored in that bedroom you are using as a love nest. On top of that, you don't know who I am or why I'm here. For all you know I might *be* ship's security. And so, as I said, Mr. Johnson, we both have problems. I'm hoping there's a way we can solve our respective problems intelligently, and to our mutual advantage." He slowly inserted two fingers inside his tuxedo pocket.

"Keep your hands in view."

Pendergast removed the fingers, which were now holding a small sheaf of crisp hundred-dollar bills.

The man stood, meaty hand clutching the gun, his face flushed and confused.

Pendergast dangled the money. "Lower the gun."

The man lowered the gun.

"Go ahead, take it."

The man reached out, snatched the money, shoved it in his pocket.

"We have to work quickly, Mr. Johnson, so that I'm gone by the time Mr. Brock returns."

"You get the hell outta here. Now."

"You take my money and still kick me out? How unsporting."

Pendergast rose with a loud sigh, turned as if to leave, but the motion accelerated with mercurial quickness into the tossing of the glass of champagne in Johnson's face while, with a simultaneous, lightning-fast motion, he brought his left fist down on Johnson's wrist. The gun bounced on the rug and skidded halfway across the room. As Johnson let out a shout and dove for it, Pendergast tripped him up, then shoved his own Les Baer 1911 in the man's ear, putting one knee at the base of his spine.

"*Doucement*, Mr. Johnson. *Doucement*."

After a long moment, Pendergast stood up. "You may rise."

The man sat up, rubbed his ear, and then stood. His face was a dark mass.

Pendergast stuck his own weapon back inside his jacket, walked across the room, picked up Johnson's gun, hefted it.

"A Walther PPK. You're a James Bond fan, I imagine. Perhaps we have less in common than I imagined." He tossed it back to Johnson, who caught it, surprised. He held it, uncertain what to do.

"Be a smart fellow and put it away."

Johnson holstered the weapon.

"Now," said Pendergast pleasantly, "here's the choice, Mr. Johnson. You could be my friend, do me the tiniest of favors, and earn another thousand. Or you could continue to act out of misplaced loyalty to a contemptuous jackass of a man who underpays you and who will fire you the very minute he learns of your indiscretion and never think about you again. So—which is it, Mr. Johnson?"

The man stared at Pendergast for a long time, then nodded curtly.

"Splendid. Open the back bedroom, my newfound friend. There's no time to waste."

Johnson turned and went to the bedroom door, unlocked it. Pendergast followed inside.

"Curt, what the hell's going on?" A woman with huge hair lay on the bed, the bedclothes pulled up to her chin.

"Get dressed and get out."

"But my clothes are on the other side of the room," she said. "I don't have anything on."

"Nobody gives a shit," said Johnson roughly. "Get going."

"You're an asshole, you know that?"

He waved the gun. "Move it!"

The woman jumped out of bed, heavy breasts flopping, snagged her clothes, and retreated into the bathroom. "Asshole!" came a second muffled insult.

Pendergast looked around. The bedroom, as he noted earlier, had been intended for storage: half a dozen large wooden crates were in view, all stamped *Fragile* and taking up much of the room.

"Do you know what is in these crates?"

"No idea," said Johnson.

"But you were hired to keep an eye on them?"

"You got it."

Pendergast walked back and forth in front of the crates for a moment. Then he kneeled before the nearest and removed a screwdriver from his bag.

"Hey, what are you doing?"

"Just taking a peek. We're going to leave everything just as we found it. Nobody will know." In a moment he had the end of the crate off, exposing green felt and padding. With a knife, he made a careful incision across several layers of padding, felt, and custom-cut pieces of Styrofoam, exposing a rack of what looked like oil paintings. Judging from the fact that the other five crates were of exactly the same dimensions, Pendergast deduced they were full of paintings as well.

He thrust his flashlight into the incision in the padding, moving it this way and that. There were eight paintings in all, unframed. From what he could see, they seemed to be all by second-tier impressionist artists—Charles Théophile Angrand, Gustave Caillebotte. There were also two German expressionist works, apparently by Jawlensky and the other, Pendergast guessed, by Pechstein. Obviously, the paintings were destined for Brock's gallery on 57th Street.

While Pendergast immediately recognized the styles of the various painters, he recognized not one of the actual paintings themselves, at least what he could see of them. They were, at best, obscure examples of their artists' oeuvre.

Reaching into his bag again, he pulled out a small leather case, which he unzipped and laid flat on the floor. He extracted several tools from the case—a jeweler's loupe, a pair of forceps, a scalpel—and set them on the nearest crate. These were followed by stoppered test tubes.

Johnson shifted his weight uneasily from foot to foot. "Whatever the hell you're doing, man, you'd better hurry it up."

"Calm yourself, Mr. Johnson. Your employer won't be back from dinner for some time yet. I'm almost finished."

Kneeling before the nearest crate, Pendergast turned his attention to the Jawlensky painting. Picking up the tweezers, he plucked off a few threads of canvas from the back of the work, where the cut canvas was nailed to the frame. Next, using both the forceps and scalpel, he shaved away a small, built-up fragment of yellow paint from the very edge of the painting and placed it in the test tube. He moved on to the Pechstein and several of the others and did the same.

He checked his watch. Eight forty-five.

He rearranged the packing to disguise the cut he had

made, screwed the end of the crate back in place, then rose with a smile. "Mr. Johnson," he said, "my apologies for interrupting your evening."

"Yeah, well, you still haven't told me who you are or what you're doing."

"Nor will I, Mr. Johnson."

They went into the living room and Pendergast turned to his host. "We have just enough time to enjoy another glass." He refilled their glasses. Johnson drank his off in a shot, then set it down. Pendergast sipped his more slowly, then pulled another sheaf of bills from his pocket.

"As promised," he said.

Johnson took them silently.

"You did well." Pendergast smiled, gave a half bow, and departed quickly.

23

Back in the suite, Constance found Pendergast hunched over a chemistry set. She watched as he dipped a cotton swab into a vial of a clear liquid and applied it to a paint chip in a test tube. Immediately, the fragment turned black.

He moved to another test tube and another, applying the same test. Finally he looked up. "Good evening, Constance."

"Any results?"

He nodded to the tests. "Indeed. These paint samples all show unacceptable levels of lead. Our Mr. Lionel Brock has six crates of impressionist paintings in his spare bedroom, and if the rest are like these, they're all forgeries. Brock must be employing a European art forger—a man of considerable talent—to imitate the work of minor artists, which he no doubt salts among his genuine paintings by major artists. Quite a clever scheme, really: nobody would question the authenticity of the *second-tier* paintings carried by a dealer known to sell the finest, most scrupulously provenanced *first-tier* works."

"Clever indeed," said Constance. "But it seems to me a man like that wouldn't risk all this on a Tibetan artifact."

"Exactly. We can strike him." With a rustle, Pendergast produced his list. "I have also crossed off Lambe—the man's as soft as risen dough."

"How did you manage that? Impersonate a doctor?"

"Ugh. Let us not speak of it. I have also struck Claude Dallas from the list, as well as Lord Cliveburgh, who is busy smuggling cocaine. Strage is illegally exporting several extremely valuable and quite genuine Greek vases, and while this might lessen the chances that he's also smuggling the Agozyen, we can't quite rule him out. Which leaves us with three: Blackburn, Calderón, and Strage." He turned his silver eyes on her. "How did your adventure belowdecks go?"

"I met the woman assigned to clean Blackburn's triplex. Luckily—for us, anyway—she took over from another worker who apparently suffered a psychotic break shortly after departure and killed herself."

"Indeed?" said Pendergast with sudden interest. "There's been a suicide on board?"

"That's what they say. She just stopped working in the middle of her shift, returned to her cabin, and had a breakdown. Later, she stabbed herself in the eye with a piece of wood and died."

"How odd. And the woman who's cleaning Blackburn's triplex—what does she say?"

"He brought his own maid, and she lords it over the ship's maid. Blackburn also had his suite redecorated for the crossing with his own furniture and artwork."

"That would include his Asian art collection."

"Yes. The same housekeeper I met also cleans Calderón's stateroom, which is next door. It seems he picked up a lot of French antiques. Apparently, he's as pleasant as Blackburn is obnoxious: he gave her a nice tip."

"Excellent." For a time, Pendergast's eyes seemed to go far away. Slowly, they came back into focus.

"Blackburn is a strong number one on our list." He reached in his pocket, withdrew yet another sheaf of crisp bills. "You are to temporarily switch places with the ship's housekeeper assigned to Blackburn and Calderón's rooms. Get in there when the suite is empty."

"But Blackburn won't let the ship's maid in without his maid being there."

"No matter—if you're caught you can always chalk it up to bureaucratic error. You know what to look for. I would suggest going late this evening—Blackburn, I've noticed, is partial to baccarat and will probably be in the casino."

"Very well, Aloysius."

"Oh—and bring me his trash, please."

Constance raised her eyebrows briefly. Then she nodded and turned toward the staircase, preparing to change for dinner.

"Constance?"

She turned back.

"Please be careful. Blackburn is one of our prime suspects—and that means he could well be a ruthless, perhaps psychopathic, killer."

21

Scott Blackburn paused at the entrance to Oscar's to button his Gieves & Hawkes bespoke suit, adjust his mauve tie, and survey the room. It was eight forty-five and the second seating was well under way: a horde of slim, elegant foreign waiters rushing in with the main courses under silver domes, which they brought to each table, laid down, and then—all at once, a waiter standing behind each diner—whipped off to reveal the dish underneath.

With a sardonic crook to his lip, Blackburn strolled over to his table. His two companions had already seated themselves and they rose obsequiously as he arrived. As well they should—Blackburn had invested several hundred million in their respective companies and sat on their boards' compensation committees. Two bottles of burgundy already stood empty on the table, among the scattered remains of hors d'oevures, antipasti, and a first course of a smallish bird that might have been squab or pheasant. As he sat down he took one bottle into his hand and examined the label.

"Richebourg Domaine de la Romanée-Conti '78," he

said. "You fellows are breaking out the good stuff." He turned and poured out the heel into his own glass. "And you've left me with nothing but sediment!"

Lambe and Calderón laughed reverentially, and Lambe gestured for a waiter. "Bring out another of these from our private cellar," he said. "One of the ones already opened."

"Right away, sir." The waiter glided off as silently as a bat.

"What's the occasion?" Blackburn asked.

"We just thought we'd indulge ourselves," Lambe said, rocking his soft, slumpy shoulders. Blackburn noticed that the man was less green about the gills than before. The weenie was, apparently, growing accustomed to the ocean.

"Why not?" Blackburn said. "This voyage is proving to be even more interesting than I anticipated. Among other things, I ran into an old girlfriend last night, and found her obliging—*very* obliging. At first, anyway."

This was greeted with a roar of laughter from his two listeners.

"And then what?" Lambe asked, eagerly leaning forward.

Blackburn shook his hand and laughed. "I don't know which was more exciting—the fucking or the fight afterward. Whew, what a wildcat."

More toadying laughter.

The waiter glided back with the bottle and a fresh glass, and Lambe indicated for him to pour Blackburn a taste. Blackburn swirled the liquid around in the glass, took a quick whiff, swirled again, then stuck his nose in and inhaled the bouquet. Then he sat back, his eyes half closed, appreciating the aroma. After a moment, he lifted the glass to his lips, drew in a small amount, rolled it around on his tongue, then drew in some air through his lips, bubbling it through the wine before swallowing. Ritual complete, he placed the glass down and waved the waiter away.

"What do you think?" Lambe asked eagerly.

"Magnificent."

They relaxed.

Blackburn raised his glass again. "And, it so happens, I have something to announce."

Both friends turned to him eagerly.

"Fill your glasses."

They did so with alacrity.

"As you know, since selling Gramnet for two billion, I've been knocking around, looking for some new little thing to mess around with. I believe I've found that thing."

"Can you talk about it?" asked Calderón.

Blackburn enjoyed the long pause.

"It has to do with scanning and searching visual databases on the web." He smiled. "When I sold Gramnet, I retained the rights to my proprietary image-compression algorithms. I'll push image content onto everybody's desktop, and it'll be content that looks a hundred times better than anything else out there."

"But Google's been working on image-matching technology for years," said Lambe. "They can't seem to get it right."

"I'm going to use a different technology: old-fashioned elbow grease. I've got thousands of programmers and researchers I can put to work on it, 24/7. I'm going to build the largest online multimedia database on the web."

"How?"

"Images can be linked just like web pages. People searching images go from one similar image to the next. Don't analyze the metadata or the images: analyze the *links*. Once they're in your own database, you can build on billions, trillions, of user-generated links. Then I'll grab the images themselves, super-high-res, and use algorithms and mathematical signatures to compress them. I've got a dozen server farms, idling, just waiting to be filled with data like this."

"But the copyrights to the images—how will you deal with that?"

"Screw copyright. Copyright's dead. This is the web. Information should be free for the taking. Everybody else is doing it—why not me?"

A reverent hush fell on the group.

"And to kick it off, I've got an ace in the hole." He raised his glass and gave a deep-throated chortle. "*And what an ace it is.*"

Then he took a three-hundred-dollar swallow of wine, closing his eyes with sheer orgiastic pleasure.

"Mr. Blackburn?" a low, deferential voice sounded at his elbow.

Blackburn turned, annoyed at having his enjoyment interrupted. A man in a rather indifferent suit stood there. He was short and ugly and had a Boston accent.

Blackburn frowned. "Who are you?"

"Pat Kemper's the name. I'm chief security officer of the *Britannia*. May I have a few words with you privately?"

"Security? What's this about?"

"Don't be alarmed, it's routine."

"My friends can hear anything you have to tell me."

Kemper hesitated a moment. "Very well. Mind if I take a seat?" And glancing quickly around the dining salon, he took a chair at Blackburn's right.

"My deep apologies for interrupting your dinner," Kemper said, his Boston accent already grating on Blackburn's nerves. The guy looked and talked like a cop. "But protocol requires that I ask you a few questions. It's about the staff member who was first assigned to clean your suite. Juanita Santamaria."

"The maid?" Blackburn frowned. "I have my own private maid, and she's supposed to supervise your people."

"Santamaria cleaned your room twice. The second time was on the first night of the voyage, around eight-thirty P.M., when she went in to turn down your beds. Do you recall her coming to your suite?"

"Eight-thirty last night?" Blackburn leaned back in his chair, took another sip of wine. "Nobody was there. My own maid was in medical, seasick and puking her guts out. I was at dinner. And on top of that, I gave strict instructions that no one was to enter my suite unsupervised."

"I apologize for that, sir. But you don't know of anything that might have happened in the suite that evening? An incident, someone she might have interacted with? Or perhaps she might have broken something, or . . . perhaps stolen something?"

"What, did something happen to her afterward?"

The security officer hesitated. "As a matter of fact, yes. Ms. Santamaria had a breakdown shortly after leaving your suite. She subsequently took her own life. Yet those who knew her, bunkmates and the like, saw no sign of impending trouble. She was, they say, a well-adjusted, religious person."

"That's what they always say about a mass murderer or suicide," Blackburn said, with a scoff.

"They also mentioned that, when Ms. Santamaria left for work that day, she was in good spirits."

"I can't help you," Blackburn said, swirling his wine and raising his glass to his nose again, inhaling. "Nobody was there. Nothing was broken or stolen. Believe me, I would know: I keep track of my stuff."

"Anything she might have seen or touched? Something that might have frightened her?"

Blackburn suddenly paused in the middle of the oenophilic ritual, the glass arrested halfway to his mouth. After a long moment he set it down without having sipped from it.

"Mr. Blackburn?" Kemper prodded.

Blackburn turned to look at him. "Absolutely not," he said in a thin, emotionless voice. "There was nothing. As I said, no one was there. My maid was in the infirmary. I was at dinner. What happened to this woman had nothing to do with me or my suite. She wasn't even supposed to be there."

"Very good," said Kemper, rising. "I assumed as much, but you know, protocol and everything. North Star would have my hide if I didn't go through the motions." He smiled. "Gentlemen, we'll speak no more about this subject. Thank you for your patience, and have a pleasant evening." He nodded at each man in turn, then quickly walked away.

Lambe watched the security chief thread his way among the tables. Then he turned to Blackburn. "Well, what do you make of that, Scott old boy? Strange doings belowdecks!" And he struck a melodramatic pose.

Blackburn did not reply.

The waiter glided up to their table. "May I recite the chef's specials for the evening, gentlemen?"

"Please. I've got two days of eating to catch up on." And Lambe rubbed his hands together.

Abruptly, Blackburn stood up, his chair tilting backward violently.

"Scott?" Calderón said, looking at him with concern.

"Not hungry," Blackburn said. His face had gone pale.

"Hey, Scotty—" Lambe began. "Hey, wait! Where are you going?"

"Stateroom." And without another word, Blackburn turned and exited the restaurant.

25

"That sounds just awful," said the kind, attractive stranger. "Would it help if I spoke to the old lady?"

"Oh, no," Inge replied, horrified at the suggestion. "No, please don't. It isn't that bad, really. I've gotten used to it."

"As you wish. If you change your mind, just let me know."

"You're very kind. It just helps to have somebody to talk to." And then she paused, blushing furiously.

Nothing like this had ever happened to Inge Larssen before. She'd always lived a cloistered existence, been painfully shy. And here she was, pouring her heart out to someone she'd just met half an hour before.

The large, gilt-edged clock on the wallpapered wall of the Chats-worth Salon read five minutes to ten. A string quartet was playing quietly in a far corner, and couples strolled by at infrequent intervals, arm in arm or holding hands. The lounge was lit by a thousand tapered candles, and they freighted the evening air with a mellow golden glow. Inge didn't think she'd ever been in a place quite so beautiful.

Perhaps it was the magical atmosphere of this place and this night that had helped her let down her guard. Or maybe it was simply the nature of her new friend: tall, self-assured, radiating confidence.

At the far end of the sofa, the stranger languidly crossed one leg over the other. "So you've lived in convents all your life?"

"Almost. Ever since I was six. That was when my parents died in an automobile accident."

"And you have no other family? No siblings?"

Inge shook her head. "None. Except my great-uncle, who was the one who put me in the convent school at Evedal instead of one of the state schools. But he's gone now. I have some friends from school. They're almost like family, in a way. And then there's my employer." *My employer*, she thought. *Why couldn't I work for somebody like this?* She began to speak, then stopped, feeling herself blushing again.

"You were about to say something."

Inge laughed self-consciously. "No, it's nothing."

"Please tell me. I'd love to hear it."

"It's just . . ." She hesitated again. "Well, you're such an important person. So successful, so . . . You've heard all about me, now—I was hoping to hear your story."

"It's nothing, no big deal," came the somewhat tart reply.

"No, really. I'd love to hear how you accomplished the impossible and got to be where you are. Because . . . well, someday I'd like . . ." Her voice trailed off as she lost the words.

There was a brief silence.

"I'm sorry," Inge said hastily. "I had no right to ask. I'm sorry." She felt a sudden awkwardness. "It's late—I should really get back to bed. The lady I take care of—if she wakes up, she'll be frightened if I'm not there."

"Nonsense," the stranger said, voice suddenly warm again. "I'd be happy to tell you my story. Let's take a turn on deck—it's stuffy in here."

Inge didn't think it was especially stuffy, but she said nothing and they made their way to the elevator and rode it four flights up, to Deck 7. "I'll show you something I'll bet you've never seen," her new friend said, leading the way down the corridor, past the Hyde Park restaurant—quiet at this late hour—and to a heavy hatchway. "We can step out here."

It was the first time that Inge had actually been on deck. It was quite chilly, and a wind moaned about the ship, while drifting spray misted her hair and shoulders. The scene could not have been more dramatic. Angry clouds scudded past a pale lemon moon. The huge ship ploughed its way through heavy waves. Above and below them, lights from countless windows and portholes turned the sea spume to molten gold. It was impossibly romantic.

"Where are we?" she breathed.

"The promenade deck. Here, I want to show you something." And her companion led the way to the aft rail at the very rear of the ship. "On a dark night like this you can see the plankton glowing in the wake. Take a look—it's unbelievable."

Holding tightly to the railing, Inge leaned over. It was a straight drop to the sea below, which creamed and boiled around the stern. Sure enough: a billion lights winked in the creamy wake, the ocean alive with phosphorescence, a separate universe of pearlescent life brought temporarily into being by the thrust of the ship.

"It's gorgeous," she whispered, shivering in the cold air.

In response, a gentle hand curled around her shoulder, drawing her near.

Inge resisted only a moment. Then she allowed herself to be pulled in close, glad of the warmth. As she stared down at the otherworldly glow in the ship's wake, she felt another hand slide up and grasp her other shoulder. The grip grew tighter.

And then—with a single, brutal tug—she felt herself lifted into the air and swung bodily over the railing.

A long, confused rush of air, and then, suddenly, a dreadful shock as she hit the icy water.

She tumbled and twisted, disoriented by the water, dazed and battered by the impact. Then she fought her way upward, her clothes and shoes like dead weight, and broke the surface, sputtering, clawing into the air as if trying to climb up into the sky.

For a moment, her mind a confused whirl, she wondered how she had fallen—if the railing had given way somehow—but then her head cleared.

I didn't fall. I was thrown.

The mere fact of it stupefied her. This couldn't be real. She looked around wildly, instinctively treading water. The great stern of the ship, like a glowing tower, was already receding into the night. She opened her mouth to scream but it was immediately filled with the churning wake. She flailed, trying to remain on the surface, coughing. The water was paralyzingly frigid.

"Help!" she cried, her voice so feeble and choked that she could hardly hear it herself above the rush of the wind, the throbbing engines, the loud hiss of rising bubbles in the wake. Above her, she heard the faint cries of the gulls that followed the ship day and night.

It was a dream. It had to be. And yet the water was so cold, so very cold. She thrashed, her bruised limbs turning to lead.

She had been thrown off the ship.

She stared in horror at the diminishing cluster of lights. She could even see, through the stern windows of the huge King George II ballroom on Deck 1, black moving dots silhouetted against the blaze of light—people.

"Help!" She tried to wave her arm and went under, clawing her way back to the surface.

Kick off the shoes. Swim.

It took but a moment to scrape off her shoes, the stupid, low-heeled pumps her employer made her wear. But it did no good. She couldn't even feel her feet anymore. She made a few feeble strokes, but swimming was hopeless; it took all her strength now just to keep her head above water.

The *Britannia* was starting to fade into the night mists that lay low on the surface of the water. The lights were getting dimmer. The cry of the gulls disappeared. The hiss of rising bubbles and the green color of the wake slowly dissipated. The water turned black, as black as it was deep.

The lights vanished. A moment later, the faint throb of the engines faded to silence.

She stared in horror at the place where the lights and sound had been. All was blackness. She kept her eyes fixed to the spot, terrified to glance away and lose the place, as if somehow that was her last hope. The sea around her was dark, heaving. The moon peeked from a bank of scudding clouds. The mist lay on the sea, momentarily silvery in the moonlight, then it darkened again as the moon slid back into cloud. She felt herself rise on a wave, top it, sink, rise again.

As she strained to see into the misty darkness, a comber broke over her with a hiss, forcing her down. She flailed and clawed. All around her there was nothing—nothing at all; just pitch black and a terrible, implacable cold.

But even as she struggled, the fierce chill seemed to ease slightly, replaced by inexplicable warmth. Her limbs disappeared. As the seconds passed, her movements grew slower, until it took an effort of immense will just to move. She made a ferocious effort to stay afloat, but her whole body had turned into a sack of useless weight. She began to realize she wasn't in the sea at all, but asleep in her bed. It had all been a nightmare. She felt flooded by relief and gratitude. The bed was warm, soft, pillowy, and she turned over and felt herself sinking into the black warmth. She sighed—and as she did so, she felt something solid and heavy on her chest, like a huge weight. A glimmer of understanding forced its way back into her consciousness: she was not in her bed after all; this was not a dream; she was truly sinking into the black bottomless depths of the North Atlantic, her lungs at their last extremity.

I was murdered, was the last thought that went through her mind as she drifted down, and then she sighed once again, the last of her air escaping her mouth in an eruption of silent horror more intense than the wildest cry.

26

It was eleven-fifteen when Kemper walked into the ship's central security station. The door was half open, and he could hear boisterous chatter and what sounded like a low cheer from within central monitoring. He put his hand on the door and eased it open.

Hundreds of video screens lined the walls of the circular room, each showing a closed-circuit feed of some place on the ship. The security officers of the watch were all crowded around a single screen, laughing and talking, so engrossed they were unaware of his entrance. They were bathed in a bluish light from the many flickering monitors. The room smelled of old pizza from a stack of greasy boxes shoved in one corner.

"Oh, yeah, grandma, take it *all*!" one cried.

"To the *root*!"

"It's the little old lady from Pasadena!"

A *Whoo-eeeh!* came from the group, mingled with catcalls and laughter. One officer swayed his hips lasciviously. "Attaboy! Ride 'em, cowboy!"

Kemper strode over. "What the hell's going on?"

The men jumped away from the closed-circuit security

screen, revealing two overweight passengers in a dim, remote hallway having vigorous sex.

"Jesus Christ." Kemper turned. "Mr. Wadle, aren't you supposed to be the supervisor this shift?" He looked around at all the officers, standing ridiculously at attention.

"Yes, sir."

"We've got a missing passenger, a suicide on the crew, we're losing thousands in the casino, and you're busy watching the Viagra Show. You think that's funny?"

"No, sir."

Kemper shook his head.

"Shall I—?" And Wadle indicated the switch to turn off the monitor.

"No. Anytime a camera is shut off it's logged, and that'll raise questions. Just . . . *avert* your eyes."

At this, someone stifled a laugh, and Kemper, despite himself, couldn't help but join in. "All right, all right. You've had your fun. Now get back to your stations."

He walked through the monitoring station to his tiny back office. A moment later his intercom buzzed.

"A Mr. Pendergast here to see you."

Kemper felt his mood sour. A moment later the private investigator entered.

"You here for the show, too?" Kemper asked.

"The gentleman in question has studied the Kama Sutra. I believe that position is called 'the Churning of the Cream.' "

"We don't have a lot of time," Kemper replied. "We're down another two hundred thousand in Covent Garden so far tonight. I thought you were going to help us."

Pendergast took a seat, throwing one leg over the other. "And that is why I'm here. May I have photographs of tonight's winners?"

Kemper handed him a sheaf of blurry photographs. Pendergast flipped through them. "Interesting—a different group from last night. Just as I thought."

"And what's that?"

"This is a large, sophisticated team. The players change every night. The spotters are the key."

"Spotters?"

"Mr. Kemper, your naïveté surprises me. While the system is complex, the principles are simple. The spotters mingle in the crowd, keeping track of the play at the high-stakes tables."

"Who the hell are these spotters?"

"They could be anyone: an elderly woman at a strategically placed slot machine, a tipsy businessman talking loudly on a cell phone, even a pimply teenager gaping at the action. The spotters are highly trained and quite often masters of creating an artificial persona to cover their activities. They count the cards—they don't play."

"And the players?"

"One spotter might have two to four players in his string. The spotters keep track of all the cards played at a table and 'count' them, which usually involves assigning negative numbers to low cards and positive numbers to tens and aces. All they have to remember is a single number—the running count. When the ratio of high cards to low cards remaining in the deck grows beyond a certain point, the odds shift temporarily in favor of the players; high cards in blackjack disfavor the dealer. A spotter who sees a table shift in this way sends a prearranged signal to one of his players, who then sits down at that table and starts betting heavily. Or, if the player is already at the table, he will suddenly up his bets. When the ratio slips back to normal or below, another signal from the spotter tells the player it's time to leave, or to drop back to smaller bets."

Kemper shifted uneasily. "How can we stop it?"

"The only foolproof countermeasure is to identify the spotters and give them the, ah, bum's rush."

"Can't do that."

"No doubt that's why they're here and not Las Vegas."

"What else?"

"Combine the cards into eight-deck shoes and then deal only a third of the shoe before reshuffling."

"We deal out of a four-deck shoe."

"Another reason you've attracted counters. You could stop them cold by instructing your dealers to shuffle up every time a new player sits down or when a player suddenly ups his wager."

"No way. That would slow play and reduce profits. Besides, the more experienced players would object."

"No doubt." Pendergast shrugged. "Of course, none of these countermeasures solve the problem of how to get *back* your money."

Kemper looked at him, eyes red-rimmed. "There's a way to get back the money?"

"Perhaps."

"We can't do anything that would involve cheating."

"*You* can't."

"We can't allow you to cheat either, Mr. Pendergast."

"Why, Mr. Kemper," Pendergast responded, his voice full of hurt, "did I say I was going to *cheat*?"

Kemper said nothing.

"A characteristic of card counters is that they stick by their system. A normal player will quit if he's losing heavily—but not a professional card counter. He knows the odds will eventually come around. That's to our advantage." Pendergast looked at his watch. "Eleven-thirty. That leaves three hours of prime play ahead. Mr. Kemper, be so kind as to extend me a half-million line of credit."

"Did you say half a *million*?"

"I'd hate to find myself short just when things got going."

Kemper thought hard for a minute. "Are you going to get back our money?"

Pendergast smiled. "I shall try."

Kemper swallowed. "All right."

"You'll need to have Mr. Hentoff warn your pit bosses and dealers that my play might be eccentric, even suspicious—although it will always remain within legal bounds. I'll take my seat at first base—on the dealer's left—and I'll be sitting out about fifty percent of the hands played, so please tell your people *not* to move me if I'm not playing. Hentoff should instruct his dealers to give me the cut at every normal opportunity, particularly when I first sit down. I'll appear to be drinking heavily, so make sure when I order a gin and tonic I'm brought only tonic water."

"All right."

"Would it be possible to lift the maximum wager at one of the high-stakes tables?"

"You mean, no upper limit to a bet?"

"Yes. It will ensure the counters mark that table, and it will make taking the money back much more efficient."

Kemper felt a bead of sweat trickling down his brow. "We can do that."

"And finally, please have Mr. Hentoff staff that table with a dealer with small hands and thin fingers. The less experienced, the better. Have him or her place the end-of-play card high up in the shoe."

"Do I dare ask why?" said Kemper.

"You dare not."

"Mr. Pendergast, if we catch you cheating, it's going to be extremely awkward for both of us."

"I will not cheat—you have my word."

"How can you possibly influence play when none of the players ever touch the cards?"

Pendergast smiled enigmatically. "There are ways, Mr. Kemper. Oh, and I shall need an assistant, one of your cocktail waitresses, someone invisible, discreet, and intelligent, who will bring me my drinks and be on call for some—how shall it put it?—*unusual* assignments I may suddenly give her. They are to be performed unquestionably and without hesitation."

"This had better work."

Pendergast paused. "Naturally, if successful, I shall expect another favor in return."

"Naturally," said Kemper.

Pendergast rose, turned, then glided through the office door into the central monitoring room beyond. Just before the door closed, Kemper could hear his honeyed southern voice raised. "My word, now it's the apadravyas position. And at their age!"

27

The elderly woman in stateroom 1039 turned slightly in her bed, mumbling in her sleep.

A moment later, she turned again, the mumbling growing fretful. Something was interfering with her slumber: a rapping sound, loud, insistent.

Her eyes opened. "Inge?" she croaked.

The only reply was another rap.

The woman raised one gnarled hand, grasping a steel bar that ran across the length of the headboard. Slowly, painfully, she raised herself to a sitting position. She had been dreaming; a rather lovely dream involving Monty Hall, door number 2, and petroleum jelly. She licked her desiccated lips, trying to recall the details, but they were already fading into a fog of elusive memories.

"Where is that girl?" she mumbled, feeling a twinge of fear.

The rapping continued. It came from somewhere beyond the bedroom.

From beneath countless layers of satin and sea-island cotton, a withered hand emerged. It plucked dentures from a dish on the bedside table, seated them over anemic gums. Then it reached out—flexing, grasping—until it closed over the handle of a cane. With a series of groans and imprecations, she raised herself to her feet. The ship was rolling noticeably and she kept one hand against the wall as she moved toward the bedroom door.

"Inge!" she called.

She felt another wash of fear. She hated being dependent, truly hated it, and she was scared and embarrassed by her frailty. All her life she had been independent, and now this rotten old age, this horrible dependency on others.

She turned on the light and looked around, trying to master her fright. Where was that damn girl? It was outrageous, leaving her alone. What if she fell? Or had a heart attack? Take pity on a girl, bring her into your service, and how did she repay you? With disrespect, disloyalty, disobedience. Inge was probably out carousing with some low element of the ship's staff. Well, this was the last straw: as soon as the ship was docked in New York, she'd send the vixen packing. No notice, no recommendations. She could use her charms—the tramp—to work her way back to Sweden.

Gaining the doorway, the old woman stopped to rest, leaning heavily on the frame. The rapping was louder here—it came from the main door of the suite: and now she could hear a voice as well.

"Petey! Hey, Pete!" The voice was muffled, coming from the corridor beyond.

"What?" the woman cried. "Who is that? What do you want?"

The rapping stopped. "Pete, come *on*!" the slurred voice replied. "We aren't going to wait all night."

"Hey, Petey-boy, get your ass out here!" said another drunken voice from beyond the door. "Remember those babes we met in Trafalgar's tonight? Well, after you left, they came back to the club. And we've been sucking down champagne ever since. Now they're back in my room, shit-faced. Come on, bud, it's your chance to get laid. And the tall blonde one's got a rack that—"

The old woman began to tremble with rage and indignation. She took a fresh hold on the doorframe. "Leave me alone!" she cried at the top of her lungs. "Get out of here!"

"What?" came the first voice, a little bewildered now.

"I said, go away!"

A pause. Then a giggle. "Oh, *shit*!" came the second voice. "Rog, we fucked up!"

"No, man, I'm sure he said 1039."

"I'm calling security!" shrilled the old woman.

From the corridor beyond the door there came an explosion of mirth, then the sound of retreating footsteps.

Breathing heavily, the woman pushed herself away from the doorframe and surveyed the room beyond, leaning on her cane. Sure enough: the couch hadn't been slept in. The clock above the couch read half past eleven. She had been abandoned. She was alone.

Turning slowly, she made her painful way back into the bedroom, her heart pounding. She eased herself onto the bed, laid the cane carefully beside her. Then, turning to the nightstand, she picked up the phone and dialed zero.

"Ship's operator," came the pleasant voice. "How may I help you?"

"Get me security," the old woman croaked.

28

Anh Minh saw the high roller immediately upon his arrival at the blackjack tables of the Mayfair Casino. Mr. Pendergast, that was the name Mr. Hentoff had given her. He looked like an undertaker in his black tuxedo, and she felt a little shiver as he stopped in the doorway and cast his pale eyes about the dim, elegantly appointed room. He must be a very high roller indeed for Mr. Hentoff to assign her solely to him as a cocktail waitress, and she wondered about the odd instructions that went along with the assignment.

"Would you like a drink, sir?" she asked, approaching him.

"Gin and tonic, please."

When she returned with the drink—tonic water only, as instructed—she found the strange-looking man over by the high-stakes tables in conversation with a very nicely groomed young blond gentleman in a dark suit. She went over and waited patiently with the drink on her tray.

". . . And so," the high roller was saying—in a completely different accent now—"I gave the guy twenty-two thousand six hundred and ten dollars, cash on the barrelhead, counting it out by hundreds, one bill at a time—one, two, three, four, and when I hit five, up came a twenty, and that's when I realized I'd been cheated. The brick of hundreds had been plugged in the middle with twenties! Hell, was I pissed. Twenties, along with tens and even some fives and ones."

"Excuse me," said the young man, suddenly angry, "I couldn't care less about your hundreds or twenties or whatever the hell it is you're talking about." He moved off quickly, scowling, his lips moving as if thinking furiously to himself.

Pendergast turned to Anh with a smile. "Thank you." He lifted off the drink, dropped a fifty on the tray, his eyes roving the room once more.

"Can I get you anything else, sir?"

"Yes, you can." He gestured faintly with his eyes, his voice now low. "Do you see that woman over there? The overweight one in the muumuu drifting among the high-stakes tables? There's a little experiment I'd like to conduct. Change this fifty and bring her a mess of bills and coins on your tray, telling her it's change from the drink she requested. She will protest that she did not buy a drink, but you will pretend you don't understand and start counting out the money. Just keep counting, reciting *as many numbers as possible*. If she is what I think she is, she may become angry like that young man I was just speaking to—so keep your cool."

"Yes, sir."

"Thank you."

Anh went to the cashier and exchanged the fifty for a

miscellany of bills and coins. Placing them on the tray, she walked over to the woman in the muumuu.

"Your change, ma'am."

"What?" the woman glanced at her, distracted.

"Your change. Ten pound, five pound, two one pound—"

"I didn't order a drink." The woman quickly tried to move off.

Anh followed her. "Your change. Ten pound, three one pound, make thirteen pound, twenty-five pence—"

A hiss of exasperation came from the woman. "Didn't you *hear*? I didn't order a drink!"

She pursued the woman. "Drink cost six pound, seventy-five pence, change come to thirteen pound, twenty-five pence—"

"You incompetent bitch!" the woman exploded, turning on her with a great swirl of color and advancing, face bright red.

"So sorry." Anh Minh retreated with the trayful of money, the woman glaring after her. She returned to the bar, poured tonic water over ice, and added a slice of lemon. She found Pendergast strolling through the crowd, gazing this way and that.

"Drink, sir?"

He looked at her, and she fancied she could now see amusement dancing in his eyes. He spoke low and rapidly. "You're a quick study. Now, do you see that man sitting at first base at the table to your right? Go spill this drink on him. I need his seat. Quick, now."

Bracing herself, Anh walked over to the specified table. "Your drink, sir?"

"Thanks, but I didn't—"

She joggled the tray and the drink fell upside down in his crotch.

The man leapt up. "Oh for God's sake—!"

"So sorry, sir!"

"My new tuxedo!"

"Sorry! So sorry!"

The man plucked a handkerchief from his breast pocket and used it to brush away the ice cubes and liquid. Pendergast glided over, ready to move in.

"So sorry!" Anh repeated.

"Just forget it!" He turned to the dealer. "Color me up, I'm outta here."

He scooped up his chips and stormed off, and as he did so Pendergast quickly slid into his seat. The dealer shuffled, laid down the deck, and handed the cut-card to Pendergast. He inserted it in the deck, and the dealer cut and loaded the shoe, inserting the end-of-play card unusually deep.

Ahn Minh hovered nearby, wondering what crazy thing Pendergast would ask her to do next.

Aloysius Pendergast looked around the table with a big grin. "How we all doing tonight? Getting lucky?" The Chinese man at third base—his mark—did not acknowledge. The two middle-aged women in between, who looked like sisters, nodded wary greetings.

"Dealing good cards tonight?" he asked the dealer.

"Doing my best," the petite woman replied evenly.

Pendergast shot a glance across the room and noticed that the lady in the muumuu, who pretended to be chatting on a cell phone, was now spotting their table. Excellent.

"I'm feeling lucky." Pendergast put a ten-thousand-pound chip into the betting circle, then dropped another in front, as a toke for the dealer.

The two women stared at his bet for a moment, and then advanced their own more modest thousand-pound wagers. The Chinese man pushed a chip into the betting circle—also a thousand.

The dealer pitched out the cards.

Pendergast stood on two eights. The two women played, and his mark drew a twelve and busted on a face card. The dealer drew a twenty in three cards and collected all their money.

The waitress came back with another drink and Pendergast took a good slug. "Rotten luck," he said, laying the drink down on a coaster and advancing his next bet.

Several more hands were played, and then Pendergast failed to bet.

"Your bet, sir?"

"Going to sit this one out," Pendergast said. He swiveled around and spoke to Anh Minh. "Gimme another gin and tonic," he slurred. "Make it dry."

The cocktail waitress scurried off.

The Chinese man bet again, five thousand this time. The look on his tired, middle-aged face had not changed at all. This time he stayed on fifteen with the dealer showing six, and the dealer busted.

The play moved deeper into the shoe. Out of the corner of his eye, Pendergast could see that another marked player, being spotted by the young blond man, was winning at the next table. The trick would be to force this one to lose bigger, to compensate. The slug of cards that he had tracked through the shuffle wasn't far off, and it promised to provide some fireworks.

The spotter in the muumuu had evidently also tracked the shuffle. Now, as the play worked up toward the beginning of the slug, Pendergast's running count was already a good plus eleven. The mark slid a pile of chips into the betting circle: fifty thousand.

A murmur rose.

"Hell, if he's doing it, I'll do it too," Pendergast said, pushing in fifty. He winked at the mark and lifted his drink. "Here's to us, friend."

The ladies each bet a thousand, and the cards were dealt.

Pendergast stood on eighteen.

The mark drew, asked to be hit on a twelve with the dealer showing a five—a violation of basic strategy—then drew an eight card.

An *oooh!* came from the crowd.

The ladies drew a series of low cards, one eventually busting. The dealer then completed her own hand: three, five, six, five: nineteen—a win for the mark.

A few more hands were played, most of the cards coming low out of the shoe. Pendergast's running count kept climbing. Many of the tens and most of the aces were still undealt. On top of that, they were now just into the slug that he had meticulously tracked in the shuffle, using his acute eyesight and prodigious memory. That—and the peek he'd gotten during the shuffle and cut—alerted him to the precise location of seven cards in that slug, along with an educated guess on the location of many others. His side count of aces stood at three—thirteen more were in the pack, and he knew the location of two of them. This would be his opportunity if he could get it right. It all depended on controlling the downstream flow of cards.

This deal he would have to bust, and do it in four cards.

He bet a thousand.

The mark put in a hundred thousand.

Another *oooh!* from the crowd.

Pendergast was dealt a fourteen.

The mark was dealt fifteen, with the dealer's upcard a ten.

Pendergast took a hit. A five: nineteen. The dealer was about to move on when Pendergast said, "Hit me again."

Bust.

There were snickers in the crowd, whispers, a derisive laugh. Pendergast took a swig from his drink. He glanced over at the mark and saw the man looking at him, a sudden faint look of contempt in his eyes.

The mark took a hit and was dealt an eight: bust. The dealer raked in his hundred thousand.

A quick mental calculation told Pendergast the running count was now twenty, the true count going even higher. Almost unheard of. The dealer was seventy-five percent through the shoe and still only three aces had been played, the rest concentrated in the remaining slug of cards. This was a combination no card counter could resist. If the mark followed the Kelly criterion—which he would if he had any brains—he would bet big. Very big. The key to controlling play, Pendergast knew, would now be to stop the good cards while sending the bad ones downstream. The problem was the two ladies between him and the mark: the cards they would get, how they would play them, and all the complications that might entail.

"Ladies and gentlemen?" asked the dealer, gesturing for the bets to be placed.

Pendergast bet a hundred thousand. The Chinese man pushed out a pile of chips: two hundred and fifty thousand. The two ladies bet their thousand each, looked at each other, and giggled.

Pendergast held up his hand. "Don't deal yet. I can't do this without another drink."

The dealer looked alarmed. "You want to pause the play?"

"I've got to have a drink. What if I lose?"

The mark did not look pleased.

The dealer cast a quizzical glance at the floorman hovering nearby, who nodded his approval.

"All right. We'll take a short pause."

"Waitress!" Pendergast snapped his fingers.

Anh Minh bustled over. "Yes, sir?"

"A drink!" he cried, handing her a fifty, which he dropped. As she bent down to pick it up Pendergast leapt up. "No, no, I'll get it!"

When their heads were close, Pendergast said, "Get those two ladies off the table. Now."

"Yes, sir."

Pendergast rose with the bill in his hand. "There it is!

Keep the change, but don't you dare come back without that drink!"

"Yes, sir." Anh bustled off.

A minute passed, then two. Word about the size of the bets had circulated and a sizable crowd was developing around the table. The impatience of the crowd—not to mention the mark—was growing. All eyes were on the tottering stacks of chips sitting on the green felt.

"Make way!" came a cry, and Hentoff, the casino manager, stepped through the crowd. He paused before the two women at Pendergast's table, flashed them a broad smile, and opened his arms. "Josie and Helen Roberts? Today is your lucky day!"

They looked at each other. "Oh, really?"

He put an arm around each and drew them up. "Once a day, we have a little lottery—all the room numbers are automatically entered. You won!"

"What did we win?"

"Ninety-minute massages with Raul and Jorge, deluxe spa treatment, a gift basket of cosmetics, and a free case of Veuve Clicquot!" He glanced at his watch. "Oh, no! If we don't hurry, we'll miss Raul and Jorge! We've been looking all over for you two!"

"But we were just—"

"We've got to hurry. The prize is good for today only. You can *always* come back." He gestured to the dealer. "Color them up."

"With the bets on the table, sir?"

"I *said*, color them up."

The dealer exchanged their chips and Hentoff, arm

around each sister, led them away through the crowd. A moment later Anh Minh arrived with the drink.

Pendergast drained it, banged it down. He looked around the table with a grin. "Okay. I'm fortified."

The dealer swept her hand over the table, calling for final bets, then she pitched out the cards. Pendergast was dealt two aces, and split. The mark got two sevens, which he also split. The dealer's upcard was a queen.

The mark advanced a new stack of chips against the split hand. Now there was five hundred thousand on the table. Pendergast added his second bet, bringing his stake to two hundred thousand.

The dealer dealt Pendergast his two cards: a king and a jack. Two blackjacks.

The crowd erupted in applause, then quickly fell into a hush as the dealer turned to the mark and dealt a card on each seven.

Two more sevens, just as Pendergast had expected. "Too bad we're not playing poker!" he brayed.

The mark split the sevens again—he had little choice—and reluctantly advanced two more piles of chips. A million pounds were now in front of him on the table.

The dealer dealt out four cards: jack, ten, queen, ace.

The crowd waited. The silence was extraordinary.

The dealer turned over her hole card—to reveal a ten.

A collective sigh rose from the crowd as it sank in: they had just witnessed a man lose a million pounds. There was no applause this time, only a high, excited murmuring, the air so thick with schadenfreude one could almost taste it.

Pendergast rose from the table, collected his own

winnings, and winked again at the Chinese man, who seemed frozen as he watched his million pounds being raked away, counted, and stacked. "Win some, lose some," he said, giving his chips a jaunty rattle.

As he exited the casino, he caught a glimpse of Hentoff, staring at him, mouth hanging open.

29

When First Officer LeSeur entered the bridge just before midnight, he immediately sensed tension in the air. Commodore Cutter was back on the bridge again, thick arms crossed over his barrel chest, pink fleshy face impassive and unreadable. The rest of the bridge complement stood at their stations, silent and on edge.

But it wasn't just Cutter's presence that created the air of tension. LeSeur was acutely aware that the level-two search had failed to turn up the Evered woman. Her husband had become unmanageable, tearing up and down, making scenes, insisting that his wife would never have jumped, that she'd been murdered or was being held hostage. His behavior was beginning to alarm the other passengers, and rumors were spreading. On top of that, the gruesome and unaccountable suicide of the housekeeper had badly spooked the crew. LeSeur had quietly checked Blackburn's alibi and found it held up; the billionaire really had been at dinner and his private maid in medical.

LeSeur was pondering these problems when the new officer of the watch arrived on the bridge and relieved the outgoing watch. While the two men discussed the change of watch in low voices, LeSeur strolled over to the bridge workstation, where Staff Captain Mason was checking the electronics. She turned, nodded, and went back to her work.

"Course, speed, and conditions?" Cutter asked the new officer of the watch. It was a pro forma question: not only was LeSeur sure that Cutter knew the answers, but even if he didn't, a glance at the ECDIS chartplotters and weather panels would have told him all he needed to know.

"Position four nine degrees 50.36 minutes north latitude and zero one two degrees 43.08 minutes west longitude, heading two four one true, speed twenty-nine knots," the officer of the watch answered. "Sea state 4, wind twenty to thirty knots on the starboard stern, seas running eight to twelve feet. Barometric pressure 29.96, dropping."

"Give me a printout of our position."

"Yes, sir." The officer of the watch tapped a few keys and a thin sheet of paper began scrolling out of a mini-printer slot in the side of the console. Cutter ripped it free, glanced at it, then tucked it into a pocket of his immaculately pressed uniform. LeSeur knew what he would do with the printout: once back in his quarters, he'd be quick to compare it to the relative position of the *Olympia* on her record-breaking crossing the year before.

Beyond the vast bank of windows that covered the forward face of the bridge, the front was getting closer and the sea was growing dramatic. It was a large, slow-moving system, which meant it would be with them for most of the crossing. The *Britannia*'s knifelike bows tore through the waves, throwing up huge frothy sprays that soared to heights of fifty feet before raining back down on the lower aft weather decks. The ship had developed a pronounced deep-ocean roll.

LeSeur's eyes roamed over the ship's system panels. He noted that the stabilizers were deployed at half position, sacrificing passenger comfort for greater speed, and he guessed it must be at Cutter's orders.

"Captain Mason?" Cutter's voice cut across the bridge.

"He'll be here any moment, sir."

Cutter did not respond.

"Under the circumstances, I suggest we give serious consideration to—"

"I'll hear his report first," Cutter interrupted.

Mason fell silent again. It was clear to LeSeur that he'd walked into the middle of an ongoing disagreement of some kind.

The door to the bridge opened again and Kemper, chief of security, stepped inside.

"There you are, Mr. Kemper, finally," Cutter said, not looking at him. "Your report, please."

"We got the call about forty minutes ago, sir," Kemper said. "An elderly woman in suite 1039, reporting that her companion is missing."

"And who is the companion?"

"A young Swedish woman named Inge Larssen. She put the old woman to bed about nine o'clock, then supposedly went to bed herself. But when some inebriated passengers mistakenly knocked on the old woman's door, she woke to find Ms. Larssen missing. We've been looking for her since, with no results."

Slowly, Commodore Cutter swiveled toward the security chief. "Is that all, Mr. Kemper? Captain Mason led me to believe it was something serious."

"We thought that this being a second disappearance, sir—"

"Have I not made it clear that the vicissitudes of the passengers are not my concern?"

"I wouldn't have troubled you, sir, except that, as I mentioned, we put out a call on the PA system, did a thorough check of the public areas. Nothing."

"She's obviously with some man." Cutter wheeled his solid form back toward the windows.

"As Mr. Kemper said, this is a second disappearance," said Mason. "I think that makes it appropriate that we bring it to your attention, sir."

Still, Cutter said nothing.

"And as Mr. Kemper reported to you on an earlier occasion, when we investigated the first disappearance, we found hair and skin samples on the port weather-deck brightwork that matched—"

"That proves nothing, it could have come from anywhere." Cutter waved an arm in a gesture that was part irritation, part dismissal. "And even if she jumped—so what? You know as well as I do that a ship in midocean is a floating suicide palace."

While LeSeur knew it was true that disappearances at sea weren't uncommon—and were always zealously covered up by the crew—this coarse reply seemed to take even Mason by surprise. The staff captain was quiet for thirty seconds or so before clearing her throat and beginning again.

"Sir," she said, taking a deep breath, "we have to consider the slim possibility that two disappearances might indicate there's a maniac on board."

"So what do you want me to do about it?"

"I would respectfully recommend we consider diverting to the nearest port."

Cutter stared at her for the first time, his eyes like coals in his pink, vein-burst flesh. He spoke slowly, voice ice-cold. "I find that recommendation ill-considered and utterly without merit, Captain Mason. This is the *Britannia*."

The pronouncement of the ship's name hung in the air as if it explained everything.

When Mason responded, her voice was low and even. "Yes, sir." Without another word, she walked past him and exited the bridge.

"Damned female fuss," Cutter muttered half under his breath. He plucked the printout from his pocket and examined it again. His scowl deepened. Even without comparing it to the *Olympia*'s navigational data, it seemed he was unhappy with their position. Ignoring the officer of the watch, he turned directly to the helmsman. "Increase speed to full ahead."

"Full ahead, aye, sir."

LeSeur didn't even think to open his mouth to object. He knew it would do no good; no good at all.

30

At precisely twenty minutes past twelve, Constance Greene emerged from the aft starboard maid station on Deck 9 and wheeled her housekeeping trolley over the plush rug toward the Penshurst Triplex. She had been loitering in the maid's station for the better part of two hours, pretending to look busy, folding and refolding linens, arranging the mouthwash and shampoo bottles in their complimentary laundry tubs, all the while waiting for Scott Blackburn to leave his suite for the casino. But the door had remained stubbornly closed all evening. Finally, just moments before, Blackburn had emerged and, with a quick glance at his watch, hurried down the corridor to the waiting elevator.

Now she stopped the trolley outside the suite; paused a moment to smooth down her maid's outfit and compose herself; then plucked out the passcard Pendergast had given her and slid it into the waiting keyslot. The lock sprang ajar and she pushed the door open, wheeling the trolley into the suite behind her as quietly as possible.

Closing the door softly, she paused in the entryway to reconnoiter. The Penshurst was one of two Grand

Triplex Suites on the *Britannia*, at 2,700 square feet remarkably large and well appointed. The bedrooms were on the upper floors, while the salon, dining room, and maid's kitchen lay before her.

Bring me his trash, Pendergast had said. Constance narrowed her eyes.

She didn't know how long Blackburn planned to spend in the casino—if that was indeed where he was going—but she had to assume there wasn't much time. She glanced at her watch: twelve-thirty. She would allow herself fifteen minutes.

She wheeled her trolley across the parquet floor of the entryway, looking curiously about her. While the suite sported the same rich wood paneling as the one she shared with Pendergast, in other ways it couldn't possibly have appeared more different. Blackburn had decorated almost every surface with items from his collection. Tibetan rugs of silk and yak wool lay strewn across the floor; cubist and impressionist paintings in heavy frames hung on the walls above. Ahead, in the salon, a Bösendorfer piano in rich mahogany sat in one corner. Prayer wheels, ritual weapons, decorative boxes of gold and silver, and a profusion of sculptures were arrayed across various tables and on the bookshelves that lined one wall. A large and intricate mandala hung over a gas fireplace. Beside it, a heavy armoire of mellow teak glowed in the subdued light.

Leaving her trolley, she walked across the salon to the armoire. She stroked the polished wood thoughtfully for a moment, then pulled the door open. Inside sat a massive steel safe, its bulk taking up almost the entire interior of the cabinet.

She stepped back, looking at the safe appraisingly. Was it large enough to hold the Agozyen?

Yes, she decided: it was large enough. She closed the door to the armoire and, taking a cloth from the pocket of her apron, polished the edges where she had touched it. One objective accomplished. She glanced around a second time and made a mental note of everything in Blackburn's extensive and wildly eclectic collections.

As she walked back toward her cart, she paused at the base of the stairway. There had been a sound—faint, but distinct—from above. She waited motionless, listening. There it was again: a muffled snore, issuing from the open door of a bedroom at the next landing.

So somebody was still in the suite. Blackburn's private maid, most likely. That would complicate things.

Grasping the handle of the trolley, she pushed it across the entryway, careful to make sure the broom and mop did not rattle in their holder. She parked it in the middle of the salon and quickly made the rounds, emptying the trash baskets and ashtrays into the fresh garbage bag she'd hung from the trolley. Leaving the trolley where it was, she darted into the dining room and kitchen in turn, repeating the process. There was precious little refuse to empty: clearly, Blackburn's own maid had done a thorough job.

Returning to the salon, she paused to consider. She did not dare go upstairs for the rest of the garbage; that would awaken the maid and precipitate an unpleasant scene. She had the most important information already:

the location and size of Blackburn's safe and a quick inventory of his collection. Perhaps she should leave now.

But as she hesitated, thinking, she noticed a curious thing. While the surfaces of the tables and the objets d'art were spotless and gleaming, and the wastebaskets had held only a few scraps, there was a surprising amount of dust on the floor, especially around the moldings along the edges of the room. It appeared that the talents of Blackburn's maid did not extend to vacuuming. She knelt and ran her finger along the base of the mahogany molding. It wasn't just dust—it was sawdust.

She lifted her gaze to the vacuum that hung from her housekeeping trolley. If she turned it on, she would wake the maid for sure. So be it. She walked over to the trolley, plucked the vacuum from its hook, pulled out the old bag and attached a fresh one. Walking to the nearest wall of the salon, she knelt, turned on the vacuum, and made several quick passes along the edge of the floor, getting as much dust as possible.

Almost immediately, there was a muffled thud from upstairs. "Hello?" came a sleepy feminine voice. "Who's there?"

Pretending not to hear over the noise, Constance crossed to the center of the room, knelt again, and made several more passes with the vacuum along the tops of the moldings, then across the rug in the entryway, checking for hair and fiber.

A minute later, the voice sounded again, much louder this time. "Hey! What are you doing?"

Constance rose, turned off the vacuum, and turned around. A short, melon-shaped woman of about thirty stood on the bottom step of the staircase, her face red, clad only in a huge terrycloth towel, which she pressed against herself with one flabby forearm. "What are you doing here?" she demanded again.

Constance curtseyed. "Sorry to wake you, mum," she said, putting on her German accent. "The maid who normally does this suite has had an accident. I've taken over her duties."

"It's after midnight!" the woman shrilled.

"I'm sorry, mum, but I was told to clean the suite as soon as it was unoccupied."

"Mr. Blackburn gave specific orders that there was to be no more maid service in this suite!"

At that moment, there was a noise from outside: the sound of a passcard being inserted into a slot, the click of a lock disengaging. The maid gasped, colored, and dashed back up the steps in the direction of her room. A moment later, the front door opened and Blackburn entered, a roll of newspapers under his arm.

Constance watched him, motionless, portable vacuum in one hand.

He stopped and stared at her, his eyes narrowing. Then he coolly turned and double-locked the door, walked across the entryway, and dropped his papers on a side table.

"Who are you?" he asked, his back still turned.

"Begging your pardon, sir, I'm your housekeeper," she said.

"Housekeeper?"

"Your new housekeeper," she went on. "Juanita—

that is, the girl who cleaned your suite—she had an accident. Now I've been assigned—"

Blackburn turned and stared at her. The words died in her throat. There was something in his expression, in his eyes, that shocked her: an intensity of purpose as hard and clean as polished steel, shot through with something like fear, or perhaps even desperation.

She tried again. "I'm sorry about the late hour. I've been doing her staterooms as well as my own, and it's been hard to catch up. I thought nobody was home, or I'd never have—"

Suddenly, a hand shot out, grasping her wrist. He squeezed it cruelly and dragged her toward him. Constance gasped with the pain.

"Bullshit," he said in a low, ugly voice, his face inches from hers. "I gave clear orders just this evening that nobody was to clean my suite but my private help." And he squeezed harder.

Constance fought back a groan. "Please, sir. Nobody told me. If you don't wish your rooms cleaned, I'll leave."

He stared at her, and she averted her eyes. He squeezed still harder, until she thought he would crush her wrist. Then he shoved her brutally away. She fell to the floor, vacuum clattering across the carpet.

"Get the fuck out of here," he growled.

Constance rose to her feet, scooping up the vacuum and smoothing her apron as she did so. She moved past him, hanging the vacuum on its hook and wheeling the trolley across the salon to the entryway of the suite. She unlocked the front door, pushed the trolley out ahead of her, and—with a single, hooded glance back at the man who was already mounting the stairs, yelling up at his own maid for admitting a stranger into the suite—stepped into the corridor.

31

The polished cherrywood table in the dining area of the Tudor Suite was covered with an incongruous clutter—a large garbage bag of clear plastic, dribbling out a host of scraps: crumpled paper, wadded tissue, cigar ash. Pendergast circled the table like a restless cat, arms behind his back, now and then bending close to examine something but never extending a hand to touch or probe. Constance sat on a nearby sofa, dressed now in one of the elegant gowns they had purchased on board ship, watching him.

"And he threw you to the ground, you say?" Pendergast murmured over his shoulder.

"Yes."

"He's an ill-mannered cur." He circled the table again, then stopped to look at her. "This is all?"

"I wasn't able to do the upstairs of the suite. Not with the maid in residence. I'm sorry, Aloysius."

"Don't be. It was an afterthought anyway. The important thing is that we know the size and location of his safe. And you've given me an excellent précis of his collections. Too bad the Agozyen doesn't seem to be among them." He dipped one hand into his pocket, pulled out a pair of latex gloves, snapped them on, then began to examine the trash. He picked up an empty seltzer bottle from the table, examined it, put it aside. This was followed by several dry-cleaning tags; a cigar butt and accumulated ash; a crumpled business card; a soiled cocktail napkin; a champagne cork; a broken compact disk case; a ship's brochure, torn in half; a swizzle stick; an empty Swan Vesta box and half a dozen spent wooden matches. Pendergast sorted through it all with great care. Once he had put the last item aside, he again circled the table, hands behind his back, pausing to examine various items with a loupe. Then, with a quiet sigh, he straightened up.

"Let's put this away where housekeeping won't take it," he said. "Just in case we want to examine anything again." He pulled off the gloves, dropped them on the table.

"What next?" Constance asked.

"Next we find a way to take a look inside that safe. Preferably when Blackburn has absented himself."

"That might be difficult. Something seems to have spooked him—he seems reluctant to leave his suite for any length of time, and he won't let anybody in."

"If it were anybody else, I'd say the two disappearances you informed me of have spooked him. But not Mr. Blackburn. Too bad we didn't narrow down my list more quickly; I could have examined his chambers with relative ease yesterday." He glanced at Constance. "And we mustn't forget that, though Blackburn may be the prime suspect, we also need to examine the rooms of Calderón and Strage, if only to rule them out."

He walked to the sideboard and poured himself a snifter of calvados, then came over to the couch and took a seat. He rolled the amber liquid gently, brought it to his nose, took a small sip, and gave a sigh that was half contentment, half regret. "Well, thank you, my dear," he said. "I'm sorry you were assaulted. In the fullness of time, I shall make sure Blackburn regrets it."

"I'm only sorry that—" Then, abruptly, Constance fell silent.

"What is it?"

"I almost forgot. I retrieved something else from his suite. I used the vacuum to pick up some odd dust samples."

"Why odd?"

"Considering the man has a live-in maid, and he's clearly a petty tyrant, I thought it was strange the room was so dusty."

"Dusty?" Pendergast repeated.

Constance nodded. "Most of it was along the walls, under the wainscoting. It looked like sawdust, actually."

Pendergast was on his feet. "Where's the vacuum bag, Constance?" He spoke quietly, but his silver eyes glittered with excitement.

"There, by the door—"

But almost before the words were out, Pendergast had flitted to the front door, scooped up the bag, plucked a clean plate from a kitchen cabinet, and returned to the table. Now his movements grew excessively careful. Taking a switchblade from his pocket, he carefully slit the vacuum bag and slowly emptied the contents onto the plate. Fixing a jeweler's loupe to his eye, he began separating the debris with the blade of his knife, scrape by tiny scrape, as if he were examining the individual grains.

"Do you know, Constance," he murmured as he bent over the table, face just inches from the surface of the wood. "I believe you're right. This is sawdust."

"Left over from construction?"

"No. *Fresh* sawdust. And if *this* is what I think it is"—here he jabbed at something with a pair of tiny forceps, then straightened up—"then we won't have to bother ourselves with Calderón or Strage."

Constance looked at Pendergast's pale, eager face. She couldn't even begin to imagine how sawdust could fit in.

As she stood up and drew near, he rummaged for an ashtray and a match. Then he motioned her to move closer. As he held the forceps over the ashtray, she could just make out, in the steel jaws, the glittering of a tiny brownish crystal.

"Pay attention," he said quietly. "This won't last long." And then he lit the match; waited a moment while the initial bloom of sulfur faded from the air; then applied the flame to the crystal.

As they watched, it flared and smoked in the forceps. And then, very briefly, Constance caught a faint scent, borne on the air of the stateroom: a rich, musky, exotic whiff of myrrh, strange, faintly intoxicating—and unmistakable.

"I know that smell," she breathed.

Pendergast nodded. "The smell of the inner monastery of Gsalrig Chongg. A special kind of incense, made only by them, used to keep a uniquely voracious species of woodworms at bay."

"Woodworms?" Constance repeated.

"Yes."

She turned to the small mound on the table. "You mean that sawdust . . . ?"

"Exactly. Some of those same woodworms must have come on board in the box that housed the Agozyen. Blackburn has done the North Star line no favors by introducing them to the *Britannia.*" He turned to face her, his eyes still glittering with excitement. "We have our man. Now all that remains is to lure him from his lair and get inside his safe."

32

Scott Blackburn walked to the front door of his suite, placed a *Do Not Disturb* card on the outside knob, then bolted it from the inside. Climbing two flights of stairs to his dressing room, he yanked off his tie, removed his suit jacket and shirt, tossed them into a corner for his maid to hang up, and slipped out of his pants. For a moment he stood in front of the full-length mirror, rippling his muscles, absently admiring his torso. Then, from a locked drawer, he drew out a set of saffron-colored Toray silk robes. He slowly dressed himself in them, first the inner robe, then the upper robe, and finally the outer robe, the fine silk slipping across his skin like quicksilver. He arranged the pleats, folding the robe over and leaving one chiseled shoulder and arm bare.

He stepped into his private sitting room, shut the doors, and stood in its center, surrounded by his Asian art collection, deep in thought. It was necessary, he knew, to calm his mind, which had been greatly disturbed by what he had heard at the dinner table that evening. So a maid had been in his room yesterday. And she had subsequently gone crazy, killed herself. The chief of security had questioned him—all allegedly routine. And then again, just now, he'd caught another ship's maid in his suite, despite his strictest orders to the hotel manager and the head of the housekeeping staff. Was it a coincidence?

Or was he, in fact, under scrutiny? Had his movements, his activities, his *acquisitions*, been tracked?

In his fierce climb to the top of the Silicon Valley hierarchy, Blackburn had long ago learned to trust his sense of paranoia. He had learned that, if his instincts told him somebody was out to get him, then somebody generally was. And here, trapped on this ship, without recourse to his usual layers of security, he was in an unusually vulnerable position. He'd heard rumors there was some kind of private investigator on board, an eccentric passenger by the name of Pendergast, looking for a thief and murderer.

Was the bastard investigating *him*?

There was no way to be certain, but the more he thought about it, the more it seemed likely. He couldn't afford to take a chance; the stakes were too high. His adversary—for, if his instincts were right, there could be no other term for him—would have to be dealt with in a special way.

A very special way.

He turned off all the lights in the room and stood in the dark, sharpening his senses. First he listened intently, teasing out every little sound—from the faint thrumming of the engines deep within the riveted steel, to the moaning of wind and sea; the splatter of rain against the glass; the sobbing of his private maid in her bedroom; the muffled footfalls in the corridor outside. He tuned in to the sensations of his own body, his bare feet on the plush nap, the scent of sandalwood and beeswax in the cabin, the sensation caused by the deep, ponderous rolling of the ship.

He inhaled, exhaled. The three enemies—hate, desire, and confusion—had to be temporarily banished. All must be calm. Of these three, hate was the most powerful of the enemies, and now it almost suffocated Blackburn in its triumphant embrace.

With iron self-control, he moved to an easel standing beside the far wall, on which something was propped up, covered by a tied shroud of the finest silk. It had been a foolish mistake not to keep it in the safe from the very beginning; but he had hated the idea of locking it away when he needed it so frequently. His own private maid had been given strict instructions never to lift the silk and look upon it. And he knew she wouldn't—it had taken him years to find someone as reliable, unimaginative, and incurious as her. But the first ship's maid—the one who killed herself—must have lifted the veil. Now, if his suspicions were true and this Pendergast was after it, even the safe wouldn't be secure enough. Hotel safes were notoriously easy to break into, and ship's safes, even a big one, were probably no different. They were designed to keep out petty thieves, and no more.

He would have to find a better hiding place.

Scrupulously avoiding looking at it, he gingerly lifted the silk covering from the object and placed it in the center of the room. With ceremonial care, he arranged thirty-six butter candles on a large silver tray, lit them, then placed them in front of the object to better illuminate it—all the while keeping his eyes averted. He placed bundles of joss sticks into two elaborately chased gold thuribles, arranging them on either side of the object.

The butter candles flickered, filling the room with their peculiar, dancing, golden light. Next, he laid out a quilted silk mat before the candles and seated himself, lotus-style, upon it. Closing his eyes, he began to chant: a strange, low, humming that the careful listener would hear as a braid of the same strange sounds linked together, without beginning or end. The warm, animal smell of the butter candles filled the air as his humming rose and fell, creating the bizarre Tibetan polyphonic effect known as *sygyt*: that of sounding two notes at once with the same voice, made famous by the Tengyo monks, among whom he had studied.

After thirty minutes of closed-eye chanting, the three enemies were gone, vanquished. Blackburn's mind was empty of all hatred and desire, and receptive to *it*. He opened his eyes suddenly, very wide, and stared at the object in the candlelight.

It was as if he'd received an electric current. His body stiffened, his muscles bulged, the cords in his neck tightened, his carotid artery pulsed. But his chanting never wavered, growing more rapid, moving into the higher registers, reaching an intensity of sound that was nothing at all like the normal tones of the human voice.

He stared, and stared, and stared. A peculiar smell began filtering into the room, a nauseating, earthy smell, like rotting toadstools. The air seemed to thicken, as if filling with smoke, which drew together in a place about four feet in front of him, clotting like dark, viscous cream into something dense, almost solid. And then . . .

It began to move.

33

It had been a voyage full of firsts, thought Betty Jondrow of Paradise Hills, Arizona, as she waited in the gilded lobby of the Belgravia Theatre, clutching a program book. Yesterday, she and her twin sister Willa had gone to the Sedona SunSpa® and gotten matching tattoos on their butts: hers of a butterfly, Willa's of a bumblebee. Both had bought ankle bracelets of real diamonds in Regent Street, one of the ship's two upscale shopping arcades, and they wore them every night. Who would have believed, Betty thought, that between them she and her sister had borne eight nine-pound babies and boasted eleven bouncing grandchildren? Thank God they had never let themselves go like so many of their high school classmates. She took great pride in the fact that, at sixty-three, she could still fit into her high school prom dress—an experiment she repeated religiously each year on the anniversary of the prom.

She looked around again and checked her watch. Almost one o'clock in the morning. Where in heck was Willa? She had gone off to buy batteries for her camera at least half an hour ago. Maybe even longer.

It was Willa who had been so anxious to meet Braddock Wiley, the movie star. One of the highlights of the cruise—and one of the reasons they had signed up—was the promise of a mid-atlantic premiere of Wiley's latest horror movie. It was supposed to happen at ten, but Braddock Wiley, or so rumor had it, was suffering a bit from seasickness due to the rough weather.

She scanned the crowd again, but still no Willa. Well, if she didn't get there soon, Betty would just have to meet Wiley for both of them. She slipped a makeup mirror out of her bag, examined her face, touched up the corners of her lips with a hankie, snapped it shut, and slid it back.

A sudden stir at the fringes of the group told her the wait had not been in vain. There was Braddock Wiley himself—dashing in nautical blue blazer, ascot, and cream-colored pants—striding into the lobby with several ship's officers. He didn't look sick at all.

As soon as he saw the group of women he beamed and came over. "Good evening, ladies!" he said, reaching inside his blazer for a pen as the women, giggling and blushing, pushed their movie programs toward him. Wiley worked his way through the crowd, chatting with everyone, signing programs and posing for photographs. He was even more handsome in person than on the silver screen. Betty hung back, hoping for a last-minute appearance of her sister—but then, finally, there was Wiley, in front of her.

"Last but not least," he said with a wink, enveloping her hand in both of his and holding it warmly. "They told me there were going to be some fine-looking ladies on board. I didn't believe them—until now."

"Come now, Mr. Wiley," said Betty, with a sassy smile. "You can't be serious. I have six grandchildren, you know."

His eyes widened in surprise. "Six grandchildren? Who could have guessed?" The movie star winked again.

Betty Jondrow could find no words in response. Flushing to the roots of her hair, for the first time in half a century she felt that delicious sensation of being a blushing, virginal, confused schoolgirl once again, holding the hand of the captain of the football team.

"Let me sign that for you," said Wiley, slipping the program from her hand, signing it with a flourish, and then moving on with a final wave to the group.

Betty raised the program and saw he had written, "To my favorite smokin' grandma—Love and French kisses, Brad Wiley."

She held the program in trembling hands. This was destined to be one of the high moments of her life. Wait until Willa saw *this*.

Wiley was gone and now the theater lobby was starting to fill with dolled-up cinemagoers. Betty came to her senses; she had better claim two good seats, and fast. Willa may have missed Braddock, but she still had time to see the premiere.

She showed her reserved ticket to the usher, went inside and found the perfect seat, right up front, and then claimed the next seat with her purse. The Belgravia Theatre was an extremely impressive space that took up much of the bow of Decks 2 through 5, very dark, trimmed in tasteful blue and amber neon, sporting plush, comfortable seats, a wide stage, and a deep balcony. Soon, despite its five-hundred-seat capacity and the late hour, the theater had filled. Within moments the lights dimmed and Braddock Wiley made another appearance, strolling out on the proscenium before the curtain, smiling in the glare of a spotlight. He spoke a few words about the film; told some amusing stories about the New York City production; thanked various producers, actors, writers, the director, and the special effects master; blew a kiss to the audience; and walked off. As applause filled the room, the 20th Century Fox logo appeared projected onto the curtains, and at that cue the curtains opened.

The audience gasped. Betty Jondrow put her hand over her mouth. There, hanging directly in front of the screen, was a brilliant bit of stagecraft—a remarkably realistic dummy of a dead woman, dripping blood, illuminated by the projector. The audience broke into excited murmurs at this unexpected piece of drama, which must have been specially arranged to spice up the premiere. The dummy had been hidden behind the curtain to shock the audience. It was amazingly realistic—almost *too* realistic.

The movie title came on, *THE VIVISECTOR*, the letters grotesquely illuminated across the body, with the word "VIVISECTOR" right on the chest, which indeed looked like it was the product of a botched operation. There were gasps of admiration from the audience at the clever, if revolting, juxtaposition.

Betty suddenly leaned forward. There was something familiar about the way the dummy was dressed—that sequined silk dress streaked with blood, the black pumps, the short blonde hair . . .

She grasped the seat in front of her, pulling herself to her feet.

"Willa!" she cried, pointing. "Oh my God! It's Willa! That's my sister! *Somebody's murdered her!"* She uttered a piercing shriek that cut through the very air of the theater, then fell back in her seat in a dead faint. The image on the screen faltered, then went dark; and with that the audience boiled to its feet and began a screaming, hollering, helter-skelter stampede for the rear exits.

31

It was approaching noon, and Patrick Kemper waited in the medical officer's quarters and tried to steady himself for what was to come. As a cruise ship security officer with thirty years of service, he thought he'd seen everything. Everything, including murder. But this went way beyond murder. Five hundred passengers had witnessed something savagely brutal. There was incipient panic aboard, not just among the passengers, but also among the belowdecks service staff, already spooked by the suicide.

Now he was faced with a hideously obvious fact: there was a homicidal maniac on board the *Britannia*, and he didn't even begin to have the resources to deal with it. Back in Boston in his cop days, they had whole teams that dealt with evidence gathering; they had the hair and fiber boys, the toxicologists, the fingerprint guys and ballistics people and the DNA teams. Here, he had no resources. Nada. And the only other ex-cop on his security team had been an MP at an airbase in Germany.

To his left stood Staff Captain Carol Mason, a blessedly steady presence. LeSeur, more obviously rattled, stood on the other side. The ship's chief medical officer—a capable but retiring internist from Johns Hopkins who relished the low-intensity, light-caseload attributes of shipboard medicine—looked the most rattled of all.

Commodore Cutter stepped briskly into the room, immaculate as usual, his face a mask of granite. Kemper glanced covertly at his watch: noon exactly.

Cutter wasted no time. "Mr. Kemper? Your report."

Kemper cleared his throat. "The victim is Willa Berkshire of Tempe, Arizona. Recently widowed, traveling with her sister, Betty Jondrow. It appears she was killed with a single blow from a machete, a stage prop kept in some locked cabinets behind the stage."

Cutter frowned. "A stage prop?"

"Yes. We don't yet know if the murderer sharpened it or simply found it that way—nobody seems to remember what condition the machete was in to begin with. She was killed just backstage—there was a large amount of blood at the scene. It appears the time of death was about half an hour to twenty minutes before curtain time; at least, that was the last time Mrs. Berkshire was seen alive. After committing the killing, the murderer used some stage pulleys and hooks to raise the body. It appears—and this is moving into speculation—the victim was lured backstage, killed with a single blow, and quickly hoisted. The entire process may have taken as little as a few minutes."

"Lured backstage?"

"It's a locked, off-limits area. The killer had a key. And I say 'lured' because it is hard to imagine a passenger going back there without some good reason."

"Any suspects?"

"Not yet. We've questioned the sister, who said only that she was to meet her sister at the theater ahead of time, hoping to get an autograph from Braddock Wiley. They knew no one else on board and hadn't made any acquaintances—their goal, she says, was to be together, not meet men or socialize. She said they have no enemies, haven't had any incidents or altercations on board. In short, Berkshire seems to have been a random victim."

"Any sign of rape or a sexual assault?"

"I'm not a doctor, Captain."

Cutter turned to the chief medical officer. "Dr. Grandine?"

The doctor cleared his throat. "Captain, this is really terrible, a shock to us all—"

"Any sign of rape or sexual assault?" came the crisp repetition.

"You must understand we have no facilities on board to do an autopsy, and in any case I'm not qualified. My training in forensic medicine is minimal and many years out of date. We've refrigerated the body for medical examination once we reach port. I haven't examined the body in detail—and any effort to do so on my part would only create a problem for the M.E. later."

Cutter stared at the doctor, his eyes glittering with his obvious low opinion of the man. "Show me the body."

This demand was met with disbelieving silence.

"Very well, but I warn you it isn't pretty—"

"Doctor, you will confine your comments to factual matters."

"Yes, of course." Very unwillingly the doctor unlocked

a door at the back of the office and they filed into a cramped room that—among other things—functioned as the ship's morgue. It smelt strongly of chemicals. Along the far wall were nine stainless steel drawers for holding cadavers. Nine seemed like a lot, but Kemper knew well that plenty of people died aboard ship, especially given the average age of the cruise ship passenger and their propensity, once on board, to overindulge in the food, drink, and sexual departments.

The doctor unlocked one of the middle compartments and slid out a drawer beyond, revealing a semi-transparent plastic body bag. Kemper could see a vague, pink thing inside. A queasy feeling formed in the pit of his stomach.

"Open it."

Kemper had already examined the body, hardly knowing what to look for. The last thing he wanted was to see it again.

Hesitantly, the doctor unzipped the bag. The commodore reached over and spread the zipper apart, exposing the naked body. A huge, cleaved wound, splitting the chest and penetrating the heart, stared back at them. The smell of formalin rose up.

Kemper swallowed.

A cultivated voice sounded behind them. "Excuse me, ladies and gentlemen?"

Kemper turned to see, in utter disbelief, Pendergast standing in the door.

"Who the devil is this?" demanded the commodore.

Kemper rushed over. "Mr. Pendergast, this is a *very* private meeting, and you must leave here immediately!"

"Must I?" Pendergast drawled.

Kemper's queasiness was replaced with irritation. This was the last straw. "Pendergast, I'm not going to warn you again—"

He paused in midsentence, mouth open: Pendergast had removed his wallet and flipped it open, revealing a gold FBI shield. Kemper stared at it in disbelief.

"Why aren't you escorting that man out of here?" the commodore asked.

Kemper couldn't quite find the words. Any words.

"I had hoped to complete this voyage incognito, as it were," Pendergast said. "But it seems the time has come to offer you my assistance, Mr. Kemper; my professional assistance this time around. The sad truth is, I *specialize* in this sort of thing." He glided past Kemper and strolled up to the body.

"Mr. Kemper, I told you to get this man *out*!"

"Commodore, I'm sorry, it seems he's a federal agent . . ." Again words failed Kemper.

Pendergast showed his shield to each person in turn, then went back to examining the body.

"He has no jurisdiction here," the commodore snapped. "We're in international waters on a British ship registered in Liberia."

Pendergast straightened up. "Quite true. I realize I have no authority here, and remain at your sufferance alone. But I should be surprised if you refused my help, seeing as how none of you appear to have the faintest idea what to do about *this*." He nodded to the body. "How would things look if it were later revealed that the ship's officers refused the help of a special agent of the FBI who was highly trained in evidence gathering and forensic work?" He smiled coldly. "At least, if you accept my help, you'll have someone to blame later—no?"

He cast a pale glance around the room.

Nobody spoke.

Pendergast clasped his hands behind his back. "Doctor? You should take vaginal, anal, and oral swabs from the victim and check for the presence of sperm."

"Swabs," the doctor repeated in a low murmur.

"I assume you have Q-tips and a microscope handy, yes? I thought as much. And surely you know what a sperm cell looks like? A drop of Eosin Y will bring up the highlights. Second, a careful visual examination of the vaginal and anal areas should reveal any telltale swelling, redness, or injury. It is essential to know as soon as possible if this is a sexual crime or . . . something else. Also, draw blood and do a blood alcohol reading."

He turned. "Mr. Kemper? I would immediately place plastic bags over the victim's hands, securing them tightly at the wrist with rubber bands. If the victim fought her attacker, the fingernails might contain traces of skin or hair."

Kemper nodded. "I'll do that."

"You've saved the victim's clothes?"

"Yes. Sealed in plastic bags."

"Excellent." Pendergast turned to address the group as a whole. "There are some unpleasant truths that need to be said. Two people have disappeared, and now this. I believe the disappearances are connected to this killing. In point of fact, I am on board this vessel to locate a stolen object whose theft also resulted in murder. I would not be at all surprised if the same person was responsible for *all four* atrocities. In short, the evidence, so far, points to a serial killer on board."

"Mr. Pendergast—" Kemper began to object.

Pendergast held up his hand. "Let me finish, if you please. A serial killer on board—who is *escalating*. He was content to toss the first two overboard. But this one—no. This was much more dramatic—much more in keeping, in fact, with the earlier murder I'm investigating. Why? That remains to be seen."

More silence.

"As you point out, the killer had a key to the backstage door. But do not be fooled into assuming the killer is a crew member."

"Who said it was a *crew* member—?" Kemper began.

Pendergast waved his hand. "Mr. Kemper, relax. If I am correct, the killer is in fact not a member of the crew. However, he may have disguised himself as one, and managed to get a passcard to off-limits areas. As a working hypothesis, I would suggest Willa Berkshire was lured backstage with the promise of meeting Braddock Wiley. Which implies that her killer was dressed as someone in authority."

He turned to the commodore. "Where are we, if I may be forgiven the question?"

The commodore stared back, then turned to Kemper. "Are you going to let this . . . *passenger* take over ship's security?" His voice was hard as steel.

"No, sir. But I would respectfully advise that we accept his help. He's . . . assisted us before."

"You're *acquainted* with this man and have used his services?"

"Yes, sir."

"In what capacity?"

"In the casino," said Kemper. "He assisted us in dealing with the card counters." He didn't add that Pendergast had walked off with more than a quarter of a million pounds extra in the process—money that had yet to be recovered.

The commodore waved his hand disgustedly, as if to abruptly distance himself from the subject at hand. "Very well, Mr. Kemper. You know as master of this ship I do not involve myself in non-nautical matters." He strode to the door, glanced back. "I warn you, Kemper: it's on your shoulders now. *All* of it." Then he turned and disappeared.

Pendergast looked at Mason. "May I ask what the *Britannia*'s present location is? Vis-à-vis the nearest body of land."

"We're about twelve hundred kilometers east of the Flemish Cap, eighteen hundred kilometers northeast of St. John's, Newfoundland."

"St. John's is the closest harbor?"

"It is now," Mason replied. "A few hours ago it would have been Galway Harbour, Ireland. We're in midcrossing."

"A pity," Pendergast murmured.

"Why is that?" the staff captain asked.

"Because it is my conviction that this killer is going to strike again. Soon."

35

As managing director of Aberdeen Bank and Trust Ltd, Gavin Bruce considered—rather grimly—that he'd had a great deal of experience taking control of impossible situations and setting things firmly in order. In the course of his career, he had taken over no fewer than four failing banks, whipped them into shape, and turned their fortunes around. Prior to that he had served as an officer in Her Majesty's Navy, seeing action in the Falklands, and the experience had served him well. But he had never faced a challenge quite as bizarre, or as frightening, as this one.

Bruce had been traveling with two other representatives of Aberdeen Bank and Trust—Niles Welch and Quentin Sharp—both ex-navy like himself, now impeccably dressed bankers of the City mold. He'd worked with them for years and he knew them both to be good, solid people. They'd been presented with this crossing by a client of his, Emily Dahlberg, as a reward for services rendered. These days, most rich clients seemed to feel that a banker owed them, but Emily understood the importance of fostering an old-fashioned relationship of mutual trust. And Bruce had repaid that trust by helping her navigate through two tricky divorces and a complex inheritance case. A widower himself, he was very appreciative of her attention and her gift.

Too bad it all seemed to be going sour.

After the discovery in the Belgravia Theatre the night before—which he had witnessed—it was immediately clear to him that the ship's personnel were in over their heads on this matter. Not only had they no idea how to investigate the killing or track down the murderer, but they seemed incapable of responding to the fear and panic that were beginning to spread through the ship, not just among the passengers but—Bruce had noticed with dismay—among the service staff as well. He'd been on enough ships to know that seafaring workers were often possessed of peculiar and superstitious maritime notions. The *Britannia* had become a fragile shell, and he was convinced that just one more shock would plunge everything into chaos.

So he had sat down after lunch with Welch, Sharp, and Ms. Dahlberg—she had insisted on being involved—and, true to form, they had come up with a plan. And now, as they strode down the plush corridors, Bruce in the lead, he took some measure of comfort in knowing they were putting that plan into action.

The small group made their way up through the decks until they reached a forward passageway leading to the bridge. There they were stopped by a nervous-looking security guard with watery eyes and a whiffle cut.

"We are here to see Commodore Cutter," said Bruce, producing his card.

The man took the card, glanced at it. "May I ask what it is in reference to, sir?"

"In reference to the recent murder. Tell him we are a group of concerned passengers and that we wish to see him immediately." After a moment's hesitation, he added, somewhat embarrassed, "Ex-captain, RN."

"Yes, sir. Just a moment, sir."

The security guard hustled away, shutting and locking the door behind him. Bruce waited impatiently, arms folded across his chest. Five minutes passed before the guard returned.

"If you'll please come this way, sir?"

Bruce and his people followed the guard through the hatch into a much more functional area of the ship, with linoleum floors and gray-painted walls framed in fake wood, illuminated with strips of fluorescent lighting. A moment later they were ushered into a spartan conference room, a single row of windows looking starboard across a stormy, endless ocean.

"Please be seated. Staff Captain Mason will be here shortly."

"We asked to see the ship's master," Bruce replied. "That would be Commodore Cutter."

The guard ran an anxious hand over his whiffle. "The commodore is not available. I'm sorry. Staff Captain Mason is second in command."

Bruce cast an inquisitive eye on his little group. "Shall we insist?"

"I'm afraid that would do no good, sir," said the guard.

"Well then, the staff captain it is."

They did not seat themselves. A moment later a woman appeared in the door, in an immaculate uniform, her hair tucked under her hat. As soon as he was over his surprise at seeing a woman, Bruce was immediately impressed by her calm, serious demeanor.

"Please sit down," she said, taking as a matter of course the seat at the head of the table—another small detail that did not escape Bruce's approval.

The banker got to the point immediately. "Captain Mason, we are clients of and representatives from one of the largest banks in the United Kingdom—a fact I mention only to impress on you our bona fides. I myself am ex-Royal Navy, former captain, HMM *Sussex*. We are here because we feel the ship is facing an emergency that may be beyond the ability of the crew to contain."

Mason listened.

"There is great anxiety among the passengers. As you probably know, some people have begun locking themselves in their rooms. There's talk of a Jack the Ripper-style killer aboard."

"I'm well aware of that."

"The crew, in case you haven't noticed, is spooked as well," Emily Dahlberg interjected.

"Again, we're aware of these problems and are taking steps to handle the situation."

"Is that so?" asked Bruce. "Well, then, Captain Mason, may I ask where the ship's security is? So far, they've been practically invisible."

Mason paused, looking at each of them in turn. "I'm going to be straight with you. The reason you see so little security is that there *is* very little security—at least, relative to the size of the *Britannia*. We're doing all we can, but this is a very, very large ship and there are four thousand three hundred people on board. All our security staff are working around the clock."

"You say you're doing all you can, but then why hasn't the ship turned around? We see absolutely no choice but to head back to port as quickly as possible."

At this, Captain Mason looked troubled. "The closest port is St. John's, Newfoundland, so if we were to divert, that's where we'd go. However, we're not going to divert. We're continuing to New York."

Bruce was aghast. "Why?"

"These were the commodore's orders. He has his . . . well-considered reasons."

"Which are?"

"Right now we're skirting the edge of a large nor'easter sitting on the Grand Banks. Diverting to St. John's will take us into its heart. Secondly, diverting to St. John's will also take us straight across the Labrador Current during the July iceberg season, which, while not dangerous, will require us to slow our speed. Finally, the diversion will only save us a single day. The commodore feels that docking in New York City would be more appropriate, given—well, given the law enforcement resources we may require."

"There's a maniac on board," said Emily Dahlberg. "Another person could be murdered in that 'single day.'"

"Nevertheless, those are the commodore's orders."

Bruce stood. "Then we insist on speaking directly with him."

Captain Mason also stood, and as she did so the mask

of professionalism slipped away for a moment and Bruce glimpsed a face that was drawn, weary, and unhappy. "The commodore can't be disturbed right now. I'm very sorry."

Bruce glared back at her. "We're sorry, too. You can be assured that this refusal of the commodore to meet with us will not be without repercussions. Now *and* later. We are not people to be trifled with."

Mason extended her hand. "I'm not unsympathetic to your point of view, Mr. Bruce, and I'll do all I can to convey to the commodore what you've said. But this is a ship at sea, we have a ship's master, and that master has made his decision. As a former captain yourself you'll surely understand what that means."

Bruce ignored the hand. "You're forgetting something. We're not only your passengers—and your customers—but we're your responsibility as well. Something can be done, and we plan to do it." And, motioning his group to follow, he turned on his heel and left the room.

36

Paul Bitterman stepped out of the elevator, swayed, and steadied himself on the polished chrome railing. The *Britannia* was in heavy swell, but that was only part of the problem; Bitterman was struggling with the combination of an exceedingly heavy dinner and nine glasses of vintage champagne.

Still gripping the railing, he looked up and down the elegant Deck 9 corridor, blinking, trying to orient himself. Raising a hand to his lips, he eased up a belch that tasted—revoltingly—of caviar, truffled pâté, crème brulée, and dry champagne. He scratched himself idly. Something didn't look right here.

After a minute or so, he figured it out. Instead of taking the port elevator, as he usually did, in the champagne fog he had somehow taken the starboard, and it had gotten him turned around. Well, it was easily fixed. Humming tunelessly, he fumbled in his pocket for the passcard to suite 961. Letting go of the railing, he struck out a little gingerly in what he thought was the right direction, only to find the room numbers moving in the wrong direction.

He stopped; turned around; belched again without bothering to raise a covering hand this time; then headed back the other way. His head really was remarkably fuzzy, and to clear it he tried to reconstruct the series of events that had brought him—for the first time in his fifty-three years—to a state approaching intoxication.

It had all started earlier that afternoon. He had been seasick ever since waking up—hadn't been able to eat a bite—and none of the over-the-counter medicines offered in the ship's pharmacy seemed to help in the least. Finally, he'd gone to the ship's infirmary, where a doctor had prescribed a scopolamine patch. Placing it behind one ear, as directed, he'd gone back to his stateroom for a nap.

Whether it was the miserable night he'd passed, or whether the patch itself had made him drowsy, Paul Bitterman didn't know. But he had awoken at nine-fifteen in the evening, blessedly free of seasickness and possessed of both a dry mouth and a superhuman hunger. He had slept right through his normal eight o'clock dinner, but a quick call to the concierge had secured a reservation at the final seating for the night—at ten-thirty—in Kensington Gardens.

As it turned out, Kensington Gardens appealed greatly to Bitterman. It was more trendy, youthful, and hip than the rather stuffy restaurant he'd been eating in, there were some truly delicious women to look at, and the food was excellent. Surprisingly, the restaurant wasn't full—in fact, it was almost half empty. Ravenous, he proceeded to order chateaubriand for two and then consume the entire portion. An entire bottle of champagne had been insufficient to slake his thirst, but the attentive wine steward had been only too happy to supply him with a second.

There had been some strange talk at the table next to him: a worried-looking couple, discussing some corpse that had apparently turned up. It seemed he might have slept through some serious event. As he made his slow and careful way down the Deck 9 corridor, he decided the first order of business tomorrow would be to get to the bottom of it.

But there was another problem. The room numbers were now headed in the right direction—954, 956—but they were all even numbers.

He paused, gripping the hallway railing again, trying to think. He'd never find 961 at this rate. Then he laughed out loud. *Paul, old buddy, you're not using your noodle.* He had come out on the starboard side, and the odd-numbered staterooms, like his, were all on the port side. How could he have forgotten? He'd need to find a transverse corridor. He set out again, weaving ever so slightly, the fog in his brain offset by a delightful floating sensation in his limbs. He decided that, deacon or not, he'd have to drink champagne more often. Domestic stuff, of course—he'd won this trip in the YMCA raffle and could never afford bottles of vintage French on his teacher's salary.

Ahead and to the left he could see a break in the line of doors: the entrance to one of the midships lobbies. This would lead to the port corridor and his suite. He stumbled through the door.

The lobby consisted of a brace of elevators opposite a cozy lounge with oak bookcases and wing chairs. At this late hour, the place was deserted. Bitterman hesitated, sniffing. There was a smell in the air here—a smell like smoke. For a moment, his sense of lazy euphoria receded: he'd attended enough safety drills to know that fire was a ship's worst danger. But this scent was unusual. It was like incense, or, more precisely, the joss sticks he had once smelled in a Nepalese restaurant in San Francisco's Chinatown.

More slowly now, he walked through the lobby to the port corridor that lay beyond. It was very quiet, and he could both hear and feel the deep thrum of the ship's diesels far below his feet. The smell was stronger here—much stronger. The strange, musky perfume was combined with other, deeper, far less pleasant scents—moldy fungus, maybe, along with something he couldn't identify. He paused, frowning. Then, taking one look back at the lobby, he turned into the port corridor.

And stopped abruptly, inebriation vanishing in an instant.

Up ahead lay the source of the odor: a dark cloud of smoke that blocked his path down the corridor. Yet it was like no smoke he had ever seen, strangely opaque, with a dense, dark grayish color and a rib-like outer surface that reminded him—in some bizarre and unpleasant way—of *linen*.

Paul Bitterman drew in his breath with an audible rasp. Something was wrong here—very wrong.

Smoke was supposed to *drift* through the air, curling, and shifting, attenuating to faint wisps at the edges. But this cloud just sat there, man-sized, strangely malignant, motionless, as if confronting him. It was so regular and even that it looked solid, an organic entity. The reek was so strong he could barely breathe. It was impossible, alien.

He felt his heart suddenly accelerate with fear. Was it his imagination, or did the thick cloud have the *form* of a man, too? There were tendrils that looked like arms; a barrel-like head with a face, strange legs that were moving, as if dancing . . . Oh, God, it looked not like a man, but a *demon* . . .

And it was then the thing slowly stretched out its ragged arms and—with a horrible, undulant purpose—began to move slowly toward him.

"No!" he shouted. "NO! Keep away! *Keep away!*"

The desperate shouts that followed quickly opened stateroom doors up and down the port-side corridor of Deck 9. There was a brief, electric moment of silence. And then, the sound of gasps; shrieks; the thud of a fainting body collapsing on the carpet; the frantic slamming of doors. Bitterman heard none of it. All his attention, every fiber of his being, was riveted to the monstrous thing that glided closer, ever closer . . .

And then it was past.

37

LeSeur stared from Hentoff to Kemper and back again. He was already feeling aggrieved that the commodore had shoved this problem onto his plate—he was a ship's officer, after all, not some casino employee. Not only that, but this problem wouldn't go away—it just kept getting worse. With at least one murder, and perhaps as many as three, he had more dangerous and alarming things to deal with than this. He shifted his stare from Hentoff to Kemper and back again.

"Let me make sure I've gotten this right," he said. "You're telling me this Pendergast fellow contrived for the card counters to lose a million pounds at the blackjack tables, in the process raking in almost three hundred thousand for himself."

Hentoff nodded. "That's about it, sir."

"It seems to me that you just got fleeced, Mr. Hentoff."

"No, sir," said Hentoff, a frosty note in his voice. "Pendergast had to win in order to make them lose."

"Explain."

"Pendergast started off by tracking the shuffle—a technique in which you observe a full shoe of play, memorizing the positions of certain critical cards or groupings, called slugs, and then follow them through the shuffle, visually. He also managed to get a glimpse of the bottom card, and since he was offered the cut, he was able to place that card inside the deck exactly where he wanted it."

"Doesn't sound possible."

"These are well-known, if exceedingly difficult, techniques. This Pendergast seems to have mastered them better than most."

"That still doesn't explain why Pendergast needed to win to make them lose."

"By knowing where certain cards were, and combining that with a counting system, he was able to control the cards going 'downstream' to the rest of the players by either jumping into a game or sitting it out—as well as by taking unnecessary hits."

LeSeur nodded slowly, taking this in.

"He *had* to shortstop the good cards in order to let bad ones go downstream. To make the others lose, he had to win."

"I get it," said LeSeur sourly. "And so you want to know what to do about this man's winnings?"

"That's right."

LeSeur thought for a moment. It all came down to how Commodore Cutter would react when he heard about this—which, of course, he would eventually have to. The answer was not good. And when Corporate heard about it, they would be even less sympathetic. One way or another, they had to get the money back.

He sighed. "For the sake of all of our futures with the company, you need to get that money back."

"How?"

LeSeur turned his weary face away. "Just do it."

Thirty minutes later, Kemper walked down the plush corridor of Deck 12, Hentoff in tow, feeling a clammy sweat building inside his dark suit. He stopped before the door of the Tudor Suite.

"You sure this is the right time for this?" Hentoff asked. "It's eleven P.M."

"I didn't get the sense LeSeur wanted us to wait," Kemper replied. "Did you?" Then he turned to the door and knocked.

"Come in," came a distant voice.

They entered to see Pendergast and the young woman voyaging with him—Constance Greene, his niece or something—in the salon, lights low, sitting around the private dining table with the remains of an elegant repast before them.

"Ah, Mr. Kemper," said Pendergast, rising and pushing aside his watercress salad. "And Mr. Hentoff. I've been expecting you."

"You have?"

"Naturally. Our business is not complete. Please sit down."

Kemper arranged himself with some awkwardness on the nearby sofa. Hentoff took a chair, looking from Agent Pendergast to Constance Greene and back again, as if trying to sort out their real relationship.

"May I offer you a glass of port?" Pendergast asked.

"No, thank you," said Kemper. An awkward silence developed before he continued: "I wanted to thank you again for taking care of those card counters."

"You're most welcome. Are you following my advice about how to keep them from re-winning?"

"We are, thank you."

"Is it working?"

"Absolutely," said Hentoff. "Whenever a spotter enters the casino, we send over a cocktail waitress to engage him in trivial conversation—always involving numbers. It's driving them crazy, but there's nothing they can do about it."

"Excellent." Pendergast turned a quizzical eye on Mr. Kemper. "Was there anything else?"

Kemper rubbed his temple. "Well, there's the question of . . . the money."

"Are you referring to *that* money?" And Pendergast nodded to the bureau, where Kemper noticed, for the first time, a stack of fat envelopes wrapped in thick rubber bands.

"If those are your casino winnings, yes."

"And there's a *question* about the money?"

"You were working for us," said Kemper, feeling the lameness of his argument even before he had made it. "The winnings rightfully belong to your employer."

"I'm nobody's employee," said Pendergast with an icy smile. "Except, of course, the federal government's."

Kemper felt excruciatingly uncomfortable under the silvery stare.

"Mr. Kemper," Pendergast continued, "you realize, of course, that I arrived at those winnings legally. Card counting, shuffle-tracking, and the other techniques I used are all legal. Ask Mr. Hentoff here. I didn't even need to draw on the line of credit you offered me."

Kemper cast a glance at Hentoff, who nodded unhappily.

Another smile. "Well then: does that answer your question?"

Kemper thought of reporting all this back to Cutter, and that helped stiffen his spine. "No, Mr. Pendergast. We consider those winnings to be house money."

Pendergast went to the bureau. He picked up one of the envelopes, slid out a thick wad of pound notes, and lazily riffled through them. "Mr. Kemper," he said, speaking with his back turned, "normally I would never even think of helping a casino recover money against gamblers who are beating the house. My sympathies would lie in the other direction. Do you know why I helped you?"

"To get us to help you."

"Only partly true. It's because I believed there was a dangerous killer on board, and for the safety of the ship I needed to identify him—with your assistance—before he could kill again. Unfortunately, he appears to still be one step ahead of me."

Kemper's depression deepened. He would never get the money back, the crossing was a disaster on every front, and he would be blamed.

Pendergast turned, riffled the money again. "Cheer up, Mr. Kemper! You two may yet get your money back. I am ready to call in my little favor."

Somehow, this did not make Kemper cheer up at all.

"I wish to search the stateroom and safe of Mr. Scott

Blackburn. To that end, I will need a passcard to the room's safe and thirty minutes in which to operate."

A pause. "I think we can manage that."

"There's a wrinkle. Blackburn is currently holed up in his room and won't come out."

"Why? Is he worried about the murderer?"

Pendergast smiled again: a small, ironic smile. "Hardly, Mr. Kemper. He's hiding something, and I need to find it. So he will need to be coaxed out."

"You can't ask me to manhandle a passenger."

"Manhandle? How crude. A more elegant way to effect his removal would be to set off the fire alarms for the starboard stern side of Deck 9."

Kemper frowned. "You want me to set off a false fire alarm? No way."

"But you must."

Kemper thought for a moment. "I suppose we could have a fire drill."

"He won't leave if it's just a drill. Only a mandatory evacuation will dislodge him."

Kemper ran his hands through his damp hair. God, he was sweating. "Maybe I could pull a fire alarm in that corridor."

This time, it was Constance Greene who spoke. "No, Mr. Kemper," she said in a strange antique accent. "We've researched the matter carefully. You need to trigger a central alert. A broken firebox would be too quickly discovered. We'll need a full thirty minutes in Blackburn's suite. And you'll have to temporarily disable the sprinkler system, which can only be done from the central fire control system."

Kemper stood up, Hentoff quickly following. "Impossible. This is a crazy thing to ask. Fire is the most dangerous thing that can happen aboard a ship, aside from sinking. A ship's officer, deliberately triggering a false alert . . . I'd be committing a criminal offense, maybe a felony. Jesus, Mr. Pendergast, you're an FBI agent, you know I can't do that! There must be some other way!"

Pendergast smiled, almost sadly this time. "There is no other way."

"I won't do it."

Pendergast riffled the fat packet of notes. Kemper could actually smell the money—it was like rusty iron.

Kemper stared at the money. "I just can't do it."

There was a moment of silence. Then Pendergast stood, went over to the bureau, opened the top drawer, placed the wad of notes inside, and then raked the rest of the envelopes off the bureau into the drawer. He shut the drawer with slow deliberation and turned to Hentoff and nodded. "See you in the casino, Mr. Hentoff."

There was another silence, longer this time.

"You're going to . . . gamble?" Hentoff asked slowly.

"Why not?" Pendergast spread his hands. "We're on holiday, after all. And you know how I adore blackjack. I was thinking of teaching it to Constance as well."

Hentoff looked at Kemper in alarm.

"I've been told I'm a quick study," Constance said.

Kemper ran his hand through his damp hair again. He could feel the wetness creeping down from his armpits. It just got worse and worse.

The atmosphere in the room grew strained. At last,

Kemper finally let his breath out with a rush. "It's going to take some time to prepare."

"I understand."

"I'll aim for a general fire alarm on Deck 9 at ten o'clock tomorrow morning. It's the best I can do."

Pendergast nodded curtly. "In that case, we'll just have to wait until then. Let us hope things are still, ah, under control by that time."

"Under control? What do you mean by that?"

But Pendergast simply bowed to each of them in turn, then sat down once again and returned to his dinner.

38

It was midnight when Maddie Edmondson slouched down the central corridor of Deck 3, bored out of her mind. Her grandparents had brought her on the voyage as a present for her sixteenth birthday, and it had seemed like a good idea at the time. But nobody had told her what to expect—that the ship would be a floating hell. All the really fun places—the discotheques and the clubs where the twentysomethings hung out, the casinos—were off-limits to a girl her age. And the shows she could get into seemed to appeal to those over the age of a hundred. Antonio's Magic Revue, the Blue Man Group, and Michael Bublé doing Frank Sinatra—it was like a joke. She'd seen all the movies, the swimming pools had been closed due to rough weather. The food in the restaurants was too fancy, and she felt too seasick to enjoy the pizza parlors or hamburger spots. There was nothing for her to do besides sit through lounge acts, surrounded by octogenarians fiddling with their hearing aids.

The only interesting thing that had happened was that weird hanging in the Belgravia Theatre. Now *that* had been something: all the old biddies leaning on their canes and squawking, the grandpas harrumphing and contracting their bushy eyebrows, the officers and deckhands running around like headless chickens. She didn't care what anybody said, it *had* to be a gag, a stage prop, some publicity stunt for the new movie. People just didn't die like that in real life, only in movies.

She passed the gold-lamé-and-green-glass entrance to Trafalgar's, the ship's hottest club. Loud, thumping house music droned from its dark interior. She paused to look in. Slender figures—college types and young professionals—were gyrating in a miasma of smoke and flickering light. Outside the door stood the requisite bouncer: thin and handsome and wearing a tux, but a bouncer no less, eager to keep underage people like Maddie from going inside to enjoy herself.

She continued morosely down the corridor. Although the clubs and casinos were hopping, some of the blue-rinse crowd that normally thronged the passageways and shops had disappeared. They were probably in their cabins, hiding under their beds. What a joke. She hoped to hell they weren't really going to institute the curfew she had heard rumored about. That would be the end. After all, it had been just a gag—hadn't it?

She rode an escalator down one level, wandered past the shops of Regent Street, the upscale shopping arcade, climbed some stairs. Her grandparents had already gone to bed but she wasn't the slightest bit tired. She'd been wandering aimlessly around the ship like this for the past hour, dragging her feet on the carpet. With a sigh, she slipped a pair of earbuds out of her pocket, stuffed them into place, and dialed up Justin Timberlake on her iPod.

She came to an elevator, stepped in, and—closing her eyes—punched a button at random. The elevator descended briefly, stopped, and she got out—another of the ship's endless corridors, this one a little more cramped than she was used to. Turning up the volume on her music player, she dragged her way down the hall, took a turn, kicked open a door bearing a sign she didn't bother to read, skipped down a set of stairs, and wandered on. The corridor took another turn, and as she went around it, she had the sudden feeling she was being followed.

She paused, turning to see who it was, but the corridor was empty. She took a few steps back and looked around the corner. Nothing.

Must have been some random ship noise: down here, the damn thing thrummed and vibrated like some monster treadmill.

She wandered on, letting herself slide along one wall, pushing away with her elbow, then tacking over to the other side to slide again. Four more days to New York City. She couldn't wait to get home and see her friends.

There it was again: that feeling she was being followed.

She stopped abruptly, this time pulling out the earbuds. She looked around but, once again, there was nobody. Where was she, anyway? It was just one more carpeted corridor with what looked like private meeting rooms or something on either side. It was unusually deserted.

She tossed back her hair with an impatient gesture: jeez, now she was getting as spooked as the old-timers. She glanced through an interior window into one of the rooms and saw a long table lined with computers—an

Internet room. She considered stepping inside and going online, but decided against it—all the good sites would certainly be blocked.

As she turned from the window, she saw a movement out of the corner of her eye and caught sight of someone just ducking around the corner behind her. No question about it this time.

"Hey!" she called. "Who's that?"

No answer.

Probably just some maid—the ship was crawling with them. She moved on, but more quickly now, keeping the earbuds in her hand. This was a depressing part of the ship anyway; she should get back up to where the shops were. As she walked, she kept an eye out for one of the diagrams posted about that told your current location. But as she did so, she could swear she heard, over the hum of the ship, the brush of feet on the carpet.

This was bullshit. She walked faster still, taking another turn, then another, still without coming to a map or an area she recognized—just more endless corridors. Except that now she noticed the carpet underfoot had given way to linoleum.

She realized she'd entered one of the off-limits areas of the ship, having missed the *Do Not Enter* sign. Maybe it had been the door she'd kicked open. But she didn't want to retrace her steps and go back: no way.

There were definite footfalls behind her, bolder now, that quickened and slowed with her pace. Was some pervert following her? Maybe she should run—she could outrun an old pervert any day. She came to a side door, ducked through, and descended a metal staircase, coming into another long corridor. She heard the clatter of footsteps on the staircase behind her.

That was when she broke into a run.

The corridor made a dogleg, then ended in a door with a label stenciled in red:

ENGINEERING ONLY

She grasped the handle. Locked. She turned in a panic, holding her breath. She could hear, echoing down the corridor, running footfalls. She frantically tried the door again, shaking it and crying out. Her iPod slipped out of her pocket and skidded across the floor, unheeded.

She turned again, looking around wildly for another door, a fire exit, anything.

The running footsteps got closer, and still closer—and then, suddenly, a figure came around the corner.

Maddie jerked violently, a scream rising in her throat—but then, looking more closely at the figure, she broke down, sobbing with relief. "Thank God it's you," she said. "I thought . . . someone was following me. I don't know. I'm lost. Totally. I'm so glad it's you—"

The knife came out so fast she didn't even have time to scream.

39

LeSeur stood in the rear of the bridge, Mason at his side. He watched Commodore Cutter, hands clasped behind his back, pace back and forth in front of the bridge workstation, alongside the array of flat-panel screens, one foot placed carefully in front of the other, moving with slow deliberation. As he strode the length of the middle bridge, his silhouetted form passed before each screen, one after another. But his eyes remained straight ahead, neither looking at the screens nor at the officer of the watch, who stood to one side, displaced and unhappy.

LeSeur glanced across the radar and weather system displays. The ship was skirting the southern flank of a large, unusual clockwise storm system. The good news was they were traveling with the wind at their backs; the bad news was this meant moving in a following sea. The stabilizers had been fully extended hours ago, but even so the ship had a slow, queasy rotational yaw that guaranteed additional discomfort for the passengers. He glanced over the displays again. Seas were running thirty feet, winds at forty knots, the radar showing a lot of scatter. Nevertheless, the ship was doing beautifully. LeSeur couldn't help but feel a twinge of pride.

Kemper appeared soundlessly at his elbow, his face a ghastly blue in the artificial light from the displays. He looked like a man with a lot on his mind.

"A word, sir," he murmured.

LeSeur glanced at Mason and gestured with his eyes. The two of them followed Kemper out to one of the covered bridge wings. Rain hammered against the windows, running down in heavy sheets. Outside, all was blackness.

Wordlessly, Kemper handed LeSeur a sheet of paper. The first officer glanced over it in the dim light. "Good Lord. Eighteen more people reported missing?"

"Yes, sir. But you'll see at the bottom that sixteen have already turned up. Someone steps out of a cabin for ten minutes and their spouse calls security. The point is, the situation on the ship is deteriorating. The passengers are getting more and more panicky. And my staff is just about paralyzed."

"What about these two that haven't been found?"

"One is a sixteen-year-old girl—her grandparents reported it. The other is a woman with a mild case of Alzheimer's."

"How long have they been missing?"

"The girl for three hours. The old lady for about an hour."

"Do you consider this a cause for serious concern?"

Kemper hesitated. "Not the old lady—I think she's probably gotten confused, maybe fallen asleep somewhere. But the girl . . . yeah, I'm concerned. We've paged her regularly, we've searched the public spaces. And then, there's *this.*" He gave LeSeur a second sheet.

The first officer read it with growing disbelief. "Bloody hell, is this true?" He stabbed his finger at the sheet. "A *monster* roaming the ship?"

"Six people on Deck 9 reported seeing it. Some kind of . . . I don't know what. A thing, covered with smoke, or made of dense smoke. Accounts vary. There's a lot of confusion."

LeSeur handed the sheets back to Kemper. "This is absurd."

"Just shows the level of hysteria. And to me, that's a troubling development—*very* troubling. Mass hysteria, on an ocean liner in the middle of the Atlantic? As it is, I don't have the staff to deal with all this. We're overwhelmed."

"Is there any way to transfer other ship's staff to temporary security duty? Pull some capable junior engineers off their usual jobs?"

"Forbidden by standing orders," said Staff Captain Mason, speaking for the first time. "Commodore Cutter's the only one who could override that."

"Can we make the request?" Kemper asked.

Mason glanced coolly toward the middle bridge where Cutter was pacing. "This is not a good time to ask the commodore anything, Mr. Kemper," she said crisply.

"What about closing the casinos and assigning Hentoff's staff to security?"

"Corporate would string us up. Forty percent of the profit margin comes from the casinos. And besides, those people are dealers and croupiers and pit bosses—they aren't trained in anything else. We might as well reassign the waitstaff."

Another long silence.

"Thank you, Mr. Kemper, for your report," said Mason. "That will be all."

Kemper nodded and left, leaving LeSeur and Mason on the bridge wing, alone.

"Captain Mason?" LeSeur finally asked.

"Yes, Mr. LeSeur?" The staff captain turned to him, the hard lines of her face dimly illuminated in the low light.

"Forgive me for raising the subject again, but have there been any more discussions about diverting to St. John's?"

A very long silence followed this question, stretching to almost a minute. Finally, Mason answered. "No official discussions, Mr. LeSeur."

"Would it be forward of me, sir, to ask why not?"

LeSeur could see Mason thinking carefully how to formulate her response. "The commodore has already expressed his firm orders on that point," she said at last.

"But what if this missing girl . . . is another victim?"

"Commodore Cutter shows no evidence of changing his mind."

LeSeur felt a swell of anger. "Excuse me for speaking frankly, Captain, but we've got a brutal murderer roaming on board this ship. If this Pendergast is to be believed, the man's killed three people already. The passengers are freaking out, half of them are hiding in their cabins, and the rest are getting drunk in the lounges and casinos. And now it seems we've got some kind of mass hysteria building, talk of an apparition roaming the ship. Our security director has as much as admitted the situation is beyond his control. Under the circumstances, don't you think we should seriously consider diversion?"

"Diverting the ship would take us deeper into the storm."

"I know that. But I'd rather weather a nor'easter than deal with an out-of-control mob—of passengers *and* crew."

"What you and I think is irrelevant," said Mason coldly.

Despite her tone, LeSeur could see this last point of his had struck home. Ship's officers were acutely aware of just how relatively small their numbers were. Along with fire at sea, passenger unrest—or worse than unrest—was always a great fear.

"You're the staff captain," he pressed. "The second in command. You're in the best position to influence him. We can't go on like this—you've *got* to persuade him to divert."

Mason turned to him, her eyes dead tired. "Mr. LeSeur, don't you realize? Nobody can change Commodore Cutter's mind. *It's that simple.*"

LeSeur stared at her, breathing hard. It was incredible, an unbelievable situation. He peered down the wing and into the main bridge. Cutter was still pacing about, immersed in his own private world, his face an unreadable mask. LeSeur was reminded of Captain Queeg in *The Caine Mutiny*, locked in denial while the ship descended inexorably into chaos. "Sir, if there's another killing . . ." His voice trailed off.

Mason said, "Mr. LeSeur, if there's another killing—God forbid—we will revisit this issue."

"*Revisit* the issue? In all frankness, sir, what's the point of more talk? If there's another—"

"I'm not alluding to more idle talk. I'm alluding to an Article V action."

LeSeur stared. Article V dealt with the removal of a captain on the high seas for dereliction of duty.

"You aren't suggesting—?"

"That will be all, Mr. LeSeur."

LeSeur watched Mason turn and walk back to the center of the bridge, pausing to confer with the navigator at the con as coolly as if nothing had happened.

Article V. Mason had guts. If it came down to that, so be it. This was quickly becoming a struggle—not just for safe operation of the *Britannia*, but for survival itself.

40

Kemper walked out of the central computer and data processing complex on Deck B, headed for the nearest elevator bank. It had taken him the better part of the night to arrange the false alarm. It had been a bitch resetting the ship's safety management systems without leaving a trail, and it had been especially difficult to disable the sprinkler system. It wasn't so long ago, he reflected grimly, that the only electronic systems on an ocean liner had been radar and communications. Now it seemed that the whole damn ship had been turned into a giant, networked system. It was like some massive floating computer.

The elevator arrived and Kemper entered, pressing the button for Deck 9. It was close to madness to set off a false alarm in the middle of an already nervous ship, with a master who was in denial at best, or deranged at worst, in a storm in the mid-Atlantic. If this ever came out, he'd not only lose his job, he'd probably rot in jail. He wondered how Pendergast had managed to talk him into it.

And then he thought of Corporate, and remembered why.

The elevator doors opened onto Deck 9. He stepped

out and checked his watch: nine-fifty. Clasping his hands behind his back, clamping a fresh smile onto his face, he strolled down the starboard corridor, nodding and smiling at the passengers returning from breakfast. Deck 9 was one of the ritziest on the ship, and he hoped to God the sprinklers wouldn't go off after all his careful work. That would be an expensive disaster for North Star, given that some of the staterooms and suites had been decorated by the passengers themselves, with costly objets d'art, paintings, and sculpture.

Not the least of which was Blackburn's own triplex.

He casually checked his watch again. Nine fifty-eight. Hentoff should be at the far end of the Deck 9 corridor with a security guard, ready to spring into action.

Eeeeeeeee! The fire alarm ripped like a screeching crow down the elegant corridor, followed by a recorded voice in a plummy English accent:

"Attention: this is a fire alarm. All passengers must evacuate the area immediately. Ship's personnel to their muster stations. Please follow the instructions posted on the inside stateroom doors or the orders of fire safety officers. Attention: this is a fire alarm. All passengers . . ."

Up and down the corridor, doors were flung open. People crowded out, some dressed, others in nightgowns or T-shirts. It was remarkable, Kemper thought, how quickly they reacted; it was almost as if they'd all been waiting for something.

"What's happening?" somebody asked. "What is it?"

"Fire?" came another voice, breathless, close to panic. "Where?"

"Folks!" cried Kemper, hustling down the hall. "There

is no need for alarm! Please leave your staterooms and move forward! Gather in the forward lounge! There is nothing to worry about, no reason to panic, everybody please head forward . . ."

"*. . . Attention: this is a fire alarm . . .*"

A large woman in a billowing nightgown came charging out of a stateroom and clutched at him with hammy arms. "Fire? Oh my God, *where*?"

"It's all right, ma'am. Please proceed to the forward lounge. Everything's going to be fine."

More people crowded around him. "Where do we go? Where's the fire?"

"Move forward to the end of the corridor and gather in the lounge!" Kemper forced his way past. Nobody had yet emerged from Blackburn's triplex. He saw Hentoff and the security guard hustling down the hall, pushing past people.

"Pepys! My Pepys!" A woman, jiggling against the flow of the crowd, careened off Kemper and disappeared back into her suite. The guard began to stop her but Kemper shook his head. The woman popped out a moment later with a dog.

"Pepys! Thank goodness!"

Kemper glanced at the casino manager. "The Penshurst Triplex," he murmured. "We have to make sure it's empty."

Hentoff took position on one side of the door while the security guard pounded on the gleaming wood. "Fire evacuation! Everyone get out!"

Nothing. Hentoff glanced to Kemper, who nodded.

The guard whipped out a master key card and swiped it. The door popped open and the two went inside.

Kemper waited by the door. A moment later, he heard raised voices from inside. A woman in a maid's uniform ran out of the triplex and down the hall. Then Blackburn appeared at the door, handled bodily by the security guard.

"Get your greasy hands off me, you bastard!" he cried.

"I'm sorry, sir, it's the rules," said the guard.

"There's no bloody fire! I don't even smell smoke!"

"It's the rules, sir," Kemper echoed.

"At least lock my door, for chrissakes!"

"Fire regulations state that all doors must remain open in a fire emergency. Now, could you please move to the forward lounge, where the other passengers are gathered?"

"I won't leave my stateroom unlocked!" Blackburn wrenched free and tried to push back toward his room.

"Sir," said Hentoff, seizing him by the coat, "if you don't come with us, we'll have to detain you."

"Detain me, my ass!" Blackburn took a swing at Hentoff, who ducked aside. He lunged for the door and Hentoff instinctively tackled him, and they rolled on the floor, two men in suits, grappling. There was the sound of tearing fabric.

Kemper rushed over. "Cuff him!"

The security guard whipped out a pair of PlastiCuffs and, as Blackburn rolled on top of Hentoff and tried to rise, skillfully threw him to the floor, pinned his hands, and cuffed them behind his back.

Blackburn jerked and quivered with rage. "Do you know who I am? You'll pay for this—!" He struggled to sit up.

Kemper moved in. "Mr. Blackburn, we're well aware of who you are. Now, please listen to me carefully: if you don't move peaceably to the forward lounge, I'll send you straight to the brig, where you will remain until disembarkation, at which time you will be turned over to local law enforcement and charged with assault."

Blackburn stared at him, nostrils dilated, blowing hard.

"Or, if you calm down and follow orders, I'll remove those handcuffs now and we'll forget all about your unprovoked attack on ship's personnel. If it's a false alarm, you'll be back in your suite in thirty minutes. Now, which is it going to be?"

A few more heaving breaths, and then Blackburn bowed his head.

Kemper gestured to the security guard, who removed the cuffs.

"Take him to the lounge. Don't let anybody leave for half an hour."

"Yes, sir."

"Then, if the all-clear has sounded, they can return to their suites."

"Very good, sir."

The guard escorted Blackburn down the now empty hall, leaving Kemper and Hentoff alone in the echoing corridor. Thank God: the sprinklers had stayed off. All his preparatory work hadn't been in vain. Firefighters were arriving, dragging out hoses and gear, entering staterooms looking for the fire, closing each stateroom door after they left. Although it was already becoming evident it was probably a false alarm, they had to go through the paces.

Kemper glanced at Hentoff and said, in a low voice, "We'd better go, too. We don't want to be here when Pendergast . . ."

"Don't even say it." And Hentoff hustled down the hall as if he couldn't get out of the area fast enough.

41

At the other end of the ship, seven decks below, Emily Dahlberg exited the Café Soho after a light breakfast of tea and scones and made her way toward the nearby shopping corridor known as Regent Street. She preferred this upscale arcade to the other, St. James's, on Deck 6. The corridor had been tricked up to look like the real Regent Street of a hundred years before, and they'd done an amazing job: streetlamps with real gas jets, cobbled alleys with small, elegant clothing boutiques lining both sides. She'd arrived just in time: unlike the casinos and clubs that were open all day and night, Regent Street kept more regular hours. It was ten o'clock and the shops were just now opening, the lights coming on, the metal grates being pulled back by staff.

Ten o'clock. Ninety minutes to kill until it was time to meet up again with Gavin Bruce and plan their next move.

Dahlberg drifted by the first shop, eyeing the goods in the window. She knew the real Regent Street well, and the stores here were even more expensive than the real thing. Imagine, she mused as she looked through the shop window, paying eleven hundred pounds for an oyster puffball cocktail dress that you could get in London for a third as much. There was something about being on an ocean liner that put one's rational mind to slumber.

She smiled vaguely as she made her way down the faux avenue, her mind wandering. Strangely, despite all the panic and confusion and apprehension that hung in the air like a pall, she found herself thinking of the elegant Mr. Pendergast. She hadn't seen him since that First Night dinner, except passing him once in the casino, but she found her thoughts returning to him again and again. She had lived fifty-one years and run through three husbands, each wealthier than the last, but she had never in her entire life met a man as intriguing as Aloysius Pendergast. And the strangest thing was, she couldn't even begin to articulate just what it was about him. But she'd known it; known it from the first moment they'd made eye contact, from the first honeyed words that had left his lips . . .

She paused to admire a sequined Cornelli jersey top, her mind wandering down various vaguely delicious and sensuous avenues before returning to the present. Her first two husbands had been English nobility, landed gentry of the old-fashioned kind, and her competence and independence had ultimately scared them away. In her third husband, an American meatpacking baron, she had finally found an equal—only to see him die of a stroke during a particularly vigorous copulation. She had hoped to meet a suitable fourth husband on the cruise—life was short, and she had a mortal fear of spending her old age alone with her horses—but now, with the uproar over this awful killing, the prospects looked poor indeed.

No matter. Once in New York, there would be the Guggenheim party, the *Elle* magazine bash, the Metropolitan Club dinner, and any number of other venues for meeting a suitable man. Perhaps, she thought, she might even be forced to lower her standards . . . but only slightly.

Then again, perhaps not. She was certain, for example, that Mr. Pendergast would not require a lowering of standards. At least, as certain as she could be without taking off the man's clothes.

She glanced over the slow-moving crowd. It was sparser than usual, no doubt due to the heavy seas, the disappearances and murder. Or perhaps everyone had hangovers—the amount of liquor she'd seen consumed in the restaurants, clubs, and lounges the previous evening had quite astonished her.

She approached another elegant shop, the last in the arcade, which was just opening its shutters. She stood idly as the metal rolled up with a hideous noise—what was charming on Regent Street was merely obnoxious on board ship—and was pleasantly surprised to see revealed the plate glass of a small fur shop. She didn't go in for wearing fur herself, but she could nevertheless appreciate a beautiful piece of couture when she saw it. One of the store clerks was in the front window, fussily adjusting a full-length Zuki basarick fur coat that had become somewhat disheveled on its old-fashioned wicker mannequin. She paused to admire the coat, which was tiered with fringe in a very full-cut style. *Thick enough to keep you warm in a Siberian gulag*, she thought with a smile.

As she watched, the clerk tugged and fussed with increasing irritation, and then realized the coat had been buttoned up crookedly. With an exaggerated rolling of the eyes he unbuttoned the coat and flicked it open. A splattering of syrupy liquid fell from the mannequin, followed by what looked like a length of reddish-white rope. The clerk, evidently feeling wetness on his hands, raised them up to his face. They were red—covered in a viscous red that could only be blood.

Blood . . .

Emily Dahlberg placed her hand over her mouth. The clerk reacted more violently, jerking back, slipping on the now bloody floor and losing his footing. He flailed, shouted, grabbed at the mannequin; and then clerk, coat, and mannequin fell heavily to the ground, the coat flying open to reveal a corpse.

But no, Emily Dahlberg realized; it was not a corpse, at least not a *whole* corpse, but instead a tangle of organs, red and white and yellow, streaming and dangling from a ragged hole cut into the wickerwork torso of the mannequin. She stared in open-mouthed shock and disbelief, temporarily unable to move. She had witnessed enough sanguinary scenes at the family meatpacking plant, on the arm of her third husband, to know that these organs did not belong to cattle. No—cattle viscera was larger. This was something else entirely . . .

All of a sudden, she realized her limbs were working again. And as she turned and began walking back down the Regent Street alley, her pace slightly unsteady, screams began to echo over her shoulder. But Emily Dahlberg did not look back, not even once.

42

At three minutes after ten o'clock, the door to a Deck 9 electrical port cracked open onto an utterly deserted corridor. The shriek of the fire alarm had ceased, and all that remained was an officious emergency message, repeating over and over from the ship's internal sound system. From one direction came the receding voices of fire control officers; from the other, a faint Babel of noise from the forward lounge. After a brief hesitation, Pendergast emerged from the darkness of the electrical port like a spider from its lair. He glanced first one direction, then the other, peering intently down the plushly carpeted and wallpapered corridor. Then, with feline quickness, he darted forward, opened the front door of the Penshurst Triplex, ducked inside, and—shutting the door behind him—slid home the heavy-duty lock.

For a moment he stood motionless in the muted entryway. Beyond, in the salon, the curtains were drawn against the dark and stormy morning, allowing only a faint light to filter into the hushed interior. He could hear the faint throbbing of the ship, the sound of rain and wind lashing the windows. He inhaled, all senses on high alert. Very faintly, he detected the same waxy, smoky, resinous smell the cab driver had described; the scent he knew from the inner monastery of Gsalrig Chongg.

He glanced at his watch: twenty-four minutes.

The Penshurst Triplex was one of the two largest suites on the ship, more like an elegant town house than a ship's stateroom, with three bedrooms and an exercise room on the upper floors and a salon, kitchen, dining area, and balcony down, connected by a spiral staircase. He moved out of the entryway and into the dark salon. Silver, gold, turquoise, and varnish gleamed dully from the shadows. Pendergast flicked on the lights and was momentarily dazzled by the extraordinary and eclectic collection of art that greeted his eyes: early cubist paintings by Braque and Picasso, mingled indiscriminately with masterpieces of Asian painting and sculpture from India, Southeast Asia, Tibet, and China. There were other treasures as well: a table displaying an array of early English repoussé silver and gold snuffboxes; several cases containing ancient Greek gold coins; an odd collection of what looked like Roman toga pins and ceintures.

The collection as a whole betrayed a collector with a fine eye, impeccable taste, and immensely deep pockets. But even more, it was the work of a man of true culture and discernment, a man with interests and knowledge that went far beyond mere business.

Was this, Pendergast wondered, the same man who had so gratuitously and sadistically mutilated Jordan

Ambrose after death? He thought again of how Ambrose's murder had been psychologically inconsistent in every conceivable way.

He went straight to the large teak cabinet at the far end of the room that, Constance had explained, housed the suite's safe. Opening the cabinet, he pulled out the magnetic passcard Kemper had supplied him with, slipped it into the slot. A moment later, the safe door sprang ajar with a faint click.

He pulled it wide and peered inside. As he did so, a strong smell of resin and smoke wafted outward. The safe was empty except for one thing: a long, rectangular wooden box covered with faded Tibetan script.

He withdrew it with exquisite care, noting its lightness. It was so riddled with insect holes that it was like a desiccated sponge, crumbling and shedding dust at the slightest touch. He unlatched the old brass keeper and gingerly opened the lid, which fell apart in his hands. Carefully, he pulled away the pieces and stared into the box's interior.

It was empty.

13

The bridge security buzzer sounded, indicating someone was entering the bridge. A moment later Kemper appeared in the hatchway. LeSeur was taken immediately aback by the man's appearance: his face was gray, his hair limp, his clothes disheveled. He looked like he hadn't slept in a week.

"What is it, Mr. Kemper?" he asked, glancing involuntarily at Commodore Cutter, still on the bridge. The man had gone back to his pacing. The ship was on autopilot—a marriage of software, mechanics, and satellite technology that was nothing short of a marvel of naval engineering, able to keep the ship on course better than any human navigator, saving significant amounts of fuel. The problem, LeSeur thought, was the autopilot was still following a course for New York City.

"They found the missing girl," Kemper said, his voice low. "Or, at least, part of her."

There was a brief silence. LeSeur felt a sudden wave of horror as he tried to process this information.

"Part of her," he repeated at last. His throat seemed to have gone dry.

"Portions of a human body—entrails, viscera—were found stuffed into a mannequin in one of the Regent Street shops. At about the same time, streaks of blood, a half-crushed bracelet, and . . . gore, other things . . . were located by one of my search parties on the port aft railing of Deck 1."

"So the rest was thrown overboard," LeSeur said, very quietly. This was a bad dream—a nightmare. It had to be.

"It would seem so, sir. The girl's iPod was located on Deck B, outside the hatch leading to the engineering spaces. It appears she was accosted down there, led or carried up to Deck 1, then killed and butchered on the weather deck and thrown overboard—with a few, ah, trophies retained. Those in turn were brought up to the Regent Street fur shop and left on a mannequin."

"Do the passengers know yet?"

"Yes. Word seems to be spreading quickly. They're taking it badly."

"How badly?"

"I've witnessed numerous scenes of hysteria. A man in the Covent Garden casino had to be restrained. I've warned you about how dangerous hysteria can become—my recommendation is that the commodore declare an ISPS Code Level One and that you take steps to increase security on the bridge immediately."

LeSeur turned to a second officer. "Activate security hatches on all bridge approaches. No one passes without authorization."

"Yes, sir."

He turned back to the security chief. "I will discuss the ISPS Code with the commodore. Any leads on the killing?"

"None. Except the killer seems to have remarkable access to the ship, including a key to Engineering and the Regent Street fur shop."

"Pendergast said the killer had somehow managed to get a security passcard."

"Or a master key," said Kemper. "Dozens have been issued."

"Motive?"

"It could be the work of a raving sociopath. Or it might be someone with a specific goal in mind."

"A goal? Such as?"

Kemper shrugged. "I don't know. Sow panic on board, maybe?"

"But why?"

When the security chief had no answer, LeSeur nodded. "Thank you, Mr. Kemper. Would you please accompany me while I report this to the commodore?"

Kemper swallowed, nodded. LeSeur strode over to the center bridge, placing himself in the path of the commodore's walk. "Commodore Cutter?"

Cutter stopped pacing, slowly raised his massive head. "What is it, Mr. LeSeur?"

"Mr. Kemper has just reported another killing on board. A young girl."

At this, Cutter's eyes flashed briefly before going dull again. He glanced over at the security chief. "Mr. Kemper?"

"Sir. A sixteen-year-old girl was murdered early this morning on Deck 1. Certain body parts were placed on a mannequin in one of the Regent Street shops; it was discovered when the shop opened this morning. The story is spreading over the ship and passengers are panicking."

"Is your staff conducting an investigation?"

"My staff, sir, is strained to the maximum just trying to keep order, answer reports of disappearances, and reassure passengers. With all due respect, we are not in any position to gather evidence, question suspects, or conduct an investigation."

Cutter continued gazing at him. "Anything else, Mr. Kemper?"

"I would recommend declaring an ISPS Code Level One on the ship."

The eyes focused briefly on LeSeur before swiveling toward the officer of the watch. "Mr. Worthington?" Cutter called out. "Estimated time to New York?"

"At current speed and heading, sixty-six hours, sir."

"St. John's?"

"Twenty-three hours, sir, again if we maintain speed."

A long silence enveloped the bridge. Cutter's eyes gleamed in the dim light from the electronics. He turned back to the security director.

"Mr. Kemper, declare a Code One. I want you to close two of the casinos and half of the nightclubs. In addition, select the shops and lounges that have been doing the least amount of business. Reassign those employees to the maintenance of order on board this ship, as far as their skills and capabilities will allow. Close the game rooms, health clubs, theaters, and spas—and again reassign the staff to security duties, whenever possible."

"Yes, sir."

"Seal any areas that may contain forensic evidence of this and the other crimes. I don't want any entry by anyone to those areas, even you."

"Already done, sir."

He turned. "Mr. LeSeur, a ten P.M. to eight A.M. curfew will remain in effect until we land. All passengers will be confined to their staterooms during those periods. Move up the restaurant dinner seatings so the last one concludes at nine-thirty."

"Yes, sir."

"All room service and other passenger services are to be canceled. All waitstaff will follow a minimal cleaning schedule. All crew are to be confined to quarters when not on duty or at mess. No exceptions. Mr. LeSeur, you will take appropriate steps to cut down on the movement of nonessential personnel about the ship."

"Yes, sir."

"You will make an appropriate announcement to the passengers declaring an International Ship and Port Security nautical emergency on board ship and outlining my orders. Infractions will be dealt with sternly. There will be no exceptions granted to these rules, no matter how rich or . . . *influential* the person might be, or claim to be."

There was a long, long silence. LeSeur waited for the most essential order to come.

"That will be all, Mr. LeSeur."

But LeSeur didn't move. "Captain Cutter, excuse me

for mentioning this, but surely you'll be diverting to St. John's?"

As Cutter's eyes rested on him, they turned cold. "No."

"Why not, sir?" LeSeur swallowed.

"I am not in the habit of explaining my reasoning with junior officers."

LeSeur swallowed again in an unsuccessful attempt to loosen his throat. "Commodore, if I may—"

Cutter interrupted him. "Mr. LeSeur, call the staff captain back to the bridge and confine yourself to your quarters until further orders."

"Yes, sir."

"That will be all. Mr. Kemper, you may vacate the bridge as well." And without another word, Cutter wheeled away and resumed his pacing.

44

Carefully, carefully, Pendergast brought the crumbling box out into the light. He fitted a jeweler's loupe to one eye and, with a pair of tweezers, began sorting through the debris inside—dead insects, particles of resin, sawdust, fibers—placing select items into small test tubes taken from his jacket pockets. When he had finished, he fitted the lid back on the box, reassembling it with exquisite care, and placed it back in the safe in the rectangle of sawdust from which he had taken it. He closed the safe, dipped the passcard into the reader to lock it, then closed the teak cabinet and stepped back.

He checked his watch: nineteen minutes left.

Blackburn had hidden the object—whatever it was—elsewhere in his suite.

He peered around the salon, examining each object in turn. Many whose dimensions exceeded that of the box he could dismiss immediately. But there were many others that could fit in the box, albeit awkwardly; too many to examine properly within a quarter of an hour.

He went upstairs and searched the bedrooms, baths, and exercise room. Blackburn, he noted, had only redecorated the salon—except for the silken bedcoverings monogrammed with a large and ostentatious "B," the upstairs rooms remained in their original decor.

He returned to the salon and paused in the center, his silvery eyes traveling around the room, fastening on each object in turn. Even if he eliminated all objects that were neither Tibetan nor Indian and more modern than the twelfth century, he was still left with an uncomfortably large number. There was an iron ritual lance damascened with gold and silver; a phur-bu dagger in massive gold with a triangular blade issuing from the mouth of Makara; several long prayer wheels in exquisitely carved ivory and silver, with sculpted mantras; a silver dorje ritual object encrusted with turquoise and coral; and several ancient thangkas and mandala paintings.

All extraordinary. But which one—if any—was the Agozyen, the terrible and forbidden object that would cleanse the earth of its human infestation?

His eye settled on the extraordinary thangka paintings that ranged about the walls: paintings of Tibetan deities and demons, bordered by rich silk brocade, used as objects of meditation. The first was an exquisite image of the Avalokiteshvara bodhisattva, the Buddha of Compassion; next, a fierce depiction of the Kalazyga demon, with fangs, three eyes, and a headdress of skulls, dancing wildly in the midst of a raging fire. He examined the thangkas at close range with his loupe, then plucked a thread of silk off the edge of each in turn and examined them as well.

Next he moved to the largest of the mandalas, hanging over the gas fireplace. It was mind-boggling: an intricate, metaphysical representation of the cosmos that was, at the same time, a magical depiction of the interior state of the enlightened Buddha, as well as being the schematic of a temple or palace. The mandalas were meant to be objects of contemplation, aids to meditation, their proportions magically balanced to purify and calm the mind. To stare at a mandala was to experience, if only briefly, the nothingness that is at the heart of enlightenment.

This was an exceptionally fine mandala; Pendergast gazed at it, his eye almost magnetically drawn to the object's center, feeling the familiar peace and freedom from attachment emanating from it.

Was this the Agozyen? No—there was no menace, no danger here.

He glanced at his watch. Blackburn would be back in twelve minutes. There was no more time to examine individual objects. Instead, he returned to the center of the room and stood there, thinking.

The Agozyen was in the room: he was certain of that. But he was also certain that further searching was a waste of precious time. A Buddhist phrase came to his mind: *When you cease searching, then you will find.*

He seated himself on Blackburn's overstuffed couch, closed his eyes, and—slowly, calmly—emptied his mind. When his mind was at rest, when he ceased caring whether he found the Agozyen or not, he opened his eyes and once again looked around the room, keeping his mind a blank, his intellect quiescent.

As he did so, his gaze gravitated toward an exquisite painting by Georges Braque hanging unobtrusively in the corner. He vaguely remembered the painting, an early masterpiece by the French cubist that had recently been auctioned at Christie's in London—purchased, he recalled, by an unknown buyer.

From his position on the sofa, he examined the painting with relaxed pleasure.

Seven minutes.

15

LeSeur intercepted Staff Captain Mason as she was entering through the outer bridge security hatchway. She paused when she saw his face.

"Captain Mason . . . ," he began, then faltered.

She looked at him, her face betraying nothing. She still appeared cool, collected, hair tucked under the captain's hat with not a single strand out of place. Only her eyes bespoke a deep weariness.

She looked through the inner hatchway toward the bridge, taking in the current operational status with a quick, professional glance, then returned her attention to him. "Is there something you wish to tell me, Mr. LeSeur?" Her voice was studiously neutral.

"You've heard about the latest killing?"

"Yes."

"Commodore Cutter refuses to divert to St. John's. We're maintaining course for New York. Sixty-five hours and change."

Mason said nothing. LeSeur turned to go and felt her staying hand on his shoulder. He felt a mild surprise: she had never touched him before.

"Officer LeSeur," she said. "I wish you to come with me when I speak to the commodore."

"I've been dismissed from the bridge, sir."

"Consider yourself reinstated. And please call the second and third officers to the bridge, along with Mr. Halsey, the chief engineer. I will need them to act as witnesses."

LeSeur felt his heart accelerate. "Yes, sir."

It was the work of five minutes to quietly round up the junior officers and Halsey and return to the bridge. Mason met them at the security hatch. Over her shoulder, LeSeur could see that the commodore was still walking back and forth before the bridge windows. His pace had slowed still further, and he was putting one foot before another with excruciating precision, head bowed, ignoring everyone and everything. At the sound of their entry, he at last paused, looked up. LeSeur knew Cutter could not help but see the bridge staff arrayed in a row behind him.

Cutter's watery eyes went from Mason to LeSeur and back again. "What is the first officer doing here, Captain? I dismissed him."

"I asked him to return to the bridge, sir."

There was a long silence.

"And these other officers?"

"I asked them to be here, as well."

Cutter continued to stare at her. "You are insubordinate, Captain."

There was a pause before Mason replied. "Commodore Cutter, I respectfully ask you to justify your decision to maintain course and heading for New York instead of diverting to St. John's."

Cutter's gaze hardened. "We've been over this already. Such a diversion is unnecessary and ill-considered."

"Pardon me, sir, but the majority of your officers—and, I might add, a delegation of prominent passengers—think otherwise."

"I repeat: you are insubordinate. You are hereby relieved of command." Cutter turned to the two security officers standing guard by the bridge hatch. "Escort Captain Mason from the bridge."

The two security guards stepped up to Mason. "Come with us, please, sir," one of them said.

Mason ignored them. "Commodore Cutter, you haven't seen what I have; what *we* have. There are four thousand three hundred terrified passengers and crew on board this vessel. The security staff is wholly inadequate to handle a situation of this magnitude, something Mr. Kemper freely acknowledges. And the situation continues to escalate. The control, and therefore the safety, of this ship is at imminent risk. I insist that we divert to the closest available port-St. John's. Any other course would endanger the ship and constitute dereliction of duty under Article V of the Maritime Code."

LeSeur could hardly breathe. He waited for an enraged outburst, or a cold, Captain Bligh-like rebuff. Instead, Cutter did something unexpected. His body seemed to relax, and he came around and leaned on the edge of a console, folding his hands. His whole demeanor changed.

"Captain Mason, we're all more than a little distraught." He glanced at LeSeur. "Perhaps I was a little hasty in my response to you, too, Mr. LeSeur. There's a reason why a ship has a master and why his orders are never to be questioned. We don't have the time or luxury to start wrangling among ourselves, discussing our reasoning, voting like a committee. However, under the circumstances, I'm going to explain my reasoning. I will explain it once, and only once. I *expect*"—he glanced over at the deck officers and the chief engineer, and his voice hardened again—"you to listen. All of you must accept the ancient and time-honored sanctity of the master's prerogative to make decisions aboard his ship, even decisions that involve life-or-death situations, such as this one. If I am wrong, that will be addressed once we reach port."

He straightened. "We're twenty-two hours to St. John's, but *only if we maintain speed*. If we did divert, we'd be plunging into the heart of the storm. Instead of a following sea, we'd be subjected to a beam sea and then, as we cross the Grand Banks, a head-on sea. We'd be lucky to maintain twenty knots of headway. By this calculation St. John's is thirty-two hours away, not twenty-two—and that's only if the storm doesn't worsen. I could easily imagine arriving in St. John's forty hours from now."

"That's still a day ahead—"

The captain held up his hand, his face darkening. "*Excuse* me. A straight heading to St. John's, however, will take us dangerously close to Eastern Shoal and the Carrion Rocks. So we will need to chart a course around those obstacles, losing at least another hour or two. That makes it forty-two hours. The Grand Banks are riddled with fishing vessels, and some of the larger factory ships will be weathering the storm offshore, with sea anchors out, immobile, making us the give-way ship in all encounters. Knock off two knots of speed and add maneuvering room, and we lose another few hours. Even though it's July, the iceberg season isn't over, and recent growler activity has been reported along the outer margins of the Labrador Current, north of the Eastern Shoal. Knock off another hour. So we're not twenty-two hours out of St. John's. We're forty-five."

He paused dramatically.

"The *Britannia* has now become the scene of a crime. Its passengers and crew are all suspects. Wherever we land, the ship will be detained by law enforcement and not released until the forensic examination of the ship is complete and all passengers and crew interviewed. St. John's is a small, provincial city on an island in the Atlantic, with a minuscule constabulary and a small RCMP detachment. It doesn't have anywhere near the kind of resources needed to do an effective and efficient job of evidence gathering. The *Britannia* could languish in St. John's for weeks, even a month or more, along with its crew and many passengers, at a loss to the corporation of hundreds of millions of dollars. The number of people on board this ship will swamp the town."

He looked around at the silent group, licked his lips.

"New York City, on the other hand, has the facilities to conduct a proper criminal and forensic investigation. The passengers will be minimally inconvenienced and the ship will probably be released after a few days. Most importantly, the investigation will be state of the art. They will find and punish the killer." Cutter closed his eyes slowly, then opened them again. It was a slow, strange gesture that gave LeSeur the creeps. "I trust I have made myself clear, Captain Mason?"

"Yes," said Mason, her voice cold as ice. "But allow me to point out a fact you've overlooked, sir: the killer has struck four times in four days. Once a day, like clockwork. Your twenty-four extra hours to New York means one extra death. An unnecessary death. *A death that you will be personally responsible for.*"

There was a terrible silence.

"What does it matter that the passengers will be inconvenienced?" Mason continued. "Or that the ship might be stuck in port? Or that the corporation might lose millions of dollars? What does it matter when *the life of a human being is at stake*?"

"That's true!" LeSeur said, louder than he intended. He was distantly surprised to hear that the voice which spoke up was his own. But he was sick at heart—sick of the killing, sick of the shipboard bureaucracy, sick of the endless talk about corporate profits—and he couldn't help but speak. "That's what this is all about: money. That's all it boils down to. How much money the corporation might lose if its ship were stuck in St. John's for a few weeks. Are we going to save the corporation money, or are we going to save a human life?"

"Mr. LeSeur," Cutter said, "you are out of line—"

But LeSeur cut him off. "Listen: the most recent victim was an innocent sixteen-year-old girl, a *kid* for God's sake, traveling with her grandparents. Kidnapped and murdered! What if she had been a daughter of yours?" He turned to face the others. "Are we going to let this happen again? If we follow the course Commodore Cutter recommends, we're very likely condemning another human being to a horrible death."

LeSeur could see the junior deck officers nodding their agreement. There was no love lost for the corporation; Mason had hit a nerve. The chief engineer, Halsey, remained unreadable.

"Commodore, sir, you leave me no choice," Mason said, her voice quiet but with a measured, almost fierce eloquence. "Either you divert this ship, or I'll be forced to call for an emergency Article V action."

Cutter stared at her. "That would be highly inadvisable."

"It's the last thing I want to do. But if you continue to refuse to see reason, you leave me no choice."

"*Bullshit!*" This profanity, so remarkable on the lips of the commodore, sent a strange shock wave rippling across the bridge.

"Commodore?" Mason said.

But Cutter did not reply. He was staring out through the bridge windows, gaze fixed on an indeterminate horizon. His lips worked soundlessly.

"Commodore?" Mason repeated.

There was no reply.

"Very well." Mason turned to the assembled group. "As second in command of the *Britannia*, I hereby invoke Article V against Commodore Cutter for dereliction of duty. Who will stand with me?"

LeSeur's heart was pounding so hard in his chest it felt like it would burst from his rib cage. He looked around, his eyes meeting the frightened, hesitant eyes of the others. Then he stepped forward.

"I will," he said.

16

Pendergast continued to look at the Braque. A small question, a nagging doubt, took root in the margins of his consciousness, spreading to fill the void he had created within his mind. Slowly, it intruded into his conscious thought:

There was something wrong with the painting.

It was not a forgery. There was no doubt it was genuine, and that it was the very painting auctioned at Christie's in the Winter Sale five months before. But there was nevertheless *something* that wasn't right. The frame, for one thing, had been changed. But that wasn't all . . .

He rose from his seat and approached the painting, pausing inches from its surface, and then stepping slowly back, staring intently at it the entire time. It came to him in a flash: part of the image was missing. The painting had lost an inch or two on the right side and at least three inches off the top.

He stood motionless, staring. He was sure the painting had been sold intact at Christie's. That could mean only one thing: Blackburn himself had mutilated it for reasons of his own.

Pendergast's breathing slowed as he contemplated this bizarre fact: that an art collector would mutilate a painting that had cost him over three million dollars.

He plucked the painting off the wall and turned it over. The canvas had recently been relined, as one might expect from a painting that had been cut down from its original size. He bent down and sniffed the canvas, coming away with the chalky smell of the glue used in relining. Very fresh: a lot fresher than five months. He pressed it with his fingernail. The glue had barely dried. The relining had been done in the last day or two.

He checked his watch: five minutes.

He quickly laid the painting face down on the thick carpeting, removed a penknife from his pocket, inserted it between the canvas and the stretcher, and—with exquisite care—pressed down on the blade, exposing the inside edge of the canvas. A dark, loose strip of old silk caught his eye.

The liner was false; something was hidden behind it. Something so valuable that Blackburn had sliced up a three-million-dollar painting to hide it.

He quickly examined the fake liner. It was held tight by the pressure between the canvas and the stretcher. Slowly, carefully, Pendergast prized the canvas away from one side of the stretcher, loosened the liner, then repeated the process on the other three sides. Keeping the painting facedown on the carpeting, he grasped the now loose corners of the liner between his thumb and forefinger, peeled it back.

Hidden between the fake liner and the real one was a painting on silk, covered by a loose silk cloth. Pendergast held it at arm's length, then laid it on the carpet and drew back the silk cover.

For a moment, his mind went blank. It was as if a sudden puff of wind had blown the heavy dust from his brain, leaving a crystalline purity. The image assembled itself in his consciousness as his intellectual processes returned. It was a very ancient Tibetan mandala of astonishing, extraordinary, utterly unfathomable complexity. It was fantastically, maddeningly intricate, a swirling, interlocking geometric fantasy edged in gold and silver, an unsettling, *disintegrating* palette of colors against the blackness of space. It was like a galaxy unto itself, with billions of stars swirling around a spinning singularity of extreme density and power . . .

Pendergast found his eye drawn inexorably to the singularity at the center of this bizarre design. Once it was fixed there, he found himself unable to move his eyes away. He made a minor effort, then a stronger one, marveling at the power of the image to hold both his mind and his gaze in thrall. It had happened so suddenly, so stealthily as it were, that he had no time to prepare himself. The dark hole at the center of the mandala seemed to be alive, pulsing, crawling in the most repellent way, opening itself like some foul orifice. He felt as if a corresponding hole had been opened in the center of his own forehead, that the countless billions of memories and experiences and opinions and judgments that made up his unique persona were being twisted, being *altered*; that his very soul was being drawn out of his body and sucked into the mandala, in which he became the mandala and the mandala became him. It was as if he were being transfigured into the metaphysical body of the enlightened Buddha . . . Except that this wasn't the Buddha.

That was the sheer, implacable, inescapable terror of it.

This was some other universal being, the anti-Buddha, the physical manifestation of pure evil. And it was here, with him, in this painting. In this room . . .

And in his head . . .

17

The sound of LeSeur's voice died out on the bridge, replaced by the howling of wind and the splatter of rain on the windows, the electronic beeping and chiming of the ECDIS electronics and radar as they went through their cycles.

No one spoke. LeSeur felt a sudden panic. He'd gotten ahead of the curve, throwing his hat into the ring with Mason. He had just made the move that would guarantee career suicide.

Finally, the officer of the watch stepped forward, a gruff mariner in the old style. Eyes downcast, hands clasped over his uniform, he was the very picture of stiff-jawed courage. He cleared his throat and began to speak. "A master's first responsibility is to the lives of the people aboard ship—crew and passengers."

Cutter stared at him, his chest rising and falling.

"I'm with you, Captain Mason. We've got to get this ship into port."

The man finally raised his eyes and faced Cutter. The captain returned the look with a gaze of such ferocity it seemed to physically assault the man. The officer of the watch dropped his eyes once more—but did not step back.

Now the second officer stepped forward, followed by two junior officers. Without a word Halsey, the chief engineer, stepped forward. They stood in a tight group in the center bridge, nervous, uneasy, their eyes avoiding the commodore's fatal stare. Kemper, the security chief, remained rooted in place, his fleshy face strained with anxiety.

Captain Mason turned to him and spoke, her voice cold, matter-of-fact. "This is a legal action under Article V. Your agreement is necessary, Mr. Kemper. You must make a decision—now. If you do not declare with us, it means you've taken the commodore's side. In that case, we will proceed to New York—and you will assume the burden of responsibility for all that entails."

"I—" Kemper croaked.

"This is a mutiny," said Cutter, his gravelly voice low and threatening. "A *mutiny*, pure and simple. You go along with this, Kemper, and you're guilty of mutiny on the high seas, which is a *criminal* offense. I will see you charged to the fullest extent. You will never set foot on the deck of a ship again as long as you live. That goes for the rest of you."

Mason took a step toward Kemper, her voice softening just slightly. "Through no fault of your own, you've been placed between a rock and hard place. On the one hand, a possible charge of mutiny. On the other, a possible charge of negligent homicide. Life is hard, Mr. Kemper. Take your pick."

The chief of security was breathing so hard he was

almost hyperventilating. He looked from Mason to Cutter and back, eyes darting around as if seeking a way out. There was none. He spoke, all in a rush. "We've got to make port as soon as possible."

"That's an opinion, not a declaration," said Mason coolly.

"I'm . . . I'm with you."

Mason turned her keen eyes on the commodore.

"You are a disgrace to your uniform and to a thousand years of maritime tradition!" Cutter roared. "This shall not stand!"

"Commodore Cutter," Mason said, "you are hereby relieved of command under Article V of the Maritime Code. I will give you one opportunity to remove yourself from the bridge, with dignity. Then I shall order you removed."

"You . . . you *vixen*! You're living proof that women have no place on the bridge of a ship!" And Cutter rushed at her with an inarticulate roar, grasping the lapel of her uniform before two security guards seized him. He cursed, clawing and roaring like a bear, as they wrestled him to the ground, pinned him, and handcuffed him.

"Brown-haired bitch! May you burn in hell!"

More security guards were called in from a nearby detail and the commodore was subdued with great difficulty. He was finally wrestled off, his thundering voice hurling imprecations down the companionway until at last silence fell.

LeSeur looked at Mason and was surprised to see a flush of poorly concealed triumph on her face. She looked at her watch. "I will note for the log that command of the *Britannia* has been transferred from Commodore Cutter to Staff Captain Mason at ten-fifty, GMT." She turned to Kemper. "Mr. Kemper, I shall need all the keys, passwords, and authorization codes to the ship and all electronic and security systems."

"Yes, sir."

She turned to the navigator. "And now, if you please, reduce speed to twenty-four knots and lay in a course for St. John's, Newfoundland."

18

The door opened softly. Constance rose from the divan with a sharp intake of breath. Pendergast slipped through the door, strolled over to the small bar, pulled down a bottle, and examined the label. He removed the cork with a faint pop, took out a glass, and casually poured himself a sherry. Carrying the bottle and glass with him, he took a seat on the sofa, put the bottle on a side table, and leaned back, examining the color of the sherry in the light.

"Did you find it?" Constance asked.

He nodded, still examining the color of the sherry, and then tossed off the glass. "The storm has intensified," he said.

Constance glanced toward the glass doors that opened onto the balcony, lashed with flecks of spume. The rain was now so heavy she couldn't see down to the water; there was only a field of gray, grading to darkness.

"Well?" She tried to control the excitement in her voice. "What was it?"

"An old mandala." He poured himself a second glass, then raised it toward Constance. "Care to join me?"

"No, thank you. What kind of mandala? Where was it hidden?" His coyness could be maddening.

Pendergast took a long, lingering sip, exhaled. "Our man had hidden it behind a Braque painting. He trimmed down and restretched the painting in order to hide the Agozyen behind it. A lovely Braque, from his early cubist period—utterly spoiled. A shame. He'd hidden it recently, too. He had evidently learned about the maid that went crazy after cleaning his rooms—and perhaps he even knew of my interest. The box was in the safe. Apparently, he felt the safe wasn't secure enough for the mandala—with good reason, as it turns out. Or perhaps he simply wanted to have it accessible at all times."

"What did it look like?"

"The mandala? The usual four-sided arrangement of interlocking squares and circles, done in the ancient Kadampa style, astonishingly intricate—but of little interest to anyone beyond a collector or a superstitious group of Tibetan monks. Constance, would you kindly sit down? It is not agreeable to speak to a standing person when one is seated."

Constance subsided into her seat. "That's all? Just an old mandala?"

"Are you disappointed?"

"I thought, somehow, that we'd be dealing with something extraordinary. Perhaps even . . ." She hesitated. "I don't know. Something with almost supernatural power."

Pendergast issued a dry chuckle. "I fear you took your studies at Gsalrig Chongg a trifle too literally." He sipped his sherry again.

"Where is it?" she asked.

"I left it in situ for the time being. It's safe with him and we know where it is now. We'll take it from him at the end of the voyage, at the last minute, when he won't have time to respond."

Constance sat back. "Somehow I can't believe it. Just a thangka painting."

Pendergast eyed the sherry again. "Our little pro bono assignment is nearly finished. All that remains is the problem of relieving Blackburn of his ill-gotten goods, and as I said, that is trifling. I have already worked out most of the details. I do hope we won't have to kill him, although I wouldn't consider it much of a loss."

"Kill him? Good God, Aloysius, I would certainly hope to avoid that."

Pendergast raised his eyebrows. "Really? I should have thought you would be accustomed to it by now."

Constance stared at him, flushing. "What are you talking about?"

Pendergast smiled, dropped his eyes again. "Constance, forgive me; that was insensitive. No, we won't kill Blackburn. We'll find another way to take his precious toy."

There was a long silence as Pendergast sipped his sherry.

"Did you hear the rumor of the mutiny?" said Constance.

Pendergast didn't seem to hear.

"Marya just informed me of it. Apparently the staff captain has taken command, and now we're heading to Newfoundland instead of New York. The ship's in a panic. They're instituting a curfew, there's supposed to be an important announcement coming over the public address system at noon"—she glanced at her watch—"in an hour."

Pendergast set down the empty glass and rose. "I am somewhat fatigued from my labors. I believe I shall take a rest. Would you see to it that upon rising at three o'clock I have a breakfast of eggs Benedict and Hojicha green tea waiting for me, fresh and hot?"

Without another word, he glided up the stairs to his bedroom. A moment later, his door eased shut behind him and the lock turned with a soft click.

19

LeSeur was one hour into the afternoon watch, and he stood at the integrated bridge workstation, before the giant array of ECDIS chartplotters and vector radar overlays, tracking the progress of the ship as it cut across the Grand Banks on a course for St. John's. There had been no sea traffic—merely a few large ships riding out the storm—and progress had been rapid.

Since the change of command the bridge had been eerily silent. Captain Mason seemed subdued by the weight of her new responsibilities. She had not left the bridge since relieving Cutter of command, and it struck him that she would probably remain there until the ship came into port. She had raised the state of emergency to ISPS Code Level Two. Then she'd cleared the bridge of all but essential personnel, leaving only the officer of the watch, helmsman, and a single lookout. LeSeur was surprised at what a good decision that turned out to be: it created an oasis of calm, of focus, that a more heavily manned bridge did not have.

He wondered just how this Article V action was going to play out with Corporate and how it would affect his career. Adversely, no doubt. He consoled himself that he'd had no choice. He had done the right thing and that was what counted. That was the best you could do in life. How others took it was beyond his control.

LeSeur's experienced eye roved over the big-screen electronics, the Trimble NavTrac and Northstar 941X DGPS, the four different sets of electronic charts, the gyro, radar, speed logs, loran, and depth sounders. The bridge would be hardly recognizable to a naval officer of even ten years before. But on one side, at a navigational table, LeSeur still charted the ship's course the old-fashioned way, on paper, using a set of fine brass navigation instruments, parallel rulers and dividers given to him by his father. He even occasionally took a sun or star sight to determine position. It was unnecessary, but it gave him a vital connection with the great traditions of his profession.

He glanced at the speed and course readouts. The ship was on autopilot, as usual, and LeSeur had to admit the *Britannia* was proving to be unusually sea-kindly, despite a thirty-foot beam sea and forty- to fifty-knot gale winds. True, there was a rather unpleasant long-period, corkscrewing roll, but he could only imagine how much worse it would be for a smaller cruise ship. The *Britannia* was making twenty-two knots, better than expected. They would be in St. John's in less than twenty hours.

He felt a great relief at the way Mason had quietly taken charge. In her noon announcement to the entire ship over the PA system, she had quietly explained that the commodore had been relieved of duty and that she had taken over. In a calm, reassuring voice she had declared an ISPS Code Level Two state of emergency and explained that they were diverting to the closest port. She had asked passengers for their own safety to spend most of their time quietly in their staterooms. When leaving their cabins for meals, she urged them to travel in groups or pairs.

LeSeur glanced at the ARPA radar. So far, so good. There had been no sign of ice, and what few ships were still on the Banks had been lying to well off their course. He touched the dial of the ECDIS and changed the scale to twenty-four miles. They were closing in on a waypoint, at which the autopilot would execute a course correction that would take them clear of the Carrion Rocks on the leeward side. After that, it was a straight shot into St. John's Harbour.

Kemper appeared on the bridge.

"How are things on the passenger decks?" LeSeur asked.

"As good as could be expected, sir." He hesitated. "I've reported the change of command to Corporate."

LeSeur swallowed. "And?"

"A lot of hard blowing, but no official reaction yet. They've dispatched a bunch of suits to meet us in St. John's. Basically, they're reeling. Their main concern is bad publicity. When the press gets hold of this . . ." His voice trailed off and he shook his head.

A soft chime from the chartplotter announced that the waypoint had been reached. As the autopilot automatically adjusted to the new heading, LeSeur felt the faintest vibration: the new course had slightly changed the ship's angle to the sea and the rolling had grown worse.

"New bearing two two zero," LeSeur murmured to the staff captain.

"New bearing acknowledged, two two zero."

The wind buffeted the bridge windows. All he could see was the ship's forecastle, half hidden in the mist, and beyond that an endless gray.

Mason turned. "Mr. LeSeur?"

"Yes, Captain?"

She spoke in a low voice. "I'm concerned about Mr. Craik."

"The chief radio officer? Why?"

"I'm not sure he's getting with the program. It seems he's locked himself in the radio room."

She nodded to a door at the rear of the bridge. LeSeur was surprised: he had rarely seen it closed.

"Craik? I didn't even know he was on the bridge."

"I need to make sure that all the deck officers are working as a team," she went on. "We've got a storm, we've got over four thousand terrified passengers and crew, and we've got a rough time ahead of us when we get to St. John's. We can't afford to have any second-guessing or dissention among the deck officers. Not now."

"Yes, sir."

"I need your help. Rather than make a big deal about it, I'd like to have a quiet word with Mr. Craik—just the two of us. I think perhaps he felt intimidated by you and the others into going along."

"That sounds like a wise approach, sir."

"The ship's on autopilot, we're still four hours from passing the Carrion Rocks. I'd like you to clear the bridge so I can speak to Craik in a nonthreatening environment.

I feel it's especially important that Mr. Kemper absent himself."

LeSeur hesitated. The standing orders stated that the bridge must be manned by a minimum of two officers.

"I'll temporarily take the watch," said Mason. "And Craik could be considered the second bridge officer—so this won't violate regulations."

"Yes, sir, but with the storm conditions . . ."

"I understand your reluctance," Mason said. "I'm asking for just five minutes. I don't want Mr. Craik feeling he's being ganged up on. I'm a little worried, frankly, about his emotional stability. Do it quietly and don't tell anyone why."

LeSeur nodded. "Aye, sir."

"Thank you, Mr. LeSeur."

LeSeur walked over to the lookout. "Join me in the companionway for a moment." He nodded to the helmsman. "You, too."

"But—"

"Captain's orders."

"Yes, sir."

LeSeur rejoined Kemper. "Captain's taking the watch for a few minutes. She'd like us to clear the bridge."

Kemper looked at him sharply. "Why?"

"Orders," LeSeur repeated in a tone he hoped would discourage further questions. He checked his watch: five minutes and counting. They withdrew to the companionway just beyond the bridge hatch and LeSeur shut the door, taking care to leave it unlocked.

"What's this all about?" Kemper asked.

"Ship's business," LeSeur repeated, sharpening his tone even further.

They stood in silence. LeSeur glanced at his watch. Two more minutes.

At the far end of the companionway, the door opened and a figure entered. LeSeur stared: it was Craik. "I thought you were in the radio room," he said.

Craik looked back at him like he was crazy. "I'm just reporting for duty now, sir."

"But Captain Mason—"

He was interrupted by a low alarm and a flashing red light. A series of soft clicks ran around the length of the bridge hatch.

"What the hell's that?" the helmsman asked.

Kemper stared at the blinking red light above the door. "Christ, someone's initiated an ISPS Code Level Three!"

LeSeur grabbed the handle of the bridge door, tried to turn it.

"It automatically locks in case of an alert," said Kemper. "Seals off the bridge."

LeSeur felt his blood freeze; the only one on the bridge was Captain Mason. He went for the bridge intercom. "Captain Mason, this is LeSeur."

No answer.

"Captain Mason! There's a Code Three security alert. *Open this door!*"

But again there was no reply.

50

At half past one o'clock Roger Mayles found himself leading a fractious group of Deck 10 passengers to the final lunch shift at Oscar's. For over an hour he had been answering questions—or rather, avoiding answering them—about what would happen when they got to Newfoundland; about how they would get home; about whether refunds would be made. Nobody had told him shit, he knew nothing, he could answer nobody—and yet they had exhorted him to maintain "security," whatever the hell that meant.

Nothing like this had happened to him before. His greatest joy of shipboard life was its predictability. But on this voyage, nothing at all had been predictable. And now he felt he was getting close to the breaking point.

He walked along the corridor, a rictus-like smile screwed onto his face. The passengers behind him were speaking in raised, querulous voices about all the same tiresome issues they'd been talking about all day: refunds, lawsuits, getting home. He could feel the slow roll of the ship as he walked, and he kept his eyes averted from the broad starboard windows lining one side of the corridor.

He was sick of the rain, the moaning of the wind, the deep booming of the sea against the hull. The truth was, the sea frightened him—it always had—and he never enjoyed looking down into the water from the ship, even in good weather, because it always looked so deep and so cold. And endless—so very, very endless. Since the disappearances began, he'd had a recurring nightmare of falling into the dark Atlantic at night, treading water while watching the lights of the ship recede into the mist. He woke up in a twisting of sheets each time, whimpering under his breath.

He could think of no worse death. None.

One of the men in the group behind him quickened his pace. "Mr. Mayles?"

He turned, not slowing, the smile as tense as ever. He couldn't wait to get into Oscar's.

"Yes, Mr.—?"

"Wendorf. Bob Wendorf. Look here—I've got an important meeting in New York on the fifteenth. I need to know how we're going to get from Newfoundland to New York."

"Mr. Wendorf, I've no doubt the company will work out the arrangements."

"Damn it, that's not an answer! And another thing: if you think we'll go by ship to New York, you're sadly mistaken. I'm never setting foot on a ship again in my life. I want a flight, first class."

A murmur of agreement rippled through the ranks behind him. Mayles stopped and turned. "As it happens, the company is already lining up flights." He knew of no such thing, but at this point he was ready to say anything to get these clods off his back.

"For all three thousand passengers?" A woman with rings on every wizened finger pushed forward, flapping her bejeweled, liver-spotted hands.

"St. John's has an international airport." Did it? Mayles had no idea.

The woman went on, voice like a buzz saw. "Frankly, I find the lack of communication intolerable. We paid a lot of money to make this voyage. We deserve to know what's going on!"

You deserve a boot up your prolapsed old ass, lady. Mayles continued smiling. "The company—"

"What about refunds?" interrupted another voice. "I hope you don't think we're going to *pay* for this kind of treatment—!"

"The company will take care of everyone," Mayles said. "Please have patience." He turned quickly to avoid more questions—and that's when he saw it.

It was a *thing;* a thing like a dense massing of smoke, at the angle of the corridor. It was moving toward them with a kind of sickening, rolling motion. He halted abruptly, paralyzed, staring. It was like a dark, malignant mist, except that it seemed to have a *texture* to it, like woven fabric, but vague, indefinite, darker toward the middle with faint interior glints of dirty iridescence. Shapes like bunching muscles came and went across its surface as it approached.

He was unable to speak, unable to move. *So it's true*, he thought. *But it can't be. It can't be . . .*

It moved toward him, gliding and roiling as if with

terrible purpose. The group stumbled to a halt behind him; a woman gasped.

"What the hell?" came a voice.

They backed up in a tight group, several crying out in fear. Mayles couldn't take his eyes off it, couldn't move.

"It's some natural phenomenon," said Wendorf loudly, as if trying to convince himself. "Like ball lightning."

The thing moved down the hall, erratically, closing in.

"Oh, my God!"

Behind him, Roger Mayles registered a general confused retreat, which quickly devolved into a stampede. The confused babble of screams and cries faded away down the hall. Still he couldn't move, couldn't speak. He alone remained rooted to the spot.

As the thing approached, he could see something inside it. It was an outline, squat, ugly, feral, with madly darting eyes . . .

No, no, no, no, noooo . . .

A low keening sound escaped Mayles's lips. As the thing drew nearer, he felt the growing breath of wetness and mold, a stench of dirt and rotting toadstools . . . The keening in his throat grew into a gargling flow of mucus as the thing slunk by, never looking at him, never seeing him, passing like a breath of clammy cellar air.

The next thing Mayles knew, he was lying on the floor, staring upward at a security officer holding a tumbler of water.

He opened his mouth to speak, but nothing came save a sigh of air leaking from between his vocal cords.

"Mr. Mayles," the officer said. "Are you all right?"

He made a sound like a punctured bellows.

"Mr. Mayles, sir?"

He swallowed, worked his sticky jaws. *"It . . . was . . . here."*

A strong arm reached down and grasped his jacket, pulling him to a sitting position.

"Your group came tearing by me, hysterical. Whatever it was that you saw, it's gone now. We've searched all the adjacent corridors. It's gone."

Mayles leaned over, swallowed unhappily, and then—as if to exorcise the very presence of the thing—vomited on the gold pile carpeting.

51

"Captain Mason!" LeSeur jammed his finger hard against the intercom button. "We've got a Code Three alert. Please answer me!"

"Mr. LeSeur," said Kemper, "she knows very well we've got a Code Three. She activated it herself."

LeSeur turned and stared. "You're sure?"

Kemper nodded.

The first officer turned back to the hatch. "Captain Mason!" He yelled into the intercom. "Are you all right?"

No response. He banged on the hatch with his fist. *"Mason!"*

He spun toward Kemper. "How do we get in there?"

"You can't," said the security chief.

"The hell I can't! Where's the emergency override? Something's happened to Captain Mason!"

"The bridge is hardened just like an airline cockpit. When the alert is triggered from within, it locks down the bridge. Totally. Nobody can get in—unless let in by someone on the inside."

"There's got to be a manual override!"

Kemper shook his head. "Nothing that would allow entry by terrorists."

"Terrorists?" LeSeur stared at Kemper in disbelief.

"You bet. The new ISPS regulations required all kinds of anti-terrorist measures aboard ship. The world's largest ocean liner—it's an obvious target. You wouldn't believe the antiterrorist systems on the ship. Trust me—you won't get in, even with explosives."

LeSeur sagged against the door, breathing hard. It was incomprehensible. Had Mason had a heart attack of some kind? Lost consciousness? He glanced around at the anxious, confused faces looking back at him. Looking to him for leadership, guidance.

"Follow me to the auxiliary bridge," he said. "The CCTVs there will show us what's going on."

He ran down the companionway, the others following, and opened the door to a service stair. Taking the metal steps three at a time, he descended a level, pulled open another door, then tore down the corridor, past a deckhand with a mop, to the hatchway leading into the aux bridge. As the group entered, a guard monitoring the security feeds within looked up in surprise.

"Switch to the bridge feeds," LeSeur ordered. "All of them."

The man typed several commands on his keyboard, and instantly a half dozen separate views of the bridge appeared on the small CCTV screens arrayed before them.

"There she is!" LeSeur said, almost sagging with relief. Captain Mason was standing at the helm, back to the camera, apparently as calm and collected as when he had left her.

"Why couldn't she hear us over the radio?" He asked. "Or the banging?"

"She could hear us," said Kemper.

"But then why . . . ?" LeSeur stopped. His carefully attuned shipboard senses felt the vibration of the huge vessel change ever so slightly, felt the sea changing. The ship was turning.

"What the *hell*?"

At the same time, there was an unmistakable shudder as the ship's engine speed increased—increased significantly.

An ice-cold knot began to harden in his chest. He glanced down at the screen displaying the course and speed, watched the sets of numbers ticking away until they steadied on a new heading and course. Two hundred degrees true, speed gradually increasing.

Two hundred degrees true . . . Quickly, LeSeur glanced at the chartplotter running on a nearby flat-panel monitor. It was all there, in glorious color, the little symbol of the ship, the straight line of its heading, the shoals and rocks of the Grand Banks.

He felt his knees go soft.

"What is it?" Kemper asked, staring closely at LeSeur's face. Then he followed the first officer's eyes to the chartplotter.

"What—?" Kemper began again. "Oh, my God." He stared at the large screen. "You don't think—?"

"What is it?" asked Craik, entering.

"Captain Mason has increased speed to flank," LeSeur

said, his voice dull and hollow in his own ears. "And she's altered course. On a heading straight for the Carrion Rocks."

He turned back to the closed-circuit television screen showing Captain Mason at the helm. Her head had turned ever so slightly, so that he caught her in profile, and he could see the faintest of smiles play across her lips.

In the corridor outside, Lee Ng paused in swabbing the linoleum corridor to listen more intently. Something big was going on, but the voices had suddenly ceased. In any case, he must have misunderstood. It was a language problem—despite diligent study, his English was still not what he wished it could be. It was hard, at the age of sixty, to learn a new language. And then there were all the nautical terms that weren't even listed in his cheap Vietnamese-English dictionary.

He resumed pushing the mop. The silence that came from the open door to the auxiliary bridge now gave way to a burst of talking. Excited talking. Lee Ng edged closer, head down, swinging the mop in broad semicircles, listening carefully. The voices were loud, urgent, and now he began to realize that he had not misheard.

The mop handle fell to the floor with a clatter. Lee Ng took a step back, and then another. He turned, began to walk, and the walk became a run. Running had saved his life in desperate situations more than once during the war. But even as he ran, he realized that this was not like the war: there was no place of refuge, no protective wall of jungle beyond the last rice paddy.

This was a ship. There was no place to run.

52

Constance Greene had listened attentively to the acting captain's announcement over the public address system, greatly relieved to hear the ship was finally diverting to St. John's. She was also reassured by the stringent security measures that were being undertaken. Any pretense that this was still a pleasure voyage had been dropped: now it was about safety and survival. Perhaps, she thought, it was karma that some of these ultra-privileged people had a glimpse of life's reality.

She checked her watch. One forty-five. Pendergast had said he wanted to sleep until three, and she was inclined to let him. He clearly needed the rest, if only to pull him out of the funk he seemed to have fallen into. She had never known him to sleep during the day before, or drink alcoholic beverages in the morning.

Constance settled on the sofa and opened a volume of Montaigne's essays, trying to take her mind off her concerns. But just as she began to lose herself in the elegant French turns, a soft knock came at the door.

She stood up and went to the door.

"It's Marya. Open, please."

Constance opened it and the maid slipped in. Her usually spotless uniform was dirty and her hair disheveled.

"Please sit down, Marya. What's going on?"

Marya took a seat, passing a hand over her forehead. "It is инсане out there."

"I'm sorry?"

"How you call it? An asylum. Listen, I bring you news. Very bad news. It's going around belowdecks like fire. I pray it's not true."

"What is it?"

"The acting captain, they say—Captain Mason—has locked herself on the bridge and is steering the ship toward rocks."

"What?"

"Rocks. The Carrion Rocks. They say we will hit the rocks in less than three hours."

"It sounds to me like a hysterical rumor."

"Maybe," said Marya, "but this one, all the crew believe it. And something big is happening up on the auxiliary bridge, many officers coming and going, lots of activity. Also that, how you say, that *ghost* has been seen again. A group of passengers this time, and the cruise director as well."

Constance paused. The ship shuddered through another massive wave, yawing strangely. She looked back at Marya. "Wait here, please."

She went upstairs and knocked on the door of Pendergast's stateroom. Usually he responded immediately, his voice as clear and collected as if he'd been awake for hours. This time, nothing.

Another knock. "Aloysius?"

A low, even voice issued from inside. "I asked you to wake me at three."

"There's an emergency you should know about."

A long silence. "I don't see why it couldn't wait."

"It can't wait, Aloysius."

A long silence. "I'll join you downstairs in a moment."

Constance descended. Several minutes later, Pendergast made his appearance, wearing black suit pants, a starched white shirt hanging open unbuttoned, black suit jacket and tie thrown over one arm. He tossed the jacket on the chair and cast his eyes about. "My eggs Benedict and tea?" he asked.

Constance stared at him. "They've shut down all room service. Food is being served only in shifts."

"Surely Marya here is clever enough to scare something up while I shave."

"We don't have time for food," said Constance, irritated.

Pendergast went into the bathroom, leaving the door open, pulled the shirt off his white, sculpted body, tossed it over the shower rail, turned on the water, and began to lather his face. He took out a long straight razor and began stropping it. Constance got up to shut the door but he gestured to her with his hand. "I'm waiting to hear what's so important that it has disrupted my nap."

"Marya says that Captain Mason—the one who took over from Cutter after he refused to change course—has seized the bridge of the ship and is sending us on a collision course with a reef."

The razor paused in its smooth progress down Pendergast's long white jaw. Almost thirty seconds passed. Then the shaving resumed. "And why has Mason done this?"

"Nobody knows. She just went crazy, it seems."

"Crazy," Pendergast repeated. The scraping continued, maddeningly slow and precise.

"On top of that," Constance said, "there's been another encounter with that thing, the so-called smoke ghost. A number of people saw it, including the cruise director. It almost seems as if . . ." She paused, uncertain how to articulate it, then dropped the idea. It was no doubt her imagination.

Pendergast's shaving continued, in silence, the only sounds the faint booming and buffeting of the storm and the occasional raised voice in the corridor. Constance and Marya waited. At last he finished. He rinsed, wiped off and folded the razor, mopped and toweled his face, pulled on his shirt, buttoned it, slipped the gold cuff links into his cuffs, threw on his tie and knotted it with a few expert tugs. Then he stepped into the sitting room.

"Where are you going?" Constance asked, both exasperated and a little frightened. "Do you have any idea what's going on here?"

He picked up his jacket. "You mean you haven't figured it out?"

"Of course I haven't!" Constance felt herself losing her temper. "Don't tell me you have!"

"Naturally I have." He slipped on his suit coat and headed for the door.

"What?"

Pendergast paused at the door. "Everything's connected, as I surmised earlier—the theft of the Agozyen, the murder of Jordan Ambrose, the shipboard disappearances and killings, and now the mad captain driving the ship up on a reef." He gave a little laugh. "Not to mention your 'smoke ghost.' "

"How?" Constance asked, exasperated.

"You have the same information I do, and I find explanations to be so tiresome. Besides, it's irrelevant now—all of it." He waved his hand vaguely around the room. "If what you say is true, all this will shortly be wedged in the abyssal muck at the bottom of the Atlantic, and right now I have something important to do. I'll be back in less than an hour. Perhaps in the meantime you might manage a simple plate of eggs Benedict and green tea?"

He left.

Constance stared at the door long after it had closed behind him. Then she turned slowly to Marya. For a moment she said nothing.

"Yes?" Marya asked.

"I have a favor to ask you."

The maid waited.

"I want you to bring me a doctor as soon as possible."

Marya looked at her with alarm. "Are you ill?"

"No. But I think *he* is."

53

Gavin Bruce and what he had begun to call his team sat in the midships lounge on Deck 8, engaged in conversation about the state of the ship and the next steps they might take. The *Britannia* seemed remarkably quiet for early afternoon. Even though a curfew had only been instituted for the nighttime hours, it seemed many of the passengers had taken to their cabins, either through fear of the murderer or exhaustion over an extremely tense morning.

Bruce shifted in his chair. While their mission to speak to Commodore Cutter had failed, it gratified him that the man had been removed and his recommendations had been acted upon. He felt that, in the end, his intervention had done some good.

Cutter had clearly been out of his depth. He was a kind of captain Bruce knew well from his own career in the Royal Navy, a commander who confused stubbornness with resolve and "going by the book" for wisdom. Such men often choked when circumstances grew chaotic. The new captain had handled the transition well; he'd approved of her speech over the PA. Very professional, very much in command.

"We're moving into the teeth of the storm," said Niles Welch, nodding at the row of streaming windows.

"Hate to be out in that mess on board a smaller ship," Bruce replied. "Amazing how sea-kindly this big ship is."

"Not like the destroyer I was a middy on during the Falklands war," said Quentin Sharp. "Now that was a squirrelly vessel."

"I'm surprised the captain increased speed back there," said Emily Dahlberg.

"Can't say I blame her," Bruce replied. "In her position, I'd want to get this Jonah ship into port as soon as possible, the hell with the passengers' comfort. Although if it were me I might just ease off on the throttle a trifle. This ship is taking quite a pounding." He glanced over at Dahlberg. "By the way, Emily, I wanted to congratulate you on how you quieted that hysterical girl just now. That's the fourth person you've managed to calm in the last hour."

Dahlberg crossed one poised leg over the other. "We're all here for the same reason, Gavin—to help maintain order and assist any way we can."

"Yes, but I could never have done it. I don't think I've ever seen anybody that upset."

"I just used my maternal instincts."

"You've never had any children."

"True." Dahlberg smiled faintly. "But I've got a good imagination."

The sound of urgent footsteps and confused shouting came echoing down the corridor.

"Not another group of drunken sods," Sharp muttered.

The voices grew louder, and an unruly group of passengers appeared, led by a man who was clearly drunk. They had fanned out and were pounding on stateroom doors, the occupants coming out into the corridor behind them.

"Did you hear?" the man in the lead shouted, his voice slurred. "You hear?" The others in the group kept banging, shouting for everyone to come out.

Bruce sat up.

"Is something wrong?" Dahlberg asked sharply.

The drunken man stopped, swaying slightly. "We're on a collision course!"

There was a babble of frightened voices. The man waved his arms. "Captain's seized the bridge! She's going to wreck the ship on the Grand Banks!"

A burst of questions, shouts.

Bruce rose. "That's an incendiary charge to make, sir, on board a ship. You'd better be able to back it up."

The man looked unsteadily at Bruce. "I'll back it up. I'll back *you* up, pal. It's all over the ship, the whole crew is talking about it."

"It's true!" a voice in the rear shouted. "The captain's locked herself on the bridge, alone. Set a course for the Carrion Rocks!"

"What nonsense," said Bruce, but he was made uneasy by the mention of the Carrion Rocks. He knew them well from his navy days: a broad series of rocky, fanglike shoals jutting up from the surface of the North Atlantic, a grave hazard to shipping.

"It's true!" the drunken man cried, swinging his arm so hard he almost pulled himself off balance. "It's all over the ship!"

Bruce could see a panic seizing the crowd. "My friends," he said in a firm tone, "it's quite impossible. The bridge on a ship like this would never, ever be manned by one person. And there must be a thousand ways to retake control of a ship like this, from the engine room or from secondary bridges. I know: I was a commander in the Royal Navy."

"That's not how it works these days, you old fool!" the drunken man cried. "The ship's totally automated. The captain mutinied and took control, and now she's going to sink the ship!"

A woman rushed forward and seized Bruce's suit. "You were navy! For God's sake, you've got to do something!"

Bruce extricated himself and raised his hands. He had a natural air of command and the frightened hubbub diminished.

"Please!" he called out. A hush fell.

"My team and I will find out if there's any truth to this rumor," he went on.

"There is—!"

"Silence!" He waited. "If there is, we'll take action—I promise you that. In the meantime, all of you should stay here and await instructions."

"If I recall," said Dahlberg, "the Admiral's Club on Deck 10 has a monitor that shows the ship's position on the crossing, including course and speed."

"Excellent," Bruce said. "That will give us independent verification."

"And then what?" the woman who had seized his suit practically shrieked.

Bruce turned to her. "Like I said, you stay here and encourage any others that happen by to do the same. Keep everyone calm, and stop spreading this rumor—the last thing we need is a panic. If it's true, we'll help the other officers retake the ship. And we'll keep you informed."

Then he turned back to his little group. "Shall we check it out?"

He led them down the hall and toward the stairs, at a fast walk. It was a crazy story, insane. It couldn't be true . . .

Could it?

51

The auxiliary bridge was crowded and getting hotter by the minute. LeSeur had called for an emergency staff meeting for all department heads, and already the ship's hospitality and entertainment chiefs were arriving, along with the chief purser, bosun, and chief steward. He glanced at his watch, then wiped his brow and looked for what must have been the hundredth time at the back of Captain Mason, displayed on the central CCTV screen, standing straight and calm at the helm, not a stray hair escaping from beneath her cap. They had called up the *Britannia*'s course on the main NavTrac GPS chartplotter. There it was, displayed in a wash of cool electronic colors: the heading, the speed . . . and the Carrion Rocks.

He stared back at Mason, coolly at the helm. Something had happened to her, a medical problem, a stroke, drugs, perhaps a fugue state. What was going on in her mind? Her actions were the antithesis of everything a ship's captain stood for.

Beside him, Kemper was at a monitoring workstation, headphones over his ears. LeSeur nudged him and the security director pulled off the phones.

"Are you absolutely sure, Kemper, that she can hear us?" he asked.

"All the channels are open. I'm even getting some feedback in the cans."

LeSeur turned to Craik. "Any further response to our mayday?"

Craik looked up from his SSB and satellite telephone. "Yes, sir. U.S. and Canadian Coast Guard are responding. The closest vessel is the CCGS *Sir Wilfred Grenfell*, hailing port St. John's, a sixty-eight-meter offshore patrol boat with nine officers, eleven crew, sixteen berths plus ten more in the ship's hospital. They are on an intercept course and will reach us about fifteen nautical miles east-northeast of the Carrion Rocks at . . . around 3:45 P.M. Nobody else is close enough to reach us before the estimated time of, ah, collision."

"What's their plan?"

"They're still working on the options."

LeSeur turned to the third officer. "Get Dr. Grandine up here. I want some medical advice about what's going on with Mason. And ask Mayles if there's a psychiatrist on board among the passengers. If so, get him up here, too."

"Aye, sir."

Next, LeSeur turned to the chief engineer. "Mr. Halsey, I want you to go to the engine room *personally* and disconnect the autopilot. Cut cables if need be, take a sledgehammer to the controller boards. As a last resort, disable one of the pods."

The engineer shook his head. "The autopilot's hardened against attack. It was designed to bypass all manual systems. Even if you could disable one of the pods—which you can't—the autopilot would compensate. The ship can run on a single pod, if necessary."

"Mr. Halsey, don't tell me why it can't be done until you've tried."

"Aye, sir."

LeSeur turned to the radio officer. "Try to raise Mason on VHF channel 16 with your handheld."

"Yes, sir." The radio officer unholstered his VHF, raised it to his lips, pressed the transmit button. "Radio officer to bridge, radio officer to bridge, please respond."

LeSeur pointing to the CCTV screen. "See that?" he cried. "You can see the green receive light. She's picking it up loud and clear!"

"That's what I've been telling you," Kemper replied. "She can hear every word."

LeSeur shook his head. He'd known Mason for years. She was as professional as they came—a little uptight, definitely by-the-book, not exactly warm, but always thoroughly professional. He racked his brains. There had to be *some* way to communicate with her face-to-face. It frustrated the hell out of him that she kept her back to them at all times.

Maybe if he could see her, he could reason with her. Or at least understand.

"Mr. Kemper," he said, "a rail runs just below the bridge windows for attaching the window-washing equipment—am I right?"

"I believe so."

LeSeur yanked his jacket off a chair and pulled it on. "I'm going out there."

"Are you crazy?" Kemper said. "It's a hundred-foot fall to the deck."

"I'm going to look into her face and ask her what the hell she thinks she's doing."

"You'll be exposed to the full force of the storm—"

"Second Officer Worthington, the watch is yours until I return." And LeSeur tore out of the door.

LeSeur stood at the port forward rail of the observation platform on Deck 13, wind tearing at his clothes, rain lashing his face, while he stared up at the bridge. It was situated on the highest level of the ship, above which rose only the stacks and masts. The two bridge wings ran far out to port and starboard, their ends projecting over the hull. Below the wall of dimly lit windows he could just barely see the rail, a single, inch-thick brass tube cantilevered about six inches from the ship's superstructure by steel brackets. A narrow ladder ran up from the platform to the port wing, where it joined the rail that encircled the lower bridge.

He staggered across the deck to the ladder, hesitated a moment, then seized the rung at shoulder level, gripping it as tightly as a drowning man. He hesitated again, the muscles of his arms and legs already dancing in anticipation of the coming ordeal.

He planted a foot on the lowest rung and pulled himself up. Fine spray washed over him and he was shocked to taste saltwater here, over two hundred feet above the waterline. He couldn't see the ocean—the rain and spray were too thick—but he could hear the boom and feel the shudder of the waves as they struck blow after blow against the hull. It sounded like the pounding of some angry, wounded sea god. At this height, the movements of the ship were especially pronounced, and he could feel each slow, sickening roll deep in his gut.

Should he attempt it? Kemper was right: it was totally crazy. But even as he asked himself the question, he knew what the answer would be. He had to look her in the face.

Grasping the rungs with all his might, he heaved himself up the ladder, one hand and one foot after the other. The wind lashed at him so violently that he was forced to close his eyes at times and work upward by feel, his rough seaman's hands closing like vises on the grit-painted rungs. The ship yawed under a particularly violent wave and he felt as if he were hanging over empty space, gravity pulling him down, down into the cauldron of the sea.

One hand at a time.

After what seemed like an endless climb, he reached the top rail and pulled his head up to the level of the windows. He peered in, but he was far out on the port bridge wing and could see nothing but the dim glow of electronic systems.

He was going to have to edge around to the middle.

The bridge windows sloped gently outward. Above them was the lip of the upper deck, with its own toe-rail. Waiting for a lull between gusts, LeSeur heaved himself up and gasped the upper rim, simultaneously planting his feet onto the rail below. He stood there a long moment, heart pounding, feeling dreadfully exposed. Plastered against the bridge windows, limbs extended, he could feel the roll of the ship even more acutely.

He took a deep, shivery breath, then another. And then he began to edge his way around—clinging to the rim with freezing fingers, bracing himself afresh with every gust of wind. The bridge was one hundred sixty feet across, he knew; that meant an eighty-foot journey along the rail before he faced the bridge workstation and helm.

He edged around, sliding one foot after the other. The rail was not gritted—it was never meant for human contact—and as a consequence it was devilishly slippery. He moved slowly, deliberately, taking most of his weight with his fingers as he crept along the polished rail, his fingers clinging to the gel-coated edge of the upper toe-rail. A big, booming wind buffeted him, sucking his feet from the rail, and for a moment he dangled, terrified, over churning gray space. He scrambled for purchase, then hesitated yet again, gulping air, his heart hammering, fingers numb. After a minute he forced himself onward.

At last, he reached the center of the bridge. And there she was: Captain Mason, at the helm, calmly looking out at him.

He stared back, shocked at the utter normality of her expression. She didn't even register surprise at his improbable appearance: a specter in foul-weather gear, clinging to the wrong side of the bridge windows.

Taking a renewed grip on the upper rail with his left hand, he banged on the window with his right. "Mason! *Mason!*"

She returned his gaze, making eye contact, but in an almost absent-minded fashion.

"What are you doing?"

No response.

"God damn it, Mason, *talk to me*!" He slammed his fist against the glass so hard it hurt.

Still she merely looked back.

"Mason!"

At last, she stepped around from the helm and walked up to the glass. Her voice came to him faintly, filtering through the glass and the roar of the storm. "The question is, Mr. LeSeur, what are *you* doing?"

"Don't you realize we're on a collision course with the Carrion Rocks?"

Another twitch of the lips, harbinger of a smile. She said something he couldn't hear over the storm.

"I can't hear you!" He clung to the rim, wondering how long until his fingers gave out and he fell away into the furious gray spume.

"I said"—she moved to the glass and spoke louder—"that I'm well aware of it."

"But why?"

The smile finally came, like sun glittering on ice. "That *is* the question, isn't it, Mr. LeSeur?"

He pressed himself against the glass, struggling to maintain his grip. He knew he wouldn't be able to hold on much longer.

"Why?" he screamed.

"Ask the company."

"But you . . . you can't be doing this *deliberately*!"

"Why not?"

He stopped himself from screaming to her that she was mad. He had to reach her, find her motives, reason with her. "For God's sake, you don't mean to murder four thousand people like this!"

"I have nothing against the passengers or crew. However, I *am* going to destroy this ship."

LeSeur wasn't sure if it was rain or tears on his face. "Captain, look. If there are problems in your life, problems with the company, we can work them out. But this . . . there are thousands of innocent people on board, many women and children. I beg you, please don't do this. *Please!*"

"People die every day."

"Is this some kind of terrorist attack? I mean"—he swallowed, trying to think of a neutral way of putting it—"are you representing a . . . a particular political or religious point of view?"

Her smile remained cold, controlled. "Since you ask, the answer is no. This is strictly personal."

"If you want to wreck the ship, stop it first. At least let us launch the lifeboats!"

"You know perfectly well that if I even slow the ship down, they'll be able to land a SWAT team and take me out. No doubt half the passengers have been e-mailing the outside world. A massive response is unquestionably under way. No, Mr. LeSeur, speed is my ally, and the *Britannia*'s destination is the Carrion Rocks." She glanced at the autopilot chartplotter. "In one hundred and forty-nine minutes."

He pounded his fist on the glass. *"No!"* The effort almost caused him to fall. He scrabbled to recover, ripping his nails on the gelcoat and watching, helplessly, as she resumed her position at the helm, her eyes focusing into the grayness of the storm.

55

At the sound of the door opening, Constance sat up. The open door brought with it the muffled noise of panic: shouts, curses, pounding feet. Pendergast stepped inside and closed the door behind him.

He walked across the entryway, something large and heavy balanced on one shoulder. As he drew closer Constance saw that it was an ivory-colored canvas duffle, snugged closed with a drawstring. He stopped at the door to the kitchen, unshouldered the duffle, dusted off his hands, then walked into the living room.

"You made the tea, at least," he said, pouring himself a cup and taking a seat in a nearby leather armchair. "Excellent."

She looked at him coolly. "I'm still waiting to hear your theory about what's going on."

Pendergast took a slow, appraising sip of tea. "Did you know that the Carrion Rocks are one of the greatest hazards to shipping in the North Atlantic? So much so that right after the *Titanic* sank, they first thought it might have fetched up on them."

"How interesting." She looked at him, sitting in the

armchair, calmly sipping his tea as if there were no crisis at all. And then she realized: perhaps there was no crisis.

"You have a plan," she said. It was a statement, not a question.

"Indeed I do. And come to think of it, perhaps now is the time to familiarize you with the details. It will save some effort later on, when we might have to react to changing situations rather quickly."

He took another languid sip. Then, putting the teacup aside, he stood and walked toward the kitchen. Tugging the laundry duffle open, he pulled something large out of it and stepped back into the living room, placing it on the floor between them.

Constance stared at it curiously. It was an oblong, hard-shelled container of white rubber and plastic, about four feet by three, lashed shut with nylon straps. Various warning labels were stamped on its face. As she watched, Pendergast removed the nylon straps and detached the faceplate. Nestled inside was a tightly folded device of Day-Glo yellow polyurethane.

"A self-inflating buoyant apparatus," said Pendergast. "Known familiarly as a 'survival bubble.' Equipped with SOLAS B packs, an EPI radio beacon, blankets, and provisions. Each of the *Britannia*'s freefall lifeboats is equipped with one. I, ah, *liberated* this from one of them."

Constance stared from the container to Pendergast and back again.

"If the officers prove unable to stop the captain, they may try to launch the ship's lifeboats," he explained. "Doing so at this rate of speed would be dangerous, perhaps foolhardy. On the other hand, we will encounter minimal risk if we launch ourselves into the water in *this* from the stern of the ship. Of course, we will have to be careful where we effect our evacuation."

"Evacuation," Constance repeated.

"It will have to be from a deck low over the waterline, obviously." He reached over to the side table, picked up a ship's brochure, and pulled out a glossy photograph of the *Britannia*. "I'd suggest this spot," he said, pointing to a row of large windows low in the stern. "That would be the King George II ballroom. It will most likely be deserted given the current emergency. We could precipitate a chair or table through the window, clear ourselves a hole, and launch. We'll of course convey the apparatus down there hidden in that duffle to avoid attracting attention." He thought for a moment. "It would be wise to wait thirty minutes or so; that will bring us close enough to the impact site to be within reasonable distance of rescue vessels, but not so close that we will be hindered by last-minute panic. If we launch ourselves from one of the ballroom's side windows, here or here, we'll avoid the worst of the ship's wake." He put the photograph aside with a sigh of self-satisfaction, as if well pleased with this plan.

"You say 'we,'" Constance said, speaking slowly. "That is, just the two of us."

Pendergast glanced at her in mild surprise. "Yes, of course. But don't be concerned: I know it may look small inside this case, but it will be certainly large enough for both of us when fully inflated. The bubble is designed to hold four, so we should find ourselves easily accommodated."

She stared at him in disbelief. "You're proposing to save yourself and just leave the rest to die?"

Pendergast frowned. "Constance, I will not be spoken to in that tone of voice."

She rose in a cold fury. "*You* . . ." She choked off the word. "Stealing that flotation device from one of the lifeboats . . . You weren't out there looking for a way to defuse the crisis or rescue the *Britannia*. You were just arranging to save your own skin!"

"As it happens, I'm rather attached to my skin. And I shouldn't have to remind you, Constance, that I'm offering to save *yours*, as well."

"This isn't like you," she said, disbelief, shock, and anger mingling. "This gross selfishness. What's *happened* to you, Aloysius? Ever since you returned from Blackburn's cabin, you've been . . . bizarre. Not yourself."

He looked back at her for a long moment. Silently, he reattached the faceplate to the plastic enclosure. Then he rose and stepped forward.

"Sit down, Constance," he said quietly. And there was something in the tone of his voice—something strange, something utterly foreign—that, despite her rage and shock and disbelief, made her instantly obey.

56

LeSeur took a seat in the conference room adjacent to the aux bridge. He was still soaked to the skin, but now, instead of being cold, he felt like he was suffocating in the heat and the smell of sweaty bodies. The room, meant to hold half a dozen people, was packed with deck officers and senior crew, and more were still arriving.

LeSeur didn't even wait for them to sort out their places before he stood up, rapped his knuckles on the table, and began.

"I just talked to Mason," he said. "She confirmed that her plan is to run the *Britannia* onto the Carrion Rocks at flank speed. So far, we haven't been able to break into the bridge or bypass the autopilot. And I haven't been able to find a doctor or psychiatrist sufficiently compos mentis to either diagnose her condition or suggest a line of reasoning that might work with her."

He looked around.

"I've had several conversations with the captain of the *Grenfell*, the only ship close enough to attempt a rescue. Other ships—civilian and Coast Guard—have been diverted. They won't get to us before the estimated collision. The Canadian CG has also dispatched two fixed-wing aircraft for surveillance and communication purposes. They have a fleet of helicopters on standby, but as of now we're still out of range of coastal rotary aircraft. We can't expect any help from that quarter. And the *Grenfell* is in no way equipped to handle four thousand three hundred evacuees."

He paused, took a deep breath. "We're in the middle of a storm, with forty-foot seas and forty- to sixty-knot winds. But our most intractable problem is the ship's speed relative to the water: twenty-nine knots." He licked his lips. "We would have many options if we weren't moving—transfer of people to the *Grenfell,* boarding by a SWAT team. But none of that's feasible at twenty-nine knots." He looked around. "So, people, I need ideas, and I need them now."

"What about disabling the engines?" someone asked. "You know, sabotaging them."

LeSeur glanced at the chief engineer. "Mr. Halsey?"

The engineer scowled. "We've got four diesel engines boosted by two General Electric LM2500 gas turbines. Shut down one diesel and nothing happens. Shut down two, and you better shut down those turbines or you'll get a gas compression explosion."

"Disable the gas turbines first, then?" LeSeur asked.

"They're high-pressure jet engines, sir, rotating at thirty-six hundred rpm. Any attempt to intervene while that bastard is running at high speed would be . . . suicide. You'd tear out the bottom of the ship."

"Cut the shafts, then?" a second officer asked.

"There are no shafts," said the engineer. "Each pod

is a self-contained propulsion system. The diesel and turbines generate electricity that powers the pods."

"Jam the drive gears?" LeSeur asked.

"I've looked into that. Inaccessible while under way."

"What about simply cutting all electric power to the engines?"

The chief engineer frowned. "Can't do it. Same reason they hardened the bridge and the autopilot system—fear of a terrorist attack. The geniuses in the Home Office decided to design a ship that, if terrorists tried to commandeer it, there'd be nothing they could do to disable or take control of the vessel. No matter what, they wanted the officers locked into the bridge to be able to bring the ship into port, even if terrorists took over the rest of the vessel."

"Speaking of the bridge," a third officer said, "what if we were to drill through the security hatch and pump in gas? Anything that will displace the air within. Hell, the kitchen has several canisters of CO_2. You know, knock her out."

"And then what? We're still on autopilot."

There was a brief silence. Then the IT head, Hufnagel, a bespectacled man in a lab coat, cleared his throat. "The autopilot is a piece of software like any other," he said in a quiet voice. "It can be hacked—in theory, anyway. Hack it and reprogram it."

LeSeur rounded on him. "How? It's firewalled."

"No firewall's impregnable."

"Get your best man on it, right away."

"That would be Penner, sir." The head of IT stood up.

"Report back to me as soon as possible."

"Yes, sir."

LeSeur watched him leave the conference room. "Any other ideas?"

"What about the military?" asked Crowley, another third officer. "They could scramble fighters, take out the bridge with a missile. Or get a sub to disable the screws with a torpedo."

"We've looked into those possibilities," LeSeur replied. "There's no way to aim a missile precisely enough. There aren't any submarines in the vicinity, and, given our speed, there's no way for one to intercept or catch us."

"Is there a way to launch the lifeboats?" a voice in the back asked.

LeSeur turned to the bosun, Liu. "Possible?"

"At a speed of thirty knots, in heavy seas . . . Jesus, I can't even *imagine* how you'd do it."

"I don't want to hear what you can't imagine. If it's even remotely possible, I want you to look into it."

"Yes, sir. I'll find out if it's possible. But to do that I'll need a full emergency launch crew—and they're all tied up."

LeSeur cursed. The one thing they lacked were experienced deckhands. Sure, they had every bloody plonker in the world on board, from croupiers to masseurs to lounge crooners—all so much ballast. "That man who came up here a while ago, what's his name? Bruce. He was ex–Royal Navy and so were his friends. Go find him. Enlist his help."

"But he was an old man, in his seventies—" Kemper protested.

"Mr. Kemper, I've known seventy-year-old ex-navy

men who could drop you in two rounds." He turned back to Crowley. "Get moving."

A voice boomed from the door, in a broad Scots accent. "No need to find me, Mr. LeSeur." Bruce pushed his way through the crowd. "Gavin Bruce, at your service."

LeSeur turned. "Mr. Bruce. Have you been apprised of our current situation?"

"I have."

"We need to know whether we can launch the lifeboats under these conditions and speed. Have you experience in that line? These are a new kind of lifeboat—freefall."

Bruce rubbed his chin thoughtfully. "We'll have to take a close look at those boats." He hesitated. "We might launch them after the collision."

"We can't wait until after the collision. Striking a shoal at thirty knots . . . half the people on board would be killed or injured by the impact alone."

This was greeted by silence. After a moment, Bruce nodded slowly.

"Mr. Bruce, I give you and your group full authority to address this issue. The bosun, Mr. Liu, assisted by Third Officer Crowley, will direct you—they are thoroughly familiar with the abandon-ship routines."

"Yes, Captain."

LeSeur looked around the room. "There's something else. We need Commodore Cutter. He knows the ship better than any of us and . . . well, he's the only one who knows the number sequence for standing down from a Code Three. I'm going to call him back to the bridge."

"As master?" Kemper asked.

LeSeur hesitated. "Let's just see what he says, first." He glanced at his watch.

Eighty-nine minutes.

57

Captain Carol Mason stood at the bridge workstation, staring calmly at the thirty-two-inch plasma-screen Northstar 941X DGPS chartplotter running infonav 2.2. It was, she thought, a marvel of electronic engineering, a technology that had virtually rendered obsolete the skills, mathematics, experience, and deep intuition once required for piloting and navigation. With this device, a bright twelve-year-old could practically navigate the *Britannia*: using this big colorful chart with the little ship on it, a line drawn ahead showing the ship's course, conveniently marked with estimated positions at ten-minute intervals into the future, along with waypoints for each course alteration.

She glanced over at the autopilot. Another marvel; it constantly monitored the ship's speed through the water, its ground speed, engine rpms, power output, rudder and pod angles, and made countless adjustments so subtle they were not even perceptible to even the most vessel-savvy officer. It kept the ship on course and at speed better than the most skilled human captain, while saving fuel—which is why the standing orders dictated that the autopilot should be used for all but inland or coastal waters.

Ten years ago, the bridge on a ship like this would have required the minimum presence of three highly trained officers; now, it required only one . . . and, for the most part, she hardly had anything to do.

She turned her attention to LeSeur's navigation table, with its paper charts, parallel rulers, compasses, pencils and markers, and the case that held the man's sextant. Dead instruments, dead skills.

She walked around the bridge workstation and back to the helm, resting one hand on the elegant mahogany wheel. It was there strictly for show. To its right stood the helmsman's console where the real business of steering was done: six little joysticks, manipulated with the touch of a finger, that controlled the two fixed and two rotating propulsion pods and the engine throttles. With its 360-degree aft rotating pods, the ship was so maneuverable it could dock without help from a single tug.

She slid her hand along the smooth varnish of the wheel, raising her glance to the wall of gray windows that stood ahead. As the wind intensified the rain had slackened, and now she could see the outline of the bows shuddering through spectacular forty-foot seas, great eruptions of spray and flying spume sweeping across the foredecks in slow-motion explosions of white.

She felt a kind of peace, an utter emptiness, that went beyond anything she had experienced before. Most of her life she had been knotted up by self-reproach, feelings of inadequacy, self-doubt, anger, overweening ambition. Now, all that was gone—blessedly gone. Decision-making had never been so simple, and afterward there had been none of that agonizing second-guessing that had tormented her career decisions. She had made a decision to destroy the ship; it had been done calmly and without emotion; and now all that remained was to carry it out.

Why? LeSeur had asked. If he couldn't guess why, then she wasn't going to give him the satisfaction of spelling it out. To her, it was obvious. There had never been—not once—a female captain on one of the great transatlantic liners. How foolish she had been to think she would be the one to break the teak ceiling. She knew—and this was not vanity—that she was twice the captain of most of her peers. She had graduated at the very top of her class at the Newcastle Maritime Academy, with one of the highest scores in the history of the school. Her record was perfect—unblemished. She had even remained single, despite several excellent opportunities, in order to eliminate any question of maternity leave. With exquisite care she had cultivated the right relationships at the company, sought out the right mentors, all the while taking care never to display careerist tendencies; she had assiduously cultivated the crisp, professional, but not unpleasant demeanor of the best captains, always genuinely pleased at the success of her peers.

She had moved easily up the ladder, to second, then first, and finally staff captain, on schedule. Yes, there had been comments along the way, unpleasant remarks, and unwelcome sexual advances from superiors, but she had always handled them with aplomb, never rocking the boat, never complaining, treating certain vile and buffoonish superiors with the utmost correctness and respect, pretending not to hear their offensive, vulgar comments and disgusting proposals. She treated them all with good humor, as if they had uttered some clever bon mot.

When the *Oceania* had been launched four years ago, she and two other staff captains were in line for the command—herself, along with Cutter and Thrale. Thrale, the least competent, who had a drinking problem besides, had gotten it. Cutter, who was the better captain, has missed it because of his prickly, reclusive personality. But she—the best captain of the three by far—had been passed over. Why?

She was a woman.

That wasn't even the worst of it. All her peers had commiserated with Cutter, even though many of them disliked the man. Everyone took him aside and expressed the opinion that it was a shame he didn't get it, that the captaincy was really his, that the company had made a mistake—and they all assured him he'd get the next one.

None of them had taken her aside like that. No one had commiserated with her. They all *assumed* that, as a woman, she didn't expect it and, moreover, couldn't handle it. Most of them had been jolly fellows together in the Royal Navy; that had been denied her as a woman. No one ever knew about the burning slight she had felt—knowing that she was the best candidate of the three, with the most seniority and the highest ratings.

She should have realized it then.

And then came the *Britannia*. The largest, most luxurious ocean liner ever built. It cost the company almost a billion pounds. And she was now the clear choice. The command was hers almost by default . . .

Except that Cutter got it. And then, as if to compound the insult, they had somehow thought she would be grateful for the bone of staff captain.

Cutter was not stupid. He knew very well that she deserved the command. He also knew she was the better captain. And he hated her for it. He felt threatened. Even before they were aboard, he had taken every opportunity to find fault with her, to belittle her. And then he had made it clear that, unlike most other liner captains, he would not spend his time chatting up the passengers and hosting cheery dinners at the captain's table. He would spend his time on the bridge—usurping her rightful place.

And she had promptly given him the ammunition he needed in his struggle to humiliate her. The first infraction of discipline in her entire life—and it occurred even before the *Britannia* left port. She must have known then, subconsciously, that she would never command a big ship.

Strange that Blackburn should have booked the maiden voyage of the *Britannia:* the man who had first proposed to her, whom she had turned down out of her own burning ambition. Ironic, too, that he had become a billionaire in the decade since their relationship.

What an amazing three hours they had passed together, every moment now seared into her memory. His stateroom had been a marvel. He had filled the salon with his favorite treasures, million-dollar paintings, sculpture, rare antiquities. He had been particularly excited about a Tibetan painting he had just acquired—apparently not twenty-four hours earlier—and in his initial flush of excitement and pride he'd taken it out of its box and unrolled it for her on the floor of the salon. She had stared at it, thunderstruck, astounded, speechless, falling to her hands and knees to see it closer, to trace with her eyes and fingers every infinite fractal detail of it. It drew her in, exploded her mind. And as she had stared—mesmerized, almost swooning—he had pulled her skirt up over her hips, torn away her panties, and, like a mad stallion, mounted her. It had been the kind of sex that she'd never experienced before and would never forget; even the smallest detail, the tiniest drop of sweat, the softest moan, every grasp and thrust of flesh into flesh. Just thinking of it made her tingle with fresh passion.

Too bad it would never happen again.

Because afterwards, Blackburn had rolled up the magical painting, returned it to its box. Still aglow with the flush of their coupling, she had asked him not to; asked him to let her gaze upon it again. He'd turned, no doubt seen the hunger in her expression. Instantly, his eyes had narrowed to jealous, possessive little points. He'd jeered, said that she'd seen it once and didn't need to see it again. And then—as quickly as lust had swept over her—a dark, consuming anger filled her. They had screamed at each other with an intensity she never knew she was capable of. The speed with which her emotions whipsawed had been as shocking as it had been exhilarating. And then Blackburn had ordered her to leave. No—she would never speak to him again, never gaze upon the painting again.

And then came the supreme irony. Their shouting had provoked the passenger in the next cabin to complain. She had been seen leaving the triplex. Someone reported her. And that had been an opportunity Cutter couldn't miss. He had humiliated her on the bridge, in front of all the deck officers. She had no doubt it had already gone into her file and would be reported back to the company.

Many of the officers and crew, even the married ones, had sexual liaisons on board; it was so easy, like shooting fish in a barrel. They never seemed to get reported—because they were men. Men were expected to do this sort of thing, discreetly and on their own time, just as she had done. But it was different for a woman . . . or so company culture seemed to say.

Her career was over. All she could hope for now was the command of a middling-size cruise ship, one of the shabbier ones that tooled aimlessly around the Mediterranean or the Caribbean, stuffed with fat, white, middle-class seniors on a floating excursion of eating and shopping. Never seeing blue water, running from every storm.

Cutter. What better way to exact revenge than to take his ship from him, rip its guts out, and send it to the bottom of the Atlantic?

58

For several minutes, Constance watched as Pendergast paced back and forth across the living room of the Tudor Suite. Once he paused as if to speak, but he merely began pacing again. At last, he turned to her. "You accuse me of selfish behavior. Of wishing to save myself at the expense of others on board the *Britannia*. Tell me something, Constance: exactly who on board ship do you consider worth saving?"

He fell silent again, waiting for an answer, the light of amusement lurking in his eyes. This was the last thing Constance had expected to hear.

"I asked you a question," Pendergast went on, when she didn't answer. "Who among the vulgar, greedy, vile crowd on board this ship do you deem worthy of being saved?"

Still, Constance said nothing.

After a moment, Pendergast scoffed. "You see? You have no reply—because there is no reply."

"That's not true," Constance said.

"Truth? You're fooling yourself. *What is truth? said jesting Pilate, and would not stay for an answer.* From the moment you boarded this vessel, you yourself were revolted by the wretched excess, appalled by the smarmy self-satisfaction of the rich and pampered. You yourself noted the shocking inequity between the serving and the served. Your behavior at dinner on that very first night, the ripostes you made to those unbearably gauche philistines we were forced to dine with, showed you had already pronounced judgment on the *Britannia*. And you were right to do so. Because I ask you again, another way: *is not this very ship a floating monument to man's cupidity, vulgarity, and stupidity?* Is not this palace of crass concupiscence richly deserving of destruction?"

He spread his hands as if the answer was obvious.

Constance looked at him in confusion. What he was saying did strike her as true. She had been repulsed by the bourgeois airs and pork-belly gentility of most of the passengers she'd met. And she was shocked and outraged by the brutal working and living conditions of the crew. Some of the things Pendergast was saying rang an uncomfortable chord in her, arousing and reinforcing her own long-held misanthropic impulses.

"No, Constance," Pendergast went on. "The only two people worth saving are ourselves."

She shook her head. "You're referring to the passengers. What about the crew and staff? They're just trying to make a living. Do they deserve to die?"

Pendergast waved his hand. "And they, for their part, are expendable drones, part of the great sea of working-class humanity that comes and goes from the shores of the world like the tide on the beach, leaving no mark."

"You can't mean that. Humanity is everything to you.

You've spent your whole life trying to save the lives of others."

"Then I've wasted my life on a useless, even frivolous, endeavor. The one thing my brother Diogenes and I always agreed on was there could be no more odious a discipline than anthropology: imagine, devoting one's life to the study of one's fellow man." He picked up Brock's monograph from the table, flipped through it, handed it to Constance. "Look at this."

Constance glanced at the open page. It contained a black-and-white reproduction of an oil painting: a young, ravishing angel bending over a perplexed-looking man, guiding his hand over a manuscript page.

"*Saint Matthew and the Angel*," he said. "Do you know it?"

She glanced at him, puzzled. "Yes."

"Then you know there were few images on this earth more sublime. Or more beautiful. Look at the expression of intense effort on Matthew's face—as if every word of the Gospel he's writing was struggling up from the very fiber of his being. And compare it to the languid approach of the angel assisting him—the way the head lolls; the half-naïve, half-coy posturing of the legs; the almost scandalously sensual face. Look at the way Matthew's dusty left foot kicks out at us, almost breaking the plane of the painting. No wonder the patron refused it! But if the angel seems effeminate, we only need to glimpse the power, the glory in those magnificent wings, to remind us that we are in the presence of the divine." He paused a moment. "Do you know, Constance, why—of all the reproductions in this monograph—this one is in black and white?"

"No, I don't."

"Because no color photograph of it exists. The painting was destroyed. Yes—this magnificent expression of creative genius was bombed into oblivion during World War II. Now, tell me: if I had to choose between this painting or the lives of a million useless, ignorant, ephemeral people—the humanity you say is so important to me—which do you think *I'd* choose to perish in that conflagration?" He pushed the image toward her.

Constance stared at him in horror. "How can you say such a vile thing? And what gives you the *right* to say it? What makes you so different?"

"My dear Constance! Don't think for a minute that I believe I'm better than the rest of the horde. I'm as guilty of the fundamental flaws of bestial man as anyone. And one of those flaws is self-interest. I am worth saving because I wish my life to continue—and I'm in a position to do something about it. This is not just the thin end of the wedge anymore: we are sailing toward catastrophe at flank speed. And on a practical level, how could I possibly save this ship? As in any catastrophe, it's every man for himself."

"Do you really think you could live with yourself if you abandoned all these people to their fate?"

"Of course I could. And so could you."

Constance hesitated. "I'm not so sure," she murmured. Deep down, a part of her found something deeply seductive in his words—and that is what disturbed her most of all.

"These people mean nothing to us. They are like the dead you read about in the newspapers. We will simply leave this floating Gomorrah and return to New York. We shall lose ourselves in intellectual pastimes, philosophy, poetry, discourse: 891 Riverside is exceedingly well furnished as a place of retirement, reflection, and seclusion." He paused. "And was this not the way of your own first guardian, my distant relation, Enoch Leng? His crimes were far more heinous than our little moment of self-interest. And yet he managed to devote himself to a life of physical comfort and intellectual satisfaction. A long, *long* life. You know this to be true, Constance: you were there with him, all along." And he nodded again, as if this were the killing stroke of his argument.

"It's true. I *was* there. I was there to see the pangs of conscience slowly eat through his peace of mind like worms through rotten wood. In the end there was so little left of a brilliant man it was almost a blessing when . . ." She could say no more. But her mind was made up now: she knew she could not be persuaded by Pendergast's nihilistic message. "Aloysius, I don't care what you say. This is horribly wrong. You've always helped others. You've devoted your entire career to it."

"Precisely! And to what advantage? What has it ever profited me other than frustration, regret, alienation, mortification, pain, and reprimand? If I were to leave the FBI, do you think my absence would be mourned? Thanks in part to my own incompetence, my only friend in the Bureau died a most unpleasant death. No, Constance: I have *at last* learned a bitter truth. All this time, I've been laboring pointlessly—the fruitless labor of

Sisyphus—trying to save that which, ultimately, is unsalvageable." With that he eased himself down again in the leather armchair and picked up his teacup.

Constance looked at him in horror. "This isn't the Aloysius Pendergast I know. You've changed. Ever since you came back from Blackburn's stateroom, you've been acting strangely."

Pendergast took another sip of tea, sniffed dismissively. "I'll tell you what happened. The scales finally fell from my eyes." Carefully, he placed the teacup back on the table and sat forward. "*It* showed me the truth."

"It?"

"The Agozyen. It's a truly remarkable object, Constance, a mandala that allows you to see through to the *real* truth at the center of the world: the pure, unadulterated truth. A truth so powerful that it would break a weak mind. But for those of us with strong intellects, it is a revelation. I *know* myself now: who I am, and—most importantly—*what I want*."

"Don't you remember what the monks said? The Agozyen is evil, a dark instrument of vengeance, whose purpose is to cleanse the world."

"Yes. A somewhat ambiguous choice of words, isn't it? *Cleanse* the world. I, of course, will not put it to such purpose. Rather, I will install it in the library of our Riverside Drive mansion, where I can spend a lifetime contemplating its wonders." Pendergast sat back and picked up his teacup again. "The Agozyen will thus accompany me into the flotation device. As will you—*assuming* you find my plan to be a palatable one."

Constance swallowed. She did not reply.

"Time is growing short. The time has come for you to make your decision, Constance—are you with me . . . or against me?"

And as he took another sip, his pale cat's eyes regarded her calmly over the rim of the teacup.

59

LeSeur had decided that the best way was to go alone.

Now he paused before the plain metal door to Commodore Cutter's quarters, trying to calm his facial muscles and regulate his breathing. Once he felt as composed as possible, he stepped forward and knocked softly, two quick taps.

The door opened so quickly that LeSeur almost jumped. He was even more startled to see the commodore in civilian dress, wearing a gray suit and tie. The ex-master stood in the doorway, his cold stare affixed somewhere above and between LeSeur's eyes, his small body projecting a granitelike solidity.

"Commodore Cutter," LeSeur began, "I've come in my authority as acting captain of the ship to . . . ask for your assistance."

Cutter continued to stare, the pressure of his gaze like a finger pushing on the middle of LeSeur's forehead.

"May I come in?"

"If you wish." Cutter stepped back. The quarters, which LeSeur had not seen before, were predictably spartan—functional, neat, and impersonal. There were no family pictures, no naval or nautical knick-knacks, none of the masculine accessories you normally saw in a captain's quarters such as a cigar humidor, bar, or red leather armchairs.

Cutter did not invite LeSeur to sit down and remained standing himself.

"Commodore," LeSeur began again slowly, "how much do you know about the situation the ship is in now?"

"I know only what I've heard on the PA," said Cutter. "Nobody has visited me. Nobody has bothered to speak to me."

"Then you don't know that Captain Mason seized the bridge, took over the ship, increased speed to flank, and is intent on driving the *Britannia* onto the Carrion Rocks?"

A beat, and he mouthed the answer. *No.*

"We can't figure out how to stop her. She locked down the bridge with a Code Three. We strike the rocks in just over an hour."

At this, Cutter took a slight step backward, wavered on his feet, then steadied. His face lost a little of its color. He said nothing.

LeSeur quickly explained the details. Cutter listened without interruption, face impassive. "Commodore," LeSeur concluded, "only you and the staff captain know the cipher sequence for shutting down a Code Three alert. Even if we managed to get on the bridge and take Mason into custody, we would still have to stand down from Code Three before we could gain control of the ship's autopilot. You know those codes. Nobody else does."

A silence. And then Cutter said, "The company has the codes."

LeSeur grimaced. "They claim to be looking for them. Frankly, Corporate is in utter disarray over this situation. Nobody seems to know where they are, and everybody is pointing fingers at everyone else."

The flush returned to the captain's face. LeSeur wondered what it was. Fear for the ship? Anger at Mason?

"Sir, it isn't just a question of the code. You know the ship better than anyone else. We've got a crisis on our hands and four thousand lives hang in the balance. We've only got seventy minutes until we hit Carrion Rocks. We *need* you."

"Mr. LeSeur, are you asking me to resume command of this ship?" came the quiet question.

"If that's what it takes, yes."

"Say it."

"I'm asking you, Commodore Cutter, to resume command of the *Britannia*."

The captain's dark eyes glittered. When he spoke again, his voice was low and resonating with emotion. "Mr. LeSeur, you and the deck officers are mutineers. You are the vilest kind of human being to be found on the high seas. Some actions are so heinous they can't be reversed. You mutinied and turned my command over to a psychopath. You and all your backstabbing, toadying, conniving, skulking lickspittles have been planning this treachery against me since we left port. Now you've reaped the whirlwind. No, sir: I will not help you. Not with the codes, not with the ship, not even to wipe your sorry nose. My remaining duty consists of only one thing: if the ship sinks, I will go down with it. Good day, Mr. LeSeur."

The flush on Cutter's face deepened still further, and LeSeur suddenly understood that it was not the result of anger, hatred, or apprehension. No—it was a flush of triumph: the sick triumph of vindication.

60

Dressed in the saffron robes of a Tibetan Buddhist monk, Scott Blackburn drew the curtains across the sliding glass doors of his balcony, shutting out the grayness of the storm. Hundreds of butter candles filled the salon with a trembling yellow light, while two brass censers scented the air with the exquisite fragrance of sandalwood and kewra flower.

On a side table, a phone was ringing insistently. He eyed it with a frown, then walked over and picked it up.

"What is it?" he said shortly.

"Scotty?" came the high, breathless voice. "It's me, Jason. We've been trying to reach your for hours! Look, everyone's going crazy, we need to get ourselves to—"

"Shut the fuck up," Blackburn said. "If you call me again, I'll rip your throat out and flush it down the toilet." And he gently replaced the receiver in its cradle.

His senses had never felt so keen, so alert, so focused. Beyond the doors of his suite he could hear shouting and cursing, pounding feet, screams, the deep boom of the sea. Whatever was happening, it did not concern him, and it could not touch him in his locked stateroom. Here he was safe—with the Agozyen.

As he went through his preparations, he thought about the strange trajectory of the last several days, and how his life had transcendentally changed. The call out of nowhere about the painting; seeing it for the first time in the hotel room; liberating it from its callow and undeserving owner; bringing it aboard ship. And then, that very same day, running into Carol Mason, staff captain on the ship—how strange life was! In the first flush of proud possession, he had shared the Agozyen with her, and then they had fucked so wildly, with such total abandon, that the coupling seemed to shiver the very foundations of his being. But then he had seen the change in her, just as he had seen the change in himself. He'd noticed the unmistakable, possessive hunger in her eyes, the glorious and terrifying abandonment of all the old and hidebound moral strictures.

It was only then he realized what he should have realized before: he had to be transcendentally careful to safeguard his prize. All who saw it would desire to possess it. Because the Agozyen, this incredible mandala-universe, had a unique power over the human mind. A power that could be *liberated*. And he, above all others, was in the perfect position to liberate it. He had the capital, the savvy, and—above all—the *technology.* With his graphical push technology he could deliver the image, in all its exquisite detail, to the entire world, at great profit and power to himself. With his unlimited access to capital and talent, he could unlock the image's secrets and learn how it wrought its amazing effects on the human mind and body, and apply that information to the creation of other images. Everyone on the earth—at least, everyone who mattered even in the least degree—would be changed utterly. He would own the original; he would control how its likeness would be disseminated. The world would be a new place: *his* place.

Except that there was another who knew about the murder he'd committed. An investigator who—he was now convinced—had pursued him onto the ship. A man who was employing every possible means, even housekeepers on the *Britannia* staff, to take from him his most precious possession. At the thought, he felt his blood pound, his heart quicken; he felt a hatred so intense that his ears seemed to hum and crackle with it. How the man learned about the Agozyen mandala, Blackburn didn't know. Perhaps Ambrose had tried to sell it to him first; perhaps the man was another adept. But in the end it didn't matter how the man had learned of it: his hours were severely numbered. Blackburn had seen the destructive work of a tulpa before, and the one he had summoned—through sheer force of will—was extraordinarily subtle and powerful. No human being could escape it.

He took a deep, shivering breath. He could not approach the Agozyen in such a state of hatred and fear, of material attachment. Trying to fulfill earthly desires was like carrying water to the sea; a never-ending task, and an ultimately useless one.

Taking deep, slow breaths, he sat down and closed his eyes, concentrating on nothing. When he felt the ripples in his mind smooth out, he stood again, walked to the far wall of the salon, removed the Braque painting, turned it over, and unfastened the false lining, exposing the thangka beneath. This he drew out with exquisite care and—keeping his eyes averted—hung it by a silken cord on a golden hook he had driven into the wall nearby.

Blackburn took his place before the painting and arranged himself in the lotus position, placing his right hand on his left, the thumbs touching to form a triangle. He bent his neck slightly and allowed the top of his tongue to touch the roof of his mouth near his upper teeth, his gaze unfocused and on the floor before him. Then, with delicious slowness, he raised his eyes and gazed upon the Agozyen mandala.

The image was beautifully illuminated by the glittering candles arrayed on silver platters, yellow and gold tints that played like liquid metal over the thangka's surface. Gradually—very gradually—it opened to him. He felt its power flow through him like slow electricity.

The Agozyen mandala was a world unto itself, a separate universe as intricate and deep as our own, an infinite complexity locked on a two-dimensional surface with four edges. But to gaze upon the Agozyen was to magically liberate the image from its two dimensions. It took shape and form within the mind; the painting's strange, intertwined lines becoming as so many electric wires flowing with the currents of his soul. As he became the painting and the painting became him, time slowed, dissolved, and ultimately ceased to exist; the mandala suffused his consciousness and his soul, owning him utterly: space without space, time without time, becoming everything and nothing at once . . .

61

The hush that had fallen over the dimly lit salon of the Tudor Suite belied the undercurrent of tension in the stateroom. Constance stood before Pendergast, watching as the agent calmly took another sip of his tea and placed the cup aside.

"Well?" he asked. "We don't have all day."

Constance took a deep breath. "Aloysius, I can't believe you can sit there, so calmly, advocating something that's against everything you've ever stood for."

Pendergast sighed with ill-concealed impatience. "Please don't insult my intelligence by protracting this pointless argument."

"Somehow, the Agozyen has poisoned your mind."

"The Agozyen has done no such thing. It has *liberated* my mind. Swept it clean of jejune and hidebound conventions of morality."

"The Agozyen is an instrument of evil. The monks knew as much."

"You mean, the monks who were too fearful to even gaze upon the Agozyen themselves?"

"Yes, and they were wiser than you. It seems the

Agozyen has the power to strip away all that is good, and kind, and . . . and *moderate* in those who gaze upon it. Look what it did to Blackburn, how he murdered to get it. Look what it's doing to you."

Pendergast scoffed. "It breaks a weaker mind, but strengthens the stronger one. Look what it did to that maid, or to Captain Mason, for that matter."

"What?"

"Really, Constance, I expected better of you. Of course Mason has seen it—what other explanation could there be? How, I don't know and don't care. She's behind the disappearances and murders—very carefully escalated, you'll notice—all to effect a mutiny and get the ship to divert to St. John's, on which heading she could contrive to run it up onto the Carrion Rocks."

Constance stared at him. The theory seemed preposterous—or did it? Almost despite herself, she could see some of the details begin to lock into place.

"But none of that is important anymore." Pendergast waved his hand. "I won't stand for any more delays. Come with me now."

Constance hesitated. "On one condition."

"And what is that, pray tell?"

"Join me in a Chongg Ran session first."

Pendergast's eyes narrowed. "Chongg Ran? How perverse—there isn't time."

"There *is* time. We both have the mental training to reach *stong pa nyid* quickly. What are you afraid of? That meditation will bring you back to normality?" This was, in fact, her own most fervent hope.

"That's absurd. There's no turning back."

"Then meditate with me."

Pendergast remained motionless for a moment. Then his face changed again. Once more, he grew relaxed, confident, aloof.

"Very well," he said. "I shall agree. But on one condition."

"Name it."

"I intend to take the Agozyen before leaving this ship. If Chongg Ran does not work to your satisfaction, then you will gaze on the Agozyen *yourself*. It shall free you, as it did me. This is a great gift I am giving you, Constance."

Hearing this, Constance caught her breath.

Pendergast gave a cold smile. "You've named your terms. Now I've named mine."

For a moment longer, she remained silent. Then she found her breath, looked into his silver eyes. "Very well. I accept."

He nodded. "Excellent. Then shall we begin?"

Just then, a knock sounded on the front door of the suite. Constance stepped over to the entryway and opened it. Outside in the hallway stood a worried-looking Marya.

"I'm sorry, Ms. Greene," she said. "No doctor to be found. I search everywhere, but this ship go crazy, crying, drinking, looting—"

"It's all right. Will you do me one last favor? Could you wait outside the door for a few minutes, please, and make sure we're not disturbed?"

The woman nodded.

"Thank you so much." Then, shutting the door softly behind her, she returned to the living room, where

Pendergast had settled himself cross-legged on the carpet, placed the backs of his wrists on his knees, and was waiting with perfect complacency.

62

Corey Penner, information technology mate second class, sat in the glow of the central server room on Deck B, hunched over a data access terminal.

Hufnagel, the IT chief, leaned over Penner's shoulder, gazing at the display through filmy glasses. "So," he said. "Can you do it?"

The question was accompanied by a wash of sour breath, and Penner tightened his lips. "Doubt it. Looks pretty heavily defended."

Privately, he was sure he could do it. There were few, if any, systems on the *Britannia* he couldn't hack his way into—but it didn't pay to advertise that, especially to his boss. The more they thought you could do, the more they'd ask you to do—he'd learned that the hard way. And the fact was he didn't really want anybody to know just how he traversed the ship's off-limits data services during his leisure hours. Close attention to the *Britannia*'s pay-for-play movie streaming, for example, had allowed him to amass a nice private library of first-run DVDs.

He tapped a few keys and a new screen came up:

HMS BRITANNIA – CENTRAL SYSTEMS
AUTONOMOUS SERVICES (MAINTENANCE MODE)

PROPULSION
GUIDANCE
HVAC
ELECTRICAL
FINANCIAL
TRIM / STABILIZERS
EMERGENCY

Penner moused over GUIDANCE and chose AUTOPILOT from the sub-menu that appeared. An error message came onto the screen: AUTOPILOT MAINTENANCE MODE NOT ACCESSIBLE WHILE SYSTEM IS ENGAGED.

Well, he'd expected that. Exiting the menu system, he brought up a command prompt and began typing quickly. A series of small windows appeared on the screen.

"What are you doing now?" Hufnagel asked.

"I'm going to use the diagnostic back door to access the autopilot." Just how he was going to get access, he wouldn't say: Hufnagel didn't need to know everything.

A phone rang in a far corner of the server room and one of the technicians answered it. "Mr. Hufnagel, call for you, sir." The technician had a strained, worried look on his face. Penner knew he'd probably be worried, too, if he didn't have such a high opinion of his own skills.

"Coming." And Hufnagel stepped away.

Thank God. Quickly, Penner plucked a CD from the

pocket of his lab coat, slid it into the drive, and loaded three utilities into memory: a systems process monitor, a cryptographic analyzer, and a hex disassembler. He returned the CD to his pocket and minimized the three programs just before Hufnagel returned.

A few mouse clicks and a new screen appeared:

HMS BRITANNIA—CENTRAL SYSTEMS
AUTONOMOUS SYSTEMS (DIAGNOSTIC MODE)
SUBSYSTEM VII
CORE AUTOPILOT HANDLING SUBSTRUCTURE

He thought he'd ask a question before Hufnagel started in again. "When—I mean, if—I transfer control of the handling routines, what next?"

"Deactivate the autopilot. Kill it completely, and switch manual control of the helm to the aux bridge."

Penner licked his lips. "It isn't really true that Captain Mason seized the—"

"Yes, it is. Now get on with it."

Penner felt, for the first time, a stab of something like apprehension. Making sure that the process monitor was active, he selected the autopilot and clicked the "diagnostics" button. A new window opened and a storm of numbers scrolled past.

"What's that?"

Penner glanced at the process monitor, sighing inwardly. *Typical IT chief,* he thought. Hufnagel knew all the latest buzzwords like "blade farmload-balancing" and "server virtualization," and he could double-talk the officers until he was blue in the face, but he didn't know jack about the real nuts and bolts of running a complex data system. Aloud, he said, "It's the autopilot data, running in real time."

"And?"

"And I'm going to reverse engineer it, find the interrupt stack, then use the internal trigger events to disrupt the process."

Hufnagel nodded sagely, as if he understood what the hell he'd just been told. A long moment passed as Penner scrutinized the data.

"Well?" Hufnagel said. "Go ahead. We have less than an hour."

"It's not quite that easy."

"Why not?"

Penner gestured at the screen. "Take a look. Those aren't hexadecimal commands. They've been encrypted."

"Can you remove the encryption?"

Can a bear shit in the woods? Penner thought. Quite suddenly, he realized that—if he played this right—he'd most likely get himself a nice fat bonus, maybe even a promotion. Corey Penner, IT mate first class, hero hacker who saved the *Britannia*'s ass.

He liked the sound of that—it even rhymed. He began to relax again; this was going to be a piece of cake. "It's going to be tough, real tough," he said, giving his tone just the right amount of melodrama. "There's a serious encryption routine at work here. Anything you can tell me about it?"

Hufnagel shook his head. "The autopilot coding was outsourced to a German software firm. Corporate can't find the documentation or specs. And it's after office hours in Hamburg."

"Then I'll have to analyze its encoding signature before I can determine what decryption strategy to use on it."

As Hufnagel watched, he piped the autopilot datastream through the cryptographic analyzer. "It's using a native hardware-based encryption system," he announced.

"Is that bad?"

"No, it's good. Usually, hardware encryption is pretty weak, maybe 32-bit stuff. As long as it's not AES or some large-bit algorithm, I should be able to crack—er, decrypt it—in a little while."

"We don't *have* a little while. Like I said, we have less than an hour."

Penner ignored this, peering closely at the analyzer window. Despite himself, he was getting into the problem. He realized he didn't care any longer if his boss saw the unorthodox tools he was using.

"Well?" Hufnagel urged.

"Just hold on, sir. The analyzer is determining just how strong the encryption is. Depending on the bit depth, I can run a side-channel attack, or maybe . . ."

The analyzer finished, and a stack of numbers popped up. Despite the warmth of the server room, Penner felt himself go cold.

"Jesus," he murmured.

"What is it?" Hufnagel asked instantly.

Penner stared at the data, confounded. "Sir, you said less than an hour. An hour until . . . what, exactly?"

"Until the *Britannia* collides with the Carrion Rocks."

Penner swallowed. "And if this doesn't work—what's plan B?"

"Not your concern, Penner. Just keep going."

Penner swallowed. "The routine's employing elliptic curve cryptography. Cutting-edge stuff. 1024-bit public key front end with a 512-bit symmetric key back end."

"So?" the IT chief asked. "How long is it going to take you?"

In the silence that followed the question, Penner suddenly became aware of the deep throb of the ship's engines, the dull slamming of the bow driven at excessive speed through a head sea, the muffled rush of wind and water audible even over the roar of cooling fans in the windowless room.

"Penner? Damn it, *how long*?"

"As many years as there are grains of sand on all the beaches in the world," he murmured, almost choking on the words from the feeling of dread.

63

The thing which had no name moved through shadow and audient void. It lived in a vague metaworld, a world that lay in the grayness between the living world of the *Britannia* and the plane of pure thought. The ghost was not alive. It had no senses. It heard nothing, smelled nothing, felt nothing, thought nothing.

It knew one thing only: desire.

It passed through the mazelike passages of the *Britannia* slowly, as if by feel. The world of the ship was but a shadow to it, an unreal landscape, a vague fabric of shade and silence, to be traversed only until its need had been fulfilled. From time to time it encountered the dull glow of living entities; their erratic movements were ignored. They were as insubstantial to the thing as the thing was to them.

Vaguely, it sensed it was approaching the prey. It could feel the tug of the living being's aura, like a magnet. Following this faint lure, it made an irregular progression through the decks of the ship, passing through corridor and steel bulkhead alike, searching, always searching for that which it had been summoned to devour, to annihilate. Its time was not the world's time; time was but a flexible web, to be stretched, broken, shrugged off, moved into and out of. It had the patience of eternity.

The thing knew nothing of the entity that had summoned it. That entity was no longer important. Not even the summoner could stop it now; its existence was independent. Nor did the thing have any conception of the appearance of the object of its desire. It knew only the pull of longing: to find the thing, to rend the entity's soul from the fabric of the world and burn it with its desire, to consume it and satiate itself—and then to cast the cinder into the outer darkness.

It glided up through a dim corridor, a gray tunnel of half-light, with the flitting presences of additional living entities; through clouds heavy with fear and horror. The aura of its prey was stronger here: strong indeed. It felt its yearning grow and stretch out, seeking the heat of contact.

The tulpa was close now, very close, to its prey.

64

Gavin Bruce and his little group—Niles Welch, Quentin Sharp, and Emily Dahlberg—followed Liu and Crowley toward a port-side hatchway onto Half Deck 7. It was marked *Lifeboats*; a similar hatch would be found on the starboard deck. A crowd milled before the hatch and, as soon as they appeared, converged on them.

"There they are!"

"Get us on the lifeboats!"

"Look, two ship's officers! Trying to save their own asses!"

They were besieged. With a shriek, a heavy woman in a disheveled tracksuit grabbed Liu.

"Is it true?" she shrieked. "That we're headed toward the rocks?"

The crowd surged forward, sweaty, smelling of panic. "*Is it true*?"

"You've got to tell us!"

"No, no, no," Liu said, holding up his hands, the grimace of a smile on his lips. "That rumor is *absolutely* false. We're proceeding on course to—"

"They're lying!" a man cried.

"What are you doing here at the lifeboats, then?"

"And why the hell are we going so fast? The ship's pounding like crazy!"

Crowley shouted to make himself heard. *"Listen!* The captain is merely bringing us into St. John's at all possible speed."

"That's not what your own crew is saying!" the woman in the tracksuit bellowed, grabbing the lapels of Liu's uniform and twisting them frantically. "Don't lie to us!"

The corridor was now packed with excited passengers. Bruce was shocked by how wild and unruly they had become.

"Please!" Liu cried, shaking off the woman. "We've just come from the bridge. Everything is under control. This is merely a routine check of the lifeboats—"

A younger man pushed forward, his suit coat hanging open, the buttons of his shirt undone. "Don't lie to us, you son of a bitch!" He made a grab at Liu, who ducked aside; the man took a swing and struck Liu a glancing blow to the side of the head. *"Liar!"*

Liu staggered, dropped his shoulders, turned, and, as the man came back at him, slammed his fist into his solar plexus. With a groan, the passenger fell heavily to the floor. An obese man charged forward, his bulk heaving, and took a wild swing at Liu while another grabbed him from behind; Bruce stepped forward, neatly dropping the fat man with a counterpunch while Crowley took on the second passenger.

The crowd, momentarily shocked by the outbreak of violence, fell silent and shuffled back.

"Return to your staterooms!" cried Liu, his chest heaving.

Gavin Bruce stepped forward. "You!" He pointed to the woman in front, wearing the tracksuit. "Step aside from that hatch, *now*!"

His voice, ringing with naval authority, had its effect. The crowd shuffled reluctantly aside, silent, fearful. Liu stepped forward, unlocked the hatch.

"They're going to the lifeboats!" a man cried. "Take me! Oh God, don't leave me!"

The crowd woke up again, pressing forward, the air filling with cries and pleadings.

Bruce decked a man half his age who tried to rush the door and won enough time for his group to pile through. Within moments they had pressed the hatch shut behind them, shutting out the crowd of panicked passengers, who began pounding and shouting.

Bruce turned. Cold spray swept across the deck, which was open to the sea along the port side. The boom and rumble of the waves was much louder here, and the wind hummed and moaned through the struts.

"Jesus," muttered Liu. "Those people have gone frigging crazy."

"Where is security?" Emily Dahlberg asked. "Why aren't they controlling that crowd?"

"Security?" said Liu. "We've got two dozen security officers for more than four thousand passengers and crew. It's anarchy out there."

Bruce shook his head and turned his attention to the long row of lifeboats. He was immediately taken aback. He had never seen anything like them in his navy days:

a line of giant, fully enclosed torpedo-shaped vessels, painted bright orange, with rows of portholes along their sides. They looked more like spaceships than boats. What was more, instead of being hung from davits, each was mounted on inclined rails that pointed down and away from the ship.

"How do these work?" he asked, turning to Liu.

"Freefall lifeboats," Liu said. "They've been deployed on oil platforms and cargo ships for years, but the *Britannia* is the first passenger vessel to use them."

"Freefall lifeboats? You can't be serious. It's sixty feet to the water!"

"The passengers are buckled into seats designed to cushion the g-forces of impact. The boats hit the water nose-down, hydrodynamically, then rise to the surface. By the time they surface they're already three hundred feet from the ship and moving away."

"What kind of engines you got on these?"

"Each has a thirty-five diesel, capable of eight knots, and they're all supplied with food, water, heat, and even a ten-minute air supply in case there's fuel burning on the water."

Bruce stared at Liu. "Good God, man, this is perfect! I thought we were going to have to launch old-fashioned boats on davits, which would be impossible in these seas. We could launch these right now!"

"I'm afraid it's not quite that simple," Liu said.

"Why the hell not?"

"The problem is our forward motion. Thirty knots. That's almost thirty-five miles an hour—"

"I know what a knot is, damn it!"

"It's just that there's no way to know how our forward speed might affect the boats. The rules are very emphatic that the boats have to be launched from a stationary ship."

"So we launch a test boat, empty."

"That wouldn't tell us how passengers might be affected by the lateral g-forces."

Gavin Bruce frowned. "I get it. So we need a guinea pig. No problem. Give me a portable VHF and put me in there. Launch the boat. I'll tell you how hard it hits."

Crowley shook his head. "You might be injured."

"What choice do we have?"

"We couldn't let a passenger do that," Liu replied. "I'll do it."

Bruce stared at him. "No way. You're the bosun. Your expertise is needed up here."

Liu's eyes darted toward Crowley, darted back. "It might be a rough landing. Like being in a car, hit broadside by another moving at thirty-five miles an hour."

"This is water we're talking about. Not steel-on-steel. Look, *somebody's* got to be the guinea pig. I've taken worse risks than this. If I get hurt, at least I'll be off the ship. As I see it, I've got nothing to lose. Let's not waste time."

Liu hesitated. "I should go."

Bruce frowned with exasperation. "Mr. Liu, how old are you?"

"Twenty-six."

"And you, Mr. Crowley?"

"Thirty-nine."

"Children?"

Both nodded.

"I'm sixty-eight. I'm a better test case because my age and condition are more in line with the other passengers. You're needed on the ship. And," he added, "your kids still need you."

Now Emily Dahlberg spoke up. "One occupant isn't a sufficient test for the launch. We'll need at least two."

"You're right," Bruce said. He glanced toward Niles Welch. "What about it, Niles?"

"I'm your man," Welch replied immediately.

"Wait a minute," Dahlberg protested. "That's not what I—"

"I know what you meant," Bruce replied. "And I'm deeply appreciative, Emily. But what would Aberdeen Bank and Trust say if I endangered one of its most important clients?" And with that, he took the VHF from Liu's unprotesting hand, moved to the stern hatch of the nearest orange spaceship, and turned the handle. It opened on pneumatic hinges with a soft hiss. He stepped into the dark interior, nodding for Welch to follow. After a moment, he poked his head out again.

"This thing is fitted out better than a luxury yacht. What channel?"

"Use 72. There's also a fixed VHF and SSB radios on board the lifeboat, along with radar, chartplotter, depth finder, loran—the works."

Bruce nodded. "Good. Now quit standing around like a bunch of sheep. Once we give you the signal, say a Hail Mary and pull the bloody lever!"

And he closed and secured the hatch without another word.

65

Constance Greene opened an ancient sandalwood box and took out a bizarre, fantastically complex knot tied from gray silken cord. Superficially, it resembled an obscure European knot known as a *Mors du Cheval*, only it was far more complex. In Tibetan it was called *dgongs*, the "unraveling."

The knot had been given to her by Tsering on her departure from the Gsalrig Chongg monastery. It had been tied in the eighteenth century by a revered lama, to be used in a particular kind of meditative exercise to expunge attachment, to rid oneself of evil thoughts or influences, or to aid in the joining of two minds. In Constance's case, the knot was to be used for cleansing herself of the stain of murder; now, she hoped it would expunge the stain of the Agozyen from Pendergast. The knot was never to be untied in the real world: to do so would be to release its power and transform it back into a mere silken cord. It was an exercise of mind and spirit only.

The stateroom was dark, the curtains drawn tightly closed over the balcony windows. Marya—who had been unable to find a doctor—stood by the salon door, anxiety and uncertainty flickering in her eyes.

Constance turned to her. "Marya, please stand guard outside. Don't let anyone interrupt us."

The woman nodded, then turned and quickly left the salon.

When she heard the door close, Constance placed the knot on a small silken pillow that lay on the floor, illuminated within a circle of candles. Then she glanced over at Pendergast. With a dry smile, the agent took his place on one side of the knot, while she sat down on the other. The knot lay between them, one loose end pointing at her, the other at Pendergast. It was a symbol, both spiritual and physical, of the interconnectedness of all life and—in particular—of the two entities that sat on either side of the knot.

Constance arranged herself in a modified lotus position, as did Pendergast. She sat for a moment, doing nothing, letting her limbs relax. Then, keeping her eyes open and contemplating the knot, she slowed her breathing and decelerated her heartbeat, as she had been taught by the monks. She allowed her mind to settle into the moment, the now, discarding past and future and closing down the endless flow of thoughts that normally afflict the human mind. Liberated from the mental chatter, her senses became acutely aware of her surroundings: the boom and shudder of the waves on the hull, the splatter of rain on the glass of the balcony door, the new-room smell, the faint scent of wax from the candles and sandalwood from the knot. She became acutely aware of the presence opposite her, a dark shape at the periphery of her vision.

Her eyes remained on the knot.

Slowly, she released each external sensation, one after the other. The trappings of the outside world vanished into darkness, like the closing of shutters in a dark house. First the room around her; then the great ship, and then the vast ocean on which they crawled. Gone were the sounds of the room, its scents, the slow roll of the ship, her own corporeal awareness. The earth itself vanished, the sun, the stars, the universe . . . gone, all gone, falling away into nonexistence. Only she remained, and the knot, and the being on the far side of the knot.

Time ceased to exist. She had reached the state of *th'an shin gha*, the Doorstep to Perfect Emptiness.

In a strange meditative state of utter awareness and yet complete absence of effort or desire, she focused on the knot. For a moment, it remained unchanged. Then—slowly, evenly, like a snake uncoiling—the knot began untying itself. The fantastically complex loops and curves, the plunging bends and rising swerves of cord, began to loosen; the bitter ends of the rope withdrew into the knot, tracing in reverse the original convoluted tying, three centuries earlier. It was a process of immense mathematical complexity, symbolizing the unraveling of the ego that must take place before a being can reach *stong pa nyid*—the State of Pure Emptiness—and merge with the universal mind.

She was there; Pendergast was there; and in the middle, the knot, in the act of untying itself. That was all.

After an indefinite period—it could have been a

second, it could have been a thousand years—the gray silken cord lay in a smooth heap, untied and loosely coiled. In its center a small, crumpled piece of silk was revealed, on which had been written the secret prayer the ancient monk had bound up in it.

She read it over carefully. Then slowly, chantlike, she began to recite the prayer, over and over again . . .

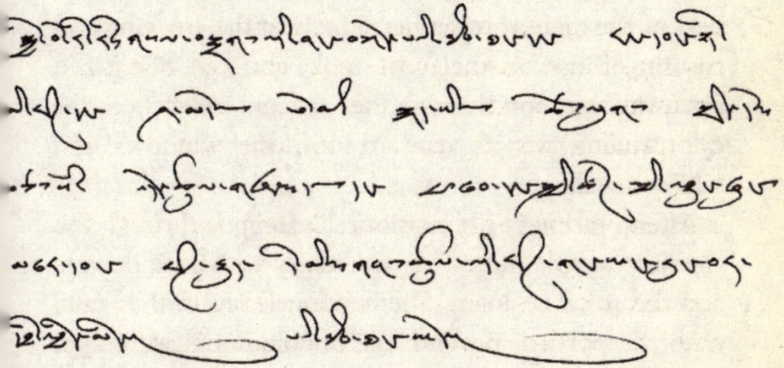

As she chanted, she extended her consciousness toward the loose end of the rope closest to her. At the same time, she was aware of the glow of the being opposite her, extending itself in the same manner toward the untied cord.

She chanted, the low, soothing tones unraveling her ego, gently parting all ties to the physical world. She felt the current as her mind touched the cord and moved along it, drawn toward the entity on the other side as he was drawn toward her. She moved along the convoluted strands, barely breathing, her heart beating with funereal slowness, coming closer, ever closer . . . Then her thought met and merged with the glow of the other, and the final stage was reached.

Abruptly, she found herself in a place both strange and familiar. She stood on a cobbled street between elegant gas lamps, staring up at a dark and shuttered mansion. It was a construct of extraordinary concentration, of pure thought alone, more real and solid than any dream she had ever experienced. She could feel the cool clamminess of the night mist on her skin; hear the creaking and rustling of insects; smell coal smoke and soot. She gazed up at the mansion through the wrought-iron fence, her eye traveling over its mansard roof, oriel windows, and widow's walk.

After a moment's hesitation, she stepped through the gate into a dark, humid garden, heavy with dead flowers and the smell of loam. She continued on up the walk, onto the portico. Beyond, the double doors were ajar, and she stepped through the entryway, passing into a grand foyer. A crystal chandelier hung overhead, dark and threatening, tinkling faintly as if disturbed by wind despite the dead air of the house. One massive doorway led into a tall library, its wing chairs and couches empty, its fireplace dark and cold. Another passage led toward a kind of refectory or perhaps exhibition hall, silent, watchful.

She crossed the foyer, her heels clicking on the marble floor, and climbed the wide stairs to the second-floor hallway. Tapestries and indistinct oil paintings lined the walls, stretching back into the dark heart of the house, interrupted by oaken doors darkened by time.

She glanced along the left wall as she moved forward. Ahead, not quite halfway down the long hall, one door was open—battered open, the doorframe smashed, splinters of wood and twisted pieces of lead scattered about the floor. The yawning black opening exhaled a cold, cellar-like stench of mold and dead, greasy centipedes.

She quickly passed by with a shudder. The door beyond drew her toward it. She was almost there.

She placed her hand on the knob, turned it. With a low creaking sound, the door swung inward and a welcome warmth flowed out around her, enveloping her with the pleasant sensation of stepping into a cozy dwelling in wintertime.

Aloysius Pendergast stood before her, dressed in black as usual, his hands clasped in front of him, smiling.

"Welcome," he said.

The room was large and beautiful, with paneled wainscoting. A fire burned in a marble fireplace, and an old clock on the mantel chimed the hours, beside an antique gasogene and several cut-glass tumblers. A stag's head mounted on the wall looked out with glassy eyes across a desk piled with leather-bound books and papers. The oak floor was covered with rich, dense carpeting, over which expensive Persian carpets had been laid in turn. Several comfortable wing chairs were scattered about, some with open books lying on their seats. It was an extremely comfortable, well-used, luxurious space.

"Come and warm yourself by the fire," he said, motioning her forward.

She moved closer to the fire, keeping her eyes on Pendergast. There was something different about him.

Something strange. Despite the utter reality of this room and this house, the edges of his form were indistinct, blurry, slightly transparent, as if he wasn't quite there.

The door shut behind her with a dull thud.

He held out his hand for hers, and she gave it to him. He grasped it, suddenly very hard, and she tried to withdraw, but he pulled her toward him. His head seemed to waver, to bulge and dissolve; the skin cracked, and a glow emerged from within; and then his face peeled away and fluttered down in burning threads, revealing a visage that Constance recognized. It was the indescribable face of the Kalazyga demon.

She stared at it, strangely unafraid, feeling its warmth, drawn to it with a mixture of fear and attraction. It seemed to fill her with fire: the ineffable, all-consuming, triumphant fire she had felt in her mad pursuit of Diogenes Pendergast. There was a purity to it that awed her.

"I am will," it said, with a voice that was not sound, but thought. *"I am pure thought burned clean of any vestige of human sentiment. I am freedom. Join with me."*

Fascinated, repelled, she again tried to withdraw her hand, but it held fast. The face, terrible and beautiful, drew closer to her. It wasn't real, she told herself, it was only a product of her mind, the image of one of the thangkas she had contemplated for hours on end, now re-created by this intense meditation.

The Kalazyga demon drew her toward the fire. *"Come. Into the fire. Burn off the dead husk of moral restraint. You will emerge like the butterfly from its chrysalis, free and beautiful."*

She took a step toward the fire, hesitated, then took

another, almost floating over the carpeting toward the warmth.

"Yes," said another voice. Pendergast's voice. "This is good. This is right. Go to the fire."

As she drew closer to the flames, the heavy guilt and mortification of murder that had lain on her shoulders melted away, replaced by a sense of exhilaration, the intense exhilaration and dark joy she felt when she saw Pendergast's brother tumble off the edge of *La Sciara* into the red-hot depths below. That momentary ecstasy was being offered to her now, forever.

All she had to do was step into the flames.

One more step. The fire radiated its warmth, licking up into her very limbs. She remembered him at the very edge, the two of them locked together in a macabre caricature of sexual union, struggling at the roaring edge of *La Sciara*; her unexpected feint; the expression on his face when he realized they were both going over. *The expression on his face:* it was the most horrifying, most pitiful, and yet most satisfying thing she had ever seen—to revel in the face of a person who realizes, without the shadow of a doubt, that he is going to die. That all hope is gone. And this bitter joy could now be hers forever; she could be free to experience it again and again, at will. And she would not even need overweening vengeance as an excuse: she could simply murder, whoever and wherever, and again and again revel in the hot blood-fury, the ecstatic, orgiastic triumph . . .

All hope is gone . . .

With a scream, she writhed in the grip of the demon, and with a sudden, immense force of will she managed to break free. She threw herself back from the fire, turned and ran through the door, and suddenly she was falling, falling through the house, through the basements, the sub-cellars, falling . . .

66

The storm raged beyond the open rails of Half Deck 7, spray sweeping across the deck despite their being sixty feet above the waterline. Liu could hardly think over the boom of the sea and the bellow of the wind.

Crowley came up, as soaked as he was. "Are we really going to try this, sir?"

"You got a better idea?" Liu replied irritably. "Give me your radio."

Crowley handed it over.

Liu tuned it to channel 72 and pressed the transmit button. "Liu here, calling Bruce, over."

"This is Bruce."

"How do you read me?"

"Five by five."

"Good. Buckle yourself into the coxswain's station at the helm. Welch should take the seat across the aisle."

"Already done."

"Need any instructions?"

"They seem to be all right here."

"The lifeboat's almost completely automatic," Liu went on. "The engine starts automatically on impact.

It'll drive the lifeboat away from the ship in a straight line. You should throttle down to steerageway speed only—they'll find you quicker that way. The master panel should be pretty self-explanatory to a nautical man."

"Right. Got an EPIRB on this crazy boat?"

"Two, and they're actually the latest GPIRBs, which transmit your GPS coordinates. On impact, the GPIRB automatically activates at 406 and 121.5 megahertz—no action required on your part. Keep the lifeboat's VHF tuned to emergency channel 16. Communicate with me through channel 72 on your handheld. You're going to be on your own until you're picked up—the *Britannia* isn't stopping. Both of you stay strapped in at all times—you're going to take a few barrel rolls in these seas, at the least."

"Understood."

"Questions?"

"No."

"Ready?"

"Ready." Bruce's voice crackled over the handheld.

"Okay. There's a fifteen-second automatic countdown. Lock down the transmit button so we can hear what happens. Talk to me as soon as possible after you hit."

"Understood. Fire away."

Liu turned to the freefall launch control panel. There were thirty-six lifeboats, eighteen on the port side and eighteen on starboard, each with a capacity of up to 150 people. Even launching one boat virtually empty like this, they still had plenty of capacity to spare. He glanced at his watch. If it worked, they'd have fifty minutes to evacuate the ship. A very doable proposition.

He murmured a short prayer.

As he initiated the launch sequence, Liu began to breathe a little easier. It *was* going to work. These damn boats were overengineered, built to withstand a sixty-foot free fall. They could take the extra strain.

Green across the board. He unlocked the switch that would began the countdown on lifeboat number one, opened the cover. Inside, the little red breaker-lever glowed with fresh paint. This was a hell of a lot simpler than in the old days, when a lifeboat had to be lowered on davits, swinging crazily in the wind and roll of the ship. Now all you had to do was press a lever; the boat was released from its arrestors, slid down the rails, and fell sixty feet to land, nose first, in the sea. A few moments later it bobbed to the surface and continued on, driving away from the ship. They'd been through the drill many times: drop to recovery took all of six seconds.

"You read, Bruce?"

"Loud and clear."

"Hang on. I'm releasing the switch."

He pulled the red lever.

A woman's voice sounded from a speaker mounted overhead. "Lifeboat number one launching in fifteen seconds. Ten seconds. Nine, eight . . ."

The voice echoed in the metal-walled half deck. The countdown ran out; there was a loud *clunk* as the steel arrestors disengaged. The boat slid forward on the greased rails, nosed off the end into open space, and Liu leaned over the side to watch it fall, as gracefully as a diver, toward the churning sea.

It struck with a tremendous eruption of spray, much larger than anything Liu had seen during the drills: a geyser that rose forty, fifty feet, swept backward in ragged petals by the tearing wind. The VHF channel let loose a squeal of static.

But instead of plunging straight into the water and disappearing, the lifeboat's forward motion, combined with the added speed of the ship, pitchpoled it sideways, like a rock skipping over the surface of a pond, and it struck the ocean a second time full force along its length, with another eruption of spray that buried the orange boat in boiling water. And then it began to resurface, sluggishly, the Day-Glo hull brightening as it shed green water. The static on the VHF abruptly died into silence.

The woman—Emily Dahlberg—caught her breath, averted her eyes.

Liu stared at the lifeboat, which was already rapidly falling astern. He seemed to be seeing the boat from a strange angle. But no, that wasn't it: the lifeboat's profile had changed—the hull was misshapen. Orange and white flecks were detaching themselves from the hull, and a rush of air along a seam blew a line of spray toward the sky.

With a sick feeling Liu realized the hull had been breached, split lengthwise like a rotten melon, and was now spilling its guts.

"Jesus . . ." he heard Crowley murmur next to him. "Oh, Jesus . . ."

He stared in horror at the stoved-in lifeboat. It wasn't

righting itself; it was wallowing sideways, subsiding back in the water, the engine screw uselessly churning the surface, leaving a trail of oil and debris as it fell astern and began to fade away in the gray, storm-tossed seas.

Liu grabbed the VHF and pressed the transmit button. "Bruce! Welch! This is Liu! Respond! *Bruce!*"

But there was no answer—as Liu knew there wouldn't be.

67

On the auxiliary bridge, LeSeur was facing a torrent of questions.

"The lifeboats!" an officer cried over the others. "What's happening with the lifeboats?"

LeSeur shook his head. "No word yet. I'm still waiting to hear from Liu and Crowley."

The chief radio officer spoke up. "I've got the *Grenfell* on channel 69."

LeSeur looked at him. "Fax him on the SSB fax to switch to channel . . . 79." Maybe choosing an obscure VHF channel to communicate with the *Grenfell*—channel 79, normally reserved for exchanges between pleasure boats on the Great Lakes—would keep their conversations secret from Mason. He hoped to God she wouldn't be scanning the VHF channels as a matter of course. She'd already seen, of course, the radar profile of the *Grenfell* as the ship approached and heard all the chatter on emergency channel 16.

"What's the rendezvous estimate?" he asked the radio officer.

"Nine minutes." He paused. "I've got the captain of the *Grenfell* on 79, sir."

LeSeur walked up to the VHF console, slipped on a pair of headphones. He spoke in a low voice. "*Grenfell*, this is First Officer LeSeur, acting commander of the *Britannia*. Do you have a plan?"

"This is a tough one, *Britannia*, but we've got a couple of ideas."

"We've got one chance to do this. We're faster than you by at least ten knots, and once we're past, that's it."

"Understood. We've got on board a BO-105 utility chopper, which we could use to bring you some shaped explosives we normally use for hull-breaching—"

"At our speed, in this sea and gale conditions, you'll never land it."

A silence. "We're hoping for a window."

"Unlikely, but have the bird stand by just in case. Next idea?"

"We were thinking that, on our pass, we could hook the *Britannia* with our towing winch and try to pull her off course."

"What kind of winch?"

"A seventy-ton electrohydraulic towing winch with a 40mm wire rope—"

"That would snap like a string."

"It probably would. Another option would be to drop a buoy and tow the wire across your course, hoping to foul your propellers."

"There's no way a 40mm wire rope could stop four 21.5-megawatt screws. Don't you carry fast rescue craft?"

"Unfortunately, there's no way we can launch our two fast rescue craft in these seas. And in any case there's no way we can come alongside to board or evacuate, because we can't keep up with you."

"Any other ideas?"

A pause. "That's all we've been able to come up with."

"Then we'll have to go with my plan," LeSeur said.

"Shoot."

"You're an icebreaker, am I right?"

"Well, the *Grenfell*'s an ice-strengthened ship, but she's not a true icebreaker. We sometimes do icebreaking duties such as harbor breakouts."

"Good enough. *Grenfell*, I want you to chart a course that will take you across our bow—in such a way as to shear it off."

A silence, and then the reply came. "I'm sorry, I don't think I read you, *Britannia*."

"You read me fine. The idea is, by opening selected bulkhead hatches we can flood forward compartments one, two, and three. That will put us down by the head enough to lift our screws almost out of the water. The *Britannia* will be DIW."

"You're asking me to *ram* you? Good God, have you lost your mind? There's a good chance I'd sink my own vessel!"

"It's the only way. If you approach head-on just a few points off our starboard side, moving not too fast—say, five to eight knots—then, just before contact, back one screw hard while engaging your bow thrusters, you could shear off our bows with your reinforced forward hullplates, swing free, and we would pass clear of each other on the starboard side. It'd be close, but it would work. That is, if you've got the helmsmanship to pull it off."

"I've got to check with Command."

"We've got five minutes to our CPA rendezvous, *Grenfell*. You known damn well you're not going to get clearance in time. Look, do you have the knackers to do this or not? That's the real question."

A long silence.

"All right, *Britannia*. We'll give it a try."

68

Constance's eyes flew open, her whole body jerking itself awake with a muffled cry. The universe came rushing back—the ship, the rolling room, the splatter of the rain, the booming seas and moaning of the wind.

She stared at the *dgongs*. It lay in an untidy coil around an ancient scrap of crumpled silk. It had been untied—for real.

She looked at Pendergast, aghast. Even as she stared, his head rose slightly and his eyes came back to life, silvery irises glittering in the candlelight. A strange smile spread across his face. "You broke the meditation, Constance."

"You were trying . . . to *drag* me into the fire," she gasped.

"Naturally."

She felt a wash of despair. Instead of pulling him out of darkness, she had almost been pulled in herself.

"I was trying to free you from your earthly fetters," he said.

"Free me," she repeated bitterly.

"Yes. To become what you will: free of the chains of sentiment, morality, principles, honor, virtue, and all those petty things that contrive to keep us enchained in the human slave-galley with everyone else, rowing ourselves nowhere."

"And that's what the Agozyen has done to you," she said. "Stripped away all moral and ethical inhibitions. Let your darkest, most sociopathic desires run rampant. That's what it offered me as well."

Pendergast rose and extended his hand. She did not take it.

"You untied the knot," she said.

He spoke, his voice low and strangely vibrant with triumph. "I didn't touch it. Ever."

"But then how . . . ?"

"I untied it *with my mind*."

She continued to stare. "That's impossible."

"It is not only possible, but it happened, as you can see."

"The meditation failed. You're the same."

"The meditation *worked*, my dear Constance. I have changed—enormously. Thanks to your insistence that we do this, I have now fully realized the power given to me by the Agozyen. The power of pure thought—of mind over matter. I've tapped into an immense reservoir of power, and so can you." His eyes were glittering, passionate. "This is an extraordinary demonstration of the Agozyen mandala and its ability to transform the human mind and human thought into a tool of colossal power."

Constance stared at him, a creeping feeling of horror in her heart.

"You wanted to bring me back," he continued. "You wanted to restore me to my old, conflicted, foolish self.

But instead, you brought me forward. You opened the door. And now, my dear Constance, it's your turn to be freed. Remember our little agreement?"

She couldn't speak.

"That's right. It is now your turn to gaze upon the Agozyen."

Still, she hesitated.

"As you wish." He rose and grabbed the neck of the canvas sack. "I'm through looking after you." He moved toward the door, not looking at her, hoisting the sack onto his shoulder.

With a shock, she realized he had no more regard for her than for anyone else.

"Wait—" she began.

A scream from beyond the door cut her off. The door flew open and Marya came backing in. Beyond, Constance caught a glimpse of something gray and unevenly textured moving toward them.

Where did that smoke come from? Is the ship on fire?

Pendergast dropped the sack and stared, taking a step backward. Constance was surprised to see a look of shock, even fear, on his face.

It blocked the door. Marya screamed again, the thing enveloping her, muffling her screams.

As the thing came through the door, it was backlit for a moment by a lamp in the entryway, and with a sense of growing unreality Constance saw a strange, roiling presence deep within the smoke, with two bloodshot eyes, a third one on its forehead—a demonic creature jerking and moving and heaving itself along as if crippled . . . or perhaps *dancing* . . .

Marya screamed a third time and fell to the floor with a crash of breaking glass, her eyes rolling and jittering in her head, convulsing. The thing was now past her, filling the salon with a damp chill and the stench of rotting fungus, backing Pendergast into a corner—and then it was on him, *in* him, swallowing him, and he issued a muffled cry of such raw terror, such agonizing despair, that it froze Constance to the marrow.

69

LeSeur stood in the middle of the crowded aux bridge, staring at the S-band radar image of the approaching ship. It loomed ever larger, a phosphorescent shape expanding dead ahead on the radar screen. The Doppler readout indicated a combined closing speed of thirty-seven knots.

"Two thousand five hundred yards and closing," said the second officer. LeSeur made a quick mental calculation: two minutes to contact.

He glanced at the more sensitive X-band, but it was awash with sea return and rain scatter. Quietly and quickly, he'd briefed the rest of the officers on his plan. He knew it was at least possible Mason had heard everything he'd said to the captain of the *Grenfell*: there was no failsafe way to block communications on the main bridge. But either way, once the *Grenfell* made its move, the *Britannia* would be hard pressed to respond.

Chief Engineer Halsey came up to his side. "I have the estimates you asked for." He spoke in a low voice so the others wouldn't hear.

So it's that bad, thought LeSeur. He withdrew Halsey to one side.

"These figures," said Halsey, "are based on a direct collision with the center of the shoal, which is what we anticipate."

"Tell me quickly."

"Given the force of that impact, we estimate the death rate at thirty to fifty percent—with almost all the rest seriously injured: broken limbs, contusions, concussions."

"Understood."

"With its draft of thirty-three feet, the *Britannia* will make initial contact with a small shoal some distance from the main portion of the reef. By the time the ship is stopped by the main rocks, it will already be ripped open from stem to stern. All the watertight compartments and bulkheads will be breached. Estimated sinking time is less than three minutes."

LeSeur swallowed. "Is there a chance it might hang up on the rocks?"

"There's a steep dropoff. The stern of the ship will pull it off and down—fast."

"Dear Jesus."

"Given the extent of injury and death, and the speed with which the *Britannia* will sink, there won't be time to institute any procedures for abandoning ship. That means nobody aboard at the time of collision has any chance of survival. That includes"—he hesitated, glancing around—"personnel remaining on the auxiliary bridge."

"*Fifteen hundred yards and closing*," said the second officer, his eyes fixed on the radar. Sweat was streaming down his face. The aux bridge had gone silent, everyone staring at the looming green blob on the radar scope.

LeSeur had debated whether to issue a general order warning passengers and crew to brace themselves, but he had decided against it. For one thing, using the PA would tip their hand to Mason. But more importantly, if the *Grenfell* did the job right, the force of the lateral impact across the bow would be mostly absorbed by the enormous mass of the *Britannia*. It would be a jolt that might startle the passengers, or at worst jar a few off their feet. But he had to take the risk.

"Twelve hundred yards."

70

Roger Mayles heard running footsteps and pressed himself into a cul-de-sac on Deck 9. A gaggle of passengers ran by shouting, gesticulating, on God knows what senseless, hysterical mission. In one sweaty hand he clutched a magnetic key that he kneaded and rubbed incessantly, like a worry-stone. With the other, he removed a flask and took a long slug of single-malt whisky—eighteen-year-old Macallan—and slipped it back into his pocket. His eye was already beginning to swell from the blow he'd received during a tussle with a hysterical passenger back in Oscar's: it felt like someone was pumping air into it, making it tighter and tighter. Blood flecked his white shirt and dinner jacket from a bloody nose that had yet to stop leaking. He must look an absolute fright.

He checked his watch. Thirty minutes to impact, if the information he'd received was correct: and he had every reason to believe it was. He checked again to see if the hall was still clear, then staggered out of the cul-de-sac. He had to avoid passengers at all costs. It was *Lord of the Flies* time on board the *Britannia*, every man for himself, and nobody descended into brutish behavior quicker than a bunch of rich assholes.

He made his way carefully down the Deck 9 corridor. Although there was nobody in sight, the distant screams, yells, pleas, and agonized sobbing were omnipresent. He couldn't believe that the ship's officers and security had virtually disappeared, leaving hospitality staff like himself at the mercy of these rampaging passengers. He had heard nothing, received no instructions. It was clear there was no plan to deal with a disaster of this scale. The ship was absolute bedlam, with no information to be had, the wildest rumors spreading like a brush fire in high wind.

Mayles slipped down the hall, the key clutched in his palm. It was his ticket out of this madhouse and he was going to spend it right now. He wasn't going to end up being one of forty-three hundred people ground to mincemeat when the ship ripped its guts open on the Grand Banks' worst shoal. The lucky ones who survived the impact would live another twenty minutes in the forty-five-degree water before succumbing to hypothermia.

That was one party he wasn't going to attend, thank you very much.

He took another slug of the whisky and slipped through a door marked by a red exit sign. He ran down a metal staircase, his short legs churning, and paused two landings below to peer into the corridor leading to the half deck where the port lifeboats were housed. While the corridor was again empty, the shouts of frantic, angry passengers were louder on this deck. He couldn't fathom why they hadn't launched the boats. He had been part of the lifeboat drills and had ridden on a couple of freefall launches. Those boats were damn near indestructible, dropping into the water while you were safely buckled into a cushioned seat, the ride no rougher than a Disneyland roller-coaster.

As he came around the corner toward the outside half deck, the noise of the crowd increased. Wouldn't you know it: a bunch of passengers had gathered at the locked lifeboat hatches, pounding and shouting to get in.

There was only one way to the port lifeboats and it was through the crowd. No doubt more frantic passengers had assembled around the starboard lifeboats as well. He advanced, still clutching the key. Maybe no one would recognize him.

"Hey! It's the cruise director!"

"The cruise director! Hey, you! Mayles!"

The crowd surged toward him. A drunken man, his face afire, grabbed Mayles by the sleeve. "What the hell's happening? Why aren't we launching the lifeboats?" He gave his arm a jerk. "Huh? Why not?"

"I don't know any more than you do!" Mayles cried, his voice high and tense, trying to pull his arm back. "They haven't told me anything!"

"Bullshit! He's going to the lifeboats—just like the others did!"

He was seized by another grasping hand and pulled sideways. He heard the cloth of his uniform tear. "Let me through!" Mayles shrilled, struggling forward. "I tell you, I don't know anything!"

"The hell you don't!"

"We want the lifeboats! You aren't going to lock us out this time!"

The crowd panicked around him, tugging at him like children fighting over a doll. With a loud rending noise, his sleeve came away from his shirt.

"Let go!" he pleaded.

"You bastards aren't going to leave us to sink!"

"They already launched the lifeboats, that's why there's no crew to be seen!"

"Is that true, you asshole?"

"I'll let you in," Mayles cried, terrified, holding up the key, "if you'll just leave me alone!"

The crowd paused, digesting this. Then: "He said he'd let us in!"

"You heard him! *Let us in!*"

The crowd pushed him forward, suddenly expectant, calmer. With a trembling hand Mayles stuck the key in the lock, threw the door open, jumped though, then spun and tried to quickly shut it behind him. It was a futile effort. The crowd poured through, knocking him aside.

He scrambled to his feet. The roar of the sea and the bellowing of the wind hit him full in the face. Great patches of intermittent fog scudded over the waves, but in the gaps Mayles could see black, angry, foaming ocean. Masses of spray swept across the inside deck, immediately soaking him to the skin. He spied Liu and Crowley standing by the launch control panel, along with a man he recognized as a banking executive, staring at the crowd in disbelief. Emily Dahlberg, the meatpacking heiress, was beside them. The knot of passengers rushed toward the first available boat, and Liu and Crowley quickly moved to stop them, along with the banker. The air grew thick with shouting and screaming, and the horrifying sound of fists impacting flesh. Crowley's radio went skipping and spinning across the deck and out of sight.

Mayles hung back. He knew the drill. He knew how to use these lifeboats, he knew the onboard launch sequence, and he would be damned if he was going to share one with a bunch of crazy passengers. Fighting between the mob and Liu's group was intensifying, and the passengers seemed to have forgotten about him in their eagerness to get into the nearest boat. He could get away before they even knew what was happening.

Liu's face was bleeding freely from half a dozen cuts. "Get word to the auxiliary bridge!" he cried to Dahlberg before the angry mob overwhelmed him.

Mayles walked past the violence, toward the far end. As he did so, he casually pressed a couple of buttons on the launch control panel. He'd get in a boat, launch it, and be safe and away. The GPIRB would go off and he'd be picked up by nightfall.

He reached the farthest boat, keyed open the control panel with a trembling hand, and began activating the settings. He watched the crowd at the other end, fighting with the banker and stamping on the now motionless forms of Liu and Crowley. A head turned toward him. Another.

"Hey! He's going to launch one! The son of a bitch!"

"Wait!"

He saw a group of passengers coming toward him.

Mayles jabbed in the rest of the settings and the stern boarding hatch swung open on hydraulic hinges. He rushed for it but the crowd was there before him. He was seized, dragged back.

"Scumbag!"

"There's enough room for all of us!" he shrilled. "Let go, you morons! One at a time!"

"You last!" An old, wiry geezer with superhuman strength belted him aside and disappeared into the boat, followed by a surging, screaming, bloody mob. Mayles tried to follow but was seized and dragged back.

"Bastard!"

He slipped on the wet deck, fell, and was kicked into the deck rail. Grasping it for support, he pulled himself to his feet. They were not going to keep him out. They were not going to take his boat. He grabbed a man crowding in front of him, slung him down, slipped again; the man rose and charged him, and they struggled in a tight embrace, staggering against the rail. Mayles braced himself with his foot, stepping on the rail to gain leverage, while the crowd surged and fought to get through the narrow hatch.

"You need me!" Mayles cried, struggling. "I know how to operate it!"

He pushed his assailant back and made another lunge for the hatch, but those inside the boat were now fighting to close the door.

"I know how to operate it!" he screamed, clawing over the backs of those trying to keep the door open.

And then it happened—with the spastic, abominable acceleration of a nightmare. To his horror he saw the wheel turn, sealing shut the hatch. He grabbed at the wheel, trying to turn it back; there was a *clunk* as the release hooks opened—and then the lifeboat shot down the ramp, jerking Mayles and half a dozen others forward.

He tumbled down the greased metal rails with them, out of control, unable to stop, and—very abruptly—suddenly found himself in a free fall toward the roiling black ocean, somersaulting in slow motion, head over heels.

The last thing he saw before he struck the water was another ship, blowing out of the sea-mist dead ahead of the *Britannia*, coming at them on a collision course.

71

LeSeur stared out the forward windows of the auxiliary bridge. As the wind had increased the rain had lessened, and now the fog was breaking up, allowing occasional views ahead across the storm-tossed seas. He stared so hard he wondered if he was seeing things.

But suddenly there it was: the *Grenfell*, emerging from a pocket of mist, bulbous bows pounding the seas. It was coming straight at them.

As the *Grenfell* appeared, there was a collective intake of breath from the aux bridge.

"Eight hundred yards."

The *Grenfell* made her move. A sudden boiling of white water along her starboard aft hull marked the reversal of the starboard screw; simultaneously, a jet of white water near the port bow signaled the engagement of the bow thrusters. The red snout of the *Grenfell* began to swing to starboard as the two ships closed in on each other, the giant *Britannia* moving much faster than the Canadian vessel.

"Brace yourselves!" LeSeur cried, grabbing the edge of the navigational table.

The maneuver of the *Grenfell* was almost immediately answered by a roar deep in the belly of the *Britannia*. Mason had taken the ship off autopilot and was reacting—alarmingly fast. The ship began to vibrate with the rumble of an earthquake, and the deck began to tilt.

"She's retracting the stabilizers!" LeSeur cried, staring at the control board in disbelief. "And—Jesus—she's rotated the aft pods ninety degrees to starboard!"

"She can't do that!" the chief engineer yelled. "She'll rip the pods right off the hull!"

LeSeur scanned the engine readouts, desperate to understand what Mason was trying to do. "She's turning the *Britannia* broadside . . . deliberately . . . so the *Grenfell* will T-bone us," he said. A horrifying, vivid split-second image formed in his mind: the *Britannia* coming about, offering her vulnerable midsection to the ice-hardened *Grenfell*. But it wouldn't be a straight T-bone; the *Britannia* would not have time to come around that far. It would be even worse than that. The *Grenfell* would strike her at a forty-five-degree angle, cutting diagonally through the main block of staterooms and public spaces. It would be a massacre, a slaughter, a butchery.

It was instantly clear to him that Mason had thought through this countermove with great care. It would be as effective as crashing the ship into the Carrion Rocks. Opportunist that she was, the staff captain had seized her chance when she saw it.

"*Grenfell!*" LeSeur cried, breaking radio silence, "back your second screw! Reverse the bow thrusters! She's turning into you!"

"Roger that," came the extraordinarily calm voice of the captain.

The *Grenfell* responded immediately, water churning up all around its hull. The ship seemed to hesitate as its bows slowed their ponderous swing and her forward motion decreased.

Underneath them, the screaming, grinding shudder grew as Mason goosed the rotating aft screws to full, 43,000 kilowatts of power deployed at a ninety-degree angle to the ship's forward motion. An insane maneuver. Without the stabilizers, and aided by a beam sea, the *Britannia* yawed as it heeled over even farther: five degrees, ten degrees, fifteen degrees from the vertical, far beyond anything envisioned by her engineers in their worst nightmares. The navigational instruments, coffee mugs, and other loose objects on the aux bridge went sliding and crashing to the floor, the men gripping whatever they could get their hands on to keep from following.

"The crazy bitch is putting the deck underwater!" Halsey cried, his feet slipping out from under him.

The vibration increased to a roar as the port side of the liner pressed down into the ocean, the lower main deck pushing below the waterline. The seas mounted, battering the superstructure, rising to the lowest port staterooms and balconies. Faintly, LeSeur could hear sounds of popping glass, the rumble of water rushing into the passenger decks, the dull noises of things crashing and tumbling about. He could only imagine the terror and chaos among the passengers as they and the contents of their staterooms and everything else on the ship tumbled to port.

The entire bridge shook with the violent strain on the engines, the windows rattling, the very frame of the ship groaning in protest. Beyond the forecastle the *Grenfell* loomed, rapidly approaching; she continued yawing heavily to port, but LeSeur could see that it was too late. The *Britannia*, with its astonishing maneuverability, had turned quartering to her, and the patrol ship was going to strike them amidships—2,500 tons meeting 165,000 tons at a combined speed of forty-five miles per hour. She would cut the *Britannia* diagonally like a pike through a marlin.

He began to pray.

72

Emily Dahlberg paused in the corridor leading from the port lifeboat deck, catching her breath. Behind her, she could hear the cries and screams of the mob—for a mob it was, and of the most primitive, homicidal kind—mingling with the roar of wind and water through the open hatches. Many other people had had the idea to head for the lifeboat stations, and a steady stream of passengers raced past her in a panic, heedless of her presence.

Dahlberg had seen enough to know that any attempt to use the lifeboats at this speed was sheer suicide. She'd seen it for herself. Now she had been tasked with getting this critical information to the auxiliary bridge. Gavin Bruce and Niles Welch had sacrificed their lives—along with another boat full of passengers—in getting that information, and she was determined to convey it.

She began moving again, trying to orient herself, when a burly man came barreling along the corridor, red-faced and goggle-eyed, crying out, "To the lifeboats!" She tried to dodge but wasn't fast enough; he clipped her and sent her sprawling to the carpet. By the time she had risen to her feet again, he had vanished from sight.

She leaned against the wall, recovering her breath, keeping back from the stream of panicked people heading for the lifeboat deck. It shocked her how people were prone to the most grotesque displays of selfishness—even, or perhaps especially, the privileged. She hadn't seen the crew and staff carrying on, shrieking and yelping and running around. She couldn't help but think of the contrast with the dignified and self-restrained end of the passengers on the *Titanic*. The world had certainly changed.

When she felt herself again, she continued down the corridor, keeping close to the wall. The auxiliary bridge was at the forward end of the ship, directly below the main bridge—Deck 13 or 14, she recalled. She was currently on Half Deck 7—and that meant she had to ascend.

She continued along the corridor, past deserted cafés and shops, following the signs for the Grand Atrium—from which, she knew, she could better orient herself. Within minutes she had passed through an archway and reached a semicircular railing overlooking the vast hexagonal space. Even at this most extreme of times, she could not help but marvel at it: eight levels high, with glass elevators running up two sides, graced with innumerable little balconies and parapets draped with passionflowers.

Grasping the railing, she looked out and down into the Atrium. The sight was shocking. The King's Arms—the elegant restaurant five levels below—was almost unrecognizable. Cutlery, half-eaten food, trampled flowers, and broken glass were strewn across the floor. Overturned tables, spilling their contents, were scattered everywhere. It looked, she thought, as if a tornado had come through. People were everywhere—some running across the Atrium, others circling aimlessly, still others helping themselves to bottles of wine and liquor. Cries and shouts filtered up toward her.

The glass elevators were still operating, and she headed toward the nearest. But even as she did so, a loud rumble filled the vast space: a growl from deep within the bowels of the ship itself.

And then the Atrium began to tilt.

At first, she assumed it was her imagination. But no: looking up at the great chandelier, she saw it was slanting to one side. As the deep growl grew in intensity, the chandelier began to vibrate, tinkling and jangling crazily. Dahlberg quickly backed into the protection of an archway as pieces of cut crystal began raining down, bouncing like hail among the tables, chairs, and railings.

My God, she thought. *What's happening?*

The heeling grew more acute and she gripped the brass railing fixed to a pillar at one side of the archway. With a scraping noise, chairs and tables in the restaurant below started sliding to one side, slowly at first, then gathering speed. Moments later, she heard the crashing and breaking of glass as the wall of bottles on the elegant bar at one side of the restaurant came down.

She clung to the railing, unable to take her eyes from the carnage occurring below. Now the great Steinway concert grand in the center of the Atrium began to move, sliding on its casters until it careened headlong into the huge statue of Britannia, which shivered into pieces and fell in a ruin of broken marble.

It was as if the ship were caught in the viselike grip of a giant and, despite the groaning, protesting engines, was being forced onto its side. Dahlberg gripped the railing as the slant grew worse and all manner of things—chairs, vases, tables, linens, glassware, cameras, shoes, purses—came tumbling past her from the balconies above to land in the Atrium with staccato thuds and crashes. Over the din of cries and yells she heard a particularly sharp scream from above; a moment later, a short, thickset woman with frizzy blonde hair and wearing a supervisor's uniform came hurtling past from an upper balcony, still screaming, and careened into the piano below with a horrifying crash, the ivory keys scattering, the strings popping in a bizarre symphony of high- and low-pitched twangs.

With a squeal of metal, the elevator nearest to her shuddered in its vertical housing, and then—with a popping of glass that ripped through the entire Atrium—the entire tube shattered all at once and began to fall in slow motion like a glittering glass curtain. The wreck of the elevator—now nothing more than a steel frame—was jarred out of its channel and swung loose on its steel cable. She could see two people aboard, clinging to brass bars inside the elevator cage and screaming. As she watched in horror, the elevator frame swung crazily across the vast interior of the Atrium, spinning as it went, then slammed into a row of balconies on the far side. The people inside were thrown into the air, tumbling down, down, to at last be lost in the chaotic jumble of furniture and fixtures now jammed up against the lower wall of the King's Arms.

Dahlberg gripped the brass rail with all her strength as the floor continued to dip. A new sound suddenly erupted from below, loud as a massive waterfall, accompanied by a rush of cold salty air so strong it nearly blew her off her perch; then white water poured into the lowest level of the Atrium and began boiling up, a vicious surge churning with pulverized furniture, fixtures, and broken bodies. At the same time the huge chandelier above her head finally ripped loose with a crack of iron and plaster; the huge glittering mass fell at an angle, crashed into the parapet just opposite her, then cartwheeled down the side of the Atrium, throwing off great masses of glittering crystal like pulverized ice.

The cold, dead smell of the sea filled her nostrils. Slowly—as if from far away—she began to realize that, despite the awful destruction taking place all around her, the ship didn't appear to be sinking; at least not yet. Instead, it was heeling over and shipping water. The engines continued to roar, the ship continued to surge forward.

Dahlberg collected her thoughts, tried to drown out the sounds of crashing glass, roaring water, and screaming. Much as she wanted to, there was nothing she could do to help anybody here. What she could do, *had* to do, was inform the bridge that the lifeboats were not an option as long as the ship was moving. She looked around and spied a nearby stairwell. Carefully gripping the rail, she half crawled, half clung her way along it until she reached the stairwell, canted at a crazy angle. Gripping the banister with all her might, she began hauling herself upward, one step at a time, heading for the auxiliary bridge.

73

Special Agent Pendergast stared at the bizarre thing of mist and darkness that enveloped him. Simultaneously, he felt the cabin shudder and lean; a deep and powerful vibration hammered up from below. Something violent was happening to the ship. He fell backward, tumbled over an armchair, and slammed into a bookcase. As the ship tilted farther he could hear a sonorous fugue of destruction and despair sounding throughout it: screams and cries, crashing, breaking, the deep thrum of water along the hull. Books came tumbling down around him as the cabin rolled to a desperate angle.

He struck it all from his mind, focusing on the thing—the most bizarre thing. Within the animate smoke, an apparition was faintly visible: rolling red eyes, fanged smile, clawed hands outstretched as it enveloped him, its expression that of need and intense hunger.

Several things flitted almost instantaneously through his mind. He knew what this was, and he knew who had created it, and why. He knew he now faced a fight, not only for his life, but for his very soul. He braced himself mentally as the thing caught him in a clammy embrace, overwhelming his senses with the cloying odor of a damp, rotting cellar, of slippery insects and sagging corpses.

Pendergast abruptly felt calm wash over him—the indifferent, liberating calm he had so recently discovered. He had been taken by surprise; he had little time to prepare; but he could tap into the extraordinary mental powers the Agozyen had set free within his mind and, in so doing, emerge victorious. This contest would be a test for those powers, a baptism by fire.

The thing was trying to enter his mind, probing with damp tendrils of will, of pure desire. He let his mind go blank. He would give it no purchase, nothing to fasten on to. With breathtaking speed, he brought his mind first to the state of *th'an shin gha*, the Doorstep to Perfect Emptiness, and then *stong pa nyid*—the State of Pure Emptiness. The thing would enter and find the room empty. No—there would not even be a room for it to enter.

Vaguely, he was aware of the entity searching the emptiness, drifting, malevolent, eyes like glowing cigarette tips. It thrashed about, seeking an anchor, like a cat sinking in a bottomless ocean. It was already defeated.

It ceased thrashing—and suddenly, like lightning, it wrapped its greasy tendrils around him, sinking fangs directly into Pendergast's mind.

A jolt of terrible pain seared through him. He responded immediately with the opposite tack. He would fight fire with fire, create an impassible mental barrier. He'd wall himself off with pure intellectual noise, deafening and impenetrable.

In the dark void, he summoned a hundred of the world's most important philosophers and set them all to conversation: Parmenides and Descartes, Heraclitus and Kant, Socrates and Nietzsche. At once, dozens upon dozens of arguments sprouted—of nature and consciousness, freedom and pure reason, truth and the divinity of numbers—forming a storm of intellectual noise stretching from horizon to horizon. Scarcely breathing, Pendergast maintained the construct through sheer force of will.

A ripple coursed through the susurrus of dialogues, like a drop of water on the surface of a black pond. As it spread outward, the nearest conversations of the philosophers fell silent. A silent hole formed in the center, like the eye of a storm. Implacably, the smoke ghost drifted through the hole, coming closer.

Instantly, Pendergast dissolved the innumerable debates, drove the men and women from his mind. With great effort, he purged himself of conscious thought once again. If such a purely rational approach would not work, perhaps a more abstract one would.

Quickly, he arrayed in his mind the thousand greatest paintings of the Western tradition. One after another, in chronological order, he allowed them to fill up to the edges the entire frame of his consciousness; he willed their colors, brushstrokes, symbols, hidden meanings, allegories subtle and obvious, to flood his entire consciousness. Duccio's *Maestà;* Botticelli's *Birth of Venus;* Masaccio's *Trinity;* Fabriano's *Adoration*; Van Eyck's *Betrothal of Arnolfini* burst again and again upon his mental landscape, drowning all thought with their complexity, their ravishing beauty. He continued through them, faster and faster, until he approached the present,

Rousseau and Kandinsky and Marin. Then he went back and started over from the beginning, moving still faster now, until all was a blur of color and shape, each image simultaneously held in his mind in overwhelming complexity, allowing the demon no foothold . . .

The blur of colors wavered, began to melt. The low rough form of the tulpa shouldered its way through the kaleidoscope of images, a sink of darkness, sucking everything in as it grew ever nearer in his mind.

Pendergast watched it approach, frozen like a mouse under the gaze of a cobra. With a huge effort, he tore his thoughts free. He was aware of his heart beating much faster now. He could sense the thing's ardent appetite for his essence, his *soul*. Desire radiated out from the smoke ghost like heat. This awareness sent a prickle of panic through him, little poppings and blisterings at the edges of his consciousness.

It was so much stronger than he had ever imagined. Clearly, anyone without the unique mental armor he now enjoyed would have succumbed to the tulpa immediately, without struggle.

The thing came closer still. With something close to despair, Pendergast fell back into the realm of absolute logic, releasing a torrent of pure mathematics across the increasingly fractured landscape of his mind. The tulpa glided through this defense more quickly than ever.

It remained unaffected by every device he had tried. Perhaps it was, in fact, invincible . . .

And now, quite suddenly, the full extremity of his peril was laid bare. For not only was the thing attacking his mind but his body as well. He could feel his muscles jerking in uncontrollable spasms; feel his heart labor; feel his hands clench and unclench. It was terrible and terrifying, a double possession of mind and physical form. Dissociation from his body, so vital to maintaining the state of *stong pa nyid*, grew ever harder to uphold. His limbs fell increasingly under the control of the tulpa; the effort needed to ignore his physical form became increasingly acute.

And then came the moment when it grew impossible. All his carefully constructed defenses, his feints and ploys and stratagems, fell away. And all Pendergast could think about was mere survival.

Now the old family mansion on Dauphine Street rose before him, the memory palace that had always promised refuge in the past. He ran toward it with desperate speed. The yard was crossed in a heartbeat, the front steps taken in a bound. And then he was inside, panting with exertion, fumbling with the locks and door chains.

He turned, back pressed against the doorframe, looking around wildly. The Maison de la Rochenoire was silent and watchful. Ahead, at the end of a long and shadow-haunted hallway, he could see the curve of the grand foyer, with its matchless collections of curiosities and objets d'art, and the double-curved sweep of staircases leading to the second floor. Still farther on, wrapped in gloom, lay the library, its thousands of leather-bound volumes dozing beneath a thin mantle of dust. Normally, this prospect filled him with tranquil pleasure.

Right now, all he felt was the atavistic dread of the hunted.

He raced down the refectory hall, heading toward

the foyer, forcing himself not to look over his shoulder. Reaching the foyer, he wheeled around, eyes searching desperately for a place of concealment.

From behind came a shiver of cold, clammy air.

His gaze fell on an arched doorway, little more than a tracery of black against black in the polished woodwork of a far wall. Beyond, he knew, lay the stairway leading down to the basement and—beyond that—to the rambling chambers and catacombs of the mansion's sub-basement. He knew of literally hundreds of niches, crypts, and hidden passages down there in which he could secret himself.

He moved quickly toward the closed door, then stopped. The thought of cowering in some dark, damp cul-de-sac—waiting, like a cornered rat, for the thing to find him—could not be borne.

With increasing desperation, he raced down the back corridor, through a set of doors and into the kitchens. Here there was a confusing warren of dusty pantries and maids' ports, and he tore through them, searching for some safe haven. It was fruitless. He whirled around again, gasping for breath. The thing was here, he could feel it—and growing closer all the time.

Without wasting another moment he ran back to the foyer. He hesitated only a second, staring wildly around at the polished wood cabinets, the glittering chandelier, the trompe l'oeil ceiling. There was only one possible bolt-hole, one place he might be safe.

He raced up the curving staircase to the second floor and ran as quickly as he could down the echoing gallery. Reaching an open door halfway down on the left, he leapt through it and slammed the door behind him, turning the lock savagely in the key and throwing the deadbolt.

His room—his own room. Although the mansion had burned long ago, he had nevertheless always been safe here. It was the one place in his memory construct so well defended that nobody—even his own brother, Diogenes—could ever penetrate.

The fire crackled in the grate, and candles guttered on the side tables. The air was perfumed by woodsmoke. He waited, his breathing gradually slowing. Just being back in the warm indirect light had a calming effect on him. His heartbeat decelerated. To think that, not long before, he had sat in this room, meditating with Constance, taking on new and unimagined mental powers. It was ironic, even slightly mortifying. But no matter. Soon—very soon—the danger would pass and he could emerge again. He'd been frightened, badly frightened, and with good reason: the thing that had already enveloped him in the physical world had almost enveloped him in the psychical world as well. He had been mere minutes from having his life, his memories, his soul, everything that defined him as a human being, rent asunder. But *it* would not penetrate here. It could not, never, never . . .

All at once he felt that sensation again, close on the back of his neck: a moist, chill breath of clammy air, heavy with the stench of damp earth and rustling, oily insects.

With a cry, he rose to his feet. It was there *already*, in his room, curling toward him, its red-and-black face contorted into the rictus of a smile, vague gray arms extending out toward him with a gesture that would have been almost tender if it were not for the claws . . .

He fell back and it was on him immediately, violating him in the most horrible fashion, spreading in and down and throughout, sucking, relentlessly sucking, until he felt something deep inside him—some essence so very deep he had never been aware that it lay at the core of his being—begin to swell, slip loose, distort . . . and he realized with a shudder of pure horror there was no hope for him anymore—no hope at all.

Constance clutched the bookshelves, rooted by fear, as Pendergast lay on the living room floor, against the wall, deathly still, haloed in mist. The ship continued to tilt, things crashing around her, the roar of water outside rising as the ship heeled. More than once she had tried to stretch out a hand to him, but she had been unable to keep hold, with the violent slanting of the cabin and the crash of books and objects around her.

Now, as she watched, the bizarre and fearful thing that had covered Pendergast like swamp vapor began to shift and break apart. Hope that had left her heart during the brief, dreadful vigil now suddenly returned: Pendergast had won. The tulpa was vanquished.

But then, with a new thrill of horror, she saw that the tulpa was not dispersing—it was instead sinking *into* Pendergast's body.

Suddenly, his clothes began to twitch and writhe, as if countless cockroaches were skittering about beneath them. His limbs convulsed, his frame animated as by a foreign presence. His facial muscles spasmed and vellicated. His eyes opened briefly, staring out at nothing, and in that brief silvery window she saw depths of terror and despair as deep as the universe itself.

A foreign presence . . .

Suddenly, Constance was conflicted no longer. She knew what she had to do.

She stood up, forced her way across the room and up the bizarrely slanting staircase, and passed into Pendergast's bedroom. Ignoring the heeling of the ship, she searched through one drawer after another until her hand closed over his Les Baer .45. She pulled out the weapon, drew back the slide to ensure there was a round in the chamber, then clicked off the safety.

She knew how Pendergast would want to live—and how he would want to die. If she couldn't help him in any other way, at least she could help him with this.

Weapon in hand, she exited the bedroom and—taking tight hold of the railing—descended the slanting stairs to the living room.

71

LeSeur stared at the plated red bow of the *Grenfell* as the Canadian ship desperately backed its screws, trying to swing itself out of the way of the *Britannia* even as the great ocean liner yawed into it at flank speed.

The deck of the aux bridge shook as the podded propulsion systems strained under the extreme maneuver forced upon them. LeSeur didn't even need to glance at the instruments to know it was over: he could extrapolate the trajectories of the two ships merely by staring out the bridge windows. He knew they were each on a course that would bring them together in the worst possible way. Even though the *Grenfell*'s headway had fallen off three or four knots while it tried to maneuver, the *Britannia* was still driving forward at full power with its two fixed screws while the aft pods, rotated ninety degrees, delivered a sideways thrust that was swinging its stern around like a baseball bat toward the *Grenfell*.

"My God, my God, my God . . ." LeSeur heard the chief engineer repeating to himself, a continuous sotto voce prayer, as he stared out the window.

The aux bridge shuddered, tilting at an even crazier

angle. The deck warning systems had lit up as the lowest decks shipped water. LeSeur heard a chorus of fresh sounds: the screeching and tearing of plated steel, the machine-gun popping of rivets, the deep groaning of the ship's immense steel frame.

"My God," whispered the engineer again.

A deep boom sounded from below, followed by a violent shimmy, as if the hull of the ship had been rung like a massive bell. The violence of it threw LeSeur to the floor; and as he rose to his knees a second boom rocked the aux bridge, slamming him sideways into the corner of the navigation table and gashing his forehead. A framed photograph of the *Britannia*'s launching, with Queen Elizabeth presiding, popped free of its screw mounts and cartwheeled along the floor, shedding pieces of glass, skidding to a halt in front of LeSeur's face. With a sense of unreality, he stared at the queen's serene, smiling visage, one white-gloved hand raised to the adoring crowd, and then for a moment he felt a horrible wash of failure—*his* failure. He had failed his queen, his country, everything he stood for and believed in. He had allowed the ship to be taken over by a monster. It was his fault.

He grabbed the edge of the table and pulled himself up, feeling a rivulet of warm blood running down into his eye. With a savage sweep of his hand he wiped it away and tried to recover his senses.

He immediately realized that something significant had just happened to the ship. The deck was righting itself at increasing speed, and the *Britannia* surged forward, no longer yawing but now moving straight ahead. Fresh alarms sounded.

"What on earth—?" LeSeur said. "Halsey, what's happening?"

Halsey had scrambled to his feet, and he stared at the engine panel, his face blanked out with horror.

But LeSeur didn't need Halsey to explain. He suddenly understood what had happened: the *Britannia* had torn off both of its aft rotating pods—essentially, its rudder. The *Grenfell* was now almost dead ahead, a few dozen seconds from impact. The *Britannia* had stopped swinging into her and was now driving toward her in a straight line.

LeSeur grabbed for the radio. "*Grenfell!*" he cried. "Stop backing and straighten out! We've lost steerage!"

The call was unnecessary; LeSeur could already see a massive boiling of water around *Grenfell*'s stern as her captain understood implicitly what he had to do. The *Grenfell* trimmed itself parallel to the *Britannia* just as the two ships closed in on each other.

There was a rush of sound as the *Grenfell*'s bows passed the *Britannia*'s, the ships so close LeSeur could hear the roaring of water, compressed into a wind tunnel formed by the narrow space between the two hulls. There was a loud series of bangs and screeches of metal as the port bridge wing of the *Grenfell* made contact with a lower deck of the *Britannia,* trailing vast geysers of sparks—and then, quite suddenly, it was over. The two ships had passed.

A ragged cheer rose up over the alarms on the auxiliary bridge, and LeSeur could make out a corresponding cheer coming over the VHF from the *Grenfell*.

The chief engineer looked over at him, his face bathed in sweat. "Mr. LeSeur, we lost both aft pods, just tore them right off—"

"I know," LeSeur replied. "And the hull's breached." He felt a swell of triumph. "Mr. Halsey, let the aft bilge spaces and compartments six and five flood. Seal the bilge bulkheads amidships."

But Halsey did nothing but stand there.

"Do it!" LeSeur barked.

"I can't."

"Why the hell not?"

Halsey held out his hands. "Not possible. The bulkheads seal automatically." He pointed at an emergency panel.

"Then *unseal* them! Get a team down there to open the hatches manually!"

"Can't," repeated Halsey helplessly. "Not when they're flooded. There's no override."

"God *damn* this automation! What's the status on the other two pods?"

"Operational. Each delivering full power to the screws. But our speed is down to twenty knots."

"And with the aft pods gone, she'll be steering with engine power now." LeSeur glanced over at the officer of the watch. "ETA Carrion Rocks?"

"At this speed and heading, thirty-five minutes, sir."

LeSeur stared out the bridge windows at the forecastle of the *Britannia*, still pounding relentlessly through the seas. Even at twenty knots they were screwed. What were their options? None that he could see.

"I'm giving the order to abandon ship," he said.

A stillness enveloped the bridge.

"Excuse me, sir—with what?" the chief engineer asked.

"With the lifeboats, of course."

"You can't do that!" cried a new voice—a feminine voice.

LeSeur looked over and saw that the female member of Gavin Bruce's team, Emily Dahlberg, had entered the auxiliary bridge. Her clothes were torn and sopping. He stared at her in surprise.

"You can't launch the lifeboats," she said. "Gavin and Niles Welch attempted a test launch—their boat ruptured."

"Ruptured?" LeSeur repeated. "Where are Liu and Crowley? Why haven't they reported back?"

"There was a mob on the lifeboat deck," Dahlberg said, breathing heavily. "Liu and Crowley were attacked. Maybe killed. The passengers launched a second boat. That one burst open when it hit the sea, as well."

This was greeted by shocked silence.

LeSeur turned to the chief radio officer. "Activate the automatic abandon-ship message."

"Sir, you heard her!" Kemper spoke up. "Those boats would be no better than floating coffins. Besides, it takes forty-five minutes to load and launch the lifeboats under ideal circumstances. We've got thirty. We'll impact when all the passengers are standing crowded on the half decks—which are open, all steel and struts. It'll be a massacre. Half of them will go overboard and the rest will be beaten to hell."

"We'll get as many on as we can, hold them on the boats until impact, and then launch."

"The force of the impact may derail the boats. They'll be jammed up in the half deck and there won't be any way to launch them. They'll go down with the ship."

LeSeur turned to Halsey. "True?"

The man's face was white. "I believe that is correct, sir."

"What's the alternative?"

"We get the passengers into their cabins and have them brace for impact."

"And then what? The ship'll go down in five minutes!"

"Then we load and launch the lifeboats."

"But I just heard the impact may *derail* the lifeboats!" LeSeur realized he was hyperventilating. He forced himself to slow down.

"At twenty knots, there'll be less damage, less of an impact. At least some lifeboats will remain railed and ready to launch. And with less of an impact, maybe we'll have more time before . . . we sink."

"Maybe? That's not good enough."

"That's all we've got," said Halsey.

LeSeur wiped the blood out of his eye again and flung it away with a snap of his fingers. He turned again to the chief radio officer. "Send a message over the PA. All passengers are to report to their quarters immediately—no exceptions. They are to don the flotation devices found under their bunks. They are then to get in their berths, feet facing forward, in fetal position, and cushion themselves with pillows and blankets. If they can't reach their cabins, they are to get into the closest chair they can find and assume a protective position—hands clasped behind the head, head between the knees."

"Yes, sir."

"*Immediately* after impact they are all to report to their lifeboat assembly stations, just as in the drills. They are to take absolutely nothing with them but their PFDs. Got it?"

"Yes, sir." He turned back toward his terminal. A moment later, a siren went off and his voice sounded over the public address system, giving the orders.

LeSeur turned to Emily Dahlberg. "I guess that goes for you, as well. You'd better return to your cabin."

She looked back at him. After a moment, she nodded.

"And Mrs. Dahlberg? Thank you."

She left the bridge.

LeSeur watched the hatch close behind her. Next he turned a baleful eye on the CCTV displaying a grainy image of the helm. Mason was still standing there, one hand draped on the wheel, the other lightly resting on the two fore pod throttles, maintaining heading by slight adjustments to the speed of the screws.

LeSeur pushed the transmit button on the internal bridge-to-bridge intercom and leaned into it. "Mason? I know you can hear me."

No answer.

"Are you *really* going to do this?"

As if in answer, her white hand moved from the throttle to a small covered panel. She flicked off the cover, pulled two levers, then returned to the throttles, pressing both as far forward as they would go.

There was a throaty rumble as the engines responded.

"Jesus," said Halsey, staring at the engine panel. "She's redlining the gas turbines."

The ship surged forward. With a sick feeling, LeSeur watched the speed indicator begin to creep up. Twenty-two knots. Twenty-four. Twenty-six.

"How is this possible?" he asked, flabbergasted. "We lost half our propulsion back there!"

"She's goosing the turbines way beyond their specs," said Halsey.

"How high can they go?"

"I'm not sure. She's pushing them past five thousand rpms . . ." He leaned over and touched one of the dials, as if in disbelief. "And now she's redlining all four Wärtsilä diesels, directing the excess power to the two remaining pods."

"Is that going to burn them out?"

"Hell, yes. But not soon enough."

"How long?"

"She could go on like this for . . . thirty, forty minutes."

LeSeur glanced at the chartplotter. The *Britannia* was back up to almost thirty knots and the Carrion Rocks were twelve nautical miles ahead. "All she needs," he said slowly, "is twenty-four."

75

Pendergast lay prostrate in a screaming night. He had made one final, almost superhuman effort to defend himself, rallying all the newfound intellectual powers the Agozyen had conferred upon him—and exhausting them in the process. It had been no use. The tulpa had sunk into the marrow of his bones, into the deepest core of his mind. He felt a dreadful alienness within himself, like the depersonalization of the worst kind of panic attack. A hostile entity was relentlessly, implacably devouring him . . . and like a man in the paralysis of a nightmare, he was incapable of resistance. It was a psychic agony far worse than the most appalling physical torture.

He withstood it for an endless, indescribable moment. And then, quite suddenly, blessed darkness rushed over him.

How long he lay—unable to think, unable to move—he did not know. And then, out of the darkness, came a voice. A voice he recognized.

"Don't you think it's time we spoke?" it said.

Slowly—hesitantly—Pendergast opened his eyes. He found himself in a small, dim space with a low, sloping roof. On one side was a plaster wall, covered with childish treasure maps and scrawled imitations of famous paintings in crayon and pastel; on the other, a latticed doorway. Weak afternoon light trickled through the lattices, revealing dust motes floating lazily in the air and giving the hidden space the otherworldly glow of an undersea grotto. Books by Howard Pyle, Arthur Ransome, and Booth Tarkington lay scattered in the corners. It smelled pleasantly of old wood and floor polish.

Across from him sat his brother, Diogenes Pendergast. His limbs were sunk into deep shadow, but the latticed light revealed the sharp contours of his face. Both his eyes were still hazel . . . as they were before the Event.

This had been their hideout, the tiny room they had fashioned beneath the back stairs in the old house: the one they'd called Plato's Cave. Its creation was one of the last things they had done together, before the bad times began.

Pendergast stared at his brother. "You're dead."

"Dead." Diogenes rolled the word around, as if tasting it. "Perhaps. Perhaps not. But I'll always be alive in your mind. And in this house."

This was most unexpected. Pendergast paused a moment to examine his own sensations. He realized that the dreadful, probing pain of the tulpa was gone, at least for the moment. He felt nothing: not surprise, not even a sense of unreality. He was, he guessed, in some unsuspected, unfathomably deep recess of his own subconscious mind.

"You're in rather dire straits," his brother continued. "Perhaps more dire than any I've seen you in before. I'm chagrined to admit that, this time, they are not of my devising. And so I ask again: don't you think it's time we spoke?"

"I can't defeat it," Pendergast said.

"Precisely."

"And it cannot be killed."

"True. It will only leavc when its mission is done. But that does not mean it cannot be mastered."

Pendergast hesitated. "What do you mean?"

"You've studied the literature. You've experienced the teachings. Tulpas are undependable, unreliable things."

Pendergast did not immediately reply.

"They might be summoned for a particular purpose. But once summoned, they tend to stray, to develop minds of their own. That is one reason they can be so very, very dangerous if used—shall we say?—irresponsibly. That is something you can turn to your advantage."

"I'm not sure I understand."

"Must I spell it out for you, *frater*? I've told you: it is possible to bend a tulpa to your will. All you have to do is *change its purpose*."

"I'm in no condition to change anything. I've struggled with it—struggled to the end of my strength—and I've been bested."

Diogenes smirked. "How like you, Aloysius. You're so used to everything being easy that, at the first sign of difficulty, you throw up your hands like a petulant child."

"All that makes me unique has been drawn from me like marrow from a bone. There's nothing left."

"You're wrong. Only the outer carapace has been torn away: this supposed superweapon of intellect you've recently taken upon yourself. The core of your being remains—at least for now. If it was gone, completely gone, you'd know it—and we wouldn't be speaking now."

"What can I do? I can't struggle any longer."

"That's precisely the problem. You're looking at it the wrong way: as a struggle. Have you forgotten all they taught you?"

For a moment, Pendergast sat staring at his brother, uncomprehending. Then, quite suddenly, he understood.

"The lama," he breathed.

Diogenes smiled. "Bravo."

"How . . ." Pendergast stopped, began again. "How do you know these things?"

"You know them, too. For the moment, you were simply too . . . *overwrought* to see them. Now, go forth and sin no more."

Pendergast glanced away from his brother, toward the stripes of gold light that slanted in through the latticed door. He realized, with a faint surprise, that he was afraid: that the very last thing he wanted to do was step out through that door.

Taking a deep breath, he willed himself to push it open.

Yawning, passionate blackness took him once again. Again came the hungry, enveloping thing: again he felt the dreadful alienness *within* him, thrusting its way through his thoughts and limbs alike, insinuating itself into his most primitive emotions, a violation more intimate and ravening and insatiable than anything he had ever imagined. He felt utterly, impossibly alone, beyond sympathy or succor—and that, somehow, seemed worse than any pain.

He took one more breath, summoning his last reserves of physical and emotional strength. He knew he would have only one chance; after that, he would be lost forever, consumed utterly.

Emptying his mind as best he could, he put aside the ravening thing and recalled the lama's own teachings on desire. He imagined himself on a lake, quite saline, precisely at body temperature, of indeterminate color. He imagined himself floating in it, perfectly motionless. Then—and this was hardest of all—he slowly stopped struggling.

Do you fear annihilation? he asked himself.

A pause. *No.*

Do you care about being subsumed into the void?

Another pause. *No.*

Are you willing to surrender everything?

Yes.

To give yourself to it utterly?

More quickly now: *Yes.*

Then you are ready.

His limbs convulsed in a long shudder, then relaxed. Throughout his mental and physical being—in every muscle, every synapse—he felt the tulpa hesitate. There was a strange, utterly inexpressible moment of stasis. Then, slowly, the thing relaxed its hold.

And as it did so, Pendergast let a new image—single, powerful, inescapable—form in his mind.

As if from far away, he heard his brother speak again: *Vale, frater*.

For a moment, Diogenes became visible again. Then, as quickly as he had come, he began to fade away.

"Wait," Pendergast said. "Don't go."

"But I must."

"I have to know. Are you really dead?"

Diogenes did not answer.

"Why did you do this? Why did you help me?"

"I didn't do it for you," Diogenes replied. "I did it for my child." And as he faded into the enfolding dark, he gave a small, enigmatic smile.

Constance sat in the wing chair at Pendergast's feet. A dozen times, she had raised the gun and pointed it at his heart; a dozen times, she had hesitated. She had hardly noticed when the ship righted itself suddenly, when it drove forward again at high speed. For her, the ship had ceased to exist.

She could wait no longer. It was cruel to let him suffer. He had been kind to her; she should respect what, she was certain, would be his wishes. Taking a strong grip on the weapon, she raised it with fresh resolve.

A violent shudder raked Pendergast's frame. A moment later, his eyes fluttered open.

"Aloysius?" she asked.

For a moment, he did not move. Then he gave the faintest of nods.

Suddenly, she became aware of the smoke ghost. It

had materialized by the agent's shoulder. For a moment it was still. Then it drifted first one way, then another, almost like a dog searching for a scent. Shortly, it began to move away.

"Do not interfere," Pendergast whispered. And for a moment Constance feared the dreadful change was still over him. But then he opened his eyes again and looked at her, and she knew the truth immediately.

"You've come back," she said.

He nodded.

"How?" she whispered.

When he answered, it was in the faintest of voices. "That which I took on when I beheld the Agozyen has been burned away in my struggle. Not unlike the lost wax process in metal casting. All that now remains is the . . . original."

Weakly, he raised one hand. Without another word, she knelt at his side, grasped it tightly.

"Let me rest," he whispered. "For two minutes—no more. Then we must go."

She nodded, glanced at the clock on the mantel. Over her shoulder, the tulpa was gliding away. As she turned to watch, it drifted—slowly, but with implacable purpose—over the still form of the unconscious Marya; through the front door of the suite; and on into mystery.

76

LeSeur stood on the aux bridge and stared out the wall of forward windows. The ship's bow bulled through the heavy seas at high speed, the hull slamming, green water periodically sweeping the forecastle. The fog was lifting, the rain had almost ceased, and visibility had risen to almost a mile.

Nobody spoke. LeSeur had been racking his mind for a way out. There was none. All they could do was monitor the electronics over which they had no control. The chartplotter showed the Carrion Rocks to be two nautical miles dead ahead. LeSeur felt the sweat and blood trickling down his face, stinging his eyes.

"ETA Carrion Rocks in four minutes," said the third officer.

The lookout stood at the window, binoculars raised and white-knuckled. LeSeur wondered why the man felt it was so important to see the rocks coming—there was nothing they could do about it. Nothing.

Kemper laid a hand on his shoulder. "Sir, I think you need to issue instructions to the bridge personnel to assume defensive positions for . . . for the upcoming collision."

LeSeur nodded, a sick feeling in his stomach. He turned and signaled for attention.

"Officers and personnel of the bridge," he said. "I want everyone on the floor, in fetal position, feet facing forward, heads cradled in hands. The collision event will not be a short one. Do not rise until the vessel is clearly DIW."

The lookout asked, "Me as well, sir?"

"You, too."

Reluctantly and awkwardly, they lay down on the floor and assumed their defensive positions.

"Sir?" Kemper said to LeSeur. "We can't afford an injured captain at the critical moment."

"In a minute."

LeSeur took one last look at the CCTV trained on the bridge helm. Mason remained calmly at the helm, as if on the most routine of crossings, one hand draped casually over the wheel, the other caressing a lock of hair that had escaped from under her cap.

Out of the corner of his eye he caught something beyond the bridge windows, and shifted his gaze.

Directly ahead and about a mile off, LeSeur could see a light-colored smudge emerge out of the mist, which resolved itself into a ragged line of white below the uncertain horizon. He immediately knew it was the immense groundswell breaking over the outer edges of the Carrion Rocks. He stared in horrified fascination as the line of white resolved into a tearing expanse of combers boiling and erupting over the outer reefs, exploding over the rocks and sending up geysers as tall as small skyscrapers. And behind the churning white water he could see a series of rocky masses looming up like the black, ruined towers of some grim castle of the deep.

In all his years at sea, it was the most terrifying sight he had ever seen.

"Get down, sir!" Kemper cried from his position on the floor.

But LeSeur could not get down. He could not take his eyes off their looming end. Very few human beings had looked into hell itself—and to him, this cauldron of writhing water and jagged rocks *was* hell, the real hell, far worse than mere fire and brimstone. A cold, black, watery hell.

Who were they kidding? Nobody would survive—nobody.

Please, God, just make it quick.

And then his eye caught a movement on the CCTV. Mason had seen the rocks herself. She was leaning forward, eagerly, as if urging the ship onward by sheer willpower, yearning it on to its watery grave. But then an odd thing happened: she jumped and turned, staring with fright at something offscreen. Then she backed up, away from the wheel, a look of pure terror on her face. Her movement carried her out of the field of the camera, and for a moment nothing happened. Then there was a strange burst of static on the screen, almost like a cloud of smoke, crossing the field of view in the direction Mason had retreated. LeSeur slapped the CCTV, assuming it was a glitch in the video feed. But then his audio headset, tuned to the bridge frequency, transmitted a gut-chilling scream—Mason. She reappeared, staggering forward. The cloud—it *was* like smoke—whirled about her and she breathed it in and out, clawing at her chest, her throat. The captain's hat tumbled off her head and her hair flew out wildly, snapping back and forth. Her limbs moved in strange, herky-jerky spasms, almost as if she were fighting her own body. With a thrill of horror, LeSeur was reminded of a marionette struggling against a controlling puppeteer. Writhing with the same, spastic movements, Mason approached the control panel. Her smoke-shrouded limbs convulsed in fresh struggle. Then LeSeur saw her stretch forth her hand—unwillingly, it seemed—and press a button. The cloud seemed to sink deeper into her, thrusting itself down her throat, while she clawed at the air, arms and legs jerking now in agony. She fell to her knees, hands up in the caricature of prayer; then she sank, shrieking, to the floor, out of sight of the camera's view.

For a second, LeSeur stood motionless, staring at the screen in surprise and disbelief. Then he grabbed the radio, punched in the frequency for the guards posted outside the bridge. "LeSeur to bridge security, what the hell's going on up there?"

"I don't know, sir," came the reply. "But the Level Three alert's been lifted. The security locks on the bridge hatch just disengaged."

"Then what the hell are you waiting for?" he screamed. "Get in there and turn hard aport, *hard aport, you son of a bitch, now, now, now*!"

77

Emily Dahlberg had left the auxiliary bridge and, as ordered, was making her way back to her cabin. The ship was still proceeding at what seemed like full speed. She descended a staircase to Deck 9, walked along a corridor, and emerged again onto a balcony overlooking the highest level of the Grand Atrium.

She paused, shocked at the sight that greeted her eyes. The water had drained away into the lower decks, leaving a tangled wreckage of sodden and broken furniture, wires, seaweed, wood paneling, ripped-up carpet, broken glass, and—here and there—a motionless body. The place stank of seawater.

She knew she had to get to her cabin and brace for the collision. She'd listened to the argument on the auxiliary bridge, heard the announcement over the PA system. But it occurred to her that her cabin, here on Deck 9, might not be a good place to be. It seemed a better place might be on one of the lower weather decks, near the stern, where she would be farthest from the point of impact and could perhaps jump into the sea afterward. It was, of course, a pathetic hope, but at least it seemed a better risk than being trapped in a cabin a hundred and twenty feet above the water.

She ran down a set of stairs, descending another eight levels, then stepped through an archway and began picking her way sternward, through the sodden debris littering the floor of the Grand Atrium. The elegant wallpaper of the King's Arms restaurant was stained and darkened, with an encircling line of kelp showing the high-water level. She passed the ruined piano, looking away when she noticed one crushed leg protruding heavily from the sound box.

With everyone in their cabins, the ship seemed strangely still, unpopulated and ghostlike. But then she heard a sound nearby—a sobbing—and, turning, noticed a bedraggled boy of perhaps eleven years old, shirtless, soaking wet, crouching amid a scatter of debris. Her heart swelled with pity.

She made her way over to him. "Hello, young man," she said, trying to keep her tone as light and as even as possible.

He stared at her and she extended a hand. "Come with me. I'll take you out of here. My name is Emily."

The boy took her hand and she helped him to his feet, then took off her jacket and placed it around his shoulders. He was shaking with terror. She put an arm around him. "Where's your family?"

"My mum and dad," he began in an English accent. "I can't find them."

"Lean on me. I'll help you. We don't have much time."

He gave one more gulping sob and she hustled him

out of the Grand Atrium, past the Regent Street shops—shuttered and deserted—and then along the side corridor leading to the weather deck. She stopped at an emergency station for two sets of life vests, which they put on. Then she led the way over to the hatch.

"Where are we going?" the boy asked.

"Outside, onto the deck. It'll be safer there."

Within moments of opening the hatchway and helping the boy step out, she found herself drenched by wind-driven spray. Above, she could see airplanes, circling uselessly. Keeping a tight hold on the boy's hand, she made her way to the rail, preparing to head aft along the deck. The engines screamed and throbbed, shaking the ship like a terrier shaking a rat.

She turned back, looking at the boy. "Let's go—" she began. Then the words died in her throat. Over the boy's shoulder, ahead of the *Britannia*'s bow, she could see a line of leaping white surf thrown up against a dead-black row of huge, tooth-like rocks. An involuntary cry escaped her lips. The boy turned and stared. The wall of death was approaching at high speed. There would be no time to reach the stern, no time to do anything but brace for the impact.

The boom of the surf against the rocks reached her, a deep vibration that seemed to thrum through her body. She put her arms around the boy. "Let's just stay here," she said breathlessly. "We'll crouch down against the wall."

They took shelter against the superstructure, the boy, now crying again, bundled in her arms. A scream sounded from somewhere above her, a forlorn sound like a lost seagull.

If she had to die, at least she would die with dignity, with another human being in her arms. She held the boy's head against her chest, closed her eyes, and began to pray.

And then the sound of the engine changed. The ship heeled over with a new motion. Her eyes flew open, almost afraid to hope. But it was true—*the ship was beginning to turn*. Rising, she brought the boy back to the rail, hardly believing her eyes as the booming line of surf edged closer, yet not quite as fast now. As the ship continued to yaw, the steepening groundswell pounded the hull, throwing up sheet after sheet of water, but in between them she could see the black rocks swinging past the bow—turning, turning—and then they were running parallel and the monstrous line of surf passed on the starboard side, the nearest rocks almost close enough to touch as they ran past, the ship's hull slamming through the steep-walled waves.

And then, suddenly, the last moiling tooth fell aft, the boom of the surf faded, and the ship headed on, noticeably slower now. And over the whine of the engines and the wrack of the surf, she could hear another sound now: the sound of cheers.

"Well," she said, turning to the boy. "Shall we go find your mum and dad?" And as she walked back to the hatch on shaking legs, Emily Dahlberg allowed herself a small smile of relief.

78

Scott Blackburn sat, cross-legged, in the ruins of the Penshurst Triplex. The stateroom salon was a perfect whirlwind of destruction—rare china, precious crystal, exquisite oil paintings, jade and marble sculptures—now so much bric-a-brac, lying strewn about and piled up against one wall in a tangled, broken heap.

Blackburn was oblivious to it all. Throughout the crisis, he had taken shelter in a closet with his precious, his most prized, his *only* possession, cradling it and protecting it from any harm. And now that the worst had passed and they were headed into port—as he'd always known they would—he had lovingly replaced it on its golden hook in his salon.

His possession—that was wrong. Because, if anything, it possessed *him*.

Pulling the monastic robes more tightly around his athletic frame, he sat on the floor in front of the Agozyen, assuming the lotus position, never once allowing his eyes to drift toward the mandala. He was alone, wonderfully alone—his private maid was gone, perhaps dead, for all he knew—and there would be nobody to disturb his communion with the unending and the infinite. His frame shivered in involuntary pleasure at the mere expectation of what was to come. It was like a drug—the most perfect, ecstatic, liberating drug—and he could never get enough of it.

Soon, the rest of the world would share his need.

He sat quietly, his heartbeat and mental restlessness slowing in turn. Finally, with a deliberation that was both delicious and maddening, he permitted his head to rise and his eyes to gaze upon the infinite wonder and mystery of the Agozyen.

But even as he did so, something intruded on his private world. An inexplicable chill caused his limbs to tremble beneath the silken wraps. He realized that a stench was settling over the room—a smell of fungus and the deep woods, completely overpowering the mellow fragrance of the butter candles. Disquiet chased away his feelings of expectation and desire. It was almost as if . . . but no, that wasn't possible . . .

In sudden apprehension, he turned to look over his shoulder. And to his transcendental horror and dismay, *it* was there—not bent on hunting down his enemy, but rather closing in on him with a hunger and desire that was palpable. He quickly rose to his feet but already it was upon him, penetrating him, filling his limbs and his thoughts alike with its burning, all-consuming need. He reared back with a gargling scream, falling over a side table and crashing to the floor, but already he felt his living essence being sucked from him, pulled relentlessly and utterly into a black and unquiet void from which there was no return . . .

Soon, quiet once again settled over the Penshurst Triplex. The guttural cries and sounds of struggle faded into the smoky, salt-heavy air. A minute passed, then two. And then the front door to the suite was opened with a passkey. Special Agent Pendergast stepped inside. He paused in the entryway, taking in the scene of devastation with pale eyes. Then, stepping over the clutter of broken objets d'art with the finicky precision of a cat, he made his way into the salon. Scott Blackburn was sprawled across the carpet, motionless, limbs shrunken and contorted into odd angles, as if bones and sinew and viscera had all been sucked from him, leaving a loose, empty sack of skin. Pendergast gave him only the most cursory of glances.

Stepping over the body, he approached the Agozyen. Taking great care to avert his eyes, he reached out as one might reach toward a poisonous snake. He let the silken shroud fall down over the face of the painting, felt carefully around the edges to ensure that every inch was covered. Then—only then—did he turn to face it, lift it from its golden hook, carefully roll it up, and tuck it under his arm. And then he withdrew silently and swiftly from the suite.

79

Patrick Kemper, chief security officer of the *Britannia*, stood on the bridge and watched Cabot Tower, perched on a bluff at the entrance to St. John's Harbour, glide past. A dull thudding of rotors sounded as yet another medevac chopper took off from the forecastle with a load of severely injured passengers. The medevac flights had been going continuously since the storm abated and the ship had come within chopper range of the coast. The sound of rotors changed timbre as the helicopter rose, temporarily passing through the bridge's view, swung round, and disappeared overhead. It was like a war zone on the ship—and Kemper felt like a shell-shocked soldier returning from the front.

The great ship passed through the Narrows and continued to slow, its two podded screws grinding and shuddering. LeSeur and the St. John's harbor pilot struggled to maintain control of the now unwieldy ship: stripped of its rotating propulsion pods, the *Britannia* had all the maneuverability of the floating carcass of a whale. The only berth at St. John's able to take the vessel was in the container port, and as two assisting tugboats pushed the ship to starboard the long, rust-streaked platform came into view, surrounded by a cluster of giant container cranes. The berth had been hastily vacated by a VLCC, which was now anchored in the harbor.

As the *Britannia* continued to turn toward the berth, Kemper saw that the quayside looked like a scene out of a disaster movie. There were dozens of emergency vehicles, ambulances, fire trucks, morgue vans, and police cars ready to receive the dead and injured, a sea of flashing lights and distant sirens.

Kemper was beyond exhausted. His head pounded and his vision was blurry from lack of sleep and non-stop stress. Now that their ordeal was over, he found himself speculating on the grim aftermath: the Maritime Board of Inquiry hearings, the testimonies, the lawsuits, the relentless press, the shame and the blame. For the first order of the day would be assigning blame. He knew well that he, as chief security officer, along with LeSeur—who was one of the most decent men Kemper had ever worked with—would bear the brunt. They would be lucky to escape criminal charges, especially LeSeur. Cutter had survived, and he would be an implacable enemy.

He glanced at LeSeur, who was huddled with the harbor pilot over the ECDIS, and wondered what the first officer was thinking. Did he know what lay ahead? Of course he did—he was no fool.

The *Britannia* was now moving only under tug power, being eased into its berth. Beyond, above the tower and on the far side of the harbor, he could see the hovering news choppers, kept out of the ship's airspace but getting in plenty of shots from a distance. No doubt the damaged and limping outline of the *Britannia* was being broadcast live on millions of television screens at this very moment. It was one of the worst—or at least most bizarre—maritime disasters of recent history.

He swallowed: he better get used to it. This was going to be his life from now on: Patrick Kemper, chief security officer on the maiden voyage of the *Britannia*. That's what he would be known as until long after he was dead. It would be his dubious claim to fame.

Forcing these thoughts out of his mind, he focused on the ship's security screens. At least all systems had been stabilized—which was more than he could say for the vessel itself. He could only imagine what it must look like from the quay: the lower port portholes and balconies bashed in by the sea, the starboard side of Deck 6 peeled open like a sardine can by the bridge wing of the *Grenfell*. The insides were even worse. As they had limped in toward St. John's, Kemper had done a security inspection of the lower decks. The sea had punched in through every piece of glass on the port side below Deck 4—portholes, plate-glass windows, and balconies alike—the water ripping through the shops, restaurants, casinos, and corridors with the force of a flash flood, smashing and piling everything up in the corners and leaving behind a mess worthy of a hurricane. The lower decks stank of seawater, old food, and dead bodies. He had been horrified to see how many people had been killed or drowned in the flood, their mangled bodies strewn about or wedged horribly among piles of debris, some even dangling from ceiling fixtures. In all, more than one hundred and fifty passengers and crew had lost their lives and nearly a thousand more had been injured.

The tugs slowly brought the great vessel into position. He could hear, faintly through the bridge windows, the sirens and bullhorns shrieking as the emergency responders geared up to receive the hundreds of injured passengers and crew still on board the ship.

He wiped his face and ran an eye once more down the security systems panels. He needed to focus on the miracle that most of them were still alive—the miracle that had happened on the bridge just before the Carrion Rocks. The miracle he could not explain, and never would be able to explain.

The ship began to creep into place alongside the quay. Great hawsers, used as springlines, were dropped on the quay and manhandled over massive bollards by teams of longshoremen. LeSeur broke away from the vector radar. "Mr. Kemper," he said, his voice the very quintessence of exhaustion, "we will be docked in ten minutes. Please make the announcement we discussed regarding evacuation procedures."

Kemper nodded, then keyed up the public address system and spoke into the bridge mike. "*Attention all passengers and crew: the ship will be docking in ten minutes. Seriously injured persons will be evacuated first. Repeat: seriously injured persons will be evacuated first. All others must remain in their staterooms or the Belgravia Theatre and await further instructions. Thank you.*"

Kemper could hear his own voice echoing over the PA system on the bridge, and he hardly recognized it. He sounded like a dead man speaking.

80

A light drizzle of rain fell from the early morning sky as LeSeur leaned against the teak rail of the *Britannia*'s bow, looking back over the enormous vessel. He could see the dark crowds of passengers pressing forward along the decks, and he could hear, drifting up with the rain, their querulous voices as they jockeyed for position before the gangway, every one trying to get off the ship as quickly as possible. Most of the emergency vehicles had left, and now it was time for the uninjured passengers to disembark. Over his shoulder, lined up on the quay, were ranks of buses ready to take people away to area hotels and homes that had been volunteered by Newfoundlanders.

As the deckhands were preparing to remove the gangway rope, the raised voices of the crew on board mingled with the shrill voices of complaint and threat from the passengers. It amazed LeSeur how these people still had the energy to be outraged. They were damned lucky to be alive.

Ropes, construction tape, and movable stanchions had been set up in a jerry-rigged effort to direct and manage the efficient processing of the passengers. At the head of the line he could see Kemper, who appeared to be giving his people the final directions on what to do: each passenger had to be identified and photographed—by orders of the RCMP—and directed to their assigned bus. No exceptions.

They were not going to like it, LeSeur knew. But the corporation had to create some kind of legal record of who had disembarked from the ship if they were ever to sort out the missing from the injured and the healthy. Corporate wanted a photograph, he was told, because they didn't want healthy passengers later suing for injuries. It was still, even after all that had happened, about money, first, foremost, and last.

The gate over the gangway was lifted and the dark stream of passengers came rolling down, like a ragged line of refugees. And wouldn't you know it: the first off was a burly man in a filthy tux, shoving his way past the women and children. He came charging down the ramp, yelling, and in the windless air his voice carried all the way to the bow. "God damn it, I want to talk to the man in charge here! I will not be photographed like some criminal!"

He burst through the press of debarkation crew members at the base of the gangway, but the St. John's stevedores and RCMP officers who had been called in to assist were not to be trifled with. They blocked his way, and when he resisted they slapped cuffs on him and took him aside.

"Get your hands off me!" came the man's shout. "How dare you! I manage a twenty-five-billion-dollar hedge fund in New York! What is this, Communist Russia?"

He was promptly bustled off to a waiting paddy wagon and shoved inside, yelling all the way. His fate seemed to have a salubrious effect on anyone else thinking of making a scene.

With effort, LeSeur tuned out the voices raised in complaint and outrage. He understood why they were upset and sympathized with them, but the bottom line was that this was the fastest way to get them off the ship. And there was still a serial killer to be found.

Kemper came up alongside him and leaned against the rail, watching the flow of people from a broader vantage point. They shared a moment of exhausted, silent commiseration. There didn't seem to be anything to say.

LeSeur's thoughts turned to the board of inquiry hearings that lay ahead. He wondered just how he was going to explain the bizarre . . . *thing* he had witnessed attack Mason. It had been like a demonic possession. Ever since it happened, he had been going over the sequence of events in his mind—dozens of times—and yet he was no nearer understanding what the hell he had seen than when he first witnessed it. What was he going to say? *I saw a ghost possess Captain Mason?* No matter how he couched it, they would think he was being evasive, or that he was crazy—or worse. No, he could never tell the truth about what he saw. Ever. He'd say, instead, that Mason had some kind of fit, an epileptic attack perhaps, and leave out the rest. Let the medical examiners figure out what happened to her limp, deflated body.

He sighed, watching the endless files of people shuffling along in the drizzle. They sure didn't look so high and mighty now; they looked like refugees.

His thoughts kept returning obsessively to what he'd seen. Maybe he hadn't seen it at all; maybe it had been a glitch in the CCTV feed. It could have been, in fact, a speck of dust trapped inside the camera, magnified a hundred times, joggled about by the vibration of the ship's engines. His stress and exhaustion had led him to see something that wasn't there.

Yes, that was it. That had to be it.

But then he thought of what they'd found on the bridge: the bizarre, sacklike corpse of Captain Mason slumped on the floor, her bones like so much mush . . .

He was shaken from his thoughts by the approach of a familiar figure: a portly man with a walking stick and a white carnation on his spotless lapel. Immediately, LeSeur felt his guts turn to water: it was Ian Elliott, principal director of the North Star Line. No doubt the man had flown here to preside personally over his public keelhauling. At his side, Kemper made a small, strangled sound. LeSeur swallowed—this was going to be even uglier than he'd imagined.

Elliott strode up. "Captain LeSeur?"

LeSeur stiffened. "Sir."

"I wanted to congratulate you."

This was so unexpected that, for a moment, LeSeur didn't understand what he'd heard. Perhaps it was all a hallucination—God knew he was tired enough to be seeing things.

"Sir?" he asked in a very different tone of voice.

"Thanks to your courage, seamanship, and levelheadedness, the *Britannia* is still afloat. I don't know the whole story yet, but from what I do know, things could have turned out very differently. I wanted to come here and thank you personally." And he stuck out his hand.

With a sense of unreality, LeSeur shook it.

"I'll let you get on with the disembarkation. But once all the passengers are off, perhaps you could fill me in on the details."

"Of course, sir."

"And then there's the question of the *Britannia*."

"Question, sir? I'm not sure I understand."

"Well, once she's been repaired and fitted out, she'll need a new captain—won't she?" And then, giving him a small smile, Elliott turned and walked away.

It was Kemper who broke the silence. "I don't frigging believe it," he murmured.

LeSeur could barely believe it either. Perhaps this was just the spin the North Star public relations people wanted to put on things—to paint them as heroes who saved the lives of over twenty-five hundred passengers. Perhaps not. In any case, he wasn't going to question it. And he'd be happy to tell Elliott everything that had happened—at least, *almost* everything . . .

His thoughts were interrupted by the approach of an RCMP officer.

"Which of you is Mr. Kemper?" the man asked.

"I'm Kemper," the chief of security said.

"There's a gentleman here from the FBI who wants to speak to you."

LeSeur watched as a thin man stepped out of the shadows of the superstructure. It was the FBI agent, Pendergast.

"What do you want?" Kemper asked.

Pendergast stepped forward into the light. He was dressed in a black suit and his face was as gaunt and corpse-like as anyone coming off the ill-fated ship. Tucked under one arm he carried a long, thin mahogany box. Next to him, linked in the other arm, was a young woman with short dark hair and dead-serious eyes.

"Thank you, Mr. Kemper, for a most interesting voyage." And with that, Pendergast eased his arm from the woman's support and slipped a hand into a valise he carried.

Kemper stared at the man in surprise. "There's no need to tip the ship's officers," he said curtly.

"I think you'll want this tip," Pendergast replied, extracting an oilskin-wrapped package from the valise. He extended it toward Kemper.

"What's this?" Kemper asked, taking the package.

The man said nothing more. He merely turned, and then he and the woman melted back into the early-morning shadows, heading toward the moving masses of people.

LeSeur watched as Kemper untied the oilskin.

"Looks like your three hundred thousand pounds," he said, as Kemper stared in silent astonishment at the soiled bundles of notes.

"Strangest man I ever met," Kemper said, almost as if speaking to himself.

LeSeur didn't hear him. He was thinking again of that demon-haunted shroud that had engulfed Captain Mason.

Epilogue

Summer had finally come to the Llölung Valley. The Tsangpo River roared over its cobbled bed, fed by melting snows in the great mountains beyond. Flowers mortared the cracks and hollows of the valley floor. Black eagles soared above the cliffs, their high-pitched cries echoing from the great wall of granite at the valley's head, mingling with the steady roar of the waterplume leaping off its rim and feathering down onto the rocks below. Beyond rose up the three massive peaks, Dhaulagiri, Annapurna, and Manaslu, swathed in eternal glaciers and snow, like three cold and remote kings.

Pendergast and Constance rode side by side up the narrow track, trailing a pack pony on whose back was tied a long box wrapped in a canvas manty.

"We should be there before sunset," Pendergast said, gazing at the faint trail that wound up the granite face.

They rode on for a while in silence.

"I find it curious," Pendergast said, "that the West, so advanced in many ways, is still in the dark ages when it comes to understanding the deepest workings of the human mind. The Agozyen is a perfect example of how much more advanced the East is in this area."

"Do you have any further thoughts on how it might work?"

"As a matter of fact, by coincidence I read an article in the *Times* that might shed some light on it. It was about a recently discovered mathematical object known as E8."

"E8?"

"E8 was discovered by a team of scientists at MIT. A supercomputer, running for four years, had to solve two hundred billion equations in order to draw an image of it—an admittedly very imperfect image. There was a crude reproduction in the newspaper, and when I saw it I was struck by its resemblance to the Agozyen mandala."

"What does it look like?"

"It's quite indescribable, an incredibly complex image of interlocking lines, points, and surfaces, spheres within spheres, occupying nearly two hundred and fifty mathematical dimensions. They say E8 is the most symmetrical object possible. Even more than that, physicists think that E8 may be a representation of the deep inner structure of the universe itself, the actual geometry of space-time. Incredible to think that, a thousand years ago, monks in India somehow discovered this extraordinary image and committed it to a painting."

"Even so, I don't understand. How could just looking at something like that alter one's mind?"

"I'm not sure. The geometry of it somehow lights up the neural networks of the brain. It creates a resonance, if you will. Perhaps on a deep level our brains themselves reflect the fundamental geometry of the universe. The Agozyen is a rare intersection of neurology, mathematics, and mysticism."

"Extraordinary."

"There are many things the dull Western mind has yet to appreciate about Eastern philosophy and mysticism. But we're starting to catch up. Scientists at Harvard, for example, have just begun to study the effect of Tibetan meditative practice on the mind—and to their amazement they discovered that it actually causes permanent physical changes in the brain and body."

They reached a crossing of the Tsangpo. The river was shallow and broad at the ford, running merrily over a shallow bed of cobbles, the rushing sound of water filling the air. Gingerly their horses stepped into the torrent and picked their way across. They came out on the far side and continued on.

"And the smoke ghost? Is there some kind of scientific explanation for that?"

"There's a scientific explanation for everything, Constance. There are no such things as miracles or magic—only science we haven't yet discovered. The smoke ghost was, of course, a tulpa, or 'thoughtform'—an entity created through an act of intense, focused imagination."

"The monks taught me some of the tulpa-creation techniques, but they warned me of the danger."

"It's extremely dangerous. The phenomenon was first described to the West by the French explorer Alexandra David-Néel. She learned the secrets of creating a tulpa not far from here, near Lake Manosawar. As a lark she tried it out and, it seems, began visualizing a plump, jolly little monk named Friar Tuck. At first, the monk existed only in her mind, but in time he began to take on a life of his own, and she glimpsed him at odd moments, flitting about her camp and frightening her fellow travelers. Things went downhill; she lost control of the monk and it began to morph into something bigger, leaner, and far more sinister. It took on a life of its own—just like our smoke ghost. She tried to destroy it by reabsorbing it into her mind, but the tulpa strenuously resisted and the end result was a psychic battle that almost killed David-Néel. The tulpa on board the *Britannia* was the creation of our friend Blackburn—and it *did* kill him."

"So he was an adept."

"Yes. He traveled and studied in Sikkim as a young man. He realized immediately what the Agozyen was, and how it could be used—much to Jordan Ambrose's misfortune. It was no concidence it ended up with Blackburn; there was nothing at all random in its movements through the world. You might say the Agozyen *sought* Blackburn out, using Ambrose as a medium. Blackburn, with his billions and his dot-com savvy, was in a perfect position to spread the image of the Agozyen across the globe."

They traveled a moment in silence. "You know," Constance said, "you never did explain to me how you sent the tulpa after Captain Mason."

Pendergast did not answer immediately. Clearly, the memory was still extremely painful. At last, he spoke. "When I freed myself from its grasp, I allowed a single image to form in my mind: the Agozyen. In essence, I implanted that image in the tulpa. I gave it a new desire."

"You changed its prey."

"Exactly. When the tulpa left us, it sought out the other living beings who had gazed on the Agozyen—and, in the case of Mason, somebody who was, indirectly at least, bent on its destruction. And the tulpa annihilated them both."

"And then?"

"I have no idea where it went. Things having come full circle, as it were, perhaps it returned to whatever plane it was summoned from. That, or it simply vanished with the death of its creator. It would be interesting to hear the views of the monks on this question."

"So it was an agent for good in the end."

"One could say that—although I doubt goodness is a concept that it would either understand or care about."

"Nevertheless, you used it to save the *Britannia*."

"True. And as a result I feel a little less mortified at having been wrong."

"Wrong? How?"

"Assuming all the killings were the work of one person—a passenger. In point of fact, Blackburn only killed one person—and he did that on dry land."

"In the most bizarre of ways. It seems that the Agozyen lifts the lid, as it were, unleashing the most buried of a person's violent and atavistic impulses."

"Yes. And that's what confused me—the similar M.O. I assumed the murders had all been committed by the same person, when I should have understood that there were two different killers under the influence of the same malevolent *effect*—the effect of the Agozyen."

They had reached the base of the trail going up the

cliff. Pendergast dismounted and, in a gesture of prayer, placed his hand upon the huge *mani* stone at the base. Constance followed, and they proceeded up the trail, leading their horses by the reins. At last, they reached the top, passed through the ruined village, and finally came around the shoulder of the mountain, spying the pinnacled roofs, towers, and sloping ramparts of the Gsalrig Chongg monastery. They passed the scree slope covered with weathered bones—the vultures had departed—and arrived at the monastery.

The gate in the outer stone wall opened almost before they had reached it. Two monks met them; one led off the two riding horses while Pendergast unpacked the cargo from the pony. He tucked the box under his arm, and he and Constance followed the monk through the ironbound doors into the monastery's dark interior, fragrant with sandalwood and smoke. Another monk appeared with a brass candleholder and led them deeper into the monastery.

They came to the room with the golden statue of Padmasambhava, the Tantric Buddha. The monks had already gathered on the stone benches, presided over by the ancient abbot.

Pendergast placed the box on the floor and seated himself on one of the benches. Constance sat next to him.

Tsering rose. "Friend Pendergast and Friend Greene," he said, "we welcome you back to monastery of Gsalrig Chongg. Please take tea with us."

Cups of sweet buttered tea were brought out and enjoyed in silence. Then Tsering spoke again.

"What have you brought us?"

"The Agozyen."

"This is not its box."

"The original box did not survive."

"And the Agozyen?"

"Inside—in original condition."

A silence. The ancient abbot spoke, and then Tsering translated. "The abbot would like to know: did anyone look upon it?"

"Yes."

"How many?"

"Five."

"And where are they now?"

"Four are dead."

"And the fifth?"

"I was the fifth."

When this was translated the abbot rose abruptly and stared. He then walked over to Pendergast, grasped him with a bony hand, and pulled him to his feet with astonishing force. He stared into his eyes. Minutes passed in the silent room—and then the abbot finally spoke.

"The abbot say this extraordinary," Tsering translated. "You burn off the demon. But you remain damaged, because once you experience ecstasy of the pure freedom of evil, you can never forget that joy. We will help you, but we can never make you whole."

"I'm already aware of that."

The abbot bowed. He bent down and picked up the box, handing it to another monk, who carried it off.

"You have our eternal thanks, Friend Pendergast," said Tsering. "You have accomplished great feat—at great cost."

Pendergast remained standing. "I'm afraid it isn't quite over yet," he replied. "You have a thief in your midst. It seems that one of your monks thought the world was ripe for cleansing and arranged for the theft of the Agozyen. We still must find that monk and stop him from doing it again—or the Agozyen will never be safe."

Once this was translated, the abbot turned and looked at him, his eyebrows slightly raised. There was a hesitation. Then the abbot began to speak. Tsering turned to translate. "The abbot say you are correct, it is not over. It is not the end, but the beginning. He ask me to tell you certain important things. Please, sit down."

Pendergast seated himself, as did the abbot.

"After you left, we discovered who released Agozyen into world, and why."

"Who?"

"It was the holy lama in the wall. The ancient one."

"The immured anchorite?"

"Yes. Jordan Ambrose fascinated by this man and speak to him. The lama let Ambrose into inner monastery, talk him into stealing Agozyen. But not to cleanse the world. Lama have other reason."

"Which was?"

"It is difficult to explain. Before you arrive in spring, his holiness the Ralang Rinpoche die. He is eighteenth incarnation of the Rinpoche who founded this monastery long time ago. We cannot continue as a monastery without our incarnated teacher. And so, when a Rinpoche dies, we must go out into world to find his reincarnation. When we do, we bring child back to the monastery and raise it as next Rinpoche. This has always been our way.

When the seventeenth Rinpoche died in 1919 Tibet was free country, and it was still possible to go out and find his reincarnation. But now the eighteenth Rinpoche is dead, and Tibet occupied. Free travel for Tibetan monks is very difficult and dangerous. Chinese arrest Tibetan monks on missions like this, beat them, sometimes kill them. The holy man in wall knows many deep things. He knew of prophecy that say: *when* we cannot go out and find new Rinpoche, then new Rinpoche *will* come to Gsalrig Chongg instead. We will know this Rinpoche, because he will fulfill the prophecy written in our founding holy text of the monastery. It say:

When the Agozyen walks the Western Sea,
And darkness upon darkness wheel,
The waters shall rise up in fury,
And batter the great palace of the deep,
And ye shall know the Rinpoche by his guardian,
Who shall return with the Green Tara,
Dancing across the waters of the Western Sea,
From the ruined palace of the deep.

"So to test prophecy, holy man release Agozyen into the world to see who will bring it back. Because man who bring it back is the guardian of the nineteenth Rinpoche."

Pendergast felt an emotion rare to him: utter surprise.

"Yes, friend Pendergast, you have brought the nineteenth Rinpoche to us." Tsering looked at Pendergast with a slightly amused expression. And then he focused a pointed gaze on Constance.

She rose. "The guardian of the . . . excuse me, are you saying *I'm* the reincarnation of the Rinpoche? But that's absurd—I was born long before he died."

The monk's smile deepened. "I do not speak of you. I speak of the child you carry."

Pendergast's surprise redoubled. He turned toward Constance, who was looking at the monk, an unreadable expression on her face.

"Child?" Pendergast said. "But you went to the Feversham Clinic. I thought—I assumed . . ."

"Yes," Constance replied. "I went to the clinic. But once there, I found I couldn't go through with it. Not even . . . knowing it was *his*."

It was Tsering who broke the silence that followed. "There is an ancient prayer. It say: *Lead me into all misfortune. Only by that path can I transform the negative into the positive.*"

Constance nodded, one hand drifting unconsciously across the slight swell of her waist. And then she smiled: a smile that seemed half secretive, and half shy.

A Word from the Authors

The Preston-Child Novels

We are very frequently asked in what order, if any, our books should be read.

The question is most applicable to the novels that feature Special Agent Pendergast. Although most of our novels are written to be stand-alone stories, very few have turned out to be set in discrete worlds. Quite the opposite: it seems the more novels we write together, the more "bleed-through" occurs between the characters and events that comprise them all. Characters from one book will appear in a later one, for example, or events in one novel could spill into a subsequent one. In short, we have slowly been building up a universe in which all the characters in our novels, and the experiences they have, take place and overlap.

Reading the novels in a particular order, however, is rarely necessary. We have worked hard to make almost all of our books into stories that can be enjoyed without reading any of the others, with a few exceptions.

Here, then, is our own breakdown of our books.

The Pendergast Novels

Relic was our first novel, and the first to feature Agent Pendergast, and as such has no antecedents.

Reliquary is the sequel to *Relic*.

The Cabinet of Curiosities is our next Pendergast novel, and it stands completely on its own.

Still Life with Crows is next. It is also a self-contained story (although people curious about Constance Greene will find a little more information here, as well as in *The Cabinet of Curiosities*).

Brimstone is next, and it is the first novel in what we informally call the Diogenes trilogy. Although it is also self-contained, it does pick up some threads begun in *The Cabinet of Curiosities*.

Dance of Death is the middle novel of the Diogenes trilogy. While it can be read as a stand-alone book, readers may wish to read *Brimstone* before *Dance of Death*.

The Book of the Dead is the culminating novel in the Diogenes trilogy. For greatest enjoyment, the reader should read at least *Dance of Death* first.

The Wheel of Darkness, which you presently hold in your hands, is a stand-alone novel that continues to follow Pendergast and takes place after the events in *The Book of the Dead*.

The Non-Pendergast Novels

We have also written a number of self-contained tales of adventure that do not feature Special Agent Pendergast. They are, by date of publication, *Mount Dragon, Riptide, Thunderhead*, and *The Ice Limit*.

Thunderhead introduces the archaeologist Nora Kelly, who appears in most of the later Pendergast novels. *The Ice Limit* introduces Eli Glinn, who appears in *Dance of Death* and *The Book of the Dead*.

In closing, we want to assure our readers that this note is not intended as some kind of onerous syllabus, but rather as an answer to the question *In what order should I read your novels?* We feel extraordinarily fortunate that there are people like you who enjoy reading our novels as much as we enjoy writing them.

With our best wishes,